Acclaim

"Hackers, treacherous villains, and unexpected twists that will leave you searching for answers alongside the characters, THE DONOR is a thrilling adventure where deciding who to trust can mean the difference between life and death. Dyer masterfully weaves together sweet romance, high-stakes, and heart-pounding excitement in a way that will leave you desperate for just one more chapter. This is an adventure readers won't want to miss!"

— C.J. Milacci, award-winning author of The Talionis Series

"Kiss your bedtime goodbye, because you won't be able to put THE DONOR down! Filled with sweet romance, crazy twists, and just enough scary, this debut thriller will take you on a fun ride."

— Katherine Briggs, author of THE ETERNITY GATE and THE IMMORTAL ABYSS

"Jennifer Dyer's newest novel, THE DONOR, is a fast-paced and addicting read. Through unique dual points of view, we are brought into the world of two hackers from opposite walks of life who discover an unimaginable secret. Hilarious dialogue, witty metaphors and a swoony romance abound in this adventure that will keep your heart racing from page one."

— V.Romas Burton, award-winning author of FORTIFIED, Book One of The Legacy Chapters

"Pure brilliance! A thrilling adventure with quirky and loveable characters and a large dose of Texas flare."
— Candace Kade, author of The Hybrid Series

"A pulse-pounding adventure full of clever twists, turns, and a shocking surprise! I was riveted on the edge of my seat!"
— AJ Skelly, author of The Wolves of Rock Falls series

"Jennifer Dyer's debut YA thriller touches on all the best elements in the genre! It has characters with brilliant minds and courageous hearts, tech that's just futuristic enough to be scary, and a mystery that keeps you guessing who's most dangerous until you turn the final pages. I can't wait for more!"
— Karyne Norton, Author of Epic Fantasy and Sci-Fi Thrillers

"Buckle up, THE DONOR is a wild ride from start to finish. Dyer knows how to keep you on your toes, with twists and turns you never see coming. Just when you think you have it all figured out, the next chapter has you questioning it all. Snarky banter, secrets, betrayal and swoon-worthy kisses; Jennifer expertly weaves it all together in an explosive narrative you won't want to put down."
— Sara K. Anderson, author of the Mindhunters Duology

THE
DONOR

THE DONOR

Quill & Flame
PUBLISHING HOUSE

JENNIFER DYER

Quill & Flame
PUBLISHING HOUSE

The Donor

Copyright ©2026 by Jennifer Dyer

Published by Quill & Flame Publishing House, an imprint of Book Bash Media, LLC.

www.quillandflame.com

All rights reserved.

No part of this publication may be reproduced, digitally stored, or transmitted in any form without written permission from the publisher, except as permitted by U.S. copyright law.

This is a work of fiction. Names, characters, and incidents are products of the author's imagination or are used fictitiously. Any similarity to actual people, living or dead, organizations, business establishments, and/or events is purely coincidental.

NO AI TRAINING: Without any limitation on the author or Quill & Flame's exclusive copyright rights, any use of this publication to train generative artificial intelligence is expressly prohibited.

Cover design by Ashley Bustamante

To every girl who's ever felt she was too much, and for Amy who
taught me that too much was just right.

Chapter One

Cameron

Nothing killed conversation faster than a kid tethered to an oxygen tank. Half the people Cameron passed in the white marble-and-glass Foster Medical Corporation lobby wouldn't look him in the eye. The others gave him that pinched "sorry for your impending demise" grimace. It didn't help that his dad owned FMC. Cameron was practically the poster boy for employee inspiration. They'd all heard the oh-so-tragic story of the only son of the Great Nigel Foster: the kid with everything but a future, thanks to his busted heart. The PR team loved it. Blah, blah. One of many reasons Cameron preferred machines to people.

Up ahead in a hallway, a scientist in a white lab coat and scrubs paused at a door, waiting for the locks to disengage. The guy's outfit blended with everything else in FMC head-quarters: white walls, white tiles, white doors. Even the air felt colorless. Lab Coat Guy glanced Cameron's way, doing a double take at the rare sight of the executive chairman's son in the flesh. After a moment of face-twitching indecision, he went with the "sorry you're about to keel over" expression.

Cameron saluted him and pressed his hand to the wall scanner next to the elevator. The sooner they got these tests over with, the sooner Cameron could get away from the constant eyeballing. And this time, the results would be better. They had to be. He'd already bought late-summer tickets for Comic-Con and DEF CON, a hacking convention. If his heart looked better, surely his dad would let him go.

His bodyguard, Jerry, caught up with him. "Would some color kill them around here?"

"And litter their precious scientific minds with something as chaotic as shading? You need to check your crazy."

Jerry snorted, swiping a meaty hand over his bald head. His deep-brown biceps flexed against his T-shirt sleeve, and the handle of his Taser showed over the waistband of his black jeans. Although he'd been a sniper in some super-secret military unit, he refused to carry anything with bullets. Fortunately, his pro-wrestler physique and suspicious squint kept most bad guys away. The few that had gotten close to Cameron had received a painful but entertaining demo of Jerry's krav maga skills.

When the elevator doors whooshed shut, Cameron exhaled.

Jerry lifted his chin in Cameron's direction. "You nervous?"

"'Course not."

"So that's why you keep tapping your thumb against your leg and blinking. And the sweat beads on your temples—"

"Thank you, Professor Profiler. Fine, yes. I hate the constant tests, and this one…" Cameron couldn't voice it. It'd be fine. It had to be.

Jerry frowned and cleared his throat. "Fair point."

The elevator doors slid open onto the fifteenth floor. Cameron's feet grew heavy, and his stomach seemed stuck back on the main level. But he lifted his chin and put one foot in front of the other. If being the only son of Nigel Foster III had taught him anything, it was how to put on his game face.

Up ahead, Dr. Grisham gestured them forward. "You're late."

Cameron spread his hands in a conciliatory motion. "I had a hot date."

As expected, Grisham's sour expression didn't crack.

"You know…because it's hot outside?"

Still nothing. Cameron was no comedian, but Grisham's sense of humor was DOA, and his personality was on life support. The guy looked half-dead too—you'd think he was the one with the heart condition. With pale skin, bulging eyes, and a pointed nose, he gave the impression of a mutated albino parrot.

Inside, Grisham's lab was as cold and sterile as the doctor, with closed blinds, dim lights, and more machines than personality. Grisham pointed Cameron to a long chair that looked like it belonged in a dentist's office. The doctor remained silent, but his pinched, constipated expression spewed volumes.

Jerry hovered by the door, probably wondering if today was when his CPR skills would be required.

Cameron pulled off his shirt and plopped into the chair, his back sticking to the low-quality fake leather. He peeled himself up and plopped his T-shirt behind him. "Last time I checked, the FMC bank statements were pretty healthy." Understatement. "I'm just saying. Would it hurt you to spring for some better chairs?"

Grisham grunted.

A reporter had once remarked that Cameron was lucky his doctor traveled the world with them. Right, because having this guy watch his every move was so awesome.

Grisham pressed sensors to Cameron's chest and spoke in his droning nasal monotone. "Be still. Breathe deep."

Brick walls had more personality. Maybe the good doc was so interested in hearts he forgot a real person was attached.

Cameron's dad chose that moment to enter. He joined Grisham and watched the screens, the space between his eyebrows wrinkling. People often remarked how much Cameron favored his dad—they shared the same brown eyes, black hair, medium build, and thick Foster eyebrows. If only Cameron possessed his dad's confidence. Nothing seemed to faze him.

The droning of the air conditioners filled the room. Grisham motioned to something on the screen. His heavy gold ring inscribed with the Greek letter gamma reflected ghostly green.

His dad nodded. The two of them murmured, probably not wanting to remind Cameron he was a ticking time bomb.

Tick. Tock. One more day off the clock.

Cameron jiggled his foot. What were Grisham's tests showing? He did everything the stupid doctor had suggested. He stuck to the sucky, mostly vegan, low-salt diet. He exercised under Jerry's supervision daily. He took handfuls of health supplements every day. And he never so much as licked a French fry. Surely, he'd done enough to put off surgery.

So why did his dad's eyebrows keep smashing together like that? Cameron tapped open his phone and scrolled through his notifications, then shut it off, unable to focus. "Hey, Dad, did you see my messages?"

His dad didn't look up. "The one about the Porsche, or the one about the Porsche?"

"I'm just saying. A small token of your affection would be a great birthday present."

Dr. Grisham huffed. "The only Porsche a seventeen-year-old boy needs is the kind that races on the carpet."

Jerk. Grisham was one of those guys who was born old, and instead of aging, petrified over time. Cameron glared at him. "Dad's parents didn't feel that way."

His dad let out the kind of fake laugh that probably gave FMC employees heartburn. "My parents also sent me to boarding school because I interfered with their yachting schedule."

Grisham pinched the bridge of his nose. "Cameron, please relax while I finish up."

In other words: shut up.

Cameron gripped his phone. Fine, if the doctor wanted him to relax, he'd do something relaxing. He angled his phone so none of the others would see and connected to the doctor's accounts. Hacking the guy was as easy as spending money at an electronics expo. He changed the auto-signature setting to Dr. Charles Grisham, M.D., Senior Vice President of Crapiology Research. Juvenile? Absolutely. But still satisfying.

While his dad and Grisham murmured, Cameron scrolled through Grisham's messages, stopping on one labeled Beneficence Donor Corp. He'd never heard of that company, but his dad was commonly called The Donor because of his support for charities and research. Maybe it was part of the Foster empire. Cameron scanned the contents. One sentence stood out: *cryo units available soon.*

That was an odd statement, but Grisham oversaw the organ R&D department. Still, Cameron wasn't sure. He took a screen shot, backed out of Grisham's account, and connected to the HUB—the Hidden Universal Browser or darknet, as some people called it. He initiated a search on Beneficence Donor Corp. When he glanced up, Grisham was staring at him, eyes full of shadows.

Chills rose on the back of Cameron's neck. He clicked his phone off and pointed to his chest. "How's it look? Better?"

Grisham stared at a blank spot on the wall. Cameron tried to swallow, but a stethoscope seemed to be lodged in his throat. The doctor finally spoke. "If you recall, hearts don't heal like a scratch on your skin. Once the heart muscle is compromised, it weakens—"

Cameron groaned. He didn't need a lecture about why his heart sucked; he needed to know what it meant. "Just tell me."

Grisham removed all the electrodes before handing Cameron a tablet. Two hearts showed on the screen. Grisham pointed to the first one. "This one's normal." He pointed to the second. "This is yours." The doctor went on to detail something about irreparable damage, but Cameron mostly heard whooshing until Grisham said, "I'm scheduling the transplant."

"But…" Cameron gripped the side of his chair. Inside, he was a computer about to overheat. "I—I feel fine. Great even." He pointed to his heart monitor watch. "My numbers seem good." Sweat broke out on his back and in his pits. "You've always said my chances of surviving the surgery were less than twenty percent."

The doctor dug around in his pocket and extracted an antacid. "Even a low percentage is better than none, yes?" He patted Cameron's hand. "We've held out as long as we could for a donor, but time is not on our side. If your mother had gotten you the proper care as an infant—"

His dad cleared his throat. "You're understandably anxious, but we've got the best scientists in the world on this."

A new heart—Cameron couldn't fathom the idea. Although FMC was the leading manufacturer in ghost protocol organs—implantable tissue grown from the recipient's DNA—the thought of a strange, lab-created *thing* beating in his chest twisted his gut into knots.

Though they'd discussed the surgery Cameron's entire life, he'd never let himself believe this day would come. "When?"

Grisham clasped and unclasped his hands. "Within six weeks."

That was practically tomorrow. How much living could he do in that tiny sliver of time? Cameron shook his head, about to protest, but his dad sank into the nearest chair, gripping his own chest. He sucked in a labored breath.

Jerry darted to him. "Whoa, Mr. Foster. You okay?"

Grisham snatched his bag and scooted to his dad's side.

Cameron jerked to his feet. "Dad?"

Though Cameron and his dad shared the same bronze coloring, in that moment his dad's skin matched Grisham's pale hue. His dad rarely got upset, not even the time they'd been mugged in Paris. If stone-faced Nigel Foster was freaking out about the surgery, Cameron was doomed.

Six weeks. Six weeks to be seventeen. Six weeks to live.

Cameron's dad waved Grisham off. "I'm fine." But he refused to look Cameron's way.

A sheen of sweat covered his dad's face. Cameron dug his fingers into his legs. The last thing he needed was his dad having a heart attack because he was so stressed about Cameron, but this whole situation sucked.

Dizziness swept over him. The lights turned harsh, glaring into his eyes. He shook his hands out, but a prickly sensation crawled over his arms and legs. He dropped back into his chair. Another low-oxygen episode—the last thing he needed. He shoved the nasal cannula deeper into his nose.

"Son? You okay?" His dad ducked closer to get Cameron's attention. "Take deep breaths and blow out like you're using a straw. It'll pass."

Cameron waved him off. "I'm fine." His dad's anxious face only made him feel worse. Cameron crammed his eyes shut. This wasn't fair. What had he done to deserve this? After all the good he'd done shutting down organ smugglers through the anonymous hacktivist board, EyeNet, the least he could wish for was time off his life sentence for good behavior.

Jerry patted Cameron's shoulder. "If percentages were true, I'd be dead a hundred times over. I've known you for three years now, and one thing I'm sure of: you and me, we're survivors."

Some of the feeling came back into Cameron's legs, but his throat was dry and raw and tight, as if he'd swallowed his T-shirt.

Dr. Grisham gave him a hesitant pat on his knee. "Everything we've done is to get you ready for this surgery, so don't worry. It's bad for your heart."

Cameron balled his hands into fists. Everything was bad for his heart, and the doctor had just given him a possible death sentence. The *least* Cameron should be allowed to do was worry. Starving for air, Cameron wheezed, "I'm not ready. I just—I haven't... Can't I have more time?"

His dad shook his head. "If people listened to odds, no one would visit Vegas. I promise, this surgery will be the beginning of a long life. Now, we must get you home to rest, and unfortunately, I have a benefit to attend."

For the first time in years, Cameron had no desire to spend the evening in front of his computer. As much as he wanted to continue doing his part in bringing down the illegal organ trade, he needed to cram as much living into the next few weeks as possible. "Didn't you say this benefit was a scholarship award dinner for that tech high school in Dallas?"

His dad went still. "The answer is no."

Nope, Cameron was getting a yes on this. He might have hacked into one of his dad's email accounts recently and viewed the guest profiles. There would be girls there. Smart and pretty ones who might want to discuss more than his trust funds. "I haven't asked yet."

His dad headed for the door. "You're not coming tonight. Too many people. Too many risks. And you know how anxious you get in crowds."

Cameron raced to head him off. In the past year, he'd grown to stand eye-to-eye with his dad. "Hear me out. The board will love it if I show up. Our stocks always go up when I make a public appearance."

His dad deployed The Foster Stare, the one that had been passed down for generations and could halt a ravenous tiger. The two of them might share the same hefty name, sharp cheekbones, and height of five ten, but Cameron would never master The Stare.

Still, he stood tall in the face of it. "Please. I won't breathe the same air as everyone else. I'll soak in hand sanitizer. Just let me come."

Jerry moved out of the shadows. It was crazy how such a big guy could be so stealthy. "Mr. Foster, sir, if I may, I would be happy to accompany the kid tonight. Maybe getting out would do him some good."

His dad turned his eye cannons on Jerry, but the big guy didn't flinch. No way would his dad give in—he never did. But this was important. And it was great to have Jerry on his side. Maybe it would be boring, but Cameron couldn't face another night inside and alone. "I'll make that speech Rahul keeps bugging me about."

"You think I would endanger my son's health for a speech and a bit of funding?"

Cameron spread his hands. "Not *a bit* of funding. A crap ton of funding."

His dad's eyebrows contracted. "Nigel Cameron Foster the Fourth, what have I said about crass language?"

If it was language he wanted… Cameron switched his argument to French and kept it up, throwing in some Spanish and Mandarin every few sentences, all the way to the waiting car.

His dad didn't say a word until they pulled into the circular drive at the house in Highland Park, a small town inside the heart of Dallas. His dad's bodyguard, Leon, opened the car door, and finally, *finally*, his dad exhaled and glanced Cameron's way. "You may come, but you will follow every health protocol. When I say it's time to leave, you will not argue."

Cameron beamed a smile at him. "Me, argue? Never."

Chapter Two

Tasha

"Does this mean we're getting another visit from the FBI?" Tasha's mom glared at the letter sitting on the white kitchen counter as if it might explode. The flowing handwritten words on the envelope glowed acidic green under the overhead lights.

Tasha Jenkins and Parent

Tasha yanked the card out and slid it across the counter. "Last time I checked, the FBI didn't employ calligraphers."

From her recliner in the adjoining living room, Gran wheezed through her nasal oxygen tubing. The O2 machine hissed out the chuffing sound that never stopped rattling Tasha's nerves. The old woman turned up the TV and glared at Tasha's mom. "You've been home ten seconds, Sarah, and already there's fussing. It's a new record."

Tasha pulled in a slow breath like her therapist had suggested. Gran's lavender essential oil hung in the air but didn't offer the promised calming effects. She pointed to the envelope. "It's the invitation to the Foster Medical Corporation scholarship dinner. Remember?"

Her mom's face screwed up like that time Tasha had accidentally used salt instead of sugar in a cheesecake recipe. The older woman tossed her purse onto the table and sank into a chair, untying her clunky nursing shoes. "This again? I already said no." She waved her hands, knocking her purse onto the floor. "I just worked a twelve-hour shift cleaning up gunshot wounds in one of the busiest trauma—"

"—units in the US. A noble career. The noblest." Tasha gave her mom a pleading look.

Her mom huffed and ran a hand through her hair. The light illuminated the growing amount of gray streaking through her blonde curls. "Since you know so much, you understand why I don't want to listen to sycophants blabber about how wonderful Nigel Foster is."

Tasha held in her groan. Barely. Her mom was so difficult sometimes. Fortunately, she'd passed down more than blonde hair and a severe case of blurting unfiltered thoughts to Tasha. "Mom," she said through a titanium-hard jaw, "remember that thing called college that costs as much as a house? This dinner is for a scholarship. A full, freaking college scholarship."

"I don't want another dime from Nigel Foster."

"Quit your yakking." Gran let loose a volley of coughs, then added, "I can't hear my program."

Her mom headed to the sink and washed her hands. "Beggin' your pardon, Majesty."

Tasha sucked in another breath, this one for volume. "You'd rather me spend the next thirty years babysitting my way toward that degree?" She focused the heat of her glare on her white Converse and frowned. She shouldn't have doodled on them during that last mind-numbing lecture on data compression algorithms. Put a pen in Tasha's hand and numbers leaked out.

When combined with her height of barely five feet, the blue Sharpie drawings made Tasha feel ten instead of seventeen.

Her mom grabbed a sponge and attacked the already spotless sink. "You've got a brilliant future ahead of you—you're smarter than anyone I know. You don't need Nigel Foster or his money. The only thing FMC has brought this family is heartache, and the sooner we forget about that place, the better."

Tasha couldn't forget, which is why she had to get to the charity dinner. When else would she have a chance for an in-person confrontation with the almighty himself? Tasha plunked a handful of chocolates in the candy dish by Gran's recliner and slid a pillow under her grandmother's ankles. Even through her socks, the soles of Gran's feet were icy. More swelling too. Tasha tucked a blanket around them. Congestive heart failure sucked.

Gran gave Tasha's hand a squeeze and spoke in a low voice. "I can tell you're up to something." She ended with a lopsided grin. "Good girl."

Her mom set a Diet Coke on Gran's side table and gave the old woman's arm a gentle squeeze. She frowned at the indentations her fingers left.

Tasha blinked hard to keep from tearing up, but that clawing sensation started in her chest and worked into her throat. Those indentations meant the heart issue was getting worse. How much longer did Gran have? According to everything she'd researched, they were down to months, not years, and the end was anything but pretty.

Her mom knew it more than most—she saw it in full color regularly at the hospital. Probably explained the crying sounds coming from her mom's room late last night. How would they bear another loss?

Tasha took a long breath. All the more reason Nigel Foster had to be called to account. He'd done enough damage.

Gran unwrapped a chocolate and winked at Tasha. "You're an angel."

"Hardly." Her grandmother wouldn't say that if she knew why Tasha wanted to go tonight. Gran's version of "up to something" probably involved flirting, not confronting a gajillionaire and calling him a murderer in front of the world. Tasha kept up the campaign on her way to the fridge. "Bethany and Gabe are going."

"They both have parents who work for FMC. I'm not on Nigel's payroll."

Tasha's insides pinched like she was wearing tight jeans after an ice cream binge. She kicked off her Converse and touched her bracelet, its tiny flash-drive charm smooth and familiar. What was it going to take to convince her mom? "In case you haven't noticed, no other scholarship opportunities are banging down our door."

"There's still time for all that."

"Fine." Tasha snatched the invitation off the counter. "I'll go by myself."

Her mom's lips pressed flat. "In case you've forgotten the most recent FBI visit regarding your little hacking hobby, you're still grounded from driving."

Gran grunted and shoved aside her blankets. "That's it. Get my keys, Natasha. I'll take you." She punctuated her proclamation with a volley of coughing.

Tasha's mom dropped onto the couch and rubbed her forehead. "Mother, you don't have a license anymore. You drove through the front door of the bank."

"How many times do I have to tell you? That kid pulled a piece. I saved the bank from a robbery."

Tasha tuned out their bickering while she changed into the dress she'd thrifted for the event. Rushing back to the kitchen, she arranged Gran's dinner on a tray and settled it beside the recliner. With a spin, she gestured to her lavender dress with a ruffled hem. "What do you think?"

Gran waved her fork around. "You look like a cupcake, but the sneakers add a classy touch." She winked and slid her gaze to Tasha's mom. "Oops. That must have been my meds talking."

"You are the wickedest-of-the-west, Gran. And Mom, I didn't buy this dress for fun." Tasha lowered her voice to a tone she hoped sounded reasonable and calm. "College. Maybe MIT." This would be a great time to conjure a starving-kitten look, but Tasha didn't have one in her. She couldn't admit the real reason she wanted to go. If her mother knew what she was planning, Tasha would spend the rest of the summer in her therapist's office. "Please. This means a lot to me."

Her mom bit her lip. "If it was anything but FMC, I'd go, but after what happened with your dad..." Her voice caught. "We're not going."

Gran tsked. "Both of you girls need to stop wallowing in the past. It's time to move on and start living."

Tasha slipped on the heeled sandals she'd bought with the dregs of her babysitting money. If stubbornness were currency, Tasha wouldn't need a scholarship, and they wouldn't have to shop in thrift stores. But tonight wasn't about some stupid handout from Foster Med Corp. Tonight was for her dad. The thought of him was a kick in the chest. Though it was cruel and snotty and sneaky, Tasha tossed down her best bargaining card. "Dad would have taken me."

Her mom's eyes bulged. Direct hit.

Tasha stared at the crocheted doily on Gran's end table. When did their lives turn into a constant battle? It wasn't what her dad would have wanted.

Her mom sputtered her best I'm-such-a-martyr sigh. "Fine, but I'm going under protest." She lifted her chin toward Gran. "You'll be okay?"

Gran pulled her handgun out of the crocheted pouch next to her chair. "Me and Elvis here will be just fine."

Her mom pinched the bridge of her nose. "Just don't shoot anyone I know. Again."

Gran tucked Elvis into her bag. "Steve deserved it."

Tasha's chest was tight, an overfilled balloon. She exhaled—triumphant, relieved, empty.

Her mom opened a package of baby carrots. "Where's this event being held?"

Tasha winced. This wouldn't go over well. "Union Station."

"Downtown Dallas?" The carrots fell at her mom's feet and scattered under the table. "That's only a few miles from Dallas General. I just spent over two hours in traffic driving away from there."

Tasha gathered the carrots. "You're the best—"

Deep barking from outside drew their attention.

Gran leaned forward. "Where's the cat?"

Tasha darted to the porch, searching under the rocking chairs and scanning the front yard. The cat was nowhere to be seen, but maybe the neighbor's dog had treed him again. She headed to the side of the house.

Her mom's footsteps banged down the porch stairs behind her. "Everything okay?"

"I don't—"

A pitiful bleat sounded from around the side of the house.

Hot darts of adrenaline shot through Tasha's neck and into her arms. She took off running for the back fence adjacent to the Gomez's cattle ranch.

Sure enough, Reyna, the neighbor's German Shepherd, had located a calf stuck in the barbed wire fence and was barking for help.

Tasha slipped in a patch of mud, and her left heel got stuck. She kicked off both shoes and shouted over her shoulder. "Mom, get the wire cutters! Have Gran call Jorge."

Reyna woofed as Tasha slid to a muddy stop by the calf. The poor baby was trying to get free, but every wiggle caused more cuts. Tasha grabbed the little guy's head, trying to hold it still, and made shushing noises. "We'll get you out of here."

Drool dripped from the calf's mouth, and it kicked clumps of dirt toward her. Where was her mom with those wire cutters?

The calf jerked again. How to stop it? Tasha shoved the skirt of her dress between the calf's ear and one of the barbs. The baby jerked again, and her skirt ripped. Her heartbeat pounded in her ears and her eyes fogged over. Why did it have to be a fence?

Her mom darted up, snapping the wires free. By the time they cut the calf loose, Jorge pulled up on his four-wheeler and started taking over vet care.

Tasha's mom put an arm around her on the way back to the house. "I told him to fix that spot last week. Think he'll listen to me now?"

Tasha snorted. "If he's anywhere near as stubborn as me, probably not."

Her mom hugged her tighter. "You come by it naturally."

On the porch, Tasha glimpsed her reflection in the glass storm door. Her dress—what was left of it—was stained with grass and mud. Dang it. She'd thrifted for three days to find it. Her wardrobe mostly consisted of jeans and T-shirts. What was she supposed to do now?

She plopped onto a rocking chair, her eyes burning and blurry. She'd just wanted one thing to go right. Just one.

The door banged shut. Guess her mom was heading inside to gloat over not having to go tonight. Maybe she was right. Tasha should give up on justice and—

"Hey," her mom's soft voice called as she pushed the glass door back open. A white halter dress, still in a department store plastic bag, hung over her arm. She shuffled her feet, eyes watery. "This..." She cleared her throat. "I got this to wear on a trip Solomon and I were planning for our anniversary. It was too young for me, and I'd have had to lose twenty pounds to fit into it, but..." Her mom bit her lip and held it out. "It might be big, but you can wear it."

It took Tasha three tries to swallow. She nodded and air hugged her mom to avoid mud transference. "I'm going to take a quick shower, then I'll be good to go."

After the world's fastest shower and change, Tasha ducked into her room, locking the door behind her. She dug into her tiny closet and yanked her ancient spare laptop from underneath a pile of school papers. Her mom would freak if she knew about the computer—the FBI had confiscated Tasha's favorite laptop and promised they'd be watching to make sure she didn't log onto the HUB.

She plopped down, jostling the shoebox where she kept mementoes and research relating to her dad's death. The lid popped open, and several printouts she'd made at the library using an incognito browser spilled from the box. The top one announced in bold black letters, "Suspicious Death for Foster Med Corp Security Guard."

For the millionth time, Tasha relived that night, her dad's last. The last time they ate dinner as a family—Tasha's attempt at lasagna, which turned out more like noodle bricks and burnt cheese. Her dad hadn't complained, even opted to choke down seconds.

His whispered conversation with her mom just before he left rang in her memory. *Something's weird at FMC…organ development…black market.*

Her mom's urging. *Don't get hurt.*

Their last goodbye, last hug, last moment, the fence at FMC.

Tasha dug her nails into her palms and flipped her computer open. She only had time for a quick check on EyeNet. *Please, please, let there be something more than online articles to use against Nigel Foster.* Several big news outlets would attend the dinner, looking for a good story, and Tasha planned to give them one.

Her mom said she wanted Tasha to move on, but that look on her face a few minutes ago had broken what was left of Tasha's heart. Solomon's death had left a huge hole in their lives. And Nigel was responsible.

While she waited for the HUB to come up, Tasha pulled her dad's half-burned FMC ID badge out of the shoebox. On the back of it, she'd taped the gum wrapper she'd found rolled up and tucked inside the pen he carried in his uniform jacket. In his tiny scrawl, he'd written, "Failstate. Organ protocol. FMC."

Failstate Global was one of many watchdog groups on the darknet that had taken an interest in organ smuggling. The anonymous members of Failstate worked much the same as Eye-Net's hacktivists—finding and exposing criminal activity. Her dad's note had to imply a connection between FMC and the organ trade. But proving it was harder than walking barefoot on asphalt in August.

So far, she'd only collected one related article in her shoebox: "Influx of organs stateside. Kidneys, heart, and liver. Failstate Global questions Foster Medical Corporation's tissue regeneration protocols." Beyond that, all she'd found was a bunch of horrible organ brokers and their victims.

After checking she'd locked the door, Tasha entered her password for EyeNet and scanned through the latest additions to her recent organ smuggling post. Maybe someone had found something that she could link to FMC.

The user with the handle Black Mask had posted about the FBI wanting Julio Cortez, a Mexican drug cartel boss, in relation to dozens of deaths, including that of an American child. Another user with the handle Cardiac had added some pictures of Cortez's alleged victims. Tasha wished she'd skipped the nachos at lunch. Gruesome.

Dozens of kid's bodies had been cleaned out, their organs removed. Those weren't drug-related killings. That was organ trafficking, which had never been Cortez's MO, at least not that she'd seen. She'd do more digging to find out where those organs were sent, but so far nothing she could use against Nigel at the banquet tonight.

Tasha ground her teeth. No matter how deep she dug, she couldn't unearth a definitive link between organ trafficking and FMC, but it had to be there. If only she could get into Nigel's computers. Surely, she'd find what she needed to ruin him.

"Tash?" Her mom called from the other end of the house. "You ready?"

"Almost." Tasha grabbed several articles from her shoebox and shoved her laptop into its hiding spot. Unfortunately, the entire mess in her closet crashed to the floor. Papers, her dad's Bible, and books sprawled on the carpet. Tasha stared at the Bible's worn black binding and the faded words *Solomon Jenkins* engraved on the cover. Almost rubbed out, like it hadn't been there in the first place, but she refused to let him be forgotten.

Tasha buried the Bible and laptop under a pile of laundry and crammed the printouts into her purse. Too bad there hadn't been some helpful watchdog group sending information to the police three years ago when her father had been murdered.

She took a long breath and squared her shoulders. Tonight, she'd have her chance to right the injustice of her dad's death. Tonight, she would nail Nigel Foster to the wall.

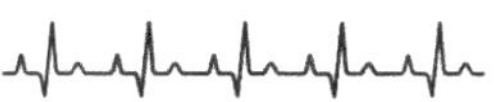

Cameron

Cameron slung his portable O2 tank over his shoulder and followed Jerry into the house. On the way to the kitchen, they passed through what Cameron called the Nigel Foster Hall of

Accomplishment, where their housekeeper Rose hung framed awards, honors, and newspaper articles. Cameron paused in front of a clipping. "Orphaned Teen Launches Medical Research Company from High School Project."

At seventeen, Cameron's father had founded FMC. At seventeen, Cameron was tethered to a stupid O2 tank, a bodyguard, and a poor prognosis. True, last year he'd started Sentinel Tech Solutions, helping small companies with tech security, but the bar was set high for Fosters. The family tree was flush with captains of industry like his dad.

What if this was it, and Cameron only had a few weeks left? There had to be more he could do, more to leave his mark before the clock stopped.

His mind wandered to EyeNet and those children who'd been killed for their organs. It seemed unlikely the Cortez cartel was behind that, but it could be the Wolf Brothers cartel. They'd been responsible for a rash of hollowed-out bodies three years back, although they'd bribed their way out of trouble.

The awards on the wall blurred into nothing but black-and-white smears. He didn't care about ceremonies, interviews, and wall plaques. No, what mattered was making a difference. His dad rarely spoke about these awards, but he did talk about the ways FMC was making the world a better place.

As a Foster, that should be Cameron's aim too. Making the world a better, safer place. No matter how much time he had left, that's what he needed to do. If nothing else, before he faced his own end, he wanted to bring justice for those kids and their families.

He found Jerry in the kitchen, leaning over the counter. The light shone on the numbers tatted on the back of his neck—one-one-nine. The few times Cameron had asked about them, Jerry had either changed the subject or refused to say anything.

The big guy straightened and pushed a small, rectangular package across the island to Cameron. "Came for you today."

Cameron tucked it under his arm. Probably the magnetic mini projector he'd ordered. It had been an impulse purchase, but he'd been bored. Ugh, he needed to get a social life. Guess he should add that to his end-of-it-all list.

Footsteps sounded in the back hall, and Leon slid into the kitchen. He carried his suit jacket over his shoulder, leaving his double gun holster exposed. Did he expect a siege inside the house? Jerry stiffened, eyeing the guns, but Leon didn't take notice. He grabbed a forbidden soda from the drink fridge and raised it to Cameron. "Your pops said he wanted to leave exactly at six. You gonna be ready?"

Like Cameron needed Leon to be his babysitter. Cameron grunted a yes and motioned Jerry toward the main hall.

Once they were alone, Jerry waved Cameron past the table holding this house's chess board—a J. Grahl set that had belonged to his grandfather. Cameron slowed. He and his dad kept games going in every house, all of them in various stages. Looked like his dad had already made another move. Dang it. He swept his gaze across the pieces to memorize their placement. He'd decide on a move later.

Jerry cleared his throat to get Cameron's attention. "Listen, I'm proud of you for standing your ground with your old man. You've had a tough life, and that's part of what tonight's about."

Cameron gripped the stair railing tighter. "The fact that I'm probably going to die in a few weeks?" Geez, why was he stressing over chess moves when death lurked over the horizon? He shoved his nasal cannula farther in and breathed deep.

Jerry eyeballed Cameron with that listen-up expression. "Your dad's company has a team of scientists and doctors working to save lives, and you're their inspiration to keep making new discoveries. There's a whole mess of sick people out there who need help. What you're doing matters."

Cameron stopped. Sometimes he forgot Jerry had a life outside of keeping Cameron safe. "How's your little sister doing with the treatments?"

Jerry stared at the Rothko painting on the opposite wall.

Cameron pulled at his snug watch band. Heart issues sucked, but he had major respect for kids like Yasmine who battled leukemia and other diseases.

Jerry cleared his throat. "She's had a setback—another infection—but your dad's been real generous to get her help from the best." Jerry shook his head as if clearing that thought. "Get changed and download some pick-up lines, kid. You've got ladies to impress."

Cameron rolled his eyes. He'd love to date, even have a girlfriend, one who liked him for *him*, not his bank accounts. But constantly moving between countries made it difficult, not to mention his dad's "people are germ incubators" mentality. He swiped a hand over his face.

The sensible side of him kept murmuring there wasn't a point, that he had too many strikes against him to think about it. Still, there was another part of him that wanted to live as much as he could while it was possible. Dr. Grisham's dire "twenty percent" kept replaying in his head. If there was ever a time to take a chance, wasn't this it?

Ugh, he didn't have time for angst. He needed to think about something else.

Jerry said something about their exercise plan tomorrow, but Cameron's mind was back on the Beneficence Donor Corp email he'd seen in Dr. Grisham's account. The name was so close to his dad's nickname, he couldn't help but wonder about it. He tapped on his phone to pull up his search.

Jerry fingered his cross necklace. "I know you're dealing with a lot, but spending all your time playing phone games isn't the same as facing life in real time."

Great. Philosophical Jerry was worse than Personal-Trainer Jerry. "Thanks for the sermon, but I need to get pretty for my speech."

Jerry grumbled about praying for Cameron's attitude and shoved off the wall, heading to his apartment at the west end of the second floor.

Cameron locked his bedroom door and crossed to the Computer Graveyard—a giant storage closet accessed through his room. Inside, chilled air raked over his skin. Hundreds of retired FMC computers lined shelves along the walls.

His dad had easily agreed to give Cameron the old computers, believing it was for a school project. No telling what he'd say if he knew the real purpose, that Cameron had hooked all the machines together to run his SpydrEye script. The program worked like a search engine, scanning all layers of the web for whatever key words he needed. It had come in handy for several of EyeNet's projects.

Cameron powered on the infrared keyboard and 3D projector connected to his phone. Several browser screens projected onto his wall. He pulled up the HUB. So far, his search had turned up a few items. From what he could see, Beneficence Donor Corp was supposedly based in the Cayman Islands, but there wasn't anything associated with it. Just a dummy website.

Heaviness settled over him as reality crashed in. Stupid surgery. Clicking mindlessly through a few darknet shopping sites, he paused on an Autonomous Navigation Tire Sensors System, or ANTS System, with which any car could self-navigate. The seller wanted stupid money for it, but Cameron purchased it anyway. It was dumb, considering he didn't have a car, but today he didn't care. In fact, he had plenty of money saved from his tech consulting work. Maybe he'd get a car, despite what his dad said, and test out the ANTS System to see if he could reverse engineer it.

Six. Weeks.

Cameron ducked into the shower and thought over his speech. Like everything else in the coming days, he had to make it count.

Chapter Three

Cameron

THE GIRL WALKED THROUGH the door like she held a grudge against it. Her thick gold hair brushed her shoulders, and when the wind stirred the hem of her white dress, Cameron got an eyeful of curvy legs.

Around her, the Grand Hall of Union Station hummed with activity. The place looked like a cross between a cathedral and the old train station it was. Ornate chandeliers cast circles of light onto the high-domed ceilings. Tan brick columns lined the walls, interspersed with arched windows over two stories tall.

Waiters carried trays of appetizers between candlelit tables, and a small orchestra warmed up in the opposite corner. Clusters of FMC scientists and executives gathered near the long bar to Cameron's right. There were a lot of people at the event, but in such a big space it didn't feel too overwhelming. Outside, the Foster security team, including Leon, prowled around the whirring escalators, but all that faded into a blur beyond *her*.

"You want me to take a picture so you can stare in peace?" Jerry asked.

Cameron glanced at Jerry, but his eyes were magnets pulled back toward her. He should stop staring. He should think of something else.

A tall and leggy girl in a designer outfit blocked Cameron's view. She tucked a tablet in the crook of her arm and gave him a thousand-watt smile. "Mr. Foster, I'm Mía. I've been assigned to make you comfortable tonight. Is there anything I can get for you?" She leaned in, her batting eyelashes and sultry tone suggesting she'd be happy to give him her phone number.

Six weeks. The words were stuck on repeat in his mind, and he couldn't stand it any longer. Who cared if it was illogical? He gestured to the girl. "I'd like her name."

Veronica frowned and tapped long, manicured nails on her tablet. "Natasha Jenkins—goes by Tasha."

"Thanks." Ducking around a chair to ditch Jerry, Cameron followed Tasha deeper into the banquet hall.

Jerry stayed on him like a car salesman. "Mía was flirting with you."

He waved Jerry off. "Too high maintenance."

Another waiter rushed past, the scent of bacon trailing behind him. Cameron loved breathing cannula-free air. So far, Jerry hadn't mentioned his O2 tank stashed behind the head table. He sped up and caught a whiff of Tasha's perfume. Vanilla and flowers.

She glanced over her shoulder, her gaze intent on something behind him. For a second, she seemed about to cry.

Jerry nudged him. "What happened to Cameron I-Don't-Like-People Foster?"

"You suggested I appreciate life. This is me appreciating it." But Jerry had a point—what was he doing, following a girl just because she was pretty? He saw beautiful girls all the time, but there was something different about Tasha, a fire burning beneath the surface. He needed to understand why.

Tasha wove between tables, hips swaying.

Jerry kept pace beside Cameron. "You going for the friendly stalker approach?"

Tasha glanced Cameron's way. Her thick lashes framed large, intelligent eyes. His heart whacked against his ribs. Instead of blood, his veins pumped hot espresso throughout every inch of him. At that moment, he could've run a marathon. He hoped this wasn't bad for his wheezing ticker, because he didn't want to die before he talked to her.

She stared past him. Her pouty lips edged up, and her face brightened. Those eyes kicked out some major wattage.

Cameron maneuvered around a table and stopped in front of her. He froze, his mind going horribly blank. Only useless gaming shortcuts batted around in his brain. *Reboot, you idiot!* "Um, hi."

Their eyes met—hers were light blue, like the sky on a perfect summer's day. "Hey." She nodded, but her gaze drifted past him.

"You come to stuff like this often?" He cringed. Guess he was, indeed, going for a creepy stalker vibe.

She raised her eyebrows. "Yeah, every day. You?"

He should have watched more romcoms and less superhero flicks. Desperate for a topic, Cameron glanced around and down. A string of numbers scribbled around the perimeter of her sneaker caught his eye. "Hey, I love pi."

"What?" Her voice held a knife-edge, and she stepped back.

"Your shoes—the digits of pi."

Her face softened and a blush lit up her cheeks. "Oh, yeah. Nervous habit."

A girl who doodles in math? More, please.

She motioned around the room. "What brings you here? You don't go to DAST-M."

"DAST-M?"

She exhaled a tiny laugh. "Obviously not. Dallas Academy of Science, Technology, and Math. I go to school there."

"Oh." Cameron groped for a response. "I'm just here with my dad."

"Poor you."

"I second that." Cameron let the moment wash over him. Tasha was talking to him like he was a normal person, not a sick kid, and not a Foster.

Another guy approached. *No, no.* Cameron sent him go-away vibes, but the guy didn't catch them. He was shorter than Cameron but had great hair. Thick black waves of it. And a Latino smolder. Ugh. Name tag read Gabriel Mendez. The joker nudged Tasha's arm. "Glad you made it. Sorry I couldn't pick you up." He held out his hand to Cameron. "Hey, I'm Gabe."

Cameron shook Gabe's hand even though he had a sudden urge to punch him. Of course, a girl like Tasha already had a boyfriend. "I'm Cameron."

Gabe lifted his chin. "What school are you from?"

Why'd Gabe have to interrupt a perfectly great conversation? Cameron took a step back and, instead of answering, he asked, "So you all go to school together?" Telling them he'd already finished an online degree from UMass would either make him seem weirder or like he was bragging. Best to shut up.

A tall, pretty girl with big brown eyes and straight black hair joined them and clasped Gabe's hand. She waved at Cameron. "Hey, I'm Bethany."

Gabe pointed. "This is Cameron."

Cameron stared at Bethany's and Gabe's joined hands and stood straighter. Perhaps Tasha wasn't taken. He glanced her way, but she was focused over her shoulder at the spot where his dad stood in front of an FMC banner. He shook hands with some guy in a tux.

Bethany snapped her fingers. "Wait, you're Cameron, as in Cameron Foster?" She drew in a quick breath. "My mom works for y'all—Dr. Liana Phan." She motioned toward a petite woman in a black dress speaking with a small group of FMC scientists.

Tasha's attention remained on the stage, like she didn't care who he was. Before Cameron could reply to Bethany, Rahul Kapoor, his dad's personal assistant, motioned him over. Cameron held up a hand to Tasha and the others. "It was nice meeting you."

When Cameron got closer, Rahul waved his hands around and spoke in a thicker-than-usual London accent, like he always did when he was stressed. "Where's your oxygen? Your dad is freaking out."

"I lost it."

Rahul snapped at one of his assistants and gestured to Cameron's face. The lady located Cameron's backpack and portable O2 way too fast. Grumbling, Rahul arranged the tubing on Cameron's face. "Smile, but look vulnerable at the same time. They'll eat you up." He shooed Cameron away and swung his phone around, filming a video for one of FMC's socials.

Did Rahul ever stop posting long enough to think how much it sucked to be the token sick kid? Probably not, but he meant well. Cameron forced his shoulders to relax.

On the raised platform, Cameron's dad patted him on the back. Even through Cameron's suit, his dad's hands radiated cold. But that was normal for Texas summers: sweltering heat outside, arctic temperatures inside.

His dad nodded at a reporter's question. "My brave son refused to miss an opportunity to support one of our education initiatives. Both of us appreciate the dedicated scientists of Foster Medical Corporation and their tireless efforts not only to help our little family, but families all over the world."

A woman joined them. She stood eye to eye with Cameron, and her custom navy suit, dark hair pulled into a neat bun, and straight posture spoke of someone ready to dish out orders. She extended a hand to Cameron. "Pleased to finally meet you. I'm Dr. Janet Dover." She nodded at his dad. "Hello, Nigel."

His dad's expression turned brittle. "Janet." He drew out her name, hardly moving his lips. "To what do we owe this pleasure?"

"Roger couldn't make it, and I couldn't pass up an opportunity to meet your handsome son. Looks so much like you." She flashed Cameron a warm yet venomous smile. "Roger O'Brien and I are on the board for DAST-M and are so pleased your father has chosen several of our exceptional students for this honor."

She looped a hand through Cameron's arm. "Your father and I went to Harvard together. Has he told you about the time we went sailing in the Cape and got stuck in that fog bank?"

"No."

"Marvelous story. Your dad's quite the navigator."

His dad scowled and motioned to Rahul. "We shouldn't detain Ms. Dover."

Wow. Cameron needed a lightsaber to slice the tension between those two. Maybe they'd dated and had a bad breakup?

To his right, the scholarship recipients formed a line to get their pictures taken with him and his dad. He had to squint against the stage lighting to glimpse Tasha and her friends toward the back. Tasha laughed at something Gabe said and punched him.

Her gaze swung up, and she caught Cameron staring. Her eyes met his and lingered for a second. She turned her lips up before glancing back down.

Outside the arched windows, the Dallas skyline shimmered against the night sky. Few stars were visible, but the buildings were lit up, outlined in green and white. It wasn't the Rocky Mountains, Dubai, or downtown Tokyo, but Dallas had its own charm…and her name was Tasha.

Cameron leaned closer to his dad. "So glad I came."

His dad tensed, his arm a metal rod behind Cameron's back. He turned away from the audience and murmured in Cameron's ear. "Don't get distracted. No matter how beautiful and charming they are, never trust a woman. They'll smile to your face only long enough to suck the life out of you."

Chapter Four

Tasha

If it hadn't been for Foster's son giving her that goofy smile, the receiving line would've been horrendous. Bethany fidgeted, probably worrying she'd say something wrong and get her mom in trouble. Gabe grumbled about his tie being a noose. Then there was Nigel Foster, a king surveying his subjects. He had a mean-girl smile, the kind that dripped with chocolate syrup and called you sweetie all while plunging a nail file into your spine. But Nigel's son seemed to be all sweetness with none of the dictator vibe. Those big eyes of his reminded her of the neighbor's Labrador puppy.

Gabe leaned closer. "Foster the Fourth keeps checking you out."

Tasha snorted but glanced at Nigel's son again. He was staring at her, although as soon as their eyes met, he snapped his gaze toward a waiter. Interesting. This could work in her favor.

She'd read about Nigel Foster's son. Apparently, the kid had some serious health problems, and it was rare for him to make a public appearance, especially without a bodyguard.

And…yep. A few feet behind Cameron lurked a brown-skinned guy with a serious face, his attention toggling between scanning the room and eyeing the kid. The low lighting cast shadows over the guard's expression, but judging by the tension in his thick arms and wide shoulders, he'd probably turn Hulk if his charge was threatened.

Posts droned on and on about Cameron's future as an eligible bachelor destined to take over The Donor's throne, but a recent insider statement indicated Foster IV's heart condition could be fatal sooner than later.

Of course, their publicist had spun it into the perfect tragedy. Poor Nigel Foster doing so much good for the world, unable to save his golden boy. He and FMC would try, and the world would benefit from the research that came from his efforts to save his precious son. Please, help their profits increase.

Boo hoo.

But Golden Boy Foster hadn't seemed sick when she met him. Sure, he currently modeled the latest in minimalist O2 backpack fashion, but he hadn't gasped for air or turned blue lipped when he'd been without it earlier. It seemed more like a publicity ploy for FMC, but his condition was well-known, so maybe she was wrong.

And why did she care? Nigel's son didn't matter. What mattered was that a viper dwelled within Nigel's custom suit, and Tasha was going to take him down.

Bethany flung her long, silky hair over a shoulder, fluttering her thick lashes. Behind her, a waiter gave Bethany's tall, perfectly proportioned frame an admiring look. He barely spared Tasha a glance.

Not that Tasha cared about that waiter, but sometimes being Bethany's friend was like living on the underside of a rock, constantly concealed in shadow. Bethany was gorgeous, intelligent, super nice, and all around awesome. And if positivity were a currency, Bethany would be a billionaire. She was everything Tasha wasn't. If they weren't friends, Tasha might frame her for a crime.

Fidgeting with her skirt, Bethany motioned to Foster IV. "He's cute in a boy-band kind of way. Or maybe a Bollywood actor. Did you know one of his great-grandmothers was a famous actress from India? Another great-grandmother was an Italian countess."

Gabe scoffed. "Your boyfriend can hear you fangirling."

Bethany waved away his comment, and the strap on her powder-blue dress drooped. She shoved it back into place. "I'm speaking for Tasha because she refuses to admit she thinks he's cute. She also thinks he has nice shoulders, and the fiber weave of his shirt looks exquisite."

Tasha rolled her eyes. "Because good fabric is so hot."

Gabe scowled, his expression reminiscent of that time his mom had signed him up for tap dance instead of karate. "Would *Tasha* like a closer look?"

Bethany rested her hand on Gabe's arm. "Don't be so grouchy. You know Padma and I did that project on fabrics for burn patients. Mom says her division at FMC is interested in our research. They have these cloned goats that excrete spider silk in their milk…" She trailed off at Tasha's glower. Unchecked, Bethany could monologue for hours.

Bethany snagged an appetizer off a passing waiter's tray. The hunk of shrimp tumbled off its toothpick and smeared a trail of pink sauce down the front of her dress. Bethany gasped and glanced at where her petite dark-haired mother, clad in a designer evening gown, chummed it up with her tuxedo-wearing FMC research partner, Dr. Andrew Winn. For a second, she thought the two doctors' fingers intertwined. Tasha's appetite tanked. Did Bethany see that?

"My mom's going to kill me!" Bethany's pitch increased with each word.

Her mom seemed too busy with Dr. Winn to notice the sauce-dress predicament. "It's not bad," Tasha said.

Bethany's glare was spiked with bubbling tears. "Liar! Your lips don't move when you're lying." She clutched her purse to her front. "I can't meet Nigel like this!"

When Tasha scanned the banquet hall, an idea sparked. "Gabe, save our spots." She motioned to Bethany and snatched a shimmery blue runner from a rectangular table.

Bethany's eyes bulged. "What're you doing?"

"Trust me." She hustled Bethany into the restroom, twisted the table runner into a scarf, and wrapped it around Bethany's neck.

Bethany glanced in the mirror, pushing the scarf to the side to cover the stain, but it kept sliding to the center again. "Why couldn't I have at least marred my dress equidistant from both edges?"

Tasha grimaced. "Wait." She dug into her purse for her pen with a clip on the side. Unfortunately, one of her printouts tumbled to the floor. The title glared back at them: "Fiery Death for Foster Med Corp Security Guard."

They both froze. Ugh, she shouldn't have shoved the paper clippings into her purse, but she'd wanted to see Nigel's face as she confronted him with his sins. She'd wanted the world to read his guilt. Then maybe he'd be caught, and her dad would receive justice.

Bethany swooped up the printout, her lips pressed tight. "You swore you were past this."

How could anyone believe she was past that? The police had ignored her when she'd asked for help digging into Nigel. She wouldn't get past this until her dad's killer paid the penalty for his crimes. Tasha grabbed for the paper. "Nothing wrong with carrying a memento."

Bethany ripped up the article and flushed it down the nearest toilet. "I know you want someone to blame for your dad's death, but if you start thinking monsters are everywhere, that's what you'll find. You'll see what you expect to see." Bethany's eyes hardened. "But this affects more than you. Gabe's dad and my mom still work for FMC. You'll wreck our futures."

Tasha crossed her arms over her chest. "Guilt? That's your tactic?"

"Yes. Plus, this'll make you look paranoid. It's—"

The door swung open. Bethany let out a startled yelp.

Tasha's mom stood in the doorway. Her gaze widened at Bethany's dress. "Oh, honey, what happened?"

The girls eyed each other. Bethany was probably debating spilling her suspicions, but they both knew what kind of scene that would invoke. Tasha spoke first. "Quick, Mom, we're trying to cover the stain."

Tasha's mom hoisted her purse onto the counter, digging safety pins out of the bag's depths. "Tash, it's almost your turn. Get out there and stall."

"Don't do anything foolish." Bethany's words chased Tasha out the door and clung to her like cheap vinyl in August.

Tasha wove her way back to the receiving line, purse pressed tight to her side. While Gabe stepped onto the platform for his moment with King Foster, stupid Bethany's stupid words clunked around in Tasha's brain. She shuffled along to the edge of the steps and twisted her purse strap, inhaling for one, two, three…

If only she hadn't nagged her dad to go to work early that day, all for a lame school project. Everything might've been different. Maybe her dad would be alive, and she'd be at a baseball game with him instead of here, about to shake hands with a devil in a custom suit.

One of Nigel's minions motioned her forward but held up his hand. She fished into her purse, clammy fingers grasping the wrinkled papers. Yes, she would do this. For her dad.

At that moment, another assistant adjusted Golden Boy's oxygen tubing. Nigel held his chin high and patted Cameron's shoulder.

A lady nearby crooned, "What a great dad."

Nigel glanced Tasha's way and seemed to be speed-reading her chapter by chapter. His eyes were like two black holes, taking everything in but letting nothing escape.

Tasha stepped onto the platform.

Nigel held out his hand. "Ms. Jenkins, how pleasant to finally meet you in person."

Without meaning to, she shook his icy hand. She sucked in air but couldn't let it out.

He glanced at her purse. "Did you have something you wished to discuss?"

This was her chance to stake him, but the road between her mouth and brain suddenly closed for construction.

Nigel kept up his stare. Up close, he and his son bore a sharp resemblance, although Nigel seemed pale compared to Cameron. He probably didn't get much sun in boardrooms and private jets.

The snake cleared his throat. "I must compliment you on your essay regarding ethics and cloning for organ production. My hope is one day you will be part of Foster Medical Corporation's work in the cloning field to aid those in need of transplants." He tilted his head toward his son. "We are going to change the world, Ms. Jenkins." Nigel paused, his eyes drilling into her psyche. "Unlike your peers, you understand the world can be a wonderful but terrible place."

His last words had an ominous ring and sent chills up her spine. "I'm sorry?" Was that a threat?

He tipped his head toward her. "You and I know the pain of losing parents in our youth. A loss like that forces you to grow up in ways others don't, and it can push you toward greatness. I know your father will be looking down on you, proud of all you will achieve."

His focus shifted. "Ah. Here comes your friend, Ms. Bethany Barrett, Dr. Phan's daughter. And what a charming dress. As I'm sure you are aware, the admissions director at Harvard is a friend of mine. I plan to speak with her on Ms. Barrett's behalf."

Nigel's assistant motioned Tasha to the other side of the stage. Time was ticking. Why had Foster mentioned Bethany's desire for Harvard? Either he was being friendly, or it was another veiled threat.

Cameron stuck out his hand. "I enjoyed meeting you." His grip was strong, and he filled out his suit nicely—*stop it!* She was acting like a fangirl meeting a hot, young Bruce Wayne. Not hot. A plain…somebody. Right? Her mouth had gone stone dry.

Cameron leaned closer. "You okay?"

Tasha popped her hand open, letting go of Cameron. What was she doing? *Get back to the plan.* She fumbled in her purse for the papers but made the double-dumb mistake of glancing into Cameron's intense eyes. Time froze. Before she could say anything, the well-dressed assistant herded her off the stage.

Her chance to pin Nigel was over. She was an utter fool. But when she glanced back, Cameron was still watching her.

Hmm…maybe her chance was only beginning.

Chapter Five

Cameron

Cameron might not have his dad's stare, but he did have
the Foster way with people. It only took a few whispered
pleas to get Tasha and her friends moved to his table. He was
probably kidding himself, but he wanted more time with the
feisty blonde. On the way off the dais, he leaned close to Jerry.
"Try not to cramp my style."

"You have to have style for it to cramp."

By the time he and Jerry made it to the round table, Tasha
and her friends were already there. Tasha sat next to a lady
who looked like an older version of her—blonde and fair, but
with green eyes instead of Tasha's blue ones. Her name tag
read Sarah Jenkins, so probably Tasha's mother.

Sarah straightened her place setting with deliberate and
precise movements, almost surgical. That word sent a shiver
through him—no, he would not spend tonight thinking about
Dr. Grisham's timeline.

Bethany sat on Sarah's other side, but Bethany's mom, Dr.
Phan, was at his dad's table chatting with Dr. Winn who
sometimes assisted Dr. Grisham in the lab.

Gabe sat next to Bethany, whispering in her ear. Bethany elbowed him and blushed. A couple pulled out the chairs on Gabe's other side. Their name tags read Alejandro and Veronica Mendez, so they must be Gabe's parents. Veronica was pretty, with highlights in her dark hair, and Alejandro's bulging arms looked almost as impressive as Jerry's. Alejandro's name tag stated he was Security Director for FMC South, one of their larger lab sites.

Cameron beat Jerry to the seat next to Tasha. In the soft candlelight, Tasha's skin glowed and the golden tones in her hair shimmered like firelight. What would it be like to run his fingers through those strands? He gulped, needing to rein in his thoughts but wanting nothing more than to let his mind wander.

Bethany inclined her head. "Mr. Foster, we had no idea you'd be sitting with us tonight."

"Please, call me Cameron." He pulled open his napkin and set it on his lap. "Jerry and I wanted to meet some of Dad's winners."

Tasha scoffed. "As in, we're Nigel's prized stallions?"

Bethany flashed Tasha a wide-eyed stare.

Cameron took a slug of water. He was a complete moron.

Tasha's phone buzzed. She yanked it out of her purse, disentangling it from a folded printout. Cameron caught sight of a headline: *"Suspicious Death for Foster Med…"* Tasha zipped her purse before he could read anything else. He stared at his plate for a moment. Whose death? There weren't any deaths surrounding FMC that he knew of. He'd ask his dad later, but why did she have that in her purse?

On her other side, Tasha's mother shot her a dark look. "I'm sorry, Cameron. My daughter seems to have gotten her personality switched with a piranha."

Tasha rolled her eyes. "It was a tragic lab mishap. I only wanted to know what the sweet little piranha was thinking. I mean, they probably have a lot of deep thoughts down there: 'To devour or not to devour, that is the question.'"

The other guy, Gabe Mendez, snorted and folded an empty sugar packet into a miniature origami creature. "Don't let Tasha get to you. Once you get past the moat filled with angry crocodiles, she's all warm and fuzzy."

Gabe's dad slipped off his suit jacket. A *Semper Fidelis* tattoo similar to Jerry's peeked out of his short-sleeved shirt. Jerry didn't seem to notice, since his eyes were zeroed in on the head table. Cameron nodded toward Alejandro's arm. "Jerry has that same ink."

Alejandro raised his chin to Jerry. "When'd you serve?"

Jerry stiffened and glared at Cameron for a second but covered his jerk-o attitude with a laugh. "Can't say."

Geez. Jerry was acting as friendly as Tasha.

"Cameron." Bethany fidgeted in her seat and twisted her napkin. "Your dad mentioned the essay I wrote for the scholarship application. Quoted from it."

Gabe paused in the middle of folding his next origami creation. "Mine, too."

Bethany nodded. "Did he, I mean…?"

Tasha leaned forward. "What she means is, how did your dad recall all that information? Did he have a hidden earpiece and an informant?"

"No, he's got a crazy good memory." Another thing the two of them shared, not that Cameron had put it to as good a use as his dad.

Bethany's eyebrows rose. "I've read his intelligence is off the charts."

Tasha sent two laser beams in Cameron's direction. "And how about yours?"

"My charts? They're fine. I keep them in my room." Cameron cringed. With cheesy lines like that, how could any girl resist giving him the boot?

Tasha's lips turned up. Whew, maybe she didn't think he was too much of an idiot. Cameron leaned closer, not caring that Jerry was watching. Tasha seemed so soft, so delicate, so likely to bite. Fascinating.

Bethany and Gabe discussed their favorite picks for college and all the great stuff they planned to do with their lives. Bethany wanted to be a doctor in genetics research. Gabe, robotic engineering, hoping for MIT. Tasha joined in about computer engineering and again, MIT. Cameron stared at his hands. Living on campus. A future. A life beyond eighteen.

All things he couldn't bet on.

He glanced at the head table. Perhaps it wasn't too late to slip away from the banquet and wait in the car. At least then he wouldn't have to spend the evening listening to endless jabbering about everyone else's amazing futures.

A waiter set a plate of broiled fish and steamed vegetables in front of Cameron. Jerry and Tasha got sauce-covered chicken and mashed potatoes lounging in a warm pool of peppered gravy with rolls and butter. Cameron tried to hide his frown. Just once, it'd be nice to have the same plate as everyone else.

Jerry didn't seem to notice Cameron's hesitation because he and Alejandro were busy discussing their workouts. Gabe was watching his dad with a strange mixture of respect and irritation.

"What's up?" Tasha took a detailed scan of Cameron's face. "You don't like fish?"

Even though his illness was international news, talking about his regimented diet seemed like flashing a neon *I'm Weird* sign over his head. But if there was anything a Foster didn't do, it was let someone see them feeling down. He forced a grin. "Oh no, I specifically asked for plain fish and flavorless vegetables. It's my favorite."

Tasha kept her eyes on him. They were marvelous. Like the Caribbean on a clear day, backed by wicked intelligence. "Sure, I bet you love fish as much as I love jogging." She pointed to her plate. "You wanna switch? I had Whataburger for lunch. I could use a few vegetables that aren't fried and drowning in ketchup."

"What's Whataburger?" Cameron asked.

Gabe choked on his bite of steak. "Seriously? You've never been to Whataburger? Are you even Texan?"

Cameron shrugged. "We're not here often."

Bethany nodded. "I read that somewhere. You live in several cities, right? Tokyo, Paris, London, Abu Dhabi, Buenos Aires, New York, and outside Denver, to name a few."

Guess Bethany read about everything. Cameron answered with a half-hearted nod.

Tasha tsked. "What, no home in Toronto or Glasgow?"

"I know. Shameful, right?" His dad did own a hotel in Toronto, but Cameron wasn't about to mention it. Their eyes met, and the edges of her mouth tilted up. He wanted to lean closer. Those lips… Oh man, he had it bad, but Tasha didn't seem impressed by him or his stuff. He suspected if he had a house on the moon, she'd still shrug one of those touchable shoulders—*stop it.* Cameron gulped water, his mind returning to her question and the word *home*. He and his dad lived all over, but where was home?

"How long are you in Dallas?" Gabe asked.

Cameron worked to keep a smile on his face, but the next trip out of Dallas might be his last. Dude, he needed a class in positive thinking. But it was hard not to freak out. He cleared his throat. "We'll probably head to Abu Dhabi in mid-July. I'm having—" Nope, he wouldn't talk about the surgery.

Beside him, Tasha went stiff, but before he could choke down a piece of fish, she switched plates with him. "I'm a piranha. We like fish. Just skip the gravy, or you'll probably regret all your life choices in two hours when the indigestion hits."

Cameron stared at the chicken and the huge mound of mashed potatoes swimming in gravy. His dad would have a coronary, but he was only going to live once. He scooped up a forkful. The potatoes melted on his tongue like clouds. He moaned—actually moaned like a complete dork.

Tasha snorted a laugh. "Taste good?"

"Like baby angels made them in Heaven's kitchen." Cameron glanced at Jerry—still talking with Gabe's dad about bicep-building techniques. Time enough to eat a few more bites before the food police arrested his plate.

Gabe heaved a forkful into his mouth and spoke around his bite. "You see that movie? The one with the hackers?"

Cameron swallowed another bite of mashed heaven. "Which one?"

Tasha waved her fork around. "The one where some guys used a cell phone to hack into an alien spaceship? 'Cause it's that easy."

Bethany spread her hands. "Well, they were good hackers."

Tasha gave a derisive snort. "Oh, yes. Everyone knows typing fast is a sign of a great hacker, especially when two people work on the same keyboard."

Gabe shrugged. "It had some great explosions. But I'd like a movie with hackers getting sent to prison for stealing people's credit cards."

Tasha took a drink and swallowed. "You're so literal. Anyway, people who use hacking to steal are big jerks. Hacking should be about getting justice for the little guy and holding the big guy accountable."

Cameron nodded. "Fighting against poverty and for human rights on behalf of those who can't fight for themselves."

Gabe shook his head. "Sounds like a bunch of vigilantes. Batman without the fashion sense."

Tasha leaned forward, her eyes intense. "Maybe that's how some see it, but are you saying it's bad to free people from oppression? The internet was started to share information and empower people."

"Exactly," Cameron said. "Knowledge should be available, not hoarded." He and Tasha glanced at each other. It sounded like she knew her stuff.

Gabe leaned forward, but Bethany put a hand on his arm. "So, Cameron, if you move often, where do you go to school? Are you planning on Harvard like your dad?"

His bite of chicken went as dry as a piece of cardboard. Always this. His future, so up in the air.

Tasha glared at Bethany, like she'd figured Cameron wasn't planning on college because he wouldn't live long enough.

Bethany stammered. "Oh, I just—"

Cameron passed off the moment with a shrug. The last thing he wanted was pity. "Since we travel so much, I was homeschooled."

Tasha groaned. "By Mr. I'm-a-Total-Genius? How horrible was that?"

Her mother pinched her arm. "You and your grandmother—subtle as bulldozers."

That was enough about him. Cameron asked Bethany what research she'd done for her scholarship application. Conversation flowed around the table, mostly bypassing Cameron. Tasha, Bethany, and Gabe chatted about their school. Apparently it was for geniuses, with classes sponsored by all the big-name universities—Harvard, Yale, MIT, Stanford, and more. Guess his early degree from UMass wouldn't seem too weird in this bunch.

When the topic rolled toward a recent DAST-M tour of the Dallas FMC South lab, Tasha's mom tensed. Her hand shook as she sipped her iced tea. After a few minutes of Gabe rambling about the infusion technology they'd seen, she shoved back from the table. "I need some air."

Bethany frowned, eyes on Tasha's retreating mom. "Did we remind her of your dad?"

Tasha looked like she'd been caught in the crosshairs. She offered an overly loud thank you when a waiter delivered dessert and stared at her plate. Layered cheesecake, something else Cameron had never tasted. He was served a bowl of melon.

She leaned over to him. "Try to grab mine, and I'll fork you."

He studied her out of the corner of his eye. This girl…was she real? A fan of free information. Willing to eat his boring fish but threatening to throw down over cheesecake. Sarcastic, and not once calling him Mr. Foster or admiring the size of his dad's estate. She was Lara Croft in Converse.

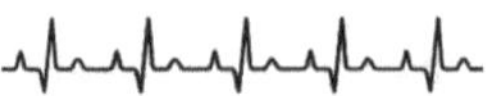

After dessert, Cameron gave his speech about the need for organ research and treatment options that reduced the black-market organ trade. When he returned to Tasha's table, she gave him a long, piercing look then stared at her nails.

His dad spoke next, tearing up when he mentioned his parents' boating accident that left him orphaned at sixteen. Gabe's mom dabbed at her eyes when Cameron's dad went into the spiel about how valuable FMC's research had proved since the birth of his only son.

Cameron had heard it a thousand times. Stares around the room zeroed in on him. This was the part he hated. It was as if they were already imagining his funeral. Everyone except Tasha. She doodled on a sugar packet, her rapid pen strokes gouging the flimsy paper. What was going on behind that beautiful face? Something raw and nuclear simmered there.

Once the presentations were over, the noise level rose again, and everyone pushed away from their tables. No, the evening couldn't end. He had to see Tasha again, but what was he supposed to say? Jerry should have spent more time teaching him about girls rather than tai chi and kung fu.

Tasha's mom put a hand on her daughter's shoulder. "I'm about to turn into a pumpkin."

Tasha gathered her purse. "I guess I should take Cinderella home."

Cameron's heart slipped into his stomach. *Say something, you idiot!*

Bethany frowned. "We were about to tour Reunion Tower. Don't you want to come?"

Tasha's mom shook her head. "I'm dead on my feet."

Gabe tilted his head toward Tasha. "You wanna come with us? I'll drive you home."

Tasha's mother yawned. "Stay or go, but the Jenkins car leaves now."

"I can take you home, Tasha. There's room in the limo." Cameron winced. Had he actually said that? He glanced at Jerry, whose eyebrows were about to climb all the way over the top of his head.

"Um, thanks, but no," Tasha said in the same way someone would thank a psycho offering a ride in his windowless van.

Gabe chuckled but lifted his chin to Cameron. "You wanna come with us to the tower?"

"What is going on, son?"

Cameron's dad headed in their direction, Grisham and Leon lurking behind him. His dad pointed to his watch. "Time to leave."

Cameron took a pull of oxygen for courage. "Actually, they just invited me to go see Reunion Tower." He gave his dad a good dose of pleading eyes.

His dad blinked as if Cameron had spoken in Klingon instead of English. Cameron's palms turned clammy, but he wasn't going to back down. Surely his dad would understand—this was about a girl. And...no. His dad shook his head, eyes on Tasha. "My son is not healthy enough to gallivant around Dallas." He gestured Cameron toward the door. "We're going home."

Tasha raised her voice. "He seems fine to me."

Cameron almost choked. Was Tasha picking a fight with Nigel Foster?

His dad's face remained pleasant. "A wonderful compliment you pay my son."

Cameron waited. In a second, his dad's voice would take on that titanium edge, and his eyes would harden to airplane-glass strength. Three, two, one…

His father blasted Tasha with *The Stare*. "While I value calculated risks in the workplace, I take the opposite approach with my son's health."

Tasha straightened her shoulders and shot his dad a haughty look, a terrier challenging a rottweiler. She was amazing.

Sarah Jenkins stepped toward his dad, but Tasha held up a hand. "I got this." Tasha fumbled in her purse and scribbled on a piece of paper. She smacked it into Cameron's palm. "Call me whenever you want a personal tour of Reunion Tower or anywhere else." She laser-beamed one last glare at his dad and marched off.

Cameron shoved Tasha's number into his pocket, staring at her retreating curves.

As if his dad heard his thoughts, he said, "Save yourself a headache and throw that number out."

The one time he found a girl remotely interesting, his dad said no. His insides tightened. This sucked. True, his dad was watching out for him, but what was the harm in letting Cameron have a little fun? "She seems nice. And smart." There was no way he'd throw out her number. In fact, he already had it memorized.

His dad grunted. "Yes, she's smart and pretty, but didn't you see the hungry look in her eyes? She's after something." His dad stared into the distance. "They're all after something, and the one who will end up getting hurt is you."

Grisham chose that moment to hand Cameron a small baggie filled with his evening medications. The vigilant doc had his meds split into five bags of seven pills each, plus powdered supplements. Thirty-five stinking pills every stinking day. As if he didn't feel weird enough.

Gesturing to Leon, his dad said, "Get the car. My son has exerted himself enough."

Cameron choked down his pills. "Honestly, I feel fine."

"And I want to keep it that way." His dad pointed to some chairs. "I'll sit with you while we wait." Jerry carried the chairs closer, and Leon lumbered away to get the car.

His dad sat and grumbled, handing his phone to Cameron. "My phone's refusing to connect to the network again."

Cameron fixed the issue while his focus remained on the escalators outside the banquet hall's main doors. By now, Tasha and the others were probably on the basement level. From what he'd seen on a map of the building, tunnels connected this building to Reunion Tower. Would he see Tasha again? He fingered his oxygen tubing. Probably not.

His father took his phone back and put a hand on Cameron's shoulder. "To be a Foster is to be exceptional. Women are drawn to us, but often for the wrong reasons. I learned that with your mother."

The mashed potatoes and chicken churned in Cameron's stomach. He was already paying a hefty price for the diet transgression, and his dad was right. Even his own mother didn't want him. She'd seen Cameron as a chance for a huge payoff. Why would any other girl be different?

When his dad's phone buzzed, Nigel glanced at it and grimaced, rubbing his neck. Cameron lifted his chin. "You okay?"

"I'm fine." His dad straightened. "Just a headache." Grisham stepped closer, but Nigel shooed him off. Squinting, his dad read the text and massaged his forehead.

Cameron leaned closer, trying unsuccessfully to glimpse his dad's screen. "What is it?"

His dad stood. "Business. I must go." He gestured to Jerry. "I'll have a car sent for you two."

Unbelievable. And awesome. Normally, his dad's constant business needs grated on Cameron's nerves, but this was perfect. A chance to do something he wanted for a change, and tonight, what he wanted was to catch up with Tasha.

Jerry's gaze followed his dad to the exit. "Must be important, at this time of night."

Cameron was already up and moving toward an elevator. "I say it's good luck."

"Whoa." Jerry caught up and clamped a hand on his shoulder. "My job is to keep you safe, and that doesn't include you running around downtown Dallas."

Cameron darted inside the elevator. "I envisioned more of a stroll than a run."

"Ha. Ha." Jerry blocked the elevator doors from shutting with his hand. "No can do. Your dad said he wanted you to go home."

Cameron leaned against the back wall. "When was the last time you were dying?"

"That won't work." But Jerry ducked his head, a definite sign he was weakening.

Cameron went for a second verbal jab. "I've been close to dying every day of my life. I just met a fascinating girl, and I'm seizing the moment." Cameron hit the down button despite the thumping in his chest. He could be having a heart attack, but he didn't feel any pain.

Jerry grumbled but stepped into the elevator with him. "Five minutes, then we head home."

"Thanks, Warden." Cameron straightened his tie, then yanked it off and stuffed it in his pocket. "Think we'll catch up to her?"

Chapter Six

Tasha

THE VIEW OF NIGHTTIME Dallas from Reunion Tower was beautiful. To Tasha's right, the giant lollipop-shaped tower offered a view of downtown's skyscrapers—outlined in green and white, tall and steady. Five hundred feet below, the freeways blurred into long streaks of red-and-white lights. And everywhere else in the three-sixty-view, the sprawling DFW metroplex was lit up like a galaxy.

It was the perfect place for a romantic moment, which Bethany and Gabe were taking advantage of. *Bleh.* It wasn't that Tasha resented them or didn't like them being together. They just had a habit of forgetting the rest of the world existed at times like this, and Tasha seemed destined to be their third wheel forever.

She moved further along the GeO-deck to put more space between herself and the kissing couple, but the annoying thing about a circular building was if she went too far, she'd find herself face-to-face with them again. Pretty much a metaphor for how her thoughts kept circling back to the evening and Cameron.

Dinner had been…interesting. It'd seemed like Foster Jr. had been flirting with her, and his eyes had lit up when she'd slapped her number into his palm. But would he call her? Did she want him to?

Sure. Yes. Obviously. It was the perfect way to get more dirt on his dad. Tasha pressed against the twinge of pain forming in her sternum. Must be heartburn from the cheesecake. Yep.

Bethany giggled, and her two friends grew quiet again. Tasha moved to the opposite side of the circular deck, by the elevators. Why hadn't she asked for Cameron's number too? Then she could've been composing emoticon-laden flirty-girl texts to get to know him better while waiting for her two best friends to come up for air.

Maybe it was better this way. At least that's what Bethany would say.

But Tasha couldn't forget what happened to her dad, and if Foster Jr. didn't reach out, Tasha would have to come up with a new plan for revenge on Nigel.

She stared at her blank phone for five whole seconds then lost patience and made use of her time to research the pictures she'd seen on EyeNet earlier. Why would the FBI blame the Cortez cartel boss for organ smuggling? True, many of the cartels were expanding their criminal bases of operations into organs, but killing kids seemed too dirty for Cortez. Something didn't add up.

She skimmed through information posted by EyeNet users Play Maker and The Ghost. Dozens of people had gone missing, and some of the bodies had been dumped in the wilderness, their organs removed. Others had been gutted, sold, and shipped across borders to be used as research cadavers.

The latest round of victims had been found last week—twenty kids. From everything Play Maker and Cardiac had posted, it seemed the organ smugglers more than likely belonged to the Wolf Brothers Cartel, a truly dirty group that left a trail of death wherever they roamed, not Cortez. And they only accounted for a fraction of human trafficking in the rest of the world.

This was big. Cortez would hang for this, and maybe she should let him. He'd made a fortune off drug smuggling. Why should she care? Her finger hovered over the screen, about to close it, but something inside her wouldn't shut up.

Three years ago, no one would help her investigate her father's death. According to the security records she'd hacked, thirty-seven employees were on the FMC campus that night. Improbable that none of them saw what happened, but no one would talk.

It was only right for her to find and share the truth like she wished someone had done for her. Wasn't that the point of hacking? She chewed a fingernail. This was different. Cortez was a drug lord. Not the best guy out there, but everyone should stand up for justice, including her.

Mind made up, it only took a few minutes of digging to find an email for Cortez. He'd listed it with pictures of his niece, Florencia, who had been missing for eighteen years. She was pretty with dark hair and thick lashes, the kind of girl who stopped conversations when she entered the room.

Before she lost her nerve, she used a series of encryption, remailers, proxys, and the anonymous HUBmail server, sending a message to Cortez himself with the relevant facts and images. The way Tasha saw it, if the Wolf Brothers Cartel was responsible, they should pay, not Cortez.

Fingers shaking, she leaned against a metal support and ignored that swirly, toilet-flush feeling in her gut—the one she got every time she did something that might come back to bite her. It would be difficult, but what if Cortez hired techy people who traced her? Having a dangerous drug lord coming after her and her family would not end well. And if the FBI caught her messing around on the darknet again, she'd be more than grounded.

"Hi."

Tasha let out a yelp and fumbled her phone. Whipping around, she stared at Cameron and put a hand over her whomping heart. "You almost gave me a heart attack."

The naughty boy had the nerve to hold out his nasal cannula. "Need some air?"

A few feet behind him, Jerry glared her way, all bristly with bodyguard irritation. The back of her neck heated like it was on fire.

Tasha attempted a charming smile. "Funny. I thought Daddy declared it was time to go."

"I changed my mind," he said.

"Oh? Was it my sparkling wit?"

"Definitely." Cameron hitched up his shoulders, his arms and chest flexing under his suit jacket. Darn, but this guy had some yummy muscles. She seriously might have to gouge out her own eyes for ogling a Foster.

But what game was he playing? Gorgeous and rich, Cameron could have almost any girl he wanted. Why was he here with her? The next thought had her heart thudding. Had he seen the articles in her purse and was plotting to take her down? Maybe Cameron was just like his father, a smooth rat.

Good. It would make what she needed to do easier. She shifted her mouth into what she hoped was a pleasant smile. From the way his guard's eyes narrowed, she had some work to do before the Oscar committee arrived. "Why do you need a bodyguard?"

Cameron lifted a shoulder. "Late night pizza runs."

"Pizza is a serious subject." A laugh bubbled from her chest. She cleared her throat. *Focus.* It wasn't like this was real socializing. "Seriously, though, is G.I. Joe just for show?" He certainly didn't appear so. He seemed more like a guy who could kill and make it look like an accident.

Cameron exhaled noisily. "There've been…moments I'd rather not relive."

Another prickle from her conscience tried to prod Tasha, but she pressed it down. "I guess being the son of Nigel Foster is a hazardous occupation." She linked her arm with his and led him around the GeO-deck. "I did promise you a tour." She pointed out the window. "There's Dallas. Do you live nearby?" Tasha knew exactly where he lived, a mansion overlooking Turtle Creek in Highland Park, the richest area in DFW, but she needed to move the conversation toward getting an invite.

"Yeah. It's not too far from here." He moved, flexing his arm.

She leaned closer. What would it be like to slide her hands up and down those biceps? Ack. Why was her brain doing this? And how did a sick guy become so fit? Of course, staying in shape was extremely important for a person with a heart condition. Gran had a friend who dragged her oxygen tank with her to jazzercise. *Stop. Just stop.* She needed to change the subject before she malfunctioned and started crushing on him. "Who was the pointy-nosed guy with your dad?"

"Dr. Grisham—my cardiologist."

"Your doctor comes to parties? How does he bill for that?"

Cameron laughed, a deep rumble. "He comes with us everywhere. Always has, since my mother—since I was little." He looked away.

Her gut pinched so hard she couldn't ignore it. What would it be like, always tethered to some doctor or bodyguard? And the bit about his mother…

Nothing she'd read had mentioned one, aside from the fact that she wasn't in the picture. Another pain hit her stupid insides—an absent bio parent was too familiar and not a subject she discussed.

Cameron continued. "Grisham used to have a big medical practice, but the stress nearly killed him. He's a cardiovascular geneticist and spends most of his time researching. I'm his side project."

Weird, but then again, weren't the rich delightfully eccentric? And what was she doing, caring? No, she needed to stay on target: charming Foster IV into an invite to his house so she could hack Nigel's private computer, or at least get some insider information. Anything she could use to prove Nigel had criminal ties. "So…your dad worries about you. Are you allowed to have friends over?"

The elevator doors whooshed open, and Cameron glanced behind them. A bunch of camera-toting tourists poured onto the deck. He sidestepped them, stiff as concrete, and swiveled until he made eye contact with his bodyguard.

The big dude closed the space between them. Did they assume a threat lurked around every corner?

Tasha cleared her throat and told her inner monologue to stop interrupting. "Did you put my number in your phone yet?"

He said nothing, eyes on the tourists.

What about the people had him so distracted? She threw out a *Star Wars* test phrase to see if she could change his focus. "We should try targeting wampa rats from here."

"We'd have more luck with a rancor. Wampa rats are rather small." He tossed a half-grin her way. "Want to walk some? It's getting crowded."

She'd hardly call a dozen tourists a crowd. "Maybe you should pull that limo out of your butt." Tasha's brain screamed at her, *shut up, shut up, shut up.* Couldn't she manage to be charming for a nanosecond? It would help if her insides would stop jumping around. She leaned against his arm. "It's just that you came up here to talk to me, but you've hardly said a word." Ugh, she sucked at this.

"You don't have a problem speaking your mind, do you?"

Tasha winced. "Unfortunately, my words run on a bullet express, while the hapless Ms. Manners in my brain is stuck on a tricycle."

He chortled, and the farther they got from the new people, the more his arm relaxed.

The guard trailed them with the air of a mother bear watching her cub. Cameron had mentioned moments he'd rather not relive, hinting that he'd needed the bodyguard's protection. What had happened? Had many people tried to hurt him? Tasha stared at her shoes, mouth suddenly dry.

As Cameron and Tasha circled the building, Bethany and Gabe looked their way, blinking as if just now remembering there were other people on the planet.

Bethany's eyes followed the lines of Cameron's oxygen tubing, and her forehead wrinkled. Oh no. Bethany was going to grill him about his heart. Tasha gave Bethany her best Jedi-mind-trick glare. *These are not the questions you're looking for.*

Oblivious, doctor-wannabe Bethany pounced. "Your dad mentioned hope for your heart condition?"

Cameron popped his knuckles, eyeing the windows. "I guess it's no secret. We're going to try surgery in a few weeks to fix it, but it's not hopeful."

Tasha's gut gave another big churn.

"Then what?" Bethany asked. "Will they give you more medications or therapy?"

Seriously? Wasn't it obvious that Cameron hated talking about this? "Hey, anyone seen that movie—"

"Well," Bethany blundered on, "there have been some big advancements in medications. Which ones do you take?"

Cameron stepped back. "I should be going."

Gabe glared Tasha and Bethany into silence and nodded at Cameron. "Hey, we're going to the new Batman movie tomorrow night. You in?"

Cameron's face lit up, but he glanced at his bodyguard as if working out a math problem. "Uh, yeah. I'd like that."

Gabe held up his phone. "Digits? I'll message you the info."

Gabe typed while Cameron recited his number, which Tasha committed to memory. Finally, something was going her way.

Cameron checked his phone and nodded at Gabe. "Got it."

Tasha leaned closer to Cameron for a better look at his phone. She'd never seen one like it before. Maybe a prototype for an upcoming release? He also had two small attachments added to it, a cylinder about the size of a lip balm tube on the top and a rectangle stuck to the bottom. Maybe an infrared projector and something else?

Was this wide-eyed boy more than he pretended to be? Hah. No. More likely, he enjoyed buying toys with Daddy's money.

Gabe stepped closer. "Nice phone."

Cameron slipped it back into his pocket. "Just an extra battery and speaker add-on."

Ooh, someone was a liar with big flaming pants.

"Mr. Foster." The bodyguard loomed over Tasha's shoulder. "Our car's here."

Cameron offered a small wave. "It was nice to meet you."

Cameron's bodyguard led him to the elevator, but the big guy said something and jogged back to Tasha. Jerry's smile was all calm seas, but his eyes promised a riptide. He spoke in low tones. "My job is to protect that kid, and he's got a big heart."

Tasha's face grew hot. Was it possible to sweat out one's eyeballs? But she held Jerry's gaze. "Yeah?"

"I thought you might need a reminder. Good night, Ms. Jenkins."

Did he just threaten her? Maybe she was that obvious, and needed to work on her flirting skills. If only her insides would stop roiling. Stomach issues or not, no way could she let Jerry expose her to Cameron before she destroyed Nigel Foster.

Chapter Seven

Cameron

CAMERON SLUMPED IN BED and stared at the ceiling fan. He and Jerry had gotten home several hours ago, but he couldn't sleep. He should text Tasha about tomorrow, but his dad would say no, that movie theaters were full of horrible diseases.

They had a theater and bowling alley downstairs, but the thought of his dad allowing friends over was every bit as laughable as the idea of going out. As for Jerry? The guy trusted no one. "Be careful with that girl," he'd warned on the drive home from the benefit.

But ever since Gabe had mentioned the movie, a single thought had smothered everything else in Cameron's mind: He could sneak out.

Those four blinking words full of promise, full of potential, full of idiocy sent his pulse slamming through his temples. Was his hard drive damaged? Sneak out of the Foster Fortress full of security cameras, eight-foot iron fencing, and Jerry, with his super-secret military intelligence background?

Impossible.

Besides, Jerry and his dad were probably right. Going out was dangerous, and getting caught sneaking out would be worse.

Cameron had never defied his dad, not like that. True, his dad had no idea about the hacking stuff, but that seemed different, even noble. But this? His dad might give him ten to twenty, and he didn't have that long.

As for Tasha, was she the villain his dad and Jerry had suggested? Although she didn't give off the hungry-to-spend-Foster-money vibe, was he missing something else?

He grunted and pulled out his phone to message her, but he had nothing interesting to say. He squeezed the metal case. What kind of guy needed tutoring to text a girl?

No sense in wasting time on brick-headed what-ifs and fantasies. His dad wouldn't let him go, and there was no getting past Jerry. He should focus on something that mattered. Something in the realm of possible…like Dr. G's email.

He pulled up the search results for Beneficence Donor Corp. One lead tied it to a corporation called Gulf Siren. And like BDC, Gulf Siren was another dead end.

Awesome. A yawn built inside Cameron's throat. It'd been a long day, and Jerry would have him up in the morning to swim laps.

No rest for the dying.

Reality performed a hard reboot on his thoughts. Five weeks and six days left.

What did he care if he got in trouble trying to sneak out? Five weeks and six days. So what if he contracted some horrible movie theater disease? Five weeks and six days. What was life without risk?

Tomorrow, he'd turn seventeen. He might as well live while he could. Opening a browser, he searched for suggestions on how to text a girl.

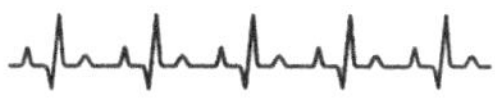

Jerry woke Cameron at the usual too-early o'clock for a swim and tai chi.

"No slacking, even on my birthday?" Cameron asked.

"Nope."

After his workout, Cameron showered and found Jerry in the kitchen. The room was a marvel of wood, stone, and metallic perfection, and the island was big enough to be seen from outer space. On most days, the vast area gleamed under Rose's housekeeping regime. She scrubbed and fussed worse than a surgeon and never left anything out of order.

Jerry pushed a tall glass of green liquid toward Cameron. Rose had taped a candle to the side of his glass and left a note on the marble counter: "Happy birthday." Cameron's throat went raw, like he'd swallowed gravel. His dad didn't encourage interaction with the staff, and they only saw Rose on the rare occasions they stayed in Dallas, but she'd remembered his birthday.

Cameron leaned on the wall next to one of the security panels that controlled things like window shades, door locks, and air systems. A perfect fit for this picture-perfect kitchen. The only thing out of place was the O2 machine in the corner. It fit in with the house the same way Cameron did with people. Maybe that's why last night had been so nice. Prickly Tasha hadn't seemed concerned about his heart condition. She treated everyone with equal hostility.

He cut his eyes to Jerry. How was he getting out of the house with a bodyguard who stuck as close as herpes?

The big guy held up a small wrapped package. "Happy birthday."

"Thanks." The box fit in the palm of Cameron's hand, and something hard rattled inside. Despite the frustration chewing on Cameron's insides, he grinned. "Keys?"

Jerry poured himself a helping of protein shake. "You won't know until you open it."

Cameron tore the wrapping off. His dad hadn't wanted him to get a license, because hiring professional drivers was safer, but through some persuasion on Jerry's part, his dad had relented. Perhaps Jerry had also convinced his dad to give him a car. He gave the box one last shake.

Lifted the lid.

And groaned. "Really funny, old man."

Jerry guffawed as Cameron held up a keychain with a palm-sized Porsche stuck to the end of it. "This will impress the ladies. Hey, baby, want to take my Porsche for a push?"

Jerry gave Cameron a playful punch on the shoulder. "You'll be the coolest among five-year-old boys."

"Just what I've always wanted."

Jerry's face cleared, and his laser-eyes narrowed at Cameron. "Here's your real gift. Food for thought."

"I was hoping for cake," Cameron said.

"You wouldn't want it if I baked it. Listen: What makes a man a man?"

Cameron knocked down a gulp of his grass-flavored smoothie. "I'm not sure I'm up for philosophy before eating cardboard muffins."

Jerry continued, unaffected. "A good man puts others first and will lay down his life for those he cares about. Like an old buddy of mine used to say: Only love and sacrifice will change the world. You hear me?"

Cameron saluted. "Yessir."

The alarm system beeped to indicate someone had opened the door in the back hall leading to the garages. A moment later, his dad's personal assistant, Rahul, bustled into the kitchen.

He held a flat, wrapped package and a gift bag. "Happy birthday!" When he snapped a picture of the package with his phone, the diamonds on his blue-faced Daytona Rolex caught the light.

Cameron glanced behind Rahul, but he seemed to have arrived alone. "I'm guessing Dad couldn't come with you."

Rahul frowned at his phone. "It's running slow."

"Try turning it off for a few seconds, if you can manage the separation."

"Someone's cheeky today." Rahul gave Cameron the stink eye but clicked the phone off and dropped it onto the counter. "Anyway, about your dad. He got called into a meeting, so we'll have to move your birthday dinner to tomorrow night."

Ten years ago, Cameron would have cried. Having such an important dad sounded great, but what it meant was spending a lot of time alone. But today, FMC's business was doing him a huge favor. He forced a frown. "Yeah. Okay."

Rahul flashed a toothy grin. "But your dad didn't want you to have to wait for your presents." He held up the wrapped package. "From me. But first ..." Rahul grunted, working to turn his phone back on. He entered the password.

Cameron snorted. "Your birthdate backwards? Are you asking to be hacked?"

Rahul snapped a picture of Cameron. "Just for that, I'm posting you on the Fashion-Fail feed."

Cameron glanced at his *There's no place like 127.0.0.1* T-shirt. "How can you be hating on *Wizard of Oz*?"

Rahul rolled his eyes and shoved the flat package toward him. "Just open it."

The present was heavy and larger than a book. Cameron tore off the paper, revealing the back of a picture frame with a certificate of authenticity. He flipped it over to find an original pencil-drawn storyboard from *Iron Man*. "Wow! This is awesome! How'd you get it?"

"I know people." Rahul insisted on more pics, then handed Cameron the large black gift bag filled with cream tissue paper. "This one's from your old man but give me a sec to call him."

"Let me guess—something educational?"

Jerry snorted. "Probably."

His dad appeared on Rahul's screen.

Cameron nodded. "Hey."

"Happy birthday, son."

Cameron yanked the tissue paper out of the bag and reached inside but caught only air. He rolled his eyes. "Dad, you messing with me?"

"If there is one thing I don't do, it is mess with my favorite son."

"I'm your only son."

"Then you should be glad you're also my favorite."

Cameron tipped the bag upside down, and a small box slid out. Jerry moved closer. The box was the same weight as the one Jerry had given him. Cameron glanced at his dad on Rahul's screen. "Haha." He opened the lid and dumped the car onto the counter. "You and Jerry are…" Except it wasn't a toy. It was a car remote. Wait… "Is that? Did you? No way!"

Rahul gestured to the hallway leading to the side drive. "Go—"

Cameron ripped off his oxygen cannula and sprinted past Rahul. He yanked open the side door and skidded to a halt on the side driveway beside a black Porsche. The others rushed after him. Cameron hugged the hood. "Dad! I love you!"

The shiny metal warmed Cameron all the way to his core. His first car. Freedom! This was perfect. Cameron had a way to meet up with Tasha, if he could escape Jerry. But wouldn't that be a kick in the pants to his dad? He'd just given Cameron this amazing gift. It'd be wrong to use it to sneak out.

But in his mind, he kept hearing the refrain. *Six weeks, six weeks.* How could he not take a chance? He wanted to grab life by the reins and make it gallop—well, something like that. Yes, destiny didn't do Cameron many favors, but perhaps she'd grown tired of kicking him while he was down.

Chapter Eight

Cameron

JERRY HANDED CAMERON a portable oxygen tank and lowered himself into the passenger seat of the car. "I've lived a long life. Might as well go for a drive." He strapped in and mouthed a prayer, holding his cross necklace.

"Thanks for the vote of confidence," Cameron said, sliding behind the wheel.

The seat was cool against his back and the steering wheel smooth. The sharp, earthy, new-leather smell permeated every-thing. He glanced over the dash—lights everywhere. This was an amazing machine. But more, it represented freedom.

Jerry held up a finger. "This car is nothing like that sleepy, arthritic Honda I used to teach you to drive stick. There's a raging psychotic stallion under the hood of this baby." He tapped the gearshift. "It might have seven gears, but if you ever drive that fast, I'll tear you up, got it?"

"Sure." Cameron pressed the ignition, and the car rumbled like a satisfied jaguar. His grin nearly jumped off his face. He slammed the car into gear and gunned it around Jerry's black truck.

He gripped the wheel and fought to keep the car off the lawn. His entire life, he'd lived by rules, and something inside him growled with the engine. He wanted more than fast. He wanted to fly.

"Whoa." Jerry pointed to the gearbox. "Remember, on this car, reverse is up and top left on the stick. And you might apologize to the flowers you just ran over."

They skidded onto the street, and Jerry grabbed his door. "So help me, if you harm someone, I'll kill you myself. And you know I can make it look like an accident."

Cameron eased off the gas enough to straighten out. Jerry lectured about safety, but Cameron hardly heard him. There had to be a way out tonight. Faking an illness wouldn't work—Jerry and Grisham would never leave him alone.

The car rolled backward at a stop sign. This wasn't as easy as it looked. He peeled out again and fishtailed around the corner. A lady glared at him like he was about to run over her purse-dog.

Jerry groaned. "Let's try not to meet Jesus face-to-face in the next five minutes."

After a few blocks, Cameron smoothed out, but he still had no idea how to escape his guard detail. He glanced Jerry's way. "You ever drive one of these?"

Jerry shook his head. "Nah."

"Want to?" Not that loaning out his car tonight would help his plan…

"Definitely. But this is your day. I'll take you up on it another time." Jerry coughed. "Speaking of your birthday, your dad had already given me the night off, and I have plans. I hate that you'll be alone today of all days."

Had he heard right? *Destiny, you beautiful, sexy thing.* Cameron tapped a rhythm on the wheel. *Don't smile, don't smile.* "Big plans?"

Jerry stared out the window. At least he'd stopped clutching the door. "Promised I'd visit Yasmine in the hospital. She thinks she can beat me at poker." Jerry chuckled, but it was hollow.

Cameron eased off the gas. Acceleration seemed insensitive. "How much longer is her treatment?"

"Not long, we hope." Jerry's voice held a husky edge.

"When she's able, you can take her out in my car. Anywhere she wants, my treat."

"You got a heart of gold."

"Too bad it doesn't work." Cameron slid the car into third gear. What was he doing, focusing on negatives when he'd been handed a gift? Breaking free to see Tasha just got two hundred times easier.

"What're you so happy about?" Jerry asked.

Dang, Yasmine wasn't the only one who sucked at a poker face. "Today's a good day."

When they returned home, Cameron made a show of yawning. "I'm going to rest." He headed up the stairs before Jerry could argue.

Inside his room, he stared at his phone. Just a simple text. If he could drive a Porsche without wrecking it, he could text a girl. But his dry mouth and empty brain protested. Everything he'd read said not to appear too eager, but with his shortened timeline, twelve hours was long enough. He went with the most brilliant thing he could think of:

Cameron

Hi.

Chapter Nine

Tasha

Tasha shoved aside the laundry she was supposed to be folding. Ever since she'd seen that picture of Cortez's niece, Florencia, Tasha couldn't stop thinking about her.

Had Florencia turned evidence and disappeared on purpose? Or had she been taken against her will? Tasha stared at the ancient brown carpet, memories stirring from the last few years. The police, reiterating that her dad's death was an accident. They'd batted around phrases like "obsessive" and "psychiatric help." Had Cortez's family been given the same treatment?

No one had seen Florencia in almost two decades. She'd be difficult to forget with her large brown eyes, thick wavy hair, and bikini-perfect figure. The last known photo of her was a grainy image taken eighteen years ago at a night club in El Paso. She was dancing with a tall, hook-nosed guy.

Tasha's phone buzzed with a message from Cameron. Tasha couldn't keep her smile under wraps as all worry about Florencia took a break. He didn't even wait an entire twenty-four hours, although he only managed one word—*Hi.*

Obviously, he wasn't sure what to say, but that was good because that meant he lacked confidence, so he'd be an easier mark. She swallowed back a wave of nausea and typed:

Tasha

Hi.

It was probably a fool's errand to think she'd find evidence in Nigel's house, but if she could hack his accounts, she could watch out for his next evil deed, maybe even find a way into the fortress that was FMC South. More lives, like her dad's, might depend on her exposing Nigel. But to do so, she had to get Cameron to trust her. She settled onto the floor and typed. An hour later, she knew a handful of earth-shattering facts such as Cameron had no pets, liked both DC and Marvel, his favorite color was green, and he preferred snow to sand. And they'd shared pictures of their shoes. Clearly, they were both skilled communicators.

Tasha

Call me?

The phone buzzed. Her insides did a stupid flip, as if this were a boy calling to speak to the real her. She straightened her hair, stamped away her unease, and answered. "Hey."

He wore a T-shirt, and his hair was messy curly like he'd run his hands through it. An improvement over last night. This boy she could almost imagine sitting next to her at DAST-M. His Adam's apple moved with a swallow. "Um, hey."

Tasha sank onto the floor. He was so shy—again, not what she'd expected from a guy whose net worth rivaled a small country. "Is this your first time calling a girl?" Ugh, that sounded more accusatory than flirty. She had to do better.

He spoke before she could clarify. "I chat up plenty of girls. Just last week there was this lovely brunette in Paris."

An image of Cameron sitting across from a sophisticated and beautiful European girl ballooned in her brain. Heads together, laughing, and dining at a Paris café. She had the ridiculous urge to scratch something. "Oh? What did you and Paris girl talk about?"

"Sushi, mainly. She was very nice."

"Sushi in Paris instead of any manner of pastries? What kind of weirdo are you?"

He rumbled a laugh—that boy had a golden voice. "Nicolette thought I was quite charming, especially when we left her a good tip."

A waitress. The tightness in Tasha's chest fizzled out. Before she knew it, they'd navigated into critical stuff like *Star Trek* versus *Star Wars* and Batman versus Iron Man. She had no idea how much time had passed when Cameron paused in the middle of reading from the French translation of Harry Potter. "Oops. Gotta go. It's time for my bo staff lesson."

Tasha sat up. "Your what-what?"

"Bo staff, quarter staff—you know, like Donatello the Ninja Turtle. Which doesn't sound manly or awesome now that I said it. Anyway, I gotta go. See you tonight?"

She shook out her leg. It'd gone numb. "Sure."

He hung up, and Tasha glanced at the phone. They'd talked for a hundred and thirty-six minutes, but it'd passed like five. The silence throbbed in her ears, and the room felt dull and empty. She paced. The important thing was to keep her objectivity. The phone grew hot in her hand, and she dropped it on the floor.

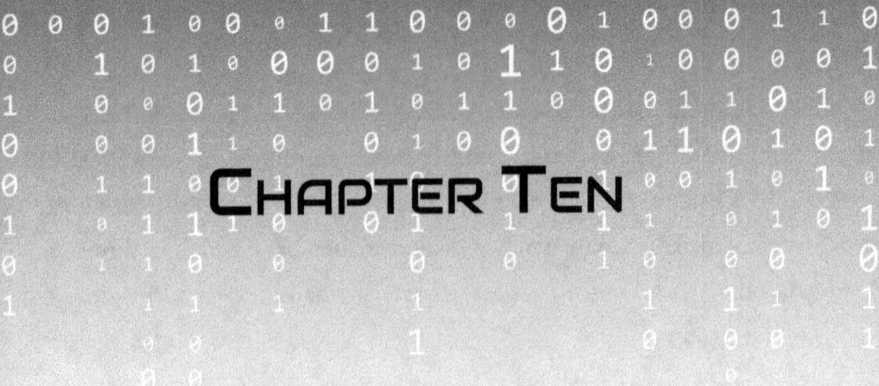

CHAPTER TEN

Cameron

Seated in his Computer Graveyard, Cameron flicked through the house's security camera feeds. Both Jerry and his dad had already left for the evening, which left Leon to watch the house and make sure Cameron didn't keel over. Considering Leon was as smart as a bowl of oatmeal, Cameron was optimistic.

For extra insurance, Cameron had left a bottle of expensive bourbon in the basement theater. That, combined with tonight's huge boxing match, should keep Leon occupied.

It didn't take long for Leon to spot the amber liquor and settle on the couch with a glass in one hand and a remote in the other. Now was Cameron's chance.

He slipped out the side door and into his Porsche. There was a small possibility his dad would notice the car had moved, especially with all its security protocols, but Cameron had made sure that if anyone checked, Cameron's phone would show he was in his room. The house cameras and the car's security system would show the car was in the garage.

Cameron eased down the driveway, headlights off, keeping an eye on the security camera footage on his phone.

For a moment, Leon sat up and cocked his head like he was listening. Cameron held his breath, as if that would help. Dang it. The engine was rumbling. He threw it into neutral and turned it off, rolling the rest of the way out of the driveway, his eyes on the screen until Leon settled back onto the couch.

He punched his fist into the air. He was free.

This was Cameron's moment, an opportunity to plot his own course. A real outing with no bodyguards, no fanfare, and no doctor watching his every move. Best birthday present yet.

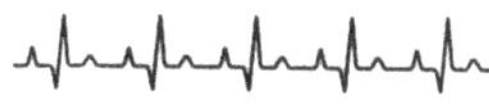

Tasha

Cameron was already waiting in front of the theater when Tasha, Gabe, and Bethany drove past, looking for a parking spot. Foster wore a T-shirt that said, *There's no place like 127.0.0.1.* Interesting, first he lied about his phone attachments being a simple speaker and battery, and now he sported the nerd code for home. He wore a simple, small backpack slung over his shoulder, but no sign of O2 tubes on his face.

As Gabe turned down another aisle in search of a parking spot, Bethany reached behind her seat to poke Tasha's knee. "I forgot how cute he is."

Gabe grunted and headed toward several open spaces at the end of the row, probably to protect his Jeep from door dings. "I wish *Tasha* would stop talking about that guy."

Bethany leaned into Gabe's side. "I just want her to enjoy something for once."

Gabe hopped out and opened both their doors, pausing to give Tasha a dubious glance, as though he could see the calculating schemer lurking under the surface.

Bethany busied herself with her phone, and Cameron waved as they got closer.

"Hey," he said.

"Hey," Tasha said. Once again, totally killer dialogue. His cologne wafted in her direction—he smelled all manly, like something spicy and warm and foresty—dang! What was she doing? This was Nigel Foster's son, not her date.

She had work to do. The night her dad died played like an earworm in her memory. The screams. The out-of-control car. The bogus report saying Solomon had driven his truck into the perimeter fence. But she knew the truth. Something had happened at Foster Med Corp that night. Something that got her dad killed. And she'd bet her good laptop that Nigel Foster was behind it.

Cameron held up his phone. "Tickets."

Gabe swiped open his phone. "How much—"

Foster shook his head. "No, I got it."

Bethany folded her arms across her chest. "That's not why we invited you."

Cameron's face fell like a scolded puppy. "I didn't mean anything by it."

Tasha waved them onward. "Thanks, but next time be a jerk and we'll all get along better." She searched for a different subject. "How'd you get your dad to let you out? Doesn't he think movie theaters are wretched hives of scum and villainy?"

"Only the ones in Mos Eisley," Cameron said.

Tasha couldn't stop a laugh from escaping. Another true *Star Wars* fan. Nice.

Bethany looked over Foster like a doctor inspecting a patient. "Shouldn't you have your oxygen?"

Cameron winced, but he shrugged the shoulder holding his backpack. "I don't need it every minute of the day."

Bethany's model-like face fell. "You don't have to be embarrassed."

He glanced behind him at the parking lot and turned one foot in that direction. Poor guy was about to bolt.

Tasha gritted her teeth and cut her eyes to Bethany. "It's none of our business what he does and when." She gestured to his bag. "Wear it or don't, but don't leave at least until after we've introduced you to movie theater popcorn."

Since Gabe and Bethany held a whispered discussion on the way into the theater, Tasha had nothing better to do than observe Cameron. He glanced at the movie posters, the crowded concession stands, and the people milling around them. His forehead scrunched up, and he dodged a group, leaning away, same as he'd done with those tourists last night.

Time to distract him. "When was the last time you went to the movies?"

Cameron slowed his pace. His eyes shifted back and forth, and he shoved his hands deep into his pockets.

"You've never been to the movies?"

"Why would you say that?"

"You have an expressive face. Don't try poker."

He gestured to the concession stand. "You want something?"

A deflection rather than an answer. "Do my questions make you uncomfortable?"

"And she asks another." He gasped and gripped his chest like he was in pain.

Tasha's knees wobbled. "You okay?" A jolt of energy burned through her chest. What should she do? Who should she call if he keeled over?

He chuckled. "Gotcha."

The nerve. She shoved his arm and stalked to the counter. "Just for that, you're buying."

"Fair enough."

Tasha ordered popcorn, chocolate candies, and a drink. She gestured to him, but he was busy scanning the crowd. His gleaming Patek Philippe watch screamed rich daddy's boy. Was he trying to get mugged?

He nodded to the guy behind the counter. "Just a bottled water."

"You want that sanitized?" She gulped. Ugh, she needed some strong tape to hold her lips shut, but Cameron seemed so tense.

He raised his eyebrows. "You ever stop?"

"No. I have a condition. It's hereditary."

Cameron smirked and pulled out his wallet, swiping one of those exclusive black credit cards. The movement dislodged another item from his pocket—a baggie filled with white powder that plopped onto the floor.

Tasha froze, her gaze stuck on the power, and her mind spun. Was he trying to get them arrested? Maybe Cameron knew she wanted revenge on his dad, so he'd come here to plant drugs on her. He'd make an anonymous tip to the police and would have her sent to jail. Then anything she said against his dad would be discounted as an attempt to divert blame. She couldn't catch her breath. She and the others needed to get away from him.

From behind them, Gabe grabbed Cameron's arm, jerking him backward and pointing at the baggie still on the floor. "What are you playing at?"

With his wide shoulders and ability to swagger, Gabe could be scary when he wanted. But Cameron looked more confused than concerned. Guess that was a side benefit from staring into the dark abyss of Nigel Foster's eyes every day.

With a flick of his wrist, Cameron twisted out of Gabe's grasp. "What?"

Gabe kicked the bag of white stuff. "You trying to get us arrested? I'm not ruining my future for some stupid rich-kid prank."

Cameron swiped up the powder, but he didn't back down. "You mean my prescribed immune booster?" His voice was every bit as needle edged as Gabe's.

Gabe's shoulders lowered a few inches. "Seriously?"

Cameron shrugged. "It's a prototype nutritional supplement from Foster Med Corp's research division." He pointed to an FMC insignia on one side of the baggie.

"But white powder in a tiny bag?" Tasha asked. "Didn't your doctor know how odd that would look?"

He shrugged. "It's a prototype. Marketing hasn't packaged it yet."

Before Tasha could dig deeper, Bethany leaned closer. A raccoon keychain swung from her purse strap. "What kinds of medications do you take again?"

Nearby, people stared. Any moment, someone might call the cops and ruin the night. Tasha spoke in a loud voice. "Glad you brought your heart meds. Let's go." She shooed them into the theater. Bethany chose a middle row and settled between Gabe and Cameron.

Guess Tasha would take the other end by Cameron. She leaned over to address all three of them and pointed to Cameron. "Okay, spill. Condition. Medications."

"What happened to it's none of your business?" Cameron asked.

Tasha raised her hands. When he'd faked having heart palpitations, it'd made her think. "If you're sick enough to carry around oxygen and strange powders, you're sick enough to need someone with you who knows how to help you." She softened her voice. "Just in case."

Cameron relented. "Fine. I have a transposition of the great vessels made worse by a viral condition I contracted as an infant. My latest X-rays and EKG show I have dilated cardiomyopathy."

"An enlarged left ventricle?" Bethany said.

He nodded. "I take digoxin, carvedilol, and spironolactone, along with an arsenal of herbal supplements."

"Fluid on your lungs?" Bethany asked.

"What, are you a doctor?" Cameron slid to the edge of his seat.

"She just plays one at the movies." Tasha glared at Bethany.

Bethany's mouth puckered. "But you're what, seventeen?"

"Yes."

Bethany was shaking her head. "There are surgeries to fix that defect at birth. Surely with all your dad's doctors—"

"My mother didn't—forget it." Cameron stood, his gaze etched on the exit.

Tasha's eyes grew hot. The knife edge in his voice covered deep wounds, ones she recognized. She put a hand on his arm. "Hey, sorry. We were out of line."

"I'm sorry," Bethany said. "I just find medical stuff so fascinating."

"We cool?" Gabe asked.

Cameron settled back in his chair, still leaning away from Bethany. "Yeah."

Good. Tasha would have done all kinds of harm to Gabe and Bethany if they'd messed this up. She picked at her popcorn, appetite gone, and snuck another peek at Cameron. What had happened with his mom?

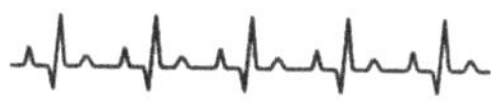

All through the movie, Tasha did the dumb thing and left her hand available on the armrest, but Golden Boy never made a move. Had she misread his interest?

After the final credits, Gabe rubbed his stomach. "Food. Now."

Bethany checked her phone. "Yeah, I wouldn't mind eating." Of course she wouldn't. Bethany's metabolism turned calories into awesomeness.

Gabe lifted his chin toward Cameron. "We're going to Whataburger. You in?"

"You keep mentioning this place." Cameron scrunched up his forehead.

Tasha grinned. "Burgers, fries, taquitos, and onion rings. It's pretty much Texas on a bun."

Cameron gave her a dubious look. "Sounds more like cholesterol on a bun."

She nudged him with her shoulder. "Tomayto, tomahto. Only one way to find out."

Cameron glanced at his phone. His olive skin glowed under the parking lot lights. Tasha was going to strangle her inner monologue if it made one more comment about his appearance.

Bethany flashed Cameron a one-point-twenty-one gigawatt smile. "Would your dad mind if you came with us?"

Cameron didn't seem fazed by Bethany's dazzle. Not even a double take. "I can come."

Gabe headed toward his car, but Cameron stepped in the opposite direction. Bethany glanced over her shoulder. "Do you know where we're going? It's just down the street."

"No, wait," Tasha said. This was a great opportunity. "I'll ride with you."

The two boys held some sort of dude staring contest that ended with Gabe giving him a stern nod. "Cool. See you two in five." The unspoken "or else" hung in the air.

Cameron tilted his head as they walked. "Do I look untrustworthy?"

"No, actually. You look as deceptive as a cow."

"I'm not sure whether to be offended. Is that good or bad?"

"You ever see a cow lie?"

"Still unsure about being offended, but until last night, I'd never even seen a chicken up close, not even on my plate. Thanks for that."

"Yeah, sure." Tasha stared at some gum smashed into the pavement. Trust-Fund Boy was not what she'd expected, nothing like his cold father. She fisted her hands, nails digging into her palms.

What was she doing, humanizing him? But dang it, he was so nice, and her plan was…well, anything but nice. She chewed a lip and fingered the tiny flash drive on her bracelet. She had to focus on the endgame, getting justice for her dad.

Not once had she spoken of what she'd seen that night, not even to her therapist. Who would believe her? And some bad people might kill her if she told, but she couldn't let it drop. Not after what those goons at FMC did.

It didn't matter how attractive or nice this boy was. When she finished with Nigel and FMC, Cameron would hate her forever.

He stopped at a shiny black Porsche with paper dealership tags and opened the door for her. After she got in, he slid into the driver's seat and fumbled around with the gearshift. "Got your seatbelt on?"

"Do I need more than one?"

"Maybe." He took a breath and closed his eyes like he was praying. "Tell me more about your school." He took off with a squeal, fishtailing out of the parking lot, and grimaced. "Sorry."

They were going to die.

Tasha gripped the door handle and distracted herself from the constant whiplash of Cameron's driving by yapping about her robotics camera project until they pulled up to Whataburger. When the car jerked to a stop, Tasha whispered her own quick prayer of thanks and tried to loosen her death-grip on the door.

Cameron rushed around to help her out like some Southern gentleman. And he wasn't out of breath.

From nearby, Gabe whistled. "Nice ride."

Cameron shoved his hands into his pockets and shrugged. "Just got it today."

The piranha in Tasha opened its big mouth. "You in the new-car-of-the-month club?"

Cameron's smile crashed and skidded off his face. "I've never had a car before. It's my birth—well, anyway. Dad got it." Cameron's face clouded, and he stared away. "I suppose he's feeling sentimental…"

"It's your birthday?" Bethany said, jumping into the conversation.

Cameron stared at the sidewalk. Was he acting self-conscious to get more attention? But a guy wanting attention would drone on about his car, his travels, his money. Cameron barely spoke about himself when asked. Maybe this car was some kind of guilty-dad offering to his sick kid.

She swallowed past the rock in her throat. "Happy birthday. I'm glad your dad let you spend it with us."

Cameron grabbed his backpack. After he looped it over his shoulder, he gestured Gabe toward the car. "Get in."

Gabe turned into a squealing three-year-old at a donut buffet. He slid inside and gripped the wheel, a grin splitting his face.

Cameron ducked into the car. "You want to drive?"

Tasha balked. "Gabe can't drive stick, and when, not if, he wrecks this thing, his life will totally suck. Come on." She grabbed Cameron's arm. "Let's corrupt you further with fast food."

Cameron slowed down. "Um, so I eat vegan."

Tasha looked at him sideways. "You eat fish."

"Okay, mostly vegan with the exception of fish."

"You ate my chicken at the banquet."

"My one and only transgression." He held the door for her and the others.

"Well, aren't you full of complexities? You'll survive this too."

Inside the fast-food restaurant, he glanced at the white plastic booths and tables highlighted with orange stripes as if he'd never seen such a sight.

Tasha tried to imitate one of Bethany's flirtatious smiles and led him to the front counter, ordering him a burger with everything. Again, Cameron tried to pay for everyone, but Gabe refused, telling the guy behind the register to put his and Bethany's food on a separate order.

Before things grew any more tense, Tasha led Cameron to a booth and settled next to him. He leaned on the table, flashing his toothpaste-ad-worthy teeth. Bethany and Gabe grabbed drinks and settled across from them. Cameron's O2 backpack rested on the bench beside him, but he wasn't using it.

Bethany sipped a Dr. Pepper and twirled her phone in circles on the table. The raccoon on her phone case became a blur of black and white.

Gabe grabbed the phone in mid spin and held it up. "What's your deal with raccoons? They're essentially scavengers, you know."

Bethany grabbed her phone back. "They're clever."

A worker dropped off a tray laden with their food, including three burgers for Gabe. Tasha rolled her eyes at him. "If I ate like you, I'd need a cardiologist."

Gabe unwrapped his burger and spoke around a bite. "Leave it to the professionals, then."

Unlike Gabe, Cameron inspected his burger with the air of a scientist, lifting the bun and peering at the contents. Instead of taking a bite, he surreptitiously poured his odd bag of white powder into yet another water bottle and stared around the restaurant as if worried someone might pull out a gun at any moment. He shoved the tiny bag with the powdery residue back into his pocket.

What was making him nervous? Was it the lack of a body-guard? His weird vitamin powder? Or perhaps the fact that he'd probably never eaten at a fast-food place.

But the restaurant seemed sedate for this time of night. Two couples in cowboy hats, boots, and skin-tight Wranglers munched their food across the aisle, leeching the smell of cigarette smoke. Gross, but not threatening, especially con-sidering the two cops hunched in a corner booth, eyeballing everyone to deter them from committing a crime during their dinner break.

On the benches outside, a rowdy group threw fries at each other and watched the cars. They were troubling, but with the cops around, they wouldn't be trolling for purses in the parking lot. Although several of them eyed Cameron's Porsche like hungry lions watching a wildebeest.

Tasha shook her head. "You don't get out much, do you?"

Cameron pinched a fry between his fingers, inspecting it. "We've established that."

She smirked. He never seemed phased by the straight pipeline of rude thoughts that she so easily blurted. Better still, he was willing to dish back. Tasha took a fry for a swim in her ketchup and popped the hot, salty, crispy deliciousness into her mouth. "Live a little."

Cameron squinted at the tiny tub of red stuff. "You know, that's essentially red dye and processed sugar."

She took a sip of her Dr. Pepper and waved a fry at him. "There's salt and vinegar in there too."

Cameron took a nibble of the ketchup-less fry she was holding. She laughed—no one had ever dared to steal her fries, especially not from her own fingers. This guy…oh, those delicious chocolate eyes. No! She should not be enjoying this, but she laughed again. "I still say fries without ketchup is like chocolate without peanut butter."

"I wouldn't know."

"Are you even American?"

"Among other things, and I thought girls were made of sugar and spice."

"Pretty sure I'm made of ketchup." She pointed to his fully loaded burger. "Try it."

Cameron took two tiny bites of bun and vegetables before burying the rest under the wrapper and chugging his water.

Tasha took a moment to refill her drink, but when it was clear he wouldn't eat more, she gathered everyone's trash and tossed it in the bin.

Gabe stretched. "Guess we need to head home."

Tasha gripped her drink. How had the night gone by so fast?

Cameron's shoulders fell. Was he as disappointed as she was—for different reasons, obviously—that the evening was over? Good. Maybe he'd invite her over to his house next. At the thought, her tattle-tale insides burned as though she'd eaten the triple jalapeno special. She took a long gulp of Dr. Pepper as they headed for the door.

Outside, the parking lot smelled of old grease and deceit. She glanced back at Cameron, her throat dry. "Call me? I know your dad doesn't like you going out, but we could come hang out with you."

Cameron's face lit up. He was so easy.

Her stomach, on the other hand, twisted.

"Hey." One of the guys eating outside stood, his gaze locked onto Cameron's fancy watch. "Got any change?"

Stupid, stupid Cameron and his rich-kid vibe was going to get them mugged. Tasha grabbed his arm and steered him to the car.

Two of the guys followed.

Tasha slammed the car door shut and pulled out her phone. "Just drive. I'll have Gabe meet us down the road."

Cameron tossed his backpack into the back and dropped his phone and wallet in the center console. He revved the engine and ground the car into gear. But instead of backing out, the car pitched forward and tapped a Ford truck, which probably belonged to the bug-eyed cowboy who'd just run out of the building.

Cameron swore. The cowboy and the group in the parking lot flooded toward the Porsche. Cameron's words jammed together. "Mydadisgoingtokillme."

Tasha held up her hand. "Easy, Golden Boy. Don't get your heart rate up."

"Stop calling me that." His voice was breathy, and he gasped for air. In that moment, he sounded like a guy with an illness.

Tasha hauled his backpack out of the back seat. "Oxygen."

But he got out of the car. What. An. Idiot. Tasha locked the doors. The cops inside could take care of this, and she didn't want to die early.

Cowboy puffed his chest out and gestured at Cameron. Their voices were muffled, but she could hear a slight slur in Cowboy's words as he called Cameron's pedigree into question.

Cameron pointed over the hood, saying, "There's no damage." Was he trying to get killed?

Cowboy took a swing. Tasha let out a scream, but Cameron shifted. He blocked the punch, twisted the guy's arm around, and let him stumble, face first, to the pavement. Tasha scrambled closer to the windshield for a better look.

A guy went for Cameron from behind, but Cameron blocked his punch and used the heel of his hand to hit the guy in the chest, knocking him backward. Tasha bounced in her seat so hard the Porsche shook. Who was this boy?

Before anyone else attacked, the cops shouted for everyone to back up. Oh no, oh no, oh no, they were going to arrest people. Tasha unstrapped her seatbelt.

One of the cops dealt with Cowboy, and the other spoke to Cameron. "All right, let's see some ID." He used that slow, exhausted manner that indicated it'd already been a long night.

Tasha shoved out of the car. "But he didn't do anything! Those jerks attacked him."

The cop held up a hand while Cameron patted his pockets, obviously forgetting he'd dropped his wallet in the car. He pulled out his money clip, and stuck to the back of it was the bag that had held the white powder.

Tasha's stomach skydived. The cop let out a super-long sigh and inspected the bag of white powder. "You wanna explain this?" He nodded to his partner. "Call K9. We got another one."

"No!" Tasha said. "It's a medicinal immune booster. Call his doctor, he'll tell you. It's for a heart condition." She ducked back into the car to grab Cameron's wallet. Maybe it had some sort of medical alert card.

"Hey!" the cop yelled. "Young lady, put your hands where we can see them."

"I'm just getting his wallet!" She held up the black billfold.

The cop flashed a light at Cameron's eyes, and Cameron made a noise like an asthmatic dog. Tasha glanced around. Gabe's car idled at the edge of the parking lot. This was her chance to run away from this mess. Get in Gabe's car and disappear.

The cop instructed Cameron to put his hands on the hood of the car and yanked his arm back to cuff him.

Cameron wheezed. "You're making a mistake."

"Yeah," Tasha said. "He's just a dumb rich kid, not a drug dealer."

"Thanks," Cameron said.

The cop patted Cameron down for weapons. "Guess Daddy will help you make bail." He held up Cameron's phone, staring at the attachments. "What's all this stuff? Place to hide your drugs?"

Tasha stepped onto the car floorboard to stand taller and glared at the cop. "No, he's a heart patient. Until tonight, he'd never been out of his house, practically. He doesn't even eat red meat."

"Looked like he was enjoying his burger."

"Two bites of bun and *lettuce*."

Cameron's face went whiter than hers.

"Seriously, he needs his oxygen! He has a transposition of the great arteries, which means his blood under-oxygenates. Cameron? You okay?"

He sputtered.

Lucky for Cameron, Tasha had excellent lungs. She screamed and bounced up and down, making the car shake. "He's having a heart attack! Call an ambulance!" Cameron gave her an odd look, but she was just getting started. "He's going to die if you don't get him help now!"

One of the cops groaned but squeezed his radio and called for an ambulance.

Tasha pointed to the car. "Let me get his oxygen."

The other cop held out his hand. "Slowly. Pass it over."

Tasha handed over the backpack and turned up the whine in her voice. "The stress could kill him."

Cameron closed his eyes, wheezing. He was either worthy of an award, or he was having an actual heart attack.

The cop searched Cameron's backpack before handing over the portable oxygen tube. "Why do you have all that cash?"

Cameron shoved his nasal cannula under his nose and gulped air, not answering. Any moment he might somersault through death's door.

Tasha's throat was tight—probably allergies. "Didn't you hear me say he's a rich idiot? That's Cameron Foster the Fourth, Nigel Foster's son."

The cop by Tasha rubbed his temple. "Should that mean something to us?"

"Lawsuits, for starters. His dad is a gajillionaire. His company, Foster Med Corp, does research in honor of his son who is dying of a heart condition. This son. Who never gets to go out alone, so he doesn't know it's stupid to carry cash."

The cop by Cameron sniffed the baggie with the white residue. "We're supposed to believe this is heart medication?"

Tasha increased her volume to Shrilling Harpy. "His dad employs a private cardiologist who prescribes all sorts of experimental treatments and supplements."

The cop winced.

Tasha went on, louder. "Call his doctor and lawyers to ask, but he needs to go to the hospital." She leaned over the hood of the car to see Cameron better. This guy made no sense. Fifteen minutes ago, she'd have sworn nothing was wrong with him, but now he looked ready to keel over. "You want me to call your dad?"

"Jerry." He murmured out the number.

An ambulance pulled into the parking lot, along with a couple more cop cars, one of them a K9 unit. Tasha told the ambulance driver to take Cameron to Dallas General and dialed Jerry. This should be interesting with a side sauce of terrifying.

Chapter Eleven

Cameron

Cameron would have preferred a heart attack to sitting in the hospital waiting for his dad to come kill him. Worse, he didn't have his phone—the police hadn't given it back before he was loaded into the ambulance. A tech had performed an EKG test and a chest x-ray on him, but so far no doctor had offered Cameron results. His stomach churned from the two bites of white bread from the restaurant. More proof he was an idiot. Why did he think he could eat like a normal person? Be a normal person?

He glanced at the door for the millionth time, but it wasn't like he could escape. His car was back at the stupid Whataburger with a giant dog tearing it apart to search for drugs. Did he seriously look like a drug dealer?

Dr. Zemke, according to his name tag, walked into the room, staring at his laptop. When the doctor looked up, he blinked several times, checked his computer screen, and glanced back at Cameron. His left hand balled up around his pen. He took a moment before squeezing some words out. "How're you feeling?"

It seemed like the doctor was the one with a medical problem. Considering his gray hair and raisin-like face, maybe he was past his prime. "Are you all right?" Cameron asked.

Dr. Zemke nodded and rubbed his eyelids. "Long night. Long career."

Cameron adjusted his oxygen tubes. "Can you prescribe something to keep my dad from killing me?"

The doctor didn't seem to hear. He kept scanning information on his computer, glancing at Cameron and back at the screen.

The familiar burn spread through Cameron's chest and numbed his hands. "What is it?"

"I just..." Dr. Zemke backed up until he bumped the door. "I need to check something." He pulled the door shut behind him.

Great. More trouble. Maybe Cameron's heart was in such bad shape they wouldn't release him from the hospital.

The door swung open. Cameron gripped the sides of the bed, waiting for his dad to burst in screaming. But it was worse. Jerry strode into the room, his mood blacker than his T-shirt. He glared at Cameron, and his arm tats did a dangerous dance as his biceps flexed. "I told you that girl was trouble."

A thousand protests whirled through Cameron's mind, and the horrid hospital gown itched. He'd never been in trouble before, not really, except for that time with the maid's chocolate syrup, but nothing like this. "I'm sorry. I totally messed up. I just wanted to have some fun, and there were these guys who were going to mug us, and I missed reverse and hit first, and I tapped some guy's car—"

Jerry held up his hand. "If you were my kid, I'd drag your hind end out back and switch you with a tree branch for sneaking out."

Cameron squeezed his eyes shut. When Jerry's weight pressed the edge of the bed down, Cameron took a breath and glanced his way again.

Instead of preparing to pound Cameron into a sheet of paper, Jerry stared out the window. "Listen, I get it. You're cooped up most of the time with thugs like Leon and old buzzards like me." When his cross necklace shifted, a beam of light glinted into Cameron's eyes, as if God himself was exposing all his inner thoughts. "But you broke trust with a lot of people tonight. And you've gotta take better care of yourself if you want to make it through this surgery."

Cameron's dry throat was made of Velcro. "You heard Dr. G. I probably won't make it through surgery. I just wanted to feel normal."

"Well, get ready to feel like a normal kid who's grounded." He let out a tiny laugh. "Tasha said you used kung fu on the guy?"

"More like tai chi—just a simple block."

Jerry tried to glare, but underneath the narrowed eyes, he looked impressed.

Someone shoved the door open again. Jerry jumped to his feet and whirled. Cameron's heart pounded, but it was only Tasha.

The pretty blonde rushed toward him. "You okay?"

Hmm. She was genuinely worried about him. Maybe he should visit the hospital more often. Cameron slumped against the pillows and tried to look sick. "They're running tests."

She handed over his car remote and glanced at some paperwork a nurse had left on a tray. Her forehead wrinkled like she'd seen something concerning.

His heart jolted all over again. "What? Is it bad?"

She waved, like she was trying to reassure him. "There's no specifics on here. Just that you're being seen by Dr. Zombie."

"Um, who?" Cameron asked, leaning forward again.

Tasha lifted a shoulder. "That's what Mom and the other nurses call Dr. Zemke. He's been here forever, and back in the day he was good." She pursed her lips. "I mean, he still knows his stuff, but sometimes he mixes up words or even patients. In fact, he's retiring at the end of the month. Mom and I are going to the party." She chewed her lip like she'd said too much. "But I'm sure you're getting great care."

Cameron groaned. The doctor had seemed a few decades past his prime. He hoped the old guy didn't try to give him the wrong patient's medicine.

Jerry crossed his arms over his chest and frowned. "You know him personally? Think we need to ask for someone else?"

She shook her head. "Mom insisted I shadow him last summer in case I suddenly decided to follow her plan for my life and go pre-med. It'll be fine."

Jerry tucked the paperwork into his pocket and headed to the door. "Still, I think I'll have a chat with the nurse. Be right back." He lifted his chin to Tasha. "Maybe you should get going. Mr. Foster will be here soon, and you don't want to be here for that." Jerry headed into the hall.

His dad... A wave of nausea hit Cameron.

Tasha put a hand on the spot where her waist tucked in and her hips curved out. Cameron had to look away to stop his mind from wandering, but she ran some fingers through her hair, reclaiming his attention. "Hope you grovel to your dad better than you drive, or else I might not see you again until you're out of college."

Cameron straightened. Even after all the weird and awkward things he'd done, she still wanted to see him again? "You sure you're up for more of this?"

Tasha leaned against the wall. "Tonight was one of the most entertaining evenings I've had in years. And your kung fu moves were…most impressive." She deepened her voice to Darth Vader level.

He couldn't hold in his grin. A beautiful girl was complimenting him on his athletic ability while quoting *Star Wars*. Though his DMs were full of pretty girls wanting his attention, Tasha was different. She wasn't tossing out *Star Wars* quotes and arguing about Batman's superiority over Iron Man to impress him. She seemed genuinely into that stuff. And she was so smart, with a wide-open future in whatever career she chose, so she didn't seem the type to only be interested in his bank accounts. *Please*, don't let his dad ground him forever.

He wanted to get out of this bed and hug her, or maybe more. Some interesting ideas fizzed in his mind, but considering he didn't have his pants, he stayed put.

"Oh." She fumbled in her purse and handed over his phone. "Thought you'd be missing this."

It was like getting part of his arm back, but Cameron didn't want to look at the display. Still, he'd have to man up sometime. When he glanced at it, his stomach sank into the uncomfortable hospital bed. Yep, his dad had called and texted numerous times—things like: "Where are you?" "Are you OK?" "I'm calling the police." "The police said you're in the hospital?! On my way."

This wouldn't end well. Before he could suggest Tasha leave, the door opened, and Cameron's dad stormed inside, followed by a frazzled Rahul and a frowning Dr. Grisham. Cameron dropped his phone as his stomach performed some major gymnastics. The fact he didn't throw up was amazing.

Rahul flashed Cameron a sideways look as though torn between giving him a high five and a lecture. Cameron's father, though, looked mad enough to high-five a hole into the wall.

Cameron sank lower in the sheets, hands going numb. He sucked hard on the O2 pumping into his nose to stave it off.

His dad rushed to his side, eyes lasering into Cameron's head. "Son, are you all right?"

Cameron opened his mouth, but his voice seemed on mute. He nodded.

"You're not hurt? Not at all?"

Cameron shook his head. Too bad he wasn't injured, because he could use some sympathy. Judging by the fire burning in his dad's eyes, a big hammer was about to fall.

His dad took a long, ragged breath and paced. "Sneaking out. Wrecking your car in the middle of the night. I thought you'd been kidnapped!" His dad's voice rose with each word. He leaned over the bed, eyes level with Cameron's. "Have you no regard for your own health and safety? I cannot believe you would risk so much this close to our surgery!" The final word echoed around the room.

Cameron leaned back. His dad never yelled. Not even when that chauffer had tried to steal a strand of pearls that had belonged to Cameron's great-grandmother.

Grisham checked Cameron's vitals, then nodded. "He's just shaken up. I'll get him discharged and monitor him at home."

His dad sagged into the one chair in the room, glancing at Dr. Grisham. "Do you think that's wise?"

Dr. G curled his lips. "And risk his health in this petri dish of infection?" Shaking his head, he rushed out the door.

His dad let out a loud exhale and smoothed his tie, motioning to Cameron. "You heard Dr. Grisham. Get dressed."

Tasha gave a tiny wave and tried to slip out the door, but not before his dad nailed her with a stare. "My son was with you?"

"It was my fault, Dad."

"I was speaking to Ms. Jenkins."

"Yes, he was with me," Tasha said, tilting her chin up.

"And you went to some restaurant establishment serving fried, processed foods?"

Those intelligent eyes of hers sparked. "You mean we got something to eat like normal seventeen-year-olds?"

This was going to escalate quickly. "I chose to go, Dad."

Neither Tasha nor his dad paid him any attention.

"Are you aware my son has a severe heart condition, and that he has a critical surgery in less than six weeks?"

Tasha glanced at Cameron, forehead wrinkling, but said, "Of course."

Cameron yanked his clothes on under the sheet, tossed aside the lame hospital gown, and slid out of the bed. Tasha looked like an angry, cornered cat. After a moment, his dad leaned back in the chair and huffed like this was too much for him to handle.

Cameron shoved his feet into his shoes. "Let's just—"

Dr. Grisham returned with Jerry in tow. Grisham said, "We can leave now." He glanced over his shoulder at the door like something concerned him, then his eyebrows wrinkled as he looked at Cameron's dad. "Everything okay?"

His dad pinched the bridge of his nose before motioning to Cameron. "We'll talk about this when we get home."

Cameron cringed. "Dad, I'm sorry. I screwed up. Just once, I wanted to know what it was like to be a regular person. She was only being nice."

The door opened again. Dr. Zemke glanced around the room and gripped his laptop. He blinked, eyes wide, staring between Cameron, his dad, and everyone else. Guess they looked like a mess.

Cameron's dad motioned to Jerry and spoke in his CEO voice. "Take my son home in his car and keep the keys and his phone." He waved toward the door.

Dr. Zemke cleared his throat. "I'd advise my patient to remain at the hospital."

Dr. Grisham shook his head. "I've already arranged for *my* patient's discharge, and I will monitor his care."

On Rahul's way out, he glanced down at Dr. Zemke's computer screen. The younger man's head did a backward jerk, like something horrible lurked on the pages.

"What?" Cameron asked.

Cameron's dad was too busy glaring at Tasha to notice. Rahul took a couple steps back and attempted a casual shrug, but he glanced sideways at Dr. Zemke. "Nothing. I'm just glad you're all right."

What did Rahul see? What about Cameron's tests concerned him?

Jerry pulled Cameron out of the room. Rahul followed but leaned against the wall opposite of them, checking his phone.

Once in the hall, Tasha turned on him. "What happened back at Whataburger? It looked like you were about to die."

"I had a low-oxygen episode. That's all."

"You have them often?" Tasha asked.

"Yeah." Cameron shook out his hands to stop the tingling that had started back up, but it wouldn't go away.

Tasha tilted her head. "What are they like? Chest pains? Headaches? Blue-tipped fingers and leg cramps?"

Enough with the questions. Cameron shoved his shaking fingers deep into his pockets. "Thanks for helping. I owe you big, and I'm sorry I got you in trouble. Where's my car?"

Tasha pointed down the hall. "I left it in the parking lot to the right of the main emergency doors."

Cameron raised his eyebrows. "Can you drive a stick?"

"I can now…mostly." Tasha lifted a shoulder and looked at him from under her thick eyelashes.

The thought of not seeing her again left an empty hole in his gut.

She grimaced. "You might need a new clutch."

Jerry grunted like a truck had backed over his toes. "What'd you do? Learn by watching YouTube?"

Tasha tossed her hands up. "I watched the video three times, and I think we should be grateful it didn't get impounded."

"Um, thanks," Cameron said. His words held a final ring. Would they be the last he spoke to her?

His dad exited the exam room without Dr. Grisham and glared at Jerry. "You were leaving." He leveled the Foster Stare at Tasha. "My son needs to be safe, which means he must avoid any pathogens that could harm his immune system."

Cameron slipped between them. "Again, it's not her fault. I initiated everything."

His dad kept his gaze on Tasha. "I will not allow any further endangerment of my son's health." He slid his eyes to Cameron. "For the foreseeable future, you are grounded."

Tasha folded her arms and straightened. No one stood up to Nigel, but Tasha had done it repeatedly. This girl was beautiful and brave and why did he get himself grounded when everything was starting to go well? The lights in the hallway glared down on them, harsh and unrelenting.

His dad ushered him down the hall. "And"—his voice dipped lower—"you are never to see Ms. Jenkins again."

Chapter Twelve

Cameron

Being grounded sucked. Before Cameron met Tasha, it wouldn't have mattered; he'd had nowhere to go. But with only four weeks and three days until surgery, every moment mattered.

The sunlight shone too bright through the upstairs lounge windows that overlooked the pool atrium and tennis courts. Jerry had scooted the couch closer to the TV to clear space for them to spar.

Though Cameron had little experience with being grounded, his dad had taken to it like a pro. No computers, no phone. He'd even cut the power to the Computer Graveyard and locked it down.

And unlike other "less fortunate kids," Cameron had the added bonus of Jerry watching him every moment of the last eight days except for Saturday, Jerry's day off. His father had filled those hours with the two of them analyzing Foster Med Corp's accounting statements.

Just how he'd always imagined spending his final days before surgery.

Worse, he could not find where his dad stashed his phones, watches, and computers. They had to be locked in the office downstairs. He'd considered ordering some pre-paid phones, but he had no way to do that, and Jerry was under strict orders to confiscate and search all Cameron's deliveries.

But today was the day Rose cleaned his dad's office, so the room would be unlocked for a few minutes. All Cameron had to do was escape Jerry and find a way around Rose, the same woman who could hear him trying to sneak into her chocolate stash from half a mile away. In hopes of a chance, Cameron had stuck a lock-picking set he'd bought years ago in a potted plant next to the stairs.

Jerry held up his rattan quarter staff. "Focus." He took a swing at Cameron's feet. "Your dad is punishing me as much as you."

Cameron sidestepped and struck with his quarter staff twice, smacking the ground, barely missing as Jerry stepped back. Cameron adjusted his tight-fitting O2 backpack and spun his staff in front of his face until it blurred. "But it wasn't your fault."

"Would you have gone out if I'd been here?" Jerry asked.

Cameron snorted and swung his weapon toward Jerry's head, but Jerry only blocked the move. "Like I could sneak out past you."

"Proving my point, professor," Jerry said.

"Can I at least check my messages?"

Jerry paused halfway in a jab toward Cameron's face. "You serious?"

Cameron groaned. He didn't want to die without contacting the outside world again, without talking to Tasha again. And he hadn't checked EyeNet since before that movie. Maybe one of the others had found something about Beneficence Donor Corp. Living without his phone was like missing part of his brain. "Can't you at least let my phone out of jail for good behavior?"

"Rules are rules." Jerry tossed his staff on the ground and directed Cameron to do the same. "Ten push-ups, then hold for ten with your nose touching the staff."

Great. Push-ups meant Jerry was ticked. Cameron grunted through the exercises and thought over his options for getting online. Fortunately, he'd detached his infrared keyboard and his 3D screen projector before the phone incarceration, but that didn't make a difference if he couldn't log into his system.

Jerry stood and stretched. "I'm going to take a shower. Can I trust you not to make a grand escape?"

With Jerry as a frontrunner for the fastest shower award, Cameron would be pushing it, but this was his chance to search the office. Cameron let out a fake yawn, but he was tensed to move. "We all know I can't outrun you."

Jerry headed for his apartment at the end of the hall. As soon as the lock on Jerry's door clicked, Cameron darted down the west staircase, grabbing the lock-picking set. He had a couple minutes, max. Dang, why did this house have to be so big? The office was located past the front door and down a long hallway on the way to his dad's bedroom.

He inched closer. The office door hung open, light spilling into the hall, and Rose's humming echoed from inside the room.

Cameron halted. Rose knew about his grounding. How could he distract her?

He darted back toward the kitchen's home security panel and set off the chime for the side delivery door. Rose backed out of his dad's office and bustled down the hall, and Cameron ducked into the office.

He only had a few minutes.

Inside the office, an orange scent hung in the air. The bookcases, file cabinets, desk, and chairs all were in perfect order, which meant she was almost finished cleaning in here. Where would his dad have put the stash?

Not on his spotless desk. Nor on any of the dark wood shelves showcasing his dad's books, sailboat model collection, and various other weird mementoes like an old medicine bottle, a money clip, and an empty wine bottle. Past the desk, a door on the east wall led to the separate garage where his dad kept the Tesla. He couldn't look in there without setting off a security beep. But that didn't seem as likely a spot. *Think.* He had to hurry.

The cabinets behind the desk. He pushed on the doors to pop them open, but the lock stuck. Cameron swore and unzipped the lock picks. If he was caught, he'd be grounded into the afterlife. He inserted the tension wrench into the bottom of the lock then slid the pick into the cylinder.

This lock wasn't big, so it wouldn't take long if he was careful. He jimmied the pick until the pins shifted and the spring pressure lessened. *Come on, come on.* Just a couple more. He chewed his tongue and ignored the beads of sweat popping out on his back.

He jolted at a banging sound down the hall. Rose had dropped something, maybe her long-handled duster. She was coming his way. He held his breath and jimmied the lock pick one last time until the door popped open.

Yes! His laptops, tablets, gaming systems, and phones loaded down several shelves. With only a moment before he was discovered, Cameron turned on his phone, hoping it still had some power. The screen lit up and—

Cameron swore. It'd been reset, and his dad had canceled the service. He dropped it back on the shelf and stood, shoving the cabinet shut with his knee. Obviously, his dad had been furious. What was he going to do? No way could he go the next several weeks without outside contact. But…he did have encrypted backups of his phone data stored on FMC servers. The only thing was, how to access it?

"What're you doing?" Jerry's voice boomed from the doorway.

When Cameron jumped nearly high enough to hit the ceiling, he scrambled for an excuse. He pointed to a book. "Just looking for something to read."

Jerry moved closer. "'Elements of Sailing.' Really?"

Yeah, that was lame. He gestured around. "It was that or corporate management, genetic organ cloning research, or quantum physics. Do any of these remotely interest you?"

"The only thing I find interesting is why you're in here." Jerry stalked around, scanning for contraband. Cameron wouldn't be surprised if the big guy frisked him. Instead, he folded his arms over his chest. "We both know you didn't come for a book."

Cameron searched for a distraction and spotted his old remote-control Jet Ski pool toy. He held it up. "Dad and I used to play with this on those rare Saturdays he didn't work. I'd use toys to create an obstacle course in the pool, and Dad would pilot the Jet Ski around, pretending to be chased by bad guys." His throat tightened. He hadn't seen that side of his dad in years. Dang, this grounding was making him lose it.

Jerry pointed to the door. "Upstairs, now."

Cameron saluted and headed to the hall, Jerry on his six.

Alone in his room, Cameron studied the digital lock his dad had installed on the Computer Graveyard's door. Inside that room, he had a lot of equipment, including a prepaid phone he'd bought to experiment on. But first he had to get past the lock.

Cameron dug through boxes in his walk-in closet. Over the years, he'd collected quite a few miscellaneous items, such as magic tricks, tech components, and spy gear. Finally, under some spy costumes and a name badge printer, he located tools and miscellaneous circuitry from a hardware class. He dumped the pile on his bed and settled in.

It was nearing midnight when he finished building a circuit board to decode the locked door. Using a butter knife he'd swiped at dinner, he jimmied the lock's screen off and plugged in his decoder. Numbers clicked by on his circuit board, but unless his dad's code was 9999991, this would take a while. He moved his desk in front of the door lock to shield the decoder from view in case anyone checked on him and went to bed.

The decoder was still checking numbers when he got up, but after a long shower, a seven-digit code had frozen on the screen: 8-6-7-5-3-0-9.

Cameron clicked the door open. He programmed a second code into the digital lock in case his dad discovered the incursion, changed the code, then grabbed the old phone and put the lock back together.

Cameron got to work importing his data into the backups. When it finally finished, he discovered thirty messages from the last few weeks. Most of them weren't from Tasha.

Many were from Dr. Zemke from the hospital.

Dr. Zemke

Cameron, we must discuss your test results. Call me at your earliest convenience, but keep this between us.

Dr. Zemke

Cameron, I'm concerned about you. Call me.

Dr. Zemke

I could lose my license for this, but you must come see me.

His dad's publicist Rahul had also called several times and left generic *contact me* messages. The last time he'd seen Rahul was at the hospital, but he was probably just checking on Cameron, maybe seeing if they could spin even his grounding into a good publicity story.

The last message came on Saturday morning.

Dr. Zemke

If I don't hear from you today, I'm going to take drastic measures. You're in danger.

Danger? Cameron's gut twisted, but wait, this was the doctor who was so old the nurses called him a zombie and the hospital was forcing him to retire because they were afraid he'd get patients mixed up. Looked like that ship had sailed.

Still, he'd said it was about Cameron's tests. Pressure shoved against Cameron's chest. His mouth tasted sour, and a rock seemed to be jammed in his throat. Cameron shut himself in his closet, shoving aside an old box of costumes, and called the doctor back. With his shaking hands, it took three taps to get the call to start. It went straight to voicemail. He hung up without leaving a message.

Cameron stared at his phone, unsure what to do. Was his heart in that bad of shape that he might need immediate surgery? Cameron tapped through his other apps, checking notifications. Most meant nothing, although Rahul had sent him a couple DMs with comic book images. He replied to one, asking Rahul to get back to him.

He leaned against the wall. What should he make of Dr. Zemke's messages? He'd studied dementia for one of his psychology classes. Sometimes people got stuck in things from the past. Surely, the doctor had him confused with some other patient.

The next set of messages were from Tasha, starting last Thursday. Basics like she had just gotten her phone back and wondered if he was still grounded.

But her last one sent his pulse pounding through his temples.

Tasha

Call me ASAP. You're not safe.

Chapter Thirteen

Tasha

Tasha stared at the crumpled letter in her fist, although *letter* wasn't the right word. A letter contained news that made sense. This was a single piece of paper ripped off an old prescription pad with only a few hastily scrawled words—a note written by a dead man.

Word had spread around Dallas General faster than a virus. Dr. Zemke was dead—an ATV accident. Tasha read and reread his name and credentials across the top of the sheet. The envelope's postmark read Saturday, and it'd been mailed from the doc's ranch in Glen Rose, southwest of DFW. It must've gone out in the mail just after his fatal accident.

The words at the bottom made her spine freeze:

Your friend. NED. No Rx in system. In danger.

NED meant "no evidence of disease." It seemed the doctor was saying Cameron had no evidence of heart issues and no prescriptions in his system. Zemke seemed to think Cameron wasn't dying but was in danger. From whom?

Tasha thrust her hands into her hair. What was going on with that boy? Sometimes he didn't move like someone with a heart condition, but then he'd wheeze like a real patient starving for air. And if he hadn't believed he had medical issues, why allow himself to be tested at the hospital?

She wrung her hair into a bun. Of course, going to the hospital had kept him out of trouble with the police, but as soon as the ambulance had taken him away, he was out of the red zone, so to speak. Why go through those tests unless he believed he had a medical issue? Either he needed a room full of Oscars, or Cameron was in a seriously weird situation.

She stared at Dr. Zemke's old prescription-pad note again. The paper was yellowing and gave off the musty smell of an ancient library book. It was rare for a hospital doctor to use prescription pads since most everything was digital.

Had he gotten the present mixed up with the past? According to her mom, lately he'd been calling nurses by the wrong names and pulling up the wrong patient charts. Then a few months ago, he'd gotten a patient's case muddled with one he'd worked as a resident.

Had he also confused Cameron's chart with someone else's?

She ran her finger over it. The info was vague. Did this imply a mentally sharp doctor avoiding HIPAA violations, or Zemke undergoing an episode of memory lapse?

She bit her nail. If she'd been asked a couple days ago who would be at the center of something fishy even the slightest bit related to Foster Med Corp, she'd have shouted Nigel's name. But he'd been genuinely freaked about Cameron's health and safety. He'd even questioned Dr. Grisham's insistence to discharge Cameron before more tests were run.

She fumbled for an explanation. Could be Munchausen by proxy, a disorder where a parent made their child appear and even feel sick. But that didn't explain the parrot-faced Dr. Grisham.

He, not Nigel, had been the one insisting Cameron go home, that the hospital was filled with dangerous germs, that Cameron was *his* patient.

After a cursory search on Grisham, she discovered his credentials checked out. Board certified cardiologist with an expertise in transposition of the great arteries.

Guess that made sense. FMC had numerous well-respected doctors on staff like Bethany's mom, Dr. Phan. The other doctors on her team were also top-notch. Dr. Grisham must be legit. Still, there was something about him that made the hairs on the back of her neck stand on end.

As for Dr. Zemke's note about Cameron, was it a simple mistake by the old doctor? Or was something suspicious going on with Dr. Grisham from FMC?

It was like she'd traveled back in time three years when she was trying to find out the truth about her dad's death. The tiny flash drive she wore as a charm on her bracelet grew heavy. She'd seen firsthand how dangerous some guys at FMC were.

But this was Cameron, the CEO's son. What danger would this pose to…

Her throat closed like someone was choking her. Cameron, the CEO's son who had a curious mind and time on his hands, might've seen something he wasn't supposed to, like her dad had.

The memory of his death tried to enter the forefront of her thoughts, but she couldn't let it. *No, shove it down and lock it in a box.* Her insides wound into a mess like that box of old computer cables in the garage. What if, like her dad, someone behind the scenes didn't want Cameron exposing them to Nigel? That could mean both Cameron and Nigel were in danger.

But if she got involved, she could be in harm's way. She should just drop it and run, but that so-called Dr. Grisham had seemed crooked enough to swallow a nail and spit up a corkscrew.

And what about Jerry, the one-man mercenary army? He'd left the hospital room supposedly to speak to Dr. Zemke but had returned with Dr. Grisham. Were he and the weird doctor a team? Did he have a score to settle with the Fosters and had somehow been a part of this? She did a quick search on Jerry Jacobs but found nothing that matched the big guy. Not even a social media reference. Jerry didn't exist. So who was he?

Her phone buzzed with an email.

??? Reply here.

It came from 1138000@junkiereadscomics.hub. A Hidden Universal Browser address? Interesting. Maybe Cameron wasn't a complete twit.

Tasha tapped out a reply. If what Zemke suspected was true, Cameron had no idea how much danger he was in. If it was a figment of the old man's imagination, then at least her conscious would be clean for trying to do the right thing.

Watch the local news tonight. Don't trust anyone.

He responded with more question marks. He'd said communication was safe, so she typed, hands shaking.

Heard from a "friend" you have no heart abnormalities. No trace of any heart meds in your system. You. Aren't. Dying.

Chapter Fourteen

Cameron

"YOU. AREN'T. DYING."

Tasha's words chased all his other thoughts away. Death had always stalked Cameron, but Tasha made it sound like he was in danger from a conspiracy. Ridiculous. Unthinkable. Possible?

Cameron gulped air. With numb fingers, he fumbled his oxygen cannula. Tasha was delusional and this proved it. It sounded like Zemke, the doctor with probable memory issues, had given her access to hospital files, proving he couldn't be trusted.

Still, he turned on the TV in the upstairs lounge. Jerry joined him, laptop in hand. Something thumped downstairs. Cameron jolted.

Jerry glanced his way. "You're as jumpy as a cat in a dog pen."

Cameron tried to think of something to say. "Have you seen Rahul lately?"

Jerry's forehead scrunched up. "No, but that's not unusual."

Cameron went back to staring at the local news. What did Tasha want him to see?

He didn't have to wait long. The breaking story was that Dr. Zemke's body had been found Saturday evening at his Glen Rose ranch after an accident on his ATV. The doctor had broken his neck. Authorities believed he died instantly.

Cameron dropped the remote. Jerry said nothing, clicking his shiny black pen and glaring at the TV. After a moment, Jerry typed on his computer, eyes furrowed.

"Jerry? You okay?"

The big guy jerked as if Cameron had sneaked up on him but collected himself by flashing a metallic smile—cold, hard, lifeless. "Yep. Great."

Dr. Zemke's message echoed in his head: *You're in danger.* Cameron watched Jerry for his next reaction. "That was the doctor who treated me at the hospital."

Jerry ran his hand over his closely shaved head. "Oh? I'd forgotten."

Yeah, and Superman lived next door. Dr. Zemke had sent his last message to Cameron on Saturday morning, saying they needed to talk. Saturday evening, Dr. Zemke was found dead. Jerry had been gone all day Saturday. He also knew where Cameron's phone had been. With the right tech and help, he could've cloned the device and snooped through messages.

Cameron locked his bedroom door and messaged Tasha.

Cameron

> You think Dr. Zemke's death was an accident?

She responded immediately.

Tasha

> No. How much do you know about your bodyguard?

Chapter Fifteen

Cameron

CAMERON PLUGGED HIS INFRARED keyboard and 3D projector into his old phone and connected to the FMC server. He sank into his desk chair, and his O2 tubing caught on the edge of his desk. He stared at the machine in the corner. Tasha could be wrong about everything, but he tossed the cannula aside. How long could he go without it?

He pulled up his browser and searched for news stories on Dr. Zemke. They all said the same thing: ATVs were known to be dangerous. The knots in Cameron's shoulders relaxed. None of the articles mentioned any police suspicion. Maybe it was a terrible accident.

He glanced at his door, the only thing separating him from a special forces sniper strong enough to snap a person's neck and skilled enough to make it look like an accident. Maybe it was murder.

But Jerry? How could he even think such a thing? Yet...how much did he know about the guy? Cameron initiated a HUB search on Jerry's name and sifted through the hundreds of Jerry Jacobs who fit his search parameters.

Back when Jerry first started working for them, Cameron had looked him up, but he'd lost interest when he found nothing. This search was no different. Doctors, lawyers, plumbers—no one matched his Jerry. This would be a lot faster if Jerry had a last name like ZXVFT. Could be that Jerry Jacobs wasn't even his real name.

Cameron tapped his finger against the desk. For the past three years, Cameron had seen Jerry more than he saw his dad, but did Cameron really know him? The only piece of personal info he knew was that Jerry had a "baby" sister named Yasmine. He didn't even know how old she was, but maybe he could find a connection that way. He took a deep breath and glanced at his O2 machine in the corner. How long before he started feeling dizzy and weak?

Cameron checked the time—one in the morning. To make sure Jerry wouldn't see any light coming from under his bedroom door, he moved into his closet, shifting aside a tub of magic tricks and spy gear—all stuff he'd collected as a kid. He settled in the back corner and began a more in-depth search, using every word he could think to combine with Jerry's name and his sister's name, provided her last name was also Jacobs.

More results popped up. Cameron clicked on an obituary dating back ten years for Clarence Jacobs, who had a son named Jerry ranked as a military sergeant. He had a wife named Thelma, which led Cameron to a listing for Thelma and Yasmine Jenkins living in the South Dallas district of Red Oak.

Jerry was a ghost, but he did have a sister named Yasmine. Still, how did this help? He stared at the carpet, drawing circles in the thick fibers while he searched his memory for everything Jerry had said about his sister.

A few months ago, Yasmine had developed a high fever and was taken to Dallas General's ER. The hospital wouldn't admit her, saying she was fine, but by the time she saw her usual doctor the next day, she was critically ill. She'd ended up in the hospital for weeks and had almost died several times.

He let that stir around in his brain. Jerry had been so angry. What if Zemke had also treated her in the ER? Maybe he'd made a mistake on her case as well. What if Jerry had recognized him? Zemke's death could've been a personal vendetta. But what did that have to do with Cameron being in danger? Unless...Zemke had recognized Jerry and knew he was dangerous. Maybe he'd wanted to notify Cameron and had gotten his medical records mixed up in the process? If the doctor was experiencing some dementia issues, he could easily confuse the past and present.

Cameron traced a few more circles in the carpet. FMC had recently started overseeing Yasmine's care, and there'd been a lot of complications. She'd gotten so sick—down to eighty pounds and running high fevers constantly. What if... No, couldn't be. But his brain insisted on asking the question: What if Jerry was angry about something that made Yasmine sick, and he was working his way through everyone he felt was at fault?

Cameron and his dad could be on that list.

He set up a crawler to search the HUB for more about Jerry, but was that enough? Maybe more answers could be found in what Dr. Zemke had seen in the hospital tests. He dug around until he found the servers for Dallas General. Once in the hospital network, he messaged Tasha.

She called him. "Are you crazy? Why are you messaging me at this unholy hour?"

Her voice blared through his earbuds, but Cameron kept his low. "You think it's unholy? I always figured Jesus would be a morning person."

"What do you want, and why are you whispering?"

"I don't want anyone to hear. I'm doing some research."

"Okay…"

Cameron scrolled through the data on his screen. "How did you know about…what you told me?"

She yawned. "Someone mailed me a letter."

"Who?"

"Dr. Zemke." Her voice held a guarded edge.

It took a moment to digest that information. The doctor's phone messages had indicated he was willing to go to great lengths to get hold of Cameron, so it made sense that he'd tried to reach Cameron through Tasha. "Follow up question. Did my paperwork refer to me by my full name?"

"And I would know how?"

"In my room, you and Jerry looked at some of my paperwork. They put those little white stickers on each page with patient information. Did you see a chart number associated with my account?"

"Why would I know that?" she asked.

"You have a thing for numbers."

"Well, aren't you smart, patient ID 246015191."

"You're scary."

"I try."

"I like scary."

"I'm sure you do. Anything else?"

Cameron checked his ID number in the hospital system. "Just a second." He scrolled through information, biting the inside of his lip.

Words like "dilated cardiomyopathy" and "anomalies detected" stood out. A chest X-ray showed the same shape of heart he'd seen dozens of times on Grisham's screen. Cameron collapsed against the wall. What an idiot he'd been to believe that his heart defect could go away.

He cleared his throat a couple times before any sound came out. "Dr. Zemke was just confused or lying. My file says the same thing it always has."

Tasha snorted, but it sounded strangled. "Are you searching the hospital server?"

"Did you hear me?"

She made a low noise. "I don't understand. Maybe Zemke had been confused lately, but he risked his medical license to reach out to me."

"He was about to retire, so was it that much of a risk?"

"I doubt a decorated doctor would want his career to end in disgrace."

"Then he just got his files mixed up."

She let out a long breath. "It seems like something weird is going on. I know you have those episodes, but a lot of the time you seem fine."

"That's what you're going on? That I *seem* fine? I take good care of myself." He'd never been given to gesture while he talked, but right now he waved both of his hands around. "I've had the best care possible, so doesn't it make sense that I'd appear *fine* most of the time?"

"But my gut tells me there's more to this."

"Well, these test results disagree with your gut." His eyes were hot. Just for a second, for a fraction of a moment, he'd allowed himself to hope. No surgery. No dire predictions of congestive heart failure. And here he was, crashing and burning all over again. He schooled his voice. "Obviously Dr. Zemke got confused, and we should just forget it and go on with our lives." What was left of them. Gah, he wanted to kick something.

"No..." She held out the word. "You got into the server in like two seconds. Maybe someone else did too. And in case you've forgotten, Zemke just died in a suspicious accident."

"He was having cognitive problems. Can't you accept that he had a tragic accident?"

"No, and maybe you don't believe me, but something is telling me that you're in the deep end and it's full of sharks."

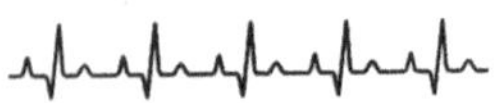

Cameron jerked awake to a banging sound. Where was he? When he blinked, rows of clothes and shoes came into focus. A closet. His closet. He'd fallen asleep last night searching for Jerry's past and his own medical records. He peeled his phone off his arm. The skin was hot, and he had the imprint of a shoe on his bicep. He gulped a few breaths. His shoulder ached. Was it from O2 deprivation? He groped for his nasal cannula, and the night before banged back to his memory. Banged…like his door.

"Kid?" Jerry called. "Seriously, are you okay?"

"Uh, yeah." Cameron shoved his 3D projector into his Nikes and his contraband phone under a box and stumbled out of the closet. "Sorry, I was sleeping hard."

Jerry's voice boomed through the door. "It's past seven. You trying to skip our swim?"

Seven? He'd only slept an hour. No wonder his head felt like someone had shoved a pillow inside it.

"You gonna open the door, or do I need to break it down?"

Cameron pawed the door handle open. "You're such a…those funny guys who do the…stuff on stage."

"You look like you spent the night juggling tarantulas." Jerry shifted his gaze to the oxygen machine. "You didn't wear your O2?"

How did he—oh. Cameron rubbed his face. No tube creases. "I forgot."

Jerry's brow scrunched up. "Any chest pains? Dizziness, nausea, headache? Should I call the doctor?"

"No!" Shoot. That came out too harsh, but the last thing Cameron wanted was to involve Grisham until he figured this out. He took stock. His head hurt, but he wasn't wheezing. "I'm fine, just tired. Can I go back to bed?"

Jerry leaned against the doorframe, his beefy arm flexing. Had he used those muscles to kill Dr. Zemke? Cameron stumbled to his bed. The faster he fell back to sleep, the better his brain would work.

"Did the news last night upset you?" Jerry asked.

Cameron froze. Why was Jerry asking about the doctor? He put on his best innocent expression. "What news?"

Jerry sat on the edge of his bed and gave Cameron the once over with X-ray eyes. "You stink at lying. Your face gets all red. The minute you found out about Dr. Zemke's death, you locked yourself in here. What's up?"

Shouldn't Cameron be the one asking that? His mind was a jumbled mess. Jerry passed over the O2 tube, his muscles expanding and flexing. Yeah, questions probably weren't the best idea at the moment. Cameron should act normal. "Maybe I'm a little freaked out. I mean, with my mortality staring me in the face, it just makes me think…"

"Ah." Jerry bumped Cameron's arm with a fist. "Get some rest and hang in there. You're going to make it."

As soon as Jerry left the room, Cameron threw the O2 tubing against the far wall. Right. The way things were going, he'd fare as well as Cheetos lip balm had in 2005.

Cameron woke around two in the afternoon. He should've been crippled with chest, shoulder, and head pain from oxygen deprivation, but so far he had no adverse symptoms. He stumbled into the bathroom, showered, then stood in front of the mirror, searching for answers the guy in the reflection didn't have.

None of this made sense. Tasha had to be wrong. Dr. Zemke too. The old guy's death was a sad, unrelated accident. He'd been known to be confused. Not only had he probably mixed Cameron up with someone else, but he might've also hit the accelerator instead of the brakes on his ATV. People had accidents on those vehicles all the time. These conspiracy theories were more like something out of a movie.

Unable to let it go, Cameron pulled up the hospital files again. There had to be a clue in there. He scrolled through information and stopped. The timestamp column was odd. Most entries occurred while Cameron had been in the hospital, but a few lines were timestamped about an hour after he'd been released. Close enough to be late data entries, but it could also mean someone altered his files. The question was why.

Cameron pulled up the results from his search on Jerry and settled at his desk, scrolling through information—some military service notes, all impeccable. Seemed to be proof Tasha was wrong about Jerry and maybe all of it.

He was about to shut it down when an Algerian blog written in French caught his attention. The post's title translated as "Hitman or Government Agent?"

Algerian police had held a Moroccan man for questioning in May the previous year on suspicion of murder. He'd come to Algeria under a Moroccan passport with the name Boka Habib, but the blogger claimed to have hacked the police's files and that the suspected gunman was American special ops soldier Jerry Jacobs. The writer also claimed the police files were altered only minutes after he'd hacked into the system.

Hunger gnawed at Cameron's stomach, but he kept reading. The gunman was released, although no reason was cited. Since the victim was running for political office but also had possible ties to the HUB's black-market drug and prostitution trade, the writer suggested the hit was carried out by either a government assassin or a professional hitman. The writer included a grainy photo of a tall, bearded, wide-shouldered man ducking into a dark-windowed car.

Cameron enlarged the photo, squinting at the screen while the whirring of the air conditioner filled his ears. The guy maybe had some similar features, but no way could this be Jerry. And he could prove it. His dad kept a meticulous calendar system, including all travel stops. Cameron pulled it up, staring at the dates from last May, unable to swallow.

Last May, when they were in France, Jerry had made an emergency trip to see his sister. Cameron's hunger evaporated—his bodyguard had been gone the week the murder took place.

Jerry refused to speak about his past, and he'd gotten all weird when Gabe's dad had asked him about his service during that banquet. Cameron pressed his fingers into his eyes. Who was this guy? A dark thought entered his mind. If he was a hitman, he could have taken out Dr. Zemke, no problem, along with anyone else who got in his way.

He churned the information over in his mind until hunger forced him out of his room. Cameron bolted downstairs, hoping he wouldn't run into anyone. What should a person grounded for the rest of his life while possibly living with a hitman eat? Certainly not tofu and green smoothies. If there was bacon in this house, he'd hoover it.

Tasha's previous message replayed. *"You. Aren't. Dying."*

Dr. Grisham had done hundreds of tests on him through the years. The results were always the same—a deformed heart, just like the hospital tests showed.

In the kitchen, Cameron scarfed three protein muffins and leaned on the counter. His head was going to explode. He snagged a vitamin-enhanced water and wandered toward the voices coming from his dad's office. He pushed open the door, ready to launch into questions, but his dad was chatting with one of his Harvard buddies, Roger O'Brien.

Though his dad always seemed to need Cameron's help with his phone, he had an affinity for high tech. A hologram of Roger sat opposite the desk from his dad. He had carefully styled sandy-blond hair, a fancy suit, and glasses, and although Cameron could only see the back of his head, he probably wore his usual smirk.

His dad was saying, "The Foster Foundation is always willing to give to charities, but this research was incomplete. I need facts, not emotional appeals." His dad spotted him in the doorway. "Glad you finally decided to wake up."

Roger turned and raised his coffee to Cameron in a salute. "Nigel tells me you were seventeen for five minutes before you sneaked out to meet some girl and wrecked your car."

Cameron shrugged. "I barely scratched it, but I seem to be grounded for life." Might as well lay on the guilt while he could.

Roger gestured to Cameron's dad with his coffee cup and glanced at one of the model sailboats. The name *Jacquelyn's Pride* was painted across the hull. Next to it sat an old-fashioned aspirin bottle. "The boy went to a movie and ate a French fry. You did way worse."

Regimented, health-conscious Nigel Foster had a rebel past? Cameron stepped further into the room. "Like what?"

His dad cleared his throat and narrowed his eyes at Roger. "I didn't have the benefit of wise parental guidance." He gave Cameron the once-over but didn't mention the O2 being MIA.

Roger slurped his coffee. "Lighten up, Nigel. Let the boy enjoy his Porsche, his summer, and girls." He gave Cameron a long look and winced, like the Grim Reaper stood behind him. The rest of his thoughts hovered in the air. *Because he doesn't have much time.*

But that might not be true.

Roger signed off with the usual "let's get together soon," giving Cameron a moment to study his dad. Another solemn face. He needed to ferret out the truth, but where to start? "Dad? Did Dr. Zemke talk to you about my test results?"

His dad leaned back in his chair with his mouth turned down and his right hand fisted. "Zemke reported your heart condition as acute and sent your test results over to Charles."

Once again, Dr. Grisham was in the middle of things. Cameron liked that guy less every second. He could be part of whatever was going on, but where did that leave Jerry? Maybe the two of them were working together. "Did you actually talk to Zemke and see the results, or did Grisham just tell you about it?"

"*Dr.* Grisham received the files, but I'm sure he'd be happy to go over the results with us." His dad tapped his fingers on the desk, studying Cameron's face. "What's this about? I'm sorry it's not better news, but Charles is gathering a team of the world's best surgeons. We're going to get through this."

Cameron shrugged.

His dad leaned forward. "I am sorry, son." After a long silence, his dad exhaled and said, "Perhaps Roger is right." He used his thumbprint to unlock a drawer and tossed Cameron his car keys, including the Porsche keychain Jerry had given him. The tiny car gleamed brighter than Cameron remembered. His dad opened the cabinet and motioned for Cameron to access his phone and other stuff. "Grounding is lifted, but I'll reinstate all restrictions if you don't act wisely. Fair enough?"

Whoa. "Yes, but—"

"Be cautious." His dad spoke over him. "I gave Jerry a few days off because his sister isn't doing well. He won't be around to watch over you."

Possible-hitman Jerry requested time off to see his sister after Dr. Zemke's death? At least two times when Jerry had time off, someone died. Cameron swallowed. Another coincidence?

His father raised his eyebrows. "I would recommend saying thank you before I change my mind."

"Uh yeah, thanks." Cameron grabbed a stack of equipment and backed out. He wanted to say more but didn't know where to begin.

His dad, though, seemed to have plenty to say. "I stand by my gut about Ms. Jenkins. Girls like that always cause trouble."

Chapter Sixteen

Tasha

Tasha's phone rang. Cameron seemed to have a sixth sense for when she was sleeping. She jabbed the screen and managed, "Whassit?"

"Can you meet, or could I come see you?"

She stretched and shook off the edges of sleep. "What happened to grounded for life?"

"Dad changed his mind."

"Nigel Foster changed his mind? What about your ninja nanny?"

"He's got the next few days off."

"When was his last day off?"

Cameron remained silent for a long time.

"Was it the Saturday Dr. Zemke was killed?"

Cameron muttered something like, "Mmhm."

Tasha swallowed. "And you don't find that suspicious?"

"I don't know what to think." He ended the sentence with a sharp exhale.

Whether he was ready to accept it or not, deep down Cameron must at least be suspicious of Jerry. Good, that guy was dangerous. They needed to talk, but did she want ultra-wealthy Foster to see

Gran's tiny, ancient house? Guess it was a risk she had to take. "If you can find my address, I'll see you in an hour."

Tasha rolled out of bed and stared at the wood paneling of her shoebox bedroom. Gran coughed, and the walls shuddered. Her great grandfather had built this house on what used to be his farm in the Middle of Nowhere, Texas. The home probably stayed in one piece out of sheer stubbornness. It was nothing like the two-story brick house they'd lived in while her dad was alive.

She ran water in the bathroom sink. Enough about her own problems. What game was someone playing with Cameron? And who was behind it? His bodyguard?

Everywhere she turned, FMC mucked with her life. Would it ever be over, and what would be left of her when that day came?

She checked the search she'd started on Dr. Zemke. Nothing so far. Her computer was already bogged down with the search on Florencia, the drug lord's niece. She'd looked into open-source programs to find a way to search faster, but that required several people to link machines to spread out the data processing. Maybe Gabe and Bethany would be willing to help, but both their parents worked for FMC.

The EyeNet people were a possibility, but their work had been related to organ smuggling, and linking machines with an unknown was a gamble. If her mother's trip to Vegas last year had taught Tasha anything, it was that gambles didn't pay off.

Chapter Seventeen

Cameron

CAMERON PULLED OVER FOR the third time on his way to Tasha's house. He wasn't that far south of Dallas, maybe forty miles, but it was like another world out here. Twisting roads covered by canopies of thick trees alternated with expansive pastures and grazing horses—the kind of place that made it seem like a tranquil, trouble-free life was possible. A few cars sped past in the other direction, and one lone black pickup meandered on the road behind him. He couldn't complain about driving the Porsche through the country roads—the car devoured each turn, and he was starting to get the hang of the gears.

While he drove, his mind wandered through all the weird things that had happened lately. His dad's publicist, Rahul, still hadn't gotten back to him. Strange for a guy who spent so much time on his phone. The last message from Rahul had been a picture of the *Tron Betrayal* comic book cover.

Since he was thinking about it, Cameron asked his phone to try Rahul, but it went to voicemail again.

The navigation signaled he'd missed a turn. Guess his thoughts distracted him. He turned onto what looked like a street but ended up in a driveway. A sign on a barbed wire fence opposite him featured a picture of a gun and said, "We don't call 911." Maybe this area wasn't as tranquil as he'd thought.

When he was back on the road, the summer sun rode high overhead, warming his skin through the sunroof. What was he hoping to prove by coming out here? For all he knew, Tasha was a crazy girl who wanted to mess with his mind. Yet still he drove.

Ahead, he spotted a narrow house with a wraparound porch that looked like it could be a movie set for an old western. An ancient tractor hunched in a ditch behind the home, and a rusty pickup begged to be put out of its misery in the neighbor's dirt driveway. Cameron pulled in and checked the address twice. The black pickup drove past.

Navigation said he'd arrived, but was he ready to face her? To face everything?

Before he could change his mind, someone tapped the car window.

Shielding her eyes from the sun, Tasha squinted down at him, her expression unreadable. Her golden hair was pulled into a messy bun and held in place with chopsticks. She wore a "Live long and prosper" T-shirt.

He pushed out of the car. "Didn't see you coming."

She pointed to the fence where a horse watched them with suspicious eyes. "I was chatting with the neighbor." She paused, glancing around. "Not exactly mansion-ville, is it?"

Cameron nodded toward the horse. "I like it, and your neighbor seems nice."

She blinked as though his sincerity had disabled her sarcasm circuit. No doubt she'd soon reboot. She crossed her arms over her un-hide-able chest. "What now, Golden Boy?"

"How about you call me Cameron?"

"No."

Right. Next time, he wouldn't pose it as a question.

She held open a rusted screen door that creaked loud enough to startle a nearby dog into a low bark. "Bienvenue à château du Watts-Jenkins."

The living room was a study in grandmother décor and smelled of lemon furniture polish. A cheery floral print covered the curtains, and the floor was made of a smooth surface that looked like wood but was probably linoleum. Picture frames covered the walls, piano, and every other available surface.

The place was clean and tidy and full of memories—a home, everything the houses he bounced between weren't. Yellowed doilies covered most non-photo surfaces except for the flat-screen TV. To his left, two end tables and a coffee table surrounded a long couch. The crown jewel, though, was the recliner hosting a shriveled old woman hunkered under two crocheted blankets and attached to an O2 machine.

She grimaced, or perhaps smiled. It was hard to tell under all those wrinkles. "Is this my early birthday present?" She sounded like she was trying to talk while gargling rocks.

"Yes, Gran. I bought you a pool boy at the store. They also come in blue and red."

"I'll take all three." The old woman's eyes lit up. She held out a puffy, arthritic hand. "You got a name, since my granddaughter isn't one to observe niceties?"

Tasha headed to the kitchen at the other end of the room, moving aside a pie on the counter. "Don't forget who controls your chocolate rations, Gran."

Cameron took the old woman's hand and, on a whim, kissed the back of it. "I'm Cameron."

She cackled and squeezed his hand. "Hazel Watts." She shifted and raised her voice. "He's a keeper, Natasha. Lock the door."

Tasha dug for something in the white fridge. The old lady's oxygen tank burbled in the corner. That was a conversation topic he could handle. Cameron gestured to her tank. His nose itched, but he wasn't out of breath. "You like the two thousand model?"

"Ooh, an O2 connoisseur? It beats the fifteen hundred series—too noisy, and the tank was always sending up condensation. How do you know so much about oxygen?"

"I—I've had to use it. Before."

He met Tasha's eyes. She held out a cold Coke can and a water. Cameron almost reached for the Coke but grabbed the water. The sugar would make him sick.

"You okay?" Tasha's voice was void of the scissor edge it usually carried.

He took a swig of icy water and settled onto the couch. A giant orange cat leapt into his lap out of nowhere. "Yah!" His dad had never allowed any pets, not even a hermit crab. The huge cat turned in circles and resettled on his legs. He stretched to set his water on the coffee table, but the cat extended its claws to imply it wouldn't tolerate any disturbances.

Tasha tilted her head toward the front door. "Wanna go outside?"

Gran tsked. "He's just made friends with Seeatee."

Cameron glanced at the cat on his lap. He spoke numerous languages but didn't recognize that word. "Seeatee? Is that a Hawaiian name?"

Tasha snorted. "It's a kindergarten name. C-A-T."

"Oh. Clever." Cameron started to pat C-A-T, but decided it wasn't worth losing a hand. He grasped at what to say. Too bad Rahul wasn't here—he was awesome at small talk.

"Look at him," Gran said. "Nothing like that double-bagger Steve your mom brought home. Now there was a guy who'd sell his own mama for cigarettes."

Um…should he thank her or run away screaming? "Double-bagger?"

Tasha shooed C-A-T down and motioned Cameron to the door. "It means someone is so ugly they have to wear more than one bag over their head. Let's go."

Gran patted a crocheted pouch at the side of her chair. "You two be careful. Elvis and I'll be watching."

Cameron could not leave that one alone. "Elvis?" Was the old woman one of those people who thought Elvis's ghost was living in her purse?

Tasha motioned Cameron toward the door. "You don't want to know."

He grabbed his drink and paused by a picture. Tasha and her mother posed with a large, brown-skinned man, his arms wrapped around their shoulders. Tasha looked several years younger and several decades less irritated. "Nice picture," he said.

Tasha's face turned stormy and dark. She yanked the door shut behind them and pointed to a porch swing on the side of the house. "Come, sit in my manicured garden. I must apologize, though. This is the groundskeeper's century off."

Cameron settled on the swing and stared at a line of trees behind Tasha's house. They had too much to talk about—he didn't know where to begin. "It's peaceful out here."

"Yeah, not much has changed in the last five or six decades."

Was she embarrassed or resigned? "Who was in the picture with you?"

"I'm not sure why you think it's any of your business."

The girl had more walls around her than a prison. "I'm curious because it's better than thinking about all my questions. And you looked happy in that picture."

"I don't now?"

"No."

Tasha groaned. "That was Solomon." Her voice caught. "My dad."

Cameron glanced her way. His own heritage was quite intercontinental, but Tasha looked fair enough to sunburn indoors. Hard to think those two were related. "*Was* Solomon?"

She huffed and gripped a charm on her bracelet that looked like a tiny flash drive. "I don't want to talk about my dad."

Cameron nodded. "There's a lot I don't want to talk about." He leaned back, enjoying the sound of the buzzing insects and nickering horses next door. On the road in front of her house, a pickup slowed. The driver, a young guy, eyed Cameron's Porsche. Cameron pushed the swing with a foot. "You know, I've never done this before."

"Sat on a porch swing in the armpit of the country with a crazy old lady trying to shoot you with Elvis?"

Cameron choked on his water. "Elvis is a gun?" Tasha's family was bursting with surprises. "I meant sit with a girl and have a conversation that isn't related to Foster Med Corp."

"How do you know this isn't about Foster Med Corp?"

Tasha

Tasha waited for Cameron to respond, but he stared at Gomez's horses in the pasture. Without a word, he wandered to the fence. Rex, the giant brown-and-white paint gelding, trotted closer and nuzzled around Cameron, looking for a treat. Tasha jogged to the pail by the back door where she kept horse treats. She handed Cameron a few and showed him how to keep his hand flat. "Rex is greedy—it'll be hard to text me if he bites off your fingers."

Cameron smiled like a toddler at Christmas. His long fingers stroked Rex's dark brown mane as if he'd never seen anything so amazing.

Tasha ran her finger over Rex's velvety coat. "Forgive my terrible manners, Your Highness. Rex, this is Cameron." She nudged Cameron with her free hand. "Maybe you should bow. He takes his royal position very seriously."

Cameron muttered, "Mmhmm."

"Cameron? You in there?"

He looked her way, his brown eyes shadowed. "Dr. Zemke said I was in danger, and now he's dead. He told you I didn't have a heart condition, but the hospital's records say I do, although the timestamp on them is odd."

Cameron leaned against the horse's muzzle. "I've tried calling Rahul—he's my dad's publicist and was at the hospital. Anyway, he noticed something on Dr. Zemke's screen that concerned him. He left me some messages, but I can't get a hold of him. I have no idea what bothered him. Was it something that made him think Zemke wanted to hurt me? Something in my medical records?

Where do I start? Is my heart condition a lie, or was Zemke lying?"

"I have a few ideas." But should she follow through? There were lines people shouldn't cross, yet here she was leaping into dangerous territory. She gestured to the chestnut mare trotting over to join them for treats. "That's Sugar, Rex's mom."

"You changed the subject. Why?"

Good grief, this guy was out of it one minute, perceptive the next. He would be the death of her. She swallowed at that last thought. "I just...I don't know if I'm ready to get into this."

"Makes two of us." He took another horse treat from her and held it out for the mare. Perhaps it was the bright sunlight, but Cameron's eyes pinched as he rubbed the horse's neck. "I never knew my mother." His voice cracked. "My dad said she didn't want me. I guess she found out about my problems then contacted Dr. Grisham and gave me over to my dad for a large sum of money. But that was after I'd contracted the virus that made my heart condition worse."

Tasha's hand froze on Rex's neck. "That sucks." His mom problems, her dad problems—maybe they had more in common than she'd thought. "For the record, I don't know my biological father either. And I don't care. Solomon was my real dad."

"And you lost him?"

Tasha stared at the mare, her muscles clenching up. "He was stolen from me."

Chapter Eighteen

Cameron

BEING WITH TASHA WAS like living in a tennis match. One moment she was lobbing wicked sarcasm at him, and the next she served up surprising depths of emotion.

She took a few heaving breaths and motioned him back toward the house. "How are you feeling?"

He shrugged but took stock. Aside from confused, he was fine. "Nothing seems wrong today, physically."

"But you're still not sure—you still think you might be sick?"

"All my episodes…" Grisham had to be behind this. Who else could pull it off? It would be almost impossible, except… Cameron's dad had trouble navigating his way through a phone, so it wouldn't be hard to show him fake test results. But why? And how did Jerry fit into this? Were they working together? It was also possible that Cameron did have an issue, just not as bad as everyone thought.

Tasha leaned against the front door, biting her lip. He wished he knew what she was thinking. She finally spoke. "Tell me more about these episodes. Are they all like the one you had when the cops were talking to us at Whataburger?"

"Talking? They were about to arrest me." He spun his key chain. It would be so easy to get into his car and drive until the road ended. He didn't want to talk about this, but she kept staring at him with that expectant look. "Okay, fine. I get dizzy, my hands and arms go numb, I have chest pain, shortness of breath, headaches, ringing in my ears, and blurred vision."

Tasha chewed her thumbnail, deep in thought. After something that looked like an internal debate, she held up a finger. "I have an idea. Give me a minute. I'll meet you in your car." She darted inside before he could protest. A few minutes later, she returned with a pie and a high-wattage smile. "You ready?"

"Where're we going?"

She stowed the pie in the back of his car. "To see the world. You drive, and I'll lead the way. Trust me?"

He couldn't answer that one, not yet. The number of people he trusted had dwindled to almost nil. They rode in silence while he eased the Porsche around turns.

Tasha leaned back and pointed for him to turn left. "You're driving better than you were the other night."

He was a different person from the other night. That Cameron had been tethered to oxygen and convinced he was as fragile as an eggshell.

Who was he now?

"How're you doing without the O2?" Tasha asked. "I saw you looking at Gran's like an alcoholic eyeing Jack Daniels."

"It's like I'm missing something, but I want to see how long I can go without it. If I had a heart condition, wouldn't I be tired or worse by now?"

"You'd think." Her voice was soft.

He glanced around. Not much traffic out here. A black pickup chugged along the road behind them and another truck whooshed past going the other way, nothing like the crowded tollways in the heart of Dallas. Certainly nothing like New York, Tokyo, Buenos Aires, all the other places he lived. "I like driving out here." Up ahead, a large office complex loomed, surrounded by open fields.

Tasha pointed. "You ever seen that?"

"No."

"Weird, since y'all own it. That's FMC South. Eight buildings. Offices in building one, and buildings three through eight are for super-secret research. Building six requires too many forms of ID to count. Only the white coats are allowed."

He slowed, and his eyes skimmed over her legs. The shorts rode high and showed off her soft skin. It would be so nice to slide his hand off the gearshift and onto her knee. The road suddenly curved, and Cameron had to jerk the wheel to keep from driving into the ditch.

Tasha grabbed her door handle. "Should I drive?"

He ignored her question. "You know a lot about FMC."

"My dad worked there."

"Oh?" Like Bethany's mom and Gabe's dad. Weird. Something about Tasha and her friends made him uneasy. "Was he a scientist?"

"A guard." She stared out the window, her hands fisted at her side. "He died there three years ago."

His gut and memory stirred. "I saw an article sticking out of your purse. It mentioned a death at FMC. Was it him?"

Instead of answering, Tasha pointed to a "Welcome to Cedar Oaks" sign squatting among trees and flowers. She blasted the a/c and unrolled her window, letting her hand wave outside. "Have you heard anything odder than Cedar Oaks? Two different kinds of trees smashed together. The city has an identity issue."

"Why are you deflecting the question?"

Instead of answering, she pointed him toward a Hardware and Lumber Supercenter. As he parked, she shifted around in her seat like she was uncomfortable.

"You need some lumber?" he asked. "And a truck to carry it?"

"Ice cream, actually, but you're going to stop for that in a bit."

"I am?"

"I made an apple pie. You can't show up to dinner with an apple pie and no ice cream. It's un-American."

He turned off the car. "I wouldn't want you committing treason, but you never mentioned dinner."

She shoved out of the low car. "C'mon, we gotta get Gabe. Then we're going to dinner at his house. His dad has info on Jerry."

Cameron slowed at the mention of Jerry. For a moment he'd felt normal, a regular guy with a regular girl walking into a hardware store that smelled of wood, dust, and potting soil. No bodyguards, no entourage, no expectations. He could have gotten used to that life.

Chapter Nineteen

Cameron

Until he stepped into the Hardware and Lumber nightmare, Cameron had never experienced the terror of a suburban super-store. The place was massive, over an acre of fifteen-foot-high shelves packed with home maintenance supplies. All around him, people pushed huge yellow carts full of stuff like grass squares, light fixtures, and wood planks. For a moment, his feet seemed cemented to the ground.

Tasha grabbed his arm and led him past a row of pasture mowers and patio furniture. "This way." She glanced back, eyebrows raised. "What's wrong? Never seen ten thousand light bulbs before?"

He paused, scanning the shelves. How many light bulbs were there? Had to be more than ten thousand.

"It wasn't a math question." She rolled her eyes. "I guess the homeschooling division of FMC neglected Sarcasm 101."

He was an idiot. "Haha. If MIT doesn't work out, you can teach comedy." Ugh. Guess he'd also missed Awesome Comebacks 101.

She pulled him onward. Gabe met them in the paint aisle and lifted his chin in greeting. He wore a yellow apron covered in a messy array of paint smears. "Be ready in a sec."

She'd dragged him here to meet Gabe? Made no sense. True, Cameron didn't have many friends, but even he knew this smacked of weird. What was her deal with this guy? He waited until Gabe was out of earshot. "Why're we here?"

Tasha fidgeted with her purse strap. "I thought, um…" Her eyes skimmed around, not meeting his.

A lady with a screaming toddler pushed a basket past them. Cameron's chest grew tight. Was that guy on the other side of the paint counter watching him? He rubbed the back of his neck and took long breaths to stop the quaking in his limbs.

Gabe returned, sans uniform apron. Tasha held out a hand to Gabe. Were her fingers trembling? Cameron's gut clenched. Wait, they were planning something. How many times had his dad warned that being a Foster came with privilege but also danger? He'd lost count of the number of kidnapping threats and attempts there'd been over the years. He took a step back. Time to get out of here.

Tasha took Gabe's keys. "I'll take your car. You two can ride together."

Um, what? "Ride where?" Cameron asked.

She gave a shrill laugh. "We're going to Gabe's house."

Cameron pulled at the collar of his T-shirt. It was getting hot, and why were the lights so dang bright? His shoulders tightened. "I thought we had to get ice cream."

Tasha backed away. "I'll get it. You two go ahead."

A nearby display of paint cans blurred. The exit—where was it again? Behind him? He scanned the shelves. When he turned back, Tasha and Gabe were gone.

The floor tile wavered in his sight. He'd never been by himself in public before, not once. And he'd never been without some guard nearby packing at least one weapon. He couldn't swallow. The room spun. Cameron shrank into a two-dimensional sketch of a person being erased one limb at a time. His lungs pressed flat, and a sharp pain hit his chest. His legs shook so hard he sank to the floor.

See? He did have a heart condition. Dr. Grisham hadn't been lying. Tasha was messing with him—this was revenge for whatever happened to her dad. He fumbled for his keys. Before he could move, a text buzzed.

Tasha

Check this out:

She'd included a link to a site detailing panic attacks. Why would she send him this garbage? He needed to get his heart medication from Dr. Grisham, not read stupid articles. Nor should he take advice from some sarcastic girl and a stupid quack in the hospital who got himself killed hunting. Why hadn't he taken his meds today? No wonder he was feeling terrible. He—

He skimmed a list of panic attack symptoms:

- Shortness of breath

- Dizziness

- Trembling

- Choking feeling

- Chest pain

- Tingling or numb fingers

A pair of Converse with scrawls of blue numbers appeared in front of him. Tasha squatted, bending her head so she could meet his eyes.

Gabe appeared beside her and held out a hand. "Sorry for the subterfuge, but Tasha's a rip-the-bandage-off kind of gal."

"What?" They weren't making sense. Cameron rubbed at the tightness in his chest. Hard to get words out.

When Tasha grabbed his wrist, her hands were warm on his clammy skin. "Look at me, Cameron."

"You called me Cameron."

"Sorry to let you down. Listen, I think you're having panic attacks, not heart episodes."

He shrank away from her. No way was that possible.

She held on. "Hear me out. I bet you've never been to a place like this, and never alone."

He'd thought the same thing but shook his head. "My heart."

She fished in her purse. Good grief, was she toting Elvis and getting ready to shoot him? Gah, this store had no air. She yanked out a small rectangle and popped it onto his finger. An oximeter? Grisham used those to check the oxygen content in Cameron's blood.

Gabe squatted with them. Cameron hated to be seen like this. The sick kid. Gabe spoke in a calm voice. "I think it might be agoraphobia, probably because you were conditioned—"

"That means you have a fear of public places," Tasha said.

"Geez, I'm not stupid." If they would give him some oxygen, he'd be fine.

Gabe scooped Cameron's keychain off the floor and studied the tiny Porsche with narrowed eyes.

"What?" Tasha asked.

"It's weird," Gabe said, "but the other night this looked less blue, more silver."

Tasha swiped the chain. "Whatever, paint guy." She inspected the device on Cameron's finger. "Your O2 reads ninety-nine percent. Normal. I tested the oximeter on myself and my grandmother just before we left. It's accurate."

He stared at his finger. No, he was having an episode. His blood oxygen levels should be lower.

She shoved the device back in her purse. "Do you hate us for forcing you to see?"

They were both crazy. He'd be out of here as soon as he could stand without wobbling.

Gabe nudged his shoulder. "Hey, it's okay. You've had a lot of stuff thrown at you. Perhaps some food will clear your head."

Tasha bumped against Gabe's side. "Thanks, Dr. Mendez."

Those two were at it again. Always inside jokes. Always touching. But they wanted his trust. No, thanks. Cameron swiped the sweat off his forehead. Tasha had articles about her dad's mysterious death at FMC. Her dad had worked security. Gabe's dad worked security. Maybe these two wanted to get something from his dad.

He stood, willing his rubbery legs to support him. Leave or stay? Cameron ignored the spinning in his head and stared at the two of them—so sure of themselves, so smug in their stupid theories. Ugh. He wanted to wipe those smiles away. His head cleared.

Hmm. On second thought, maybe he'd stay, and if they were after his dad, he'd find out. No one beats a Foster.

Gabe gestured toward the exit. "You up to driving, or you wanna let me try?"

"I'm fine." Cameron rolled his shoulders as the feeling gradually returned to his extremities. He took long, even breaths, willing himself to be fine. No way would he let Gabe chauffeur him around like an invalid. He should leave them both here, but the only way to see what they were up to was to play along.

Tasha held up Gabe's keys. "Bethany and I will meet y'all at the house." Her voice broke, and she sped toward the exit. Why was she upset? Cameron was the one being played.

In the parking lot, Cameron slammed the car into gear, and they roared onto the street. Gabe pointed the way and made appreciative noises for the car's athletic ability, but Cameron didn't listen to the specifics. His thoughts revved harder than the engine. For years, his medical tests had shown he had a heart condition. Why was Tasha trying so hard to prove otherwise? What would she get out of it? He gripped the gearshift so hard his hand went numb.

Grisham was his dad's oldest friend. The two had known each other back in boarding school. The doctor had no reason to lie about Cameron's health. Cameron had known Tasha only a few weeks, and she had plenty of reasons to trick him. Then there was Jerry, who might be leading a double life as an assassin. Cameron should talk to his dad, but before tossing down any serious accusations, he needed proof.

Where to get some? If he could get inside the hospital's server room, he could check for another version of those files.

Gabe directed him through a neighborhood and nodded to a nice two story with a brick-and-stone façade. "That's where Tasha used to live."

"Why'd she move?"

"Man, it sucked. Her mom was really sad after Tasha's dad died, but she got some money from the death settlements—you probably knew that, right?"

"Why would I?"

"I just figured with it being your dad's company."

Was this about money?

Gabe went on. "Anyway, a year later, her mom went to Vegas and came home remarried to this guy Steve Kramer she'd known in high school." Gabe made a disgusted sound. "Three months after the wedding, Steve took off with all the money. Sold all of Solomon's things except his old Bible and a work jacket Tasha kept in her bedroom. Left them with a dumpster of debt. They lost the house, everything."

"How did that happen?" Cameron asked. "Wasn't the money in trusts and such? Can't Sarah sue Steve?"

Gabe laughed, but it sounded hollow. "Man, we're just normal people, you know? Sarah didn't have an attorney in her back pocket. Lawyers cost money."

No wonder Tasha seemed brittle. People she'd trusted had either died or tricked her. Cameron jammed the clutch onto the floorboard. That still didn't make her trustworthy.

"That's not all," Gabe said. "Tasha's never met her biological dad. Her mom won't talk about him, not even his name."

Cameron's gut twisted for Tasha. Guess of all people, she'd understand about his mother. "Why're you telling me?"

"'Cause you need to know you're not the only person who's been screwed over, and Tasha won't talk about it." Gabe pointed to a modest brick house with cheerful flowers lining the beds and a "Welcome" sign on the front porch. "There's my place." When

Cameron pulled to the curb, Gabe shoved out of the car. "Let's eat."

Cameron let the car idle a moment longer. Gabe could be telling the truth, or Tasha could be out for revenge, and Cameron was the dummy she needed for inside information. She could have asked Gabe to play on his sympathy. He squeezed the bridge of his nose. All this guessing was giving him a headache. Only one way to find out the truth. Cameron grabbed Tasha's pie and followed Gabe inside.

Gabe's house smelled like grilled meat and spicy vegetables, but getting past the Golden Retriever at the front door was difficult. The dog got very personal with its nose, and its tail *bam-bam-bammed* against the wall.

"Down, Nikki." Gabe tossed his wallet on a table to the right of the door. Cameron followed suit and set his car remote down while Nikki danced between them.

Sizzling noises drifted from the back of the house. Cameron's mouth watered, but he wasn't sure his stomach could handle food. What did he think he could accomplish?

To his left, a dining table held a half-sanded shelf resting on newspaper. To his right, the office featured a clean desk and a giant framed box displaying a Marine sword and various awards of service.

Straight ahead, the family room's sectional sofa faced a TV and a giant dog bed. Nikki trotted past the dog bed and hopped onto the couch. The kitchen off to the side of the family room looked nothing as grand or neat as Rose's domain, but the counters were loaded down with dips, chips, beans, rice, brownies, and more. Stuff he'd seen on menus but never tasted. He set the pie on the counter and turned, spying a narrow stairway leading to a second floor.

Each Foster residence was filled with museum-quality art and perfection, but no pets or projects or a mom cooking dinner. A heaviness settled inside him. This wasn't just a residence. Like Tasha's place, it was a home.

Gabe kicked aside a pair of old sneakers by the back door. "Sorry for the mess, man."

Cameron's throat was tight, but he managed to say, "Don't be."

Gabe's mom—Veronica, Cameron remembered from the banquet—backed out of the laundry room. Her thick hair was pulled into a ponytail. She wore workout clothes, but her makeup was still fresh. "Oh good, you're here." She hugged them both and pointed to the bowl of chips on the counter. "Eat."

Gabe snagged a chip and dunked it into thick, yellow cheese dip. "You're the best, Mom."

"Ick." Veronica glared at Gabe. "Are you an animal, raised in a barn? Wash your hands. Guests first." She handed Cameron a plate and indicated a series of bowls on the far side of the counter. "Tasha mentioned you eat mostly vegan and fish, so I made some things special for you."

The dog woofed and padded to the front. Gabe followed. "Bethany's here."

Tasha and Bethany came into the house without knocking, like they were family. Nikki wagged and pranced around their feet. Tasha carried some grocery bags to the kitchen while Bethany gave the dog's ears a good rub and hugged Cameron. He kept his arms flat at his sides. So much hugging.

The backdoor from the garage opened, and Gabe's dad entered, sniffing the air. He wore a suit and an Arlington Police Department badge clipped to his belt. Guess he also worked as a cop. "I have died and gone to heaven." He kissed Veronica. "And dinner smells good too." He play-punched Gabe's shoulder and wrapped an arm around each girl.

Cameron felt like an explorer on another planet. A mom. Hugging. Everyone was happy. Almost everyone. Once the conversation started, things would surely go sideways.

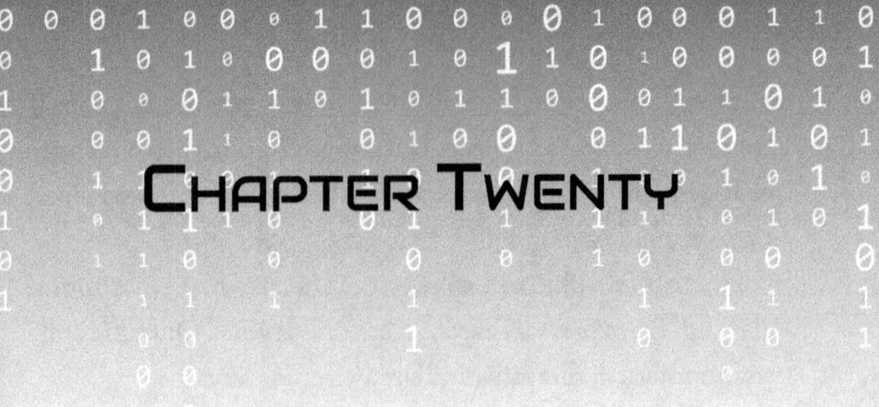

Chapter Twenty

Tasha

There was something refreshing about watching Cameron eat. It was as if each bite drove him to a new location in Flavor Town. Same as the way he looked around the house—not a narrowing of eyes at the fluffs of dog fur or Veronica's half-finished craft project, but like he wanted to touch each surface. Not what she'd expected from a trust-fund boy.

After dinner, Alejandro leaned forward and nailed Cameron with a glare. "Tasha says you've got some questions about your bodyguard."

Cameron didn't answer, so Tasha jumped in. "What's up with this Jerry? Think he's capable of murder?"

Cameron gave her an odd sideways look, but too bad if he was mad. They needed to know. Jerry could have been involved in Dr. Zemke's murder.

Alejandro tapped his fingers on the table. He'd changed into a T-shirt, so all his muscles and tats put on a scary show. When they were little, Alejandro had acted like a giant seesaw, lifting Tasha and Gabe on his arms. At that thought, other pre-FMC memories flooded her mind—Alejandro and Solomon playing soccer with them at the park, dinners where their two families would laugh and play games until midnight. No—she couldn't dwell on the memories. Like her dad, those days were gone.

Alejandro took a swig of his drink. "I did some digging. Took a while because Jerry's government service records have been erased."

"Why would they do that?" Tasha asked. And did Cameron just twitch his head?

Alejandro spread his arms wide. "No idea. I made a call to a buddy. He said Jerry was Special Forces—a sniper, one of the best. Then one day he was gone."

Tasha's mouth fell open. "He went AWOL?" She glanced at Cameron, who sat stonelike.

Alejandro leaned back, rubbing his hands through his short graying hair. "That doesn't explain why he's got no record. Bottom line." His eyes bored holes into Cameron's before turning their wattage on Tasha. "This guy's scary dangerous. He can shoot the corner off a Dorito from four hundred yards out. You'd best use caution."

Nikki padded to the front room, ears up. She growled and jogged back to the kitchen, woofing at Alejandro. He wrinkled his forehead and followed her to the front room. Cameron and Gabe trailed after them.

"What is it, mi amor?" Veronica asked.

Alejandro peered out the window. "Just a black pickup stopped a few houses down."

"Weird," Cameron said. "I've been seeing black pickups like that one all day…" His voice trailed off.

Tasha and the others stood from the table and crowded the doorframe between the kitchen and front room. "What is it?" Tasha asked Cameron.

"Jerry drives a black truck like that."

Alejandro stared at Cameron for a long moment then typed something on his phone. He glanced at Veronica and put on a smile as fake as Gran's Elvis-Asked-Me-Out story. "Did I see one of Tasha's apple pies? How about we all go back to the kitchen and slice that up?"

They ate pie in silence. Cameron and Alejandro kept checking things on their phones and eyeing each other. Tasha had the urge to peek out the window to see if the black truck was still there. Was Special Forces Jerry following them? Had Alejandro called a cop buddy to check out the truck?

A chill ran through her. Had Gabe's dad herded them away from the front windows, worried that the sniper might be targeting them?

About halfway into his second piece, Gabe's dad glanced at his phone and shoved back from the table. "I'm going to check out that Porsche. It's not every day a man's got a machine like that in his front yard." Without asking for permission, he grabbed Cameron's remote and headed outside.

Gabe and Bethany stayed in the kitchen, but Tasha followed Cameron to the front window. Alejandro poked around inside Cameron's car, and it wasn't long before a white Ford pickup pulled up. A sandy-haired guy carrying a big toolbox joined Gabe's dad. The new guy hauled out a handheld remote-type thing and waved it inside the car.

"What are they doing?" Tasha asked.

Cameron yanked open the front door. "Checking for bugs, and not the crawly kind."

Chapter
Twenty-One

Cameron

ALEJANDRO STARED AT A handheld frequency scanner, indeed checking his car for surveillance bugs. Cameron glanced up the street. No more black pickup. Gabe's dad held a finger to his lips and reached under the driver's seat, extracting a small metal button. The pit of Cameron's stomach burned. He was being watched.

The other guy held up a black pen and tapped his ear. A listening device? Cameron took it and turned it around in his fingers. He'd seen one like this before—it was the kind where the end popped out with a click so people with nervous habits could drive everyone else nuts. But where had he seen it?

It came to him a second later. Jerry. While they were watching the news about Grisham the other night, Jerry had been clicking this pen.

Cameron dropped the thing like it was on fire. It bounced on the pavement. He stomped on it, grinding his heel until the casing cracked. Sure enough, small wires protruded.

Alejandro popped the back hatch on his car and ran his hands along the spare tire well, yanking out a small GPS locating device.

Someone—*Jerry?*—was following and watching Cameron. Betrayal stung like wasps inside his throat. Alejandro tossed what they'd found into a thick metal case and motioned Cameron away from the car. "Seems like something a Special Forces guy could pull off. Question is, why?"

Cameron's mind spun. This looked bad, but…they were talking about Jerry. The guy who'd been like an older brother to him. "He could've been looking out for my safety."

Alejandro shook his head. "Why wouldn't your dad just use the GPS system installed in the car? Or track your phone?"

His dad had been especially paranoid since that kidnapping close call several years ago, which had led to him hiring Jerry. Cameron had been grabbed and his phone had been tossed away. An off-duty police officer had been nearby, so Cameron had been rescued quickly. But even one more minute, and Cameron might've been gone for good.

As for cars, most thieves knew how to disconnect car tracking systems, so if his dad wanted to keep tabs on his locale, it'd make sense that he'd employ extra measures, especially considering this was the first bit of true freedom he'd ever given Cameron.

But Jerry could be using that as an excuse to keep tabs on Cameron for some other reason.

Cameron glanced down at his clothes. He remembered a show where a kid was tracked by something put in his shoe. He motioned for Alejandro to check him.

After waving the sensor over him, Alejandro nodded. Clear.

That brought Cameron's thoughts back to his previous questions. His dad was one of the wealthiest men in the world, which made Cameron a big target for all kinds of schemes and scams.

Could he trust this group whom he hardly knew? Who could he trust, outside of his dad?

He rubbed his throbbing temple. He had to untangle this mess, and until he did, he wasn't putting up with things like listening devices and people tracking his location.

He checked his phone. Rather than disabling the GPS, he spoofed it to make it look like he was at the park nearby their house. He leaned into the car, checking the Porsche's GPS. Someone had turned it back on. He fixed that too.

Tasha scooted up behind him. "Still think Zemke's death was an accident?"

Cameron followed Bethany, Tasha, and Gabe to the back porch, which was crammed with rattan furniture, bird feeders, and dog toys. He wasn't sure where else to go. So many questions, but no answers. Jerry could be spying on him, but whether it was to protect him or to harm him, Cameron didn't know. His dad would obviously want to track his location, but who else had access to that information, and what intentions did they have?

His hands prickled, cold and stiff. Not again. Whatever these episodes were, he would not succumb.

He shook out his arms. Jerry had been like an older brother. Hard to believe the guy was dirty. What motivated him? Was it his sister Yasmine or something more sinister?

Bethany sat cross-legged on one of the chairs and gestured to Cameron. "What are you thinking?"

Cameron stared at their earnest faces. He had a decision to make. He could tell them what was on his mind or walk away and go it alone. His gaze fell on Tasha. No matter the motive behind those eyes, he needed help. "I want to see Dr. Zemke's files."

Bethany tapped a fingernail on the arm of her chair. "Have you tried to get into the hospital servers? They're not exactly secure."

Cameron nodded. "Yes. The timestamps were odd, but that doesn't necessarily mean anything bad."

Tasha sat up straighter. "What if your real records were erased? Dallas General has a secure internal backup system that might have a record of the original files. Then you'll see that I'm right."

Cameron leaned back. "I could ask—"

Tasha shook her head. "But what if whoever erased the other files figures out what we—you want and gets to the backups before we do?"

"We? And if it's an internal system, we can't hack it externally."

Bethany shrugged. "We'll go there tomorrow and download your files from the server."

Gabe gaped at them. "How do any of you know about hacking hospital servers?"

Tasha snorted. "We attend a school for kids with big brains, remember?"

"Yeah, I'm in the club," Gabe said, shoulders tight, "but I don't break the law."

Bethany picked at the hem of her shorts. "It's his information. He has a right to it."

Gabe crossed his arms. "Y'all are either freaks or criminals. Either way, I hate orange jumpsuits. Leave me outta this."

While Tasha and Gabe bickered, Cameron stood. "I should go."

Bethany put out a hand to stop him. "No. You need to get into the hospital's backups, and we can help you." She tugged on a strand of her hair. "If only we had an RFID reader. Then we could clone and print an ID badge for you to get past all their digital locks."

Bethany was getting scarier by the minute. He should walk away from all three of them, but the truth might be in the hospital backups.

Someone else must have seized control over Cameron's mouth, because he said, "I have an RFID scanner."

Tasha and Gabe quit arguing. Tasha studied him with what appeared to be admiration. "You have a radio frequency scanner?"

Bethany tapped her fingers against her lips. "But we'd have to make an ID."

No and no. He should not, but his mouth said, "I have a badge maker too."

Tasha leaned closer. "Do tell, bad boy."

He lifted a shoulder. "School project on security analysis."

Gabe threw his hands in the air. "You're seriously breaking into the hospital?"

Tasha rolled her eyes. "Of course not. We're *walking* in. Tomorrow. And Cameron will see that I'm right."

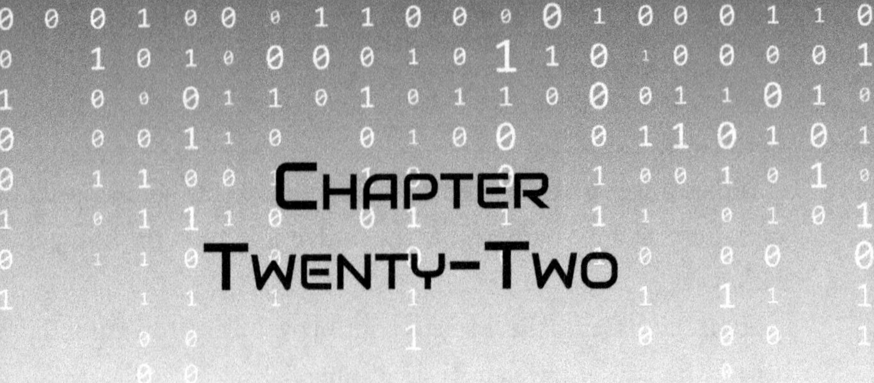

Chapter Twenty-Two

Cameron

Nothing like a shot of adrenaline to start the day.

Cameron shouldn't have agreed to this, but here he was, pulling into in the hospital parking lot at seven thirty in the morning and waiting for Tasha to create a diversion in the tech department so he could get into the server room. Bethany was also nearby somewhere, watching them on her computer.

This promised to be a disaster.

He leaned over the steering wheel and stared at the looming hospital complex. The structure was a steel and glass marvel, almost like someone had taken huge rectangular building blocks and stacked them into an L shape. Rows of square windows dotted the sides of the building and overlooked an acre of green space. He parked on the edge of a visitor lot and sat in the idling car, staring at the blueprints for the tech department.

He couldn't decide if it was better or worse having Tasha nearby. Being with her was like petting a tiger. Fascinating, but touch the wrong spot, and goodbye arm.

Bethany seemed nice on the surface, but something about her made his palms itch. She'd been far too quick with her hacking information last night. Gabe seemed straight up, but one wrong word to his dad could get them in all kinds of trouble.

Cameron donned on a stick-on camera disguised to look like an earring that Tasha had designed for a robotics class.

The girls' plan was simple, or so they said. Tasha's mom had made her volunteer at the hospital numerous times, so she would take a shift today and visit the tech department with a computer issue. She'd assured Cameron the employees down there were easily distractible. Cameron would use his fake ID badge to get in.

Cameron closed the hospital blueprints and checked to make sure the programming on the Porsche's GPS held—yep, both his phone and car showed he was still at the park. Maybe Alejandro had removed all the bugs, but someone could have added more once he got home. His dad's bodyguard Leon had eyed him as he pulled out of the garage that morning. Jerry was still supposedly with his sister, but he could be working with Leon to keep planting equipment in Cameron's car. Last night, Cameron had ordered bug detecting equipment of his own.

What were they listening for? And were they keeping tabs on his location to find a place to grab him?

He breathed deep. Time to focus on the task, not his fears. He was an actor playing a role—a network guy at a hospital. If he played his part convincingly, everything would be fine. Maybe if he repeated that enough, he'd believe it.

After he slipped on the Dallas General lanyard he'd made last night, a glance in the mirror showed a professional with a goatee dressed in black business casual. *I'm a network technician named Raj.* He topped the look with glasses that tinted in bright lights.

The trick was to add layers of costume elements. That way, people would focus on external things like clothes, glasses, and facial hair instead of his actual features.

He put in his earbuds so he'd appear occupied, grabbed his computer bag, and headed toward the building. Just another day at the office. Many of the business shifts started around eight, so he only needed to get close enough to another employee for the RFID scanner in his bag to read their badge.

According to the blueprints, the server room with the backups was located behind the ER within the tech offices. A tap on his phone screen sent the script he'd written last night into the hospital phone systems. For the next hour, phones in the tech department would ring randomly every twenty-five seconds. A little extra distraction in case Tasha failed.

Shoulders back, he walked through a garden patio and into the main entrance, heading for the coffee shop. The line did not disappoint. Visitors and employees crowded the counter. Glancing at his phone like he was reading something fascinating, he moved past people until he saw a lady with a badge from the tech offices. He tapped his phone screen to turn on his RFID scanner and slid past her on his way out.

Ducking into a nearby restroom, Cameron pulled out the small black RFID reader and slid his ID badge into the card slot, waiting for it to program. Now for the hard part.

Bethany called and spoke before he could say hello. "Get in place. Once Tasha starts, you're on."

The map of the complex bloomed in his brain like a 3D projection—the legendary Foster memory at work. At least he had that in common with his dad. He headed for the locked door that would take him toward the tech offices. Taking a breath, he swiped his newly manufactured card. If this didn't work, he'd have to come up with another plan. He stared at the digital door lock. It seemed to take an hour, but the mechanism finally clicked, and the door opened.

Cameron let out a breath and headed down the hall. Next, he had to get the code to the server room door. Sure, no problem…

He wound through the corridors, passing patients, orderlies, doctors, nurses, and security guards. They each stared at him. Could they tell he didn't belong? Sweat dripped between his shoulder blades.

He pushed through the next lock-protected door. The place smelled of harsh cleaners and burnt popcorn. His shoes squeaked against the white tile—too loud, too noticeable. Any moment, someone would turn him in for trespassing. Which would be worse? Facing jail, or his dad?

No time to panic. If he wanted answers and definitive proof for his dad, he had to get to that backup server. When he pushed into a suite of offices filled with cubicles and small glass-walled offices, a sultry laugh floated from the back of the room. Was that Tasha? Cameron wandered in that direction, passing a dozen empty desks on his way. A nearby phone rang. Someone answered it then slammed the receiver down with a grunt. As soon as that call ended, another phone started ringing.

"Sounds like your program to make the phones ring is working," Bethany said in his ear. "Just don't blow it by getting caught."

Cameron ducked his head and muttered a reply. "Wow. Helpful."

At the back of the room, Cameron turned a corner and spotted shapely legs…legs that were attached to Tasha. Wearing a short dress, she leaned over a desk with a computer in front of her and six guys at her side all stretching to see her computer screen. "See?" she said. "Each time I click on it, this happens. I just don't get it."

Cameron ducked into the hall behind her. Three doors down on the left was the server room. Just as Cameron had figured, a coded lock kept the room secure. He cleared his throat and typed a text to Bethany.

Cameron

Need door code.

She answered in his ear. "I'm on it. Give me a second. Move a few feet closer and lean against the wall, pretending you're on a call."

"Aren't we already?"

"Talk computer to me and wait. I changed the temperature in the server room. Someone will come check it any moment. Take off your camera earring and stick it to the wall two feet to your left and a foot down. I'll tell you when it's in a good spot." He peeled the earring off and endured a few seconds of "not there, a few more centimeters to the right, the other way" before Bethany was satisfied.

"How do you know so much about this stuff?"

"I read a lot of spy novels."

Yeah...same as Leon was a Mensa member. Trusting her had *bad idea* written all over it, but he wanted to know what that file said and if her idea of acting like he was answering an IT question was a good one. Cameron settled into position against the wall and pretended he was talking someone through changing their password.

A few seconds later, a woman hustled to the server room. When she passed, the numbing feeling started in his feet, and his hands went clammy. What if she saw through his ruse and had him arrested? What was he thinking? No way could he pull this off.

The lady typed her code and shoved into the server room. Cameron counted the seconds, taking deep breaths to combat the dizziness that accompanied his episodes—panic attacks?

Why would Grisham invent the heart condition? Money? He had acquired his job with FMC because of Cameron's heart issues. But what did that have to do with Jerry? When he got home, Cameron would have to do some deeper digging on them both.

The lady shoved out of the server room, slowing to glare at him.

He pointed to his phone, making several open-and-close motions with his hand to indicate the person on the other end wouldn't shut up. Shaking his head, he said into the phone, "No, tap the gear icon. That's your settings." He rolled his eyes at the woman, as if to imply *can you believe this idiot?*

She rolled her eyes back and banged through another office door, cursing when a phone starting ringing. Now or never.

Bethany gave him the code, and he was in. Frigid air washed over him, chilling the sweat around his temples. The door clicked closed, leaving him alone with the soothing hum of machines.

He scanned the rows of metal cabinets. Thousands of blue cables fed into stacks and stacks of servers, all in beautiful, organized rows. He rolled out a keyboard and plugged in a thumb drive, starting to download files from the timespan he'd been in the hospital. He took long breaths while the data transferred. *Please, please let no one come in and find me.*

Fifty percent complete. *Come on.*

"I can help you look through the data," Bethany said in his ear. "But we'd have more processing speed if we linked up our systems. It'd be like a hot date for our computers."

Seventy-five percent. He glanced at the door, and the hairs on the back of his neck stood on end. Linking machines? That could allow her to get more than this data from him. What was she after?

One hundred percent. He exhaled, yanking his thumb drive out and shoving the keyboard back in place.

Bethany hummed in his ear. "Speaking of dates, you should ask Tasha out."

"Bit busy right now." He shoved out of the room and grabbed the earring camera, then headed toward an exit. Though his heart banged against his ribs, he moved at a normal speed, head high, shoulders back, and arms out. His dad always told him if he acted as though he owned the place, people would think it was true. His hands were shaky and numb, but he kept them out of his pockets and kept heading toward the exit. Was it a right and two lefts? His temples pulsed.

"Wait!" someone shouted from behind him.

Cameron's heart jolted.

"Sir, hold up," a woman called. Was it the lady who'd checked the server room earlier? Did she know he'd broken in? Pounding footsteps followed him. Overhead, a droning voice announced some sort of code. Was security coming to get him?

Behind him, a bearded guy lumbered closer, his gait like…Leon's. Cameron's chest pounded. He turned a corner, doing everything he could to focus on the door ahead. Was it

Leon, stalking him and getting ready to grab him? Or was he becoming more paranoid by the minute?

He ducked around another corner. *Keep the pace normal, don't look back.* Bethany prattled in his ear, but he didn't hear what she said. Footsteps drew closer. Each of his heartbeats seemed to scream, *run!* Eyes on the door, he sped up his pace.

"Sir, stop!"

Cameron couldn't breathe. They'd caught him, and he'd never know what the doctor had found. Worse, his dad would be so angry he wouldn't believe anything Cameron told him about Jerry and Grisham.

A nurse pounded past him, catching up to an old man limping out the door. Cameron hadn't even noticed the old guy wearing a hospital gown and slippers, tottering along with his walker. Although Cameron's body sagged with relief, he didn't slow. Once he reached the door, he jogged to his car. He cranked the a/c on the highest setting and breathed. In. Out.

"Did you hear anything I said?" Bethany asked.

He jumped. He'd forgotten about her. "Um, what?"

"Send Tasha some flowers. She'll love them."

Cameron leaned his head on the steering wheel until his pulse returned to normal. His upper lip felt naked without his O2, but still no issues. That download better have some clear information. Then he could get on with his life. Right?

He groaned. "Flowers for Tasha. She might set them on fire." And what was with Bethany's pushiness? She wanted to connect with his computer, connect him to Tasha. Why?

Hand on the gearshift, he froze. Bethany's mother worked for FMC, so what if her daughter was after some kind of insider information to help her mom get an edge at work? Was she using

Tasha to help gain Cameron's trust to get information out of him?

Or was he so twisted up he'd never trust anyone again? Still, maybe sticking close to Tasha wasn't a bad idea. It would give him more time to figure both girls out. Right. A little data theft always made for perfect date conversation.

Chapter Twenty-Three

Tasha

Bethany and Cameron were waiting in her yard when Tasha got home. Seeing Bethany so interested in something that might get her into trouble was weird. She'd always seemed straightlaced. They'd first met at an FMC employee day at Six Flags Amusement Park when Bethany had scarfed a funnel cake then hopped on The Texas Giant roller coaster next to Tasha. Their moms had refused to ride. The funnel cake had made an awful encore, but their friendship was cemented.

Though they'd attended different schools at first, they'd teamed up to study. Tasha had already been a top student, but Bethany's rigid study charts and drive for perfection helped Tasha step it up another notch.

It had been Bethany who'd encouraged her and Gabe to apply to DAST-M, where Bethany was a model student. She never broke rules at school or at home. She did her own laundry and kept her room perfectly neat. Until now, that funnel cake was Bethany's biggest transgression. What was up with her?

Cameron leaned against his car. He waved, his chest flexing under his *Don't matter if you're #000000 or #FFFFFF* T-shirt. Her ancient Honda Civic creaked and groaned to a stop. She yanked the keys out of the ignition and gripped her Wonder Woman keychain until it dug into her palm. What was she doing helping him? On the off chance it didn't get her killed, being a part of data theft could end her MIT dreams. She did not need some good looking, kind-hearted jerk mucking up her future. He'd already screwed up her plans to get revenge for her father's death.

Her cheeks prickled. That wasn't fair. Her dad's death wasn't Cameron's fault, and maybe, just maybe, if she were honest, it might not be his dad's fault either.

She exhaled. Okay, since she was having this Sunday school moment of honesty with herself, Nigel wasn't what she'd expected. He'd been strict and definitely had a pole up his rear, but from what she'd seen, he was a doting father worried about his son.

And…she had no actual proof Nigel had been involved in what happened to her dad. She swallowed past her dry throat. Giving up on what she'd believed for so long was difficult, like a kid getting candy pried from their fist. But maybe it was time to let that go.

It seemed someone else at FMC was messing with the Fosters. But why? Money? Perhaps Cameron's private doctor had some major gambling or drug issues and needed cash.

Tasha waved Cameron and Bethany inside. They gathered around the dining table, speaking in low voices to keep Gran snoozing in her recliner. Until the doorbell rang.

Gran jerked awake. Tasha grumbled. It wasn't Gran's oxygen delivery day, so who was bothering them now? Outside, some delivery guy in a uniform held up two bundles. A big arrangement of roses and a gold box of what looked like expensive chocolates. She jerked the door open. "You've got the wrong address."

He held up the card. "Says this is for a Hazel Watts."

Flowers for Gran. Really? Tasha glared back at the table. Cameron and Bethany were on their phones, although Bethany's fingernails were tip-tapping a nervous rhythm on a raccoon rescue sticker on her case. Was it the low kitchen lighting, or were Cameron's ears turning red?

Delivery guy whined from outside. "Did I get the wrong address?"

Tasha took both items from him. "I guess not."

Delivery guy stood there, expectant, eyebrows raised.

Tasha bit her lip. Right, a tip, but it wasn't like she kept stacks of cash around. There was a little left in her babysitting stash, but—

Cameron appeared beside her and pressed a bill into the guy's palm. The delivery guy grinned and trotted off to his car.

She whirled on Cameron. "Stop doing that."

The goof opened his eyes in perfect *who-me* innocence. "What?"

"Throwing your money around."

He stepped closer, smelling delicious, and those lips…good enough to bite. Oh, how she hated him.

"I didn't throw anything." His voice was low and sultry.

Gran snorted awake. Tasha ducked around Cameron. "Look, Gran, you got roses."

A smile practically cracked the old woman's face. "I haven't gotten flowers since the last millennium. Who're they from?"

Tasha's heart thudded, and she peeked at Cameron again, but they were for Gran, not her, and it wasn't like he'd send Tasha flowers anyhow. She yanked out the card. "It says, 'To Hazel, a beautiful lady. From a secret admirer.'" Tasha stared at the card so long the message blurred.

Gran pointed to the chocolates. "Those for me too? My, my, I must have made quite an impression on my admirer." Her gaze cut to Cameron.

He ignored them as if the gifts had nothing to do with him. But who else would they be from? Tasha handed Gran one piece of chocolate and put the rest away. "You can't eat them all at once, or you'll die in a horrible diabetic coma."

"Death by chocolate. Sounds delicious."

"I'll ration—" Tasha's phone buzzed, cutting her off.

Unknown Number

> Will you have dinner with your grandmother's secret admirer tonight at 7?

It *had* been him. Tasha's face turned lava hot, and it was all she could do not to glance at Cameron. Tasha punched her reply into the screen.

Tasha

> Maybe.

She sank into her seat at the table, face still on fire. That jerk, asking her out in a totally thoughtful, romantic way. Seriously, who did he think he was, making Gran's day like that? And Bethany needed to put that Cheshire-cat smile away before it blinded someone.

Instead of spoiling the moment with commentary, Cameron turned on that fancy phone attachment she'd suspected was a projector and filled the wall with screens. "Let's get to work."

Cameron and Bethany started discussing search parameters to help them avoid looking at anyone else's data, but Tasha couldn't focus. She exhaled, buffing a scratch on the table. It'd been there since the night her dad was killed.

Cameron said something and Bethany responded, but the noise in the room faded. A strong floral scent wafted off Gran's roses, taking her back to the night her dad died. A bouquet of flowers had sat on the table—an anniversary gift from her dad to her mom.

That night, she'd been connected to her dad via a camera similar to the one Cameron had used earlier. It'd been for a robotics project. Everything was fine until her dad's work SUV started acting funny before it slammed into the fence in the FMC parking lot. She'd screamed and smashed the vase on the table, destroying the last thing her dad had given her mom.

She snapped back to the present, and a wave of nausea hit her so hard she ran to the bathroom, sick as a junkyard dog. She stayed there, brushing her teeth, splashing water on her face, washing her hands, wiping, wiping, wiping away the memories. She squeezed the flash drive charm on her bracelet.

Were the people who'd killed him somehow involved with Cameron too? If that was the case, she was a complete moron for letting him into her house and life.

When she finally collected herself, she stopped to pour a glass of iced tea then slunk back to the table.

Cameron was still working through the data, chin resting on his hand. Another fancy watch gleamed in the light. The guy had so much patience. He stopped, indicating a file. "I think this is it. Look at the timestamp. That's an hour earlier than the file I downloaded."

He hesitated, face freezing into something like dread. Tasha's heart squeezed. Would this show he did have a heart condition and that she'd gotten his hopes up for nothing? Or that someone evil was lying to him? She squeezed his hand, unable to think of something to say.

He swallowed and opened the file.

Tasha stood. The screen showed Cameron's test results, the ones Dr. Zemke must have seen. *Heart normal. No defects or anomalies noted.*

Cameron went statue still. Only his eyes moved, scanning the information up and down. He looked like he was about to be sick.

Tasha swallowed. "Who do you think changed this?"

Bethany let out a hiss. "Tasha said Jerry was there that night, and that he left the room. He could have done this."

Tasha cleared her throat. "Your doctor left the room too, but he said he spoke to the nursing staff."

Cameron shook his head, sagging in his chair. "Why?"

Tasha rubbed a cramp out of her neck. "Jerry's a disgraced soldier, so what if Dr. Grisham is blackmailing him to help keep your condition a secret? As for the doctor, FMC is into medical stuff. Maybe Grisham wants to make sure he has his big paycheck plus access to FMC's organ research, and being your private doctor gives him that? Are there competitors they could sell information to?"

Cameron ran his finger back and forth across the table. "We have several competitors—GeneAlytics, PharmaLyfe, and MedRxSystems. One major area of research is in organ cloning and development—growing organs to match host DNA, which would make transplants available to more people. We're rolling out a huge announcement later this year. Dad always talks about how I'm his inspiration. We also have a huge pharmaceutical division and conduct chemo and immune suppressant research. Plus, FMC has some equipment divisions, most of them surgical and life support systems."

He nodded at Bethany. "Your mom works in the ghost organ protocol division. Has she ever mentioned issues with competitors or espionage?"

Bethany twisted hair around her fingers and didn't meet his eyes. "Mom won't discuss work." She tapped a nail on her keyboard, shifting in her seat. "You know, there are groups, crooked ones like the mafia, involved in the organ trade. They can set up chains of dummy websites to get their broker's information. It's big money. They often kidnap people in third-world countries, stealing their organs and leaving them for dead, and some of them harvest organs from prisoners. What if they're behind this? They could be promising Jerry a big payout."

Tasha choked on her tea. Guess Bethany had researched the organ black market too?

Cameron folded his arms over his chest. "What's with you two and the organ trade?"

Bethany shrugged and tugged on the hem of her T-shirt. "School project."

Liar. Bethany hadn't done any projects on the organ trade. Perhaps, though, she might be interested in EyeNet. Black Mask had recruited Tasha last year, so surely he'd be interested in another dedicated member.

Bethany ran a finger through Cameron's keyboard projection. "Love your setup, but how do you have so much processing power from a phone?"

"It's linked to some servers."

"Nice," Bethany said. "If you want our help finding more on Jerry and your dad's competitors, we should link together."

Cameron leaned away from Bethany, eyes narrowed.

Weird that Bethany would be willing to link up with someone she hardly knew, but they'd sorta broken the law together. Guess that could count as trust.

Before Tasha could comment, Cameron waved his hands at both their laptops. "I'll link you two together."

Bethany's hands gripped the sides of her laptop. "I meant link with you." Her request made sense from a processing speed standpoint, but Cameron said no. Why was she being so stubborn?

Cameron's face took on a pleasant yet blank expression. In that moment, he looked just like his father. "Yeah, but as we just discussed, someone might be going after my dad's company, so I can't take more risks. Speaking of"—he glanced at Tasha—"do you have a hammer?"

"Um, yeah, in the garage."

Cameron followed her to the garage, and when she handed over the tool, he dropped the thumb drive he'd used on the floor and smashed it into pieces. He swept them into a pile then headed inside, flushing the detritus down the toilet.

Some of the tension in Tasha's shoulders melted. They'd still broken a lot of laws, but at least they hadn't looked at or kept anyone else's data.

When they returned to the dining room, Bethany had packed up her computer. "I promised Gabe I'd meet him for a picnic tonight at the lake." She gave Cameron a pointed look. "See y'all later."

Tasha waved, focused on Cameron. "What does your dad think you're doing today?"

"Studying, which is true in a sense. He'll be in meetings until after ten tonight." Cameron glanced at his phone. "But I need to go too."

"Good," Tasha said. "I've got a hot date with Gran's secret admirer."

"I wouldn't want to make him jealous." Cameron headed to the door.

Tasha blinked. "Umm…you're leaving?" Had she accepted a date from some creepy unknown person? Or…maybe he didn't feel in a date mood anymore. Understandable. "Look, it's fine if you don't want to go—"

He studied her for a long moment. "I do, but there's a few things I need to do first. See you at seven." He let himself out.

Tasha stared at the door. It didn't make sense to go out tonight, not with everything they'd just discovered, but they needed to keep collaborating, and humans had to eat and…she wanted to see him again. Too bad that when he found out the whole truth about her, especially that she'd been using him in the beginning, he'd never want to see her again.

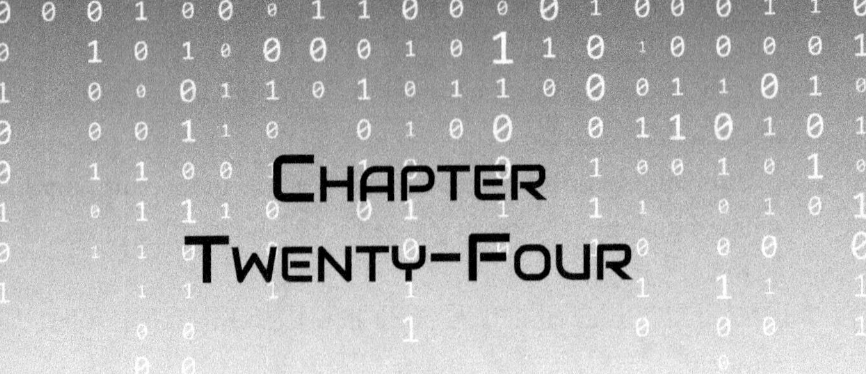

Chapter Twenty-Four

Tasha

CAMERON KNOCKED AT SEVEN. When she opened the door, he handed her a bag of takeout from a local bakery. "For Hazel," he said. "Soup and pie."

Tasha stared at the bag. He'd brought dinner for Gran? This boy was either a great guy or a total player. Either way, she had to keep her guard up…for both their sakes.

Cameron walked her to the car, opening her passenger door, then slid into the driver's seat. He turned on the engine but paused and itched the tip of his nose. Was he missing his oxygen? Tasha wadded up her purse strap. "How're you doing with all this?"

Cameron pulled out, shifting gears and maneuvering around a corner without giving her whiplash. "Which part of 'all this' do you mean?"

"You're not dying, and your episodes are panic attacks. The doctor who wanted to warn you is dead, and you're on your own without Jerry, who might be trying to kill you. And you're crazy enough to take me on a date. It's safe to say you might be experiencing some mental instability."

He laughed. It was deep and full with no rasps or wheezing. How could anyone believe this boy was sick? Tasha leaned her head back and imagined a world without mortal danger and murders, where only the two of them and this moment existed, this feeling of hope blooming inside her chest. What would it be like if he wrapped an arm around her and pulled her close? Gave her some stupid nickname and took her out often? Held her hand? Kissed—

Tasha almost slapped herself. They were working together to solve his death issues, and she needed his help to figure out how her dad died. Even if his dad wasn't behind it, it was still their company and could cause them trouble.

She fingered the flash drive charm on her bracelet. She needed to show him what was on it. Maybe then she could find out the truth about what happened to her dad.

Tasha dug her nails into her wrist. No matter how she justified it, she was still using Cameron Foster.

The road streaked by, and Cameron turned off the main highway onto a deserted country road. She glanced around at the scenery—nothing but trees and dirt. Wait, there weren't any restaurants out here. Where was he taking her?

A burning feeling spread in the center of her chest. She gripped the door handle, and the flash drive grew heavier by the second. Three years ago, some faceless guy with a deep voice had threatened if she told the truth about what had happened to her dad, they'd kill everyone she loved.

What if Cameron and his dad had been in on it, and they knew what she'd seen? What if all of this had been his way of gaining her trust so that he could get rid of her quietly? Out here in the country could be a good place to do it. She gulped in a breath. "I thought we were going to dinner."

"We are," he said.

Like heck. "If you're taking me to some remote place to murder me, I will so kill you back."

Cameron slowed the car and glanced her way, eyes wide. "What?"

"Why else are you driving me to the middle of nowhere at this time of day?"

"Bethany told me you loved the lake beach, so I thought you'd like a picnic. She said she and Gabe were planning to be nearby, so plenty of witnesses."

Tasha sagged against her seat. "Right. A picnic. Sounds great." She forced a laugh. This stuff about her dad was making her certifiable. If she didn't get it off her chest soon, the weight might crush her.

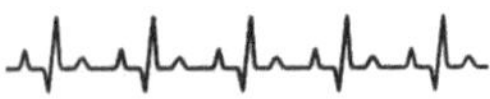

They shared a picnic of Italian takeout and triple chocolate cheesecake—well, she had ravioli and cheesecake. He ate fish, veggies, and fruit. She offered to share hers, but apparently after seventeen years of eating vegan, it wasn't easy to suddenly tolerate new foods.

Though it was past eight, the sun still shone on the western horizon, and the temperature had cooled all the way down to ninety-five. Tasha leaned back on the soft blanket Cameron had spread for them on the sandy lake beach. She kicked off her sandals, digging her feet into the warm, soft sand. Nearby, a few families wrapped up cookouts and retreated to campers parked up the hill.

Her shoulder brushed Cameron's, and a sense of warmth rose in Tasha's cheeks that had nothing to do with the warm night. She glanced at the almost-empty beach. So far, they hadn't seen Bethany and Gabe. She bet they'd lost track of time. All the better. Tasha didn't want to share this moment with anyone else. She cleared her throat. "Do you want to talk about…everything?"

He grunted and leaned back on an elbow. "Not at the moment."

"That's fair." Tasha stretched out her arm, the lake's breeze tickling her skin. If only they didn't have that *everything* hanging over them. Cameron was more interesting than any boy she'd met. What did a normal girl say on a normal date? They'd covered the fascinating topic of weather twice already. She exhaled and blurted, "I guess this is pretty lame compared to the beaches you've seen."

Cameron leaned closer to her. "It has its own charm."

Did Cameron truly like her? Would he still like her after he knew the truth? She tossed a small stone into the lake, watching it sink beneath the surface. Her heart was that rock, sinking deeper into this risky territory, yet any moment the current could turn against her. Tasha searched for something to say. "What's the best vacation you've ever taken?"

He leaned all the way back and stared at the sky. "Dad never takes time off. For him, work is life."

"Well, that sucks." She scooted closer. Barely an inch separated them. Heat billowed off his bronze arms. Everything in her wanted to touch his skin, to feel the hard muscles underneath. She clenched her fists and focused on a plane overhead flying north toward DFW airport. "Do you want to be like your dad? Always working?"

"Until this week, I didn't think I'd live long enough to have to worry about it."

The breeze tossed his dark hair, and he gazed at the water, his face full of…something. What was it? Longing? Sometimes she was so buried beneath her own pain she forgot others hurt too. She squeezed his hand. "I'm sorry."

He held on. "Perhaps it's been worth it. I met you."

"You're an idiot."

"And yet you say it with such affection."

She took a long drink of the sweet tea Cameron had ordered for her. Small waves lapped at the shoreline, always moving, always changing. "What do you want out of life? And don't waste my time with something generic like world peace and homes for all the puppies. What do you, Cameron, want?"

He stared at the horizon. An answer lurked in his mind somewhere, but he seemed to be debating whether to trust her with it. Finally, he exhaled. "I've always wanted to be *something*." He dragged a hand through his hair. "That sounds lame."

Tasha had read a good interrogation tactic was to sometimes keep quiet. She managed. Barely.

"What I mean is my dad has always been everywhere. He started Foster Med Corp when he was seventeen. Granted, he'd inherited the money to do it, but he's always done everything he set his mind to." Cameron chewed his lip. "There was this time with a reporter, when we were in New York several years ago. She was asking me questions about my life and my heart issue. She just… She looked at me like I was something to be pitied." His voice caught. "She said I was lucky to have such an amazing dad to care for me, as if I'd never be able to take care of myself."

Tasha's throat felt too thick to talk.

He went on. "That night I did my first hack. I'm not proud of it." He shifted around. "I broke into a bank's computers. It was a small-town bank, and I didn't take anything. The next day, I alerted them to the issue, which ended in me starting a security consulting business. I donated my first paycheck to an activist group, and that led me into hacktivism…"

He let out a long breath. "I didn't want my dad to have a son who never achieved anything. I wanted to measure up." He lifted his very nice shoulder. "I wanted to make him proud."

Dang, if they'd met under any other circumstances, she'd probably be grosser than Bethany, making puppy eyes and falling all over herself to keep his attention. "You started your own company; don't you see that's already amazing?" Her eyes grew hot. Cameron was truly a noble person, inside and out.

And what was she? Yes, she was into hacktivism, but why? Not for some noble cause like Cameron. No, it was all tied up in finding the truth about her dad.

He shifted his weight, and their legs brushed.

She let her weight tip toward him until their skin made contact. He was warm and smelled of something musky. She dug her fingers into the sand, and her senses drilled down to his even breathing and the water lapping the shore.

Cameron, though, kept glancing around.

"Who're you looking for?" Tasha sat straighter. "You think someone followed us?"

"We should've seen Gabe and Bethany by now."

She sagged back on the blanket. "They lose track of time." Besides, their presence would destroy *this*, the first time in forever that she didn't feel like punching something.

Yet the longer she sat next to him, the heavier her flash drive charm became. She couldn't pretend to be all date-y when she had all these huge secrets burning her up. "I have something I need to show you."

"Wait, can I go first?" He let go of her hand and sat up straight. "I have something for you."

She shoved her toes deeper in the sand. If he delayed, she might lose her nerve, but the excitement in his eyes lit up the lakeshore. "Sure. What is it?"

He dug in his pocket and pulled out a necklace—a simple silver chain with a heart pendant. A few light-blue stones glittered in the center of the heart.

Tasha dusted off her feet. It took her a moment to think of something to say because the gift made no sense. "What's this for?"

He shrugged and stared at the water. "I saw the heart and... I don't know, it felt symbolic. If you hadn't tried so hard to help me, I'd never have known."

He looked at her expectantly, like maybe he was hoping for some sort of kissing marathon in exchange for the gift. What a jerk. She stood. "No thanks."

His face fell. "You don't like it?"

"My affection's not for sale."

He got to his feet too. "I just—you're the first person not on Dad's payroll who's cared about me—"

"And you bought me something? Don't you realize how that looks?"

He blinked, eyes popping wide. "It's not like that. Geez. It's a necklace. I saw it and thought you might like it. End of story."

She groaned. He'd been locked up like Rapunzel most of his life, so she should give him a break. "Normal people don't give jewelry on the first date." She shook her head. "You're such an idiot. Why do I like you?" Whoa—why'd she admit that out loud?

His back stiffened. "I can return it if you'd like."

"Don't be a moron." She chewed her lip and heard her therapist's voice. *True relationships only develop with honesty and trust.* An hour ago, she'd thought he was going to kill her, and he'd bought her a gift. Cameron made no sense. Or maybe Tasha was the one with a problem. She was a busted, hollowed-out shell. Her next thought dug claws into her insides—the real problem with his gift was that it represented something nice, while these days she seemed only capable of anger.

She fingered the chain. "It's beautiful."

He stared at the sand, a muscle working in his jaw.

Time for a truce. She held up the pendant. "Help me put it on?"

He stepped behind her and clasped it around her neck, his fingers dragging along her collarbone. Tingles danced on her skin and sank deep into her chest. She grasped the heart pendant and faced him. "Just so we're clear, if you ever think you can buy me, I'll punch a hole in your face."

"Is that your version of thank you?"

"It's a warning." She sputtered an exhale. "And thank you. I love it."

He moved closer, saying nothing, staring at her with eyes full of fire.

Her heart thrummed in her ears. She either wanted to scream or kiss him.

His gaze darkened and dropped to her lips. He wanted to kiss her too.

Something heated inside her, like warm oil seeping through her muscles. Cameron leaned forward. An invisible force pulled Tasha closer. Resistance was futile. She didn't care about revenge, not anymore. It was just her and this incredible boy. She crashed toward him, all in.

Their lips met, soft and thrilling. A lightning bolt shivered from her lower lip down through her belly as he ran a hand up her arm. Her nerve endings came alive as if they'd been plugged into a reactor. His fingers brushed her neck. She leaned closer, her mouth molding to his, or his to hers. She didn't want to think, just wanted to savor this moment.

She ran her hands over his broad shoulders.

He pulled back, panting. His eyes glazed over, and it took him a moment to speak. "You said you had something to show me."

She blinked a few times and flopped back onto the blanket. No, not this, not now. She had finally let it go. "We just had this incredible moment! How can you be so smart and so stupid?"

He ran his hands over his face. "I didn't want you to think I thought you were kissing me because of the necklace. Or that I expected—"

"Shut up. I don't."

He settled beside her. "Okay. We can kiss some more."

She held up a finger. "You had your chance, but maybe later." Definitely later. She pulled off her bracelet, closing her fist around it. In her gut, the cheesecake had started a war with the ravioli. "I don't want to show this to you because it sucks, and it might make you mad. Or you'll hate me."

His eyes wrinkled, and the warm expression evaporated, replaced by something firmer. He leaned away from her.

"No, it's nothing I did, nothing against you, not really, it's…it sucks." Heat pressed against her eyes. Oh, crud. She could not cry. She didn't cry on dates. Of course, this was the only date she'd been on, so how would she know? And why was she determined to ruin the perfect night by showing a guy she just met the most horrible day of her life?

Because he needed to know. Because it might have to do with him—some bad people could be targeting both him and his dad. Because she didn't want any secrets and wanted more than anything to build something real with this guy who had the nicest broken heart she'd ever known. But there was always the chance it'd end with him hating her.

Her hand shook. Worse, this could put him in danger too, but not knowing would be just as bad for his health. She pressed her bracelet into his palm. "I'll totally understand if you want your necklace back."

He turned the bracelet's charm over, eyes narrowed. "It looks like a flash drive."

"Yes, and I'm trusting you with what's on it. Don't tell anyone about it—our lives depend on it."

His eyes did that cute scrunch-up thing. He probably thought she was being sarcastic, but at least he pulled out his phone. Yeah, she'd definitely seen a small plugin on the side of his projector.

"Tasha!"

Gabe pounded across the sand in their direction. He leaned over his knees, panting. His shirt was wet with sweat and his hair looked like it'd been in a tornado. "Have you seen Bethany?" Gabe's eyes were wild.

"No." Instinct made her grab Cameron's hand. "She said y'all were meeting here. Were you late? Maybe she went home."

Gabe turned in a circle, scanning the trees. "Her car's still here."

Tasha's throat burned. "What're you saying?"

Gabe gripped his hair. "I can't find her—she isn't—something's wrong."

"You're overreacting," Tasha said. "I'm sure she just…took a walk." Even to Tasha, the words sounded pathetic and wrong, wrong, wrong.

"You're not getting it!" Gabe turned on his heel, shouting. "She's gone."

Chapter Twenty-Five

Cameron

Cameron and Tasha followed Gabe to the parking lot. Sirens wailed in the distance, their red-and-blue lights splattering across the trees.

Cameron pulled out his phone. There had to be some way of finding her on the traffic cameras. "Can we trace her somehow? What about her phone?"

Gabe shook his head. "It's off."

"Which car is hers?"

Gabe scoffed. "You're not Ethan Hunt, and you can't key something into your phone and find her." He wrung his hands. "My dad's gonna be here any minute."

Cameron ignored the outburst. Gabe was obviously panicked. Instead, he stepped aside and started searching. Finally, he found Bethany's white coupe on a city camera headed toward the lake, but there was not a camera in the parking lot. He leaned against his car—leaden and guilty. He was kissing Tasha while Bethany was in trouble, and this couldn't be a coincidence, not with everything that had happened. Were Grisham and Jerry behind this?

Gabe's dad pulled up in a police SUV, grim-faced and tense. Gabe ran over to him, and whatever his dad said caused Gabe to ball up his fists and curse. He whirled on them. "Bethany's mom just got a ransom text."

Tasha grabbed Cameron's arm.

Cameron's gut pinched. "My dad will help. I have some money too—"

Alejandro held up his hand. "Your dad has already offered."

Tasha exhaled. "Wow. That's nice."

Cameron nodded. "He comes across as tough, but he's got a good heart." His mind whirled into action. There had to be something he could do. "We can trace the phone it came from and maybe triangulate—"

"We got this, kid." Alejandro nodded to one of the officers and stepped away but paused and glared back at Cameron. "But stick around."

For the next hour, Cameron leaned on his car, watching cops swarm the park, his stomach twisting. Dr. Zemke had ended up dead after trying to help him. Bethany and Tasha were trying to help him. What if…? He couldn't think the rest but couldn't stop thinking about it either. What if this was his fault?

Because old habits die hard, Cameron started to call Jerry. But instead, he logged onto EyeNet. Black Mask had left a message with several links, but before he could read it, Tasha's mom careened into the parking lot, her Toyota sedan throwing up gravel.

She pulled up next to Cameron's car and gave him a look that could scorch the devil. "You," she said, unrolling the window and slamming the car into park. "This is your fault!"

Tasha jogged closer. "Mom, what are you doing?"

Sarah had a slap fight with her seatbelt and tumbled out of the car. She must have gotten tangled with her purse because it scattered on the pavement. Lipstick, wallet, change, and papers spewed everywhere. "Veronica called about Bethany. How come you didn't?" Without taking her eyes off Tasha, she jabbed a finger toward Cameron. "You have to stay away from him—"

"How is this Cameron's fault?" Tasha matched her mother's volume.

"His dad's evil. You of all people know that."

"This isn't Nigel's fault. I think he's a victim too."

"How can you be calm when your friend is missing?" Sarah dragged both hands through her hair. "Think about it. Everything was fine until Foster Jr. showed up."

Cameron held up his hands. "What does this have to do with my dad? I—"

Sarah slammed her car door. "Stay away from my daughter."

Cameron wanted to yell back. His dad was a great man who donated more money to charitable causes than most people made in a lifetime. How could Sarah say such horrible things?

He took a cleansing breath. Sarah was obviously freaking out. Instead of responding, he knelt and shoved the spilled contents back into her purse. Sarah yanked it away. He picked up one last piece of scrap paper under her car. It was heavy with something hard folded inside it. The writing on top looked like letterhead or a prescription pad. He handed the wadded-up bundle to her, and she threw it onto her car's floorboard.

Tasha wrung her hands. "Mom, you're humiliating me!"

"Oh, I'm causing you problems? I'm so sorry." She spread her arms wide. "It was his dad who ruined our lives! First, some nut-job doctor puts a weird note in my work mailbox, and then this?"

Tasha and Cameron glanced at each other. Something else from Dr. Zemke?

Before they could follow up, a black SUV screeched into the parking lot. Jerry jumped out of the passenger seat. "Kid! You okay?"

Fire spread across Cameron's chest. What if Jerry tried to kidnap him?

Tasha grabbed Cameron's hand. "I won't let him get you."

Jerry ran toward them. "I heard about Dr. Phan's daughter. What happened?"

"How'd you know I'd be here?" Cameron asked.

Jerry gave him the side eye. "I'm good at my job."

Alejandro, thankfully, appeared just then. "Jerry Jacobs. We'd like to talk to you."

Jerry held up his hand to Cameron. "Don't go anywhere."

The two former Marines stormed across the parking lot. At first, Alejandro's body language was aggressive—he gestured wildly, pointing at Jerry's face. Jerry responded in kind. They paced, folded arms over their chests. Alejandro jerked out his phone. Jerry followed suit, also making a call.

Another police cruiser pulled into the parking lot, its flashing lights blinding him. By the time the bright spots faded from Cameron's vision, Alejandro and Jerry were headed his way, and there weren't any handcuffs involved. What the what?

Alejandro jerked his head to Cameron. "You two can head home."

Cameron wasn't going anywhere with Jerry, and why would Alejandro betray him like this? "I don't think so."

Tasha quit arguing with her mom long enough to jump into their conversation. "What happened to Jerry being super scary and staying away from him?"

Alejandro held a finger out to her. "Not now, Natasha."

Cameron couldn't swallow past his tight throat. Gabe's dad worked part time for FMC. He could be in on this. How deep did this go?

Alejandro motioned Cameron a few feet away from the others. "I was wrong."

"He's not a scary ex-sniper?" Cameron asked.

"That he is, but you can trust him."

Jerry joined them and rubbed his forehead. He looked tired, like he'd aged ten years since yesterday. "Join me over by the squad car. We need to talk."

Cameron wanted to be anywhere but near Jerry, but he also needed answers. Jerry leaned on the black SUV. The flashing red-and-blue lights gave him an eerie glow. Cameron kicked the pavement. His first date had gone perfectly until everything bricked into one huge mess.

Jerry waved a bug detector over Cameron. "You're clean."

"Why're you searching me with a bug detector when you're the one who bugged my car?" Cameron asked.

Jerry raised his eyebrows. "First, where's your O2?"

A police cruiser skidded out of the parking lot, mixing the smell of burnt rubber with the fishy odor from the lake.

Cameron studied Jerry. He'd trusted the guy like an older brother. In truth, Jerry had been Cameron's best friend, his only friend. How pathetic was that? "It turns out I'm not dying."

Jerry's face wrinkled up like a linen shirt after a plane ride. "What do you mean, not dying? Did you have more tests run or something?"

This guy expected him to dish everything but was keeping more secrets than the Pentagon. "Why does Alejandro suddenly trust you?"

Jerry crossed his arms over his chest. "I'm not at liberty to talk about it."

"Guess we're deadlocked."

Jerry rubbed his eyes. "Let me make a phone call." He moved a few feet away from his SUV and pulled out a phone Cameron hadn't seen him use before, speaking in rushed murmurs. "Yeah. He needs to know."

Over on the other side of the parking lot, Tasha and her mother stood with their hands on their hips, eyes narrowed, mouths moving at light speed. Gabe gestured with his hands, and Alejandro's shoulders were so tight they almost eclipsed his neck.

Jerry shook his head at whatever the person on the other end of the phone said. "He's gotta know more than that." After a few more grunts, he shoved the phone into his pocket.

Cameron forced words out through his teeth. "Who was that? Your secret mafia warlord trying to get information from Dad's company to sell organs on the black market?"

Jerry's brow furrowed. "You're smart, I'll give you that."

Cameron moved backward until his body pressed against the SUV. "It's true?"

Jerry huffed. "Don't be ridiculous. I work against the mafia. You think Alejandro would let me go otherwise?"

"Maybe you threatened him. Maybe you're together on this."

Jerry nodded toward Alejandro, who was berating a uniformed cop. "He look like the type who takes threats?"

"You were a sniper, and all your service records are gone. Tell me you wouldn't find that suspicious."

Jerry looked away.

"What happened?" Cameron asked.

Jerry's shoulders slumped, and his voice dropped to a whisper. "I did something stupid a few years ago, and I'm paying for it now."

Two cops walked in their direction. Cameron stepped closer. "What'd you do?"

"Not going to talk about it."

"Oh, there's a shock," Cameron said.

"You don't understand," Jerry said.

"Exactly. Guess I never will."

They stared at each other, facing off in some game with rules Cameron didn't know.

Jerry glanced around and seemed satisfied that no one was listening. He pointed to the one-nineteen tat on the back of his neck. "I was a government gunman, once upon a time. That's my number of sniper kills."

Whoa.

Jerry's neck muscles flexed, and his eyes became unfocused. "The last hit turned out to be…a kid. Two days before, me and my unit were out searching for a kidnap victim in some rocky, desert mountains. Came across a group dressed as women, but something felt off. We'd rescued dozens of refugees before—good people in need of help—but a feeling deep down told me these women weren't right. But how can you know?" He shoved off the car and paced.

"One of the women stumbled. My buddy Eric went over to help." Jerry rubbed the back of his neck. "My spine tingled like maybe someone was about to shoot us. I kept looking for snipers, but the area was clean. Everything was fine until the person Eric was helping blew them all to bits."

His voice cracked, and a vein on his temple stood out. "I should've shot when I first had that feeling, but I hesitated. I didn't want to murder an innocent."

His voice dropped to monotone. "Next day, there we were again, searching for the kidnapped victims. We saw a couple kids climbing on rocks. One fell. Grabbed his ankle like he'd broken it, but I couldn't tell. Was he faking? Maybe he wanted to lure us to the kill zone. This chill ran up my spine, like a ghost was at my back, shouting at me to run. All I could see in that moment was Eric being blown away."

Jerry dragged both hands over his head. "But the kid could've been running for his life. Maybe he needed help. Just then, the other kid with him reached for his backpack. He had something in his hand. I thought, 'detonator,' and pulled the trigger."

Jerry went quiet and stared at the SUV, shaking his head at the ghosts haunting him. "The kid tumbled down the rocks, dead before he hit the ground."

A police radio crackled, and Cameron jolted. He'd been half a world away, lost in Jerry's desert tragedy. "But the kids had a bomb, right?"

Jerry huffed. "Yeah, in the backpack. His friend tried to detonate it, so we had to shoot him too. Two kids. Dead. Wired to blow us all away. Who makes kids carry bombs or dresses like a woman to blow people up?" He spat on the ground, as if he couldn't stand the taste of those words. "After that, I couldn't do it anymore. When we made it back to the base, I walked away. And just kept walking."

"It wasn't your fault."

"Doesn't matter. Like a coward, I left my buddies back there to die. And tried to disappear. But you can't disappear, not anymore."

Cameron stared at the asphalt. This explained a lot, from Jerry's dislike of Leon's gun to why he never talked about his past. "And now?"

"Now I work for a government-adjacent branch called UNITED, a terrorism task force, among other things. It's big—bigger than you'd think."

"Why work for them?"

"It was either this, paying the penance for the people I abandoned, or ruin my father's good name and have my momma see her son sitting in jail."

"So that's why you were in Algeria a while back?"

Jerry went still. "I'm not even gonna ask where you got that information."

No denials. Cameron couldn't catch his breath. He grabbed his sides. Why was the world so messed up? Jerry saw his friend blown up then was forced to continue killing. Bethany was taken from a suburban lake. Dr. Zemke murdered. Cameron's feet went numb. This wasn't one of his panic episodes. This was something inside him breaking. "So…you're a spy?"

Jerry snorted. "More like a trained dog on a short leash. Had to give up pretty much everything I cared about, but I'm here to protect you. I swear it on my baby sister's health. Now, are you gonna trust me?"

"Why're you working for my dad? And don't insult me with lies."

Jerry's mouth worked as though he chewed a big wad of gum. "We're investigating some other organizations that might be trying to use part of your dad's holdings as a front."

"Does Dad know?"

"No, and he can't, not yet."

Cameron ran his hands through his hair. "But—"

"But nothing. I'm watching out for your dad as much as I am for you. You go blabbing about this, you'll get both of you killed. These people don't play. I wouldn't have told you if you weren't already in deeper than stink in an outhouse."

Across the parking lot, Tasha's mom hustled her to their car. Their sedan tore out of the lot. "I'll trust you on one condition," Cameron said.

"What?"

"That UNITED helps us find Bethany."

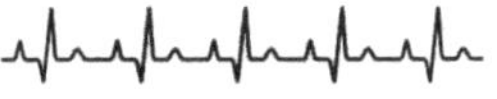

"What now?" Cameron asked Jerry, his throat so tight he couldn't swallow. Even though Jerry had gotten permission from UNITED to help with the search, finding Bethany seemed impossible. Sure, Cameron had set up facial-recognition scripts and searches for her online, but millions of people lived in Dallas—it would take forever, if it even worked.

Jerry slid behind the wheel of the Porsche and ran the bug detector over the interior. With a final nod, he climbed out.

Cameron waved him back into the seat and headed for the passenger side. "You drive." He grabbed his bag from the backseat and set up the docking station for his phone and projector. "If you're not behind this mess, who is? Leon? Grisham?"

Jerry pulled out of the parking lot. "Could be Leon. I don't like him."

"What do you know about him?"

Jerry turned onto the main road that led back to the highway. "Nothing good. Where're we headed?"

"Let's see what I can find on Leon and Grisham. Maybe there's something that will help. Head to Tasha's. Since you followed me earlier, you know where it is."

Jerry shifted into third gear. "What makes you think I followed you?"

"I kept seeing a black truck like yours, and I found the bugs you left in my car, including that pen you always click. I just can't believe you'd spy on me like that."

Jerry fished in his jeans pocket and yanked out his black pen. "You mean this pen?"

Cameron grabbed it, turning it over in his hands. A memory trickled back—Mexico City. Masked men carrying guns and aiming to kidnap Cameron. Jerry took a bullet for Cameron and then drove them out of danger, bleeding all over the car. "You didn't bug my Porsche, and you weren't following me?"

The streetlights slashed across Jerry's face. "No."

"Then who did?"

Jerry steered the car through a sharp turn. "The question you want to ask is why?"

Cameron stared out the window, thinking.

A black pickup, the same black pickup from earlier, zoomed past them so hard it rocked the Porsche. Cameron pointed. "That's the truck." It skidded onto a country road, kicking up dust. Cameron's stomach seemed to fall out of the car. "That's the way to Tasha's house. What if they're after her?"

Tasha

TASHA SLUMPED IN THE passenger seat next to the crazy person who'd once been a normal mom before they heard of Foster Med Corp, before Solomon's death, before Steve.

But tonight…tonight was one of the best times of her life. Until it became one of the worst.

Tasha dug her nails into her thighs. A scream was building deep down, banging around in her chest, pressing up through her throat to rage free. Memories bounced around in her head. Her dad calling her "princess" only moments before his car hit the wall and exploded. The night she and her mom came home to find out Steve, Tasha's so-called stepfather, hadn't been making the mortgage payments. Instead, he'd been draining money from their bank accounts and had sold almost everything they'd owned, then disappeared, leaving them with nothing but debt.

And the moment when her faith in her fellow man might have been restored by a ridiculous boy with a golden heart, Bethany was kidnapped, and it probably had something to do with Cameron and FMC.

As if her mom knew what she was thinking, she said, "I miss Solomon like crazy. I know you do too."

Tasha stared out the window.

Her mom reached for her hand but stopped short and patted her arm. "Listen, baby, I'm so sorry about everything. After Solomon was killed, I was dead inside. It was stupid to think Steve would help. I wanted to believe…" She sniffled. "I got lost in my own grief, and I haven't been the best mom these past three years, spending all my time at work and letting you run wild on your computer. I'm so sorry."

Tasha rubbed her burning eyes. She didn't have the energy for this. "What do you want me to say?"

"That you'll use your head more than your heart. I wasn't much older than you when I met your bio father, Wade, if that was even his real name." She scraped her fingers through her hair and groaned. "Sounds so terrible when I say it out loud." She waved her hand like she was whisking away a bad smell. "I got lucky with Solomon, and I wouldn't trade you for the world, but I don't want you to make my same mistakes. I know Cameron's a handsome, interesting young man, but—"

"Cameron's not what you think. Solomon would've liked him. And I don't think Nigel is bad either. He's a dad who loves his son and is being targeted by greedy criminals."

Her mom chewed her lip. "What a mess." She grabbed Tasha's hand and squeezed. "You remember what Solomon used to say? Sometimes the only way out is through. We'll get through this too."

Her mom probably wanted her to agree, to remember all the things Solomon used to say about how the way to change the world is through love and sacrifice, but the words tasted sour in her mouth. A lump of clay sat where Tasha's heart should be, and she couldn't say what her mom needed to hear. Tasha cleared her throat. "That reminds me. What were you saying about a weirdo doctor putting something in your mailbox?"

"Today at work, I found a note taped to the top of my message box. I put it in my purse. Someone making a joke, I'm sure, but they wrote the note on one of Dr. Zemke's prescription pads. Isn't that horrible? What kind of creep—"

Something slammed into the car. Tasha's body flew to the left. The high-pitched screech of brakes and crunching metal eclipsed the radio. The airbag let out a giant *pop*, and dust filled the car. She caught flashing glimpses of trees, the road, air. Her head jerked to the right and a horrid pain splintered across her skull. Everything went black.

Chapter Twenty-Seven

Cameron

THEY'D CAUGHT A GLIMPSE of Tasha's mom's taillights when the black truck rammed into it. Cameron yelled and reached forward, as if that would stop the crash.

Tasha's car hit a metal barrier and flipped over it. The pickup veered off the road too. Clouds of dust exploded, and Cameron couldn't breathe. Had Tasha been wearing her seatbelt? Did their airbags go off? Would she lose another parent tonight?

Jerry spun them to a stop just off the road where the crash had occurred.

Cameron fumbled with his seatbelt and jumped out, already dialing nine-one-one. Tasha's car was down in a ravine—*too far, too far*. Steam and dirt swirled, and everything was too quiet. No screaming, no moans of pain. *No, no, no.* He yelled details to the operator while skidding down the incline. *Please be okay, please, please.*

Ahead, next to the car, a light swung around on the ground. In the dim beams of the moon, a tall, beefy guy crouched next to the car.

Cameron yelled, "Hey!"

The guy ducked out of sight.

Jerry sped ahead, his Taser out, telling Cameron to stay back.

Like heck he would. Cameron slid toward the car, but a light flashed, and a boom rang through the trees. Pain sliced into his arm. He grabbed it, warm liquid making his skin slick. His brain supplied the word *gunshot*.

"Sir? Are you okay?" The voice came from his phone.

"Uh, I just got shot."

Jerry yelled, and the other guy grunted like he'd been punched.

The operator peppered him with questions. Cameron gritted his teeth and shined his phone light onto his arm. A cut—not too deep, but a few inches long—sliced down his forearm. "Just a flesh wound."

Coming to his senses, he scrambled up, swinging his light over the car. The rear was smashed flat. He skidded over debris, yanking on the passenger door, but it wouldn't open. "Tasha? Are you okay?"

Tasha hung upside down, arms dangling over her head toward the car's ceiling. She wasn't moving.

Cameron shouted her name over and over. He raced around the car, yelling at Tasha and her mom to wake up.

Sarah jerked, eyes opening, screaming for Tasha. She fumbled with the lock button. Jerry returned, and together they pried Sarah's door open. The big guy checked her and gave the operator information while Cameron wrenched Tasha's door open and patted her face. "Come on, Tasha. Please, wake up." She moaned and fluttered her eyes. Cameron slid closer so she could see him without moving. "You okay?"

"My head hurts. What happened?" Her voice was soft and groggy.

How badly was she injured? "Try not to move. Help is on the way."

A firetruck pulled up, lights casting halos in the dusty air. Two paramedics jumped out of the truck and ran to the car. One gently motioned Cameron away from Tasha and went to work getting her neck stabilized.

Jerry said a few words to the other firefighters and joined Cameron.

"Did you catch the guy?" Cameron asked.

Jerry shook his head. "He ran, and I didn't want to leave you."

Two police cruisers and an ambulance pulled up.

Jerry zeroed in on Cameron's injury and swore. "Let me see that."

Cameron waved him off, but Jerry had his hands on his head. "You could've been killed. I told you to wait in the car."

"And I chose to ignore you. My—" He wasn't sure what Tasha was to him yet, but no way would he leave her unprotected while he hid in a car.

Paramedics ran over with two stretchers and worked to extract Tasha and her mother from the car. At some point, the police arrived and got Cameron's statement while one of the EMTs wrapped Cameron's bleeding arm in gauze.

Another officer asked Sarah a barrage of questions and demanded to see her license. She pointed behind her while the paramedic tended a cut on her cheek. "My purse is in the car."

A few officers pointed their giant flashlights at the sedan, illuminating the interior. "No purse in here."

As soon as the police finished with him, Cameron jogged over to Tasha's stretcher. She looked so small and vulnerable with all the equipment holding her down. He swallowed. "Are you okay? What hurts? What can I do?"

She moaned. "I don't want to go to the hospital. What if some horrible person comes to get me? And who will take care of Gran?" She lowered her voice. "My mom said she got a note from Dr. Zemke, but she didn't have a chance to tell me what it said."

Cameron thought back. "Earlier at the park, she dropped a paper with something folded inside of it. She threw it on her floorboard."

Tasha moaned. "Think that's what they were after?"

"Hang on a sec." Cameron strode to the car. Trying to appear nonchalant, he squatted next to the driver's side.

"What are you doing?" An officer shined a light in his face.

Cameron turned on his phone's light with his right hand to draw the officer's attention and reached under the seat with his left hand, which was awkward with the car hanging upside down. "My girlfriend can't find her phone. She's dying to update her status. Maybe it's silly, but she's the one strapped to the stretcher."

The officer waved him off. "It might not be safe. Step away, please."

"Sure thing." Cameron reached one last time until his fingers closed around some paper caught in a seat spring. He crumpled it in his fist and stepped away. Back at Tasha's side, he whispered, "Got it."

She whispered something back, and he had to lean down to hear. "Be careful and play dumb, Cameron. I'll call you as soon as I'm free."

Her breath tickled his ear. Despite the terrible circumstances, energy shot through his limbs. He'd never been on a roller coaster, but this had to be what it felt like. High in the air one moment, crashing low the next, then jerked around unexpected corners. He barely knew her, but the thought of losing her had his insides writhing.

He squeezed her fingers. "What about Gran?"

"Oh my gosh, are you flirting with me?" She spoke in a low, rapid voice. "Our neighbor's a cop. Mom's already called him—he promised to watch over her. Listen, it's all connected. You, me, Dr. Zemke. Bethany. Just find the common denominator."

The EMT patted Cameron on the shoulder and loaded Tasha into an ambulance.

He stared after her, heat rising in his chest as he curled his hands into fists. Whoever did this needed to be stopped.

After making sure the police would follow up if they needed more information, he motioned Jerry up the hill back to his car. The doors stood open, and the Porsche's interior light spilled onto the dirt. He glanced inside. His bag and projectors were gone.

Cameron slid behind the wheel. "Let's go." Who had hit Tasha, and how was it connected to Bethany's disappearance?

Jerry climbed into the passenger side of the Porsche.

Cameron took off. "You think there's a chance we've been bugged again?"

"Can't say. They stole my detector."

Great. Where should they go? Heading home seemed too much like doing nothing. He drove onto a main highway and revved the engine high, turning over possibilities, but he couldn't discuss them because the car might be bugged. Up ahead, Cameron spotted a strip mall with a coffee shop and screeched into the parking lot.

Two guys glanced over. One of them stood, probably thinking about beating Cameron up and taking his car, but when Jerry got out, the guy's eyes bugged, and he headed in the other direction. Now that Cameron knew he was healthy, he was determined to increase his weight training. Someday, guys would see him and turn around too.

Jerry led them into the busy coffee shop and ordered two frozen coffees. While the blender ran, Jerry leaned closer. "What'd you find in the car?"

"Something from the doctor. Sarah had it in her purse earlier."

"And the guy who tried to kill them also stole her purse." Jerry hardly moved his lips. Did he think someone was watching them even here? "You got it?"

Cameron dug into his pocket.

"Actually, grab a napkin and a sweetener. I'm going to drop my jacket. Squat down like you're going to help me and bundle it up in the sleeve."

They sat, and Jerry glanced into his jacket folds. He acted like he was passing his coffee to Cameron, but something tiny glinted under his finger. A small data drive. Which would be no problem if his phone attachments hadn't been stolen.

Cameron took a sip of his drink, grimaced, and put it down. It tasted like coffee-flavored sugar. "Tasha said to find the common denominator. My gut says it's Leon and Grisham."

Jerry scanned the area. "Good choices, but what's your rationale?"

Cameron pulled out his phone and scrolled around. "Leon's resume is all references from employers who hired him for things like *personal assistant* and *security team*. Most of them are guys with police records. He likes girls—young ones—expensive whiskey, and cigars."

Jerry bunched his forehead. "What kind of website tells you all that?"

"Facebook and LinkedIn. With a password like ChickMagnet, he's asking to be hacked."

Jerry glanced Cameron's way. "How did you figure out Chick-Magnet?"

"He's got a picture of a baby chicken holding a magnet in his past profile pics. Maybe if he'd chosen AwesomeSoccerMom I'd have had more trouble. Now…let's see if he uses that password for everything else."

Jerry rubbed the stubble on his chin. "You do this often?"

"No. Never." Cameron typed more. "And…yep, email."

"Hacking your way through private information is illegal."

"So is attempted murder." Cameron ran Leon's email through a search to pick out words like "work," "meet," "package," and "problem." "Yeesh. Dude doesn't delete emails. Here's something about a delivering a 'package' to an address…five months ago. February nineteenth." Cameron closed his eyes. "We were in New York at the time, right?"

"Yep. We'd just returned from Mexico City."

Cameron set a search to run on Leon and pulled up Google Maps. "I'll need some time to find out for sure, but I wonder if we can discover what he delivered." The delivery address was a restaurant in New York. He checked his search and found some images of good-old Leon chumming up with some interesting looking dudes. He pulled up a couple images and cross-refer-enced them. A storm brewed in his stomach. He opened an image of Leon standing with a tall, skinny, middle-aged woman and showed it to Jerry. "Know her?"

Jerry choked on a sip of his coffee. "Do you?"

Cameron switched to a copy of a police report. "Albina Bogdanov—Russian Mafia." He flipped to another image of Leon with an Asian guy. "Here he's with—"

"Gen Lee—known associate of the Chinese Mafia." Jerry swore. "Kid, you shouldn't be anywhere near this stuff."

"Neither should my dad's bodyguard." Cameron went back to Leon's email, but his phone buzzed with incoming texts.

Dad

> When I said I was giving you freedom, I didn't mean you could stay out all night.
>
> Get home ASAP or you'll be grounded again.

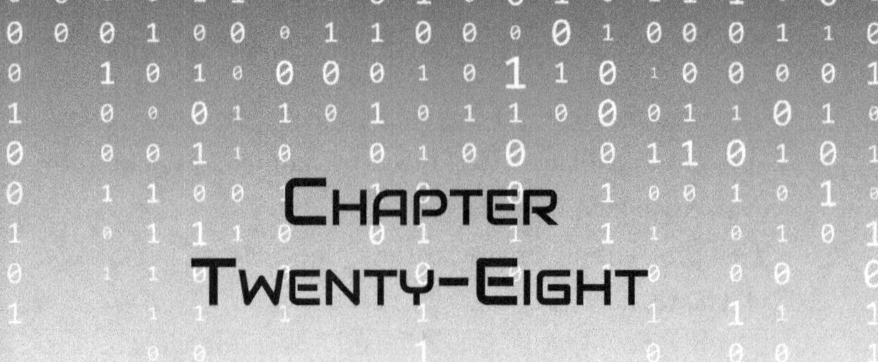

Chapter Twenty-Eight

Cameron

Nothing tested his heart's reflexes like sneaking into the house late at night. The halls were quiet, sterile, and empty. Maybe his dad had gone to bed. Still, he tiptoed up the stairs, stopping every three steps to listen. He snapped on his light.

"Hello, son."

Cameron staggered backward, his heart flopping and flailing.

His dad sat on a chair in the middle of the room. "Late night?"

Excuses spun through Cameron's mind as he wheezed like a sick kid again. "I…"

That stare. Even lawyers shied away from it. Everything that had happened spilled to the edge of his tongue, but Jerry's warning about his dad's safety helped him bite the words back. "How was your day?"

"A diversion. How delightful. Let's discuss your flagrant disregard for your own health, starting with the bandage on your arm."

Cameron gulped. His dad would freak out if he knew he'd been shot. "It's just a scratch, but I know how important it is to maintain my 'health." Gah, the lies were piling up.

His dad folded his arms. "How deep do you want to dig this hole for yourself?"

What was he supposed to say? Forget Jerry and his own misgivings. This was his dad, and he deserved truth. "I don't even know where to begin." He started to mention the bugs in his car but stopped. If someone had put listening devices in his car, there could be more in the house, even his room. Anything he said could endanger his dad.

"Did you kiss her?"

Cameron blinked. Not where he'd expected his dad to go next. Would that be the thing that pushed Nigel Foster over the edge? "Um…"

"I can see the answer is yes." His dad inhaled and tapped his fingers together. "I know what's going on here. You are rebelling. You've felt restricted because of your illness, and people assume you're fine because you don't look sick."

"She's not like—"

His dad held up a finger. No one interrupted Nigel Foster. "I have been very protective of you, and I am paying the price with your disrespect for the rules. You've skipped your medication, got a cut on your arm, and you don't even have your oxygen." His dad sagged against the chair. "I've been sitting in your room for an hour waiting for you, worried almost to the point of death."

"Dad, I'm sorry, I…" Cameron should have called, but he'd been so caught up in the circumstances, he hadn't thought about it. Not his best moment as a son.

He ran a hand through his hair. It was time to tell his dad he wasn't sick. Despite what Jerry had said, Nigel Foster was powerful and could take care of himself and Cameron too. He'd be the best person to fix all this, but Leon could have the room bugged. Cameron imagined him waiting at the bottom of the stairs, gun loaded and pointed at his dad's chest.

His dad stood, brushing off his trousers. "When I was your age with a trust fund and the world at my disposal, there was no internet to announce my identity to everyone. You must be more cautious. A simple virus for some people could be devastating for you. Even kissing this girl could lead to your death."

Cameron covered his face with his hands. How did everything get so messed up so fast?

"Oh, and one more thing. Necklaces at Tiffany's are not the best way to spend your allowance." He headed to the door. "I will extend you leniency today, but do not test me again unless you wish to be disappointed."

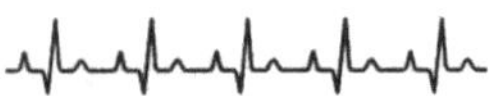

Cameron sat in the corner of his closet, under his long coats, same as he used to do when reading his vintage Batman comics. Only then, he'd dreamed of being a hero. Stuffing in his ear buds, he synced his phone with a pair of smart glasses.

He plugged in the flash drive Dr. Zemke had taped inside the note to Tasha's mom and illuminated the note with his phone light. *In case something happens to me. Keep this safe.*

The info on Zemke's flash drive turned out to be Cameron's medical report. Conclusion to all tests: Cameron's heart was totally normal. Finally, proof he could take to his dad. But why would anyone fake a heart condition? Guess Grisham was willing to go to great lengths to get to Cameron's dad, but why? Still, the only thing Cameron could fathom was money.

Another file was attached. Cameron clicked on it, but there wasn't much: *Nigel II and Jacquelyn. Midazolam. Foster, Nigel III—medical records missing.* He'd also included a photo of an old memo from a Dallas General admin regarding missing drugs from a supply closet.

Nigel II was his grandfather, Jacquelyn his grandmother. And why were his dad's medical records missing? So weird. He drummed his fingers on his phone. Tasha said to solve this he had to find the common denominator. That had to be Grisham.

Cameron called Tasha, but she didn't answer. He paced. He searched online. He doodled on paper. At some point, he fell asleep.

He jerked awake when Tasha called. His clock read nine in the morning. He answered on the first ring. "Are you okay? Shouldn't you be resting?"

"Sure."

"Did you get out of the hospital?"

"Yeah."

Why was she being so short? "Anything broken?" he asked.

"My sense of humor has been shattered beyond repair, but the rest of me's okay. The doctor said I have a minor concussion and a terrible attitude. Listen, do you remember last night?"

"Um…yeah." He yawned and scrolled through the information from Zemke again. "There was some medical—"

"No, not that." Her words spilled out in a rush. "There's something small but totally important you're forgetting. Call me when you remember."

"You mean about the medical records?"

"No." She said something muffled, like she was talking to someone else. "I've gotta go."

"Wait, any news on Bethany?" he asked.

"None. Just try to remember." She ended the call.

He stared at his phone. What was she talking about, and why so brief? Cameron paced, double-checking his bedroom door locks. He glanced at the oxygen machine in the corner of his room. Again, his face felt naked, but it was only his mind trying to kick a habit, like a coffee drinker quitting cold turkey. He'd live.

Maybe.

He rubbed his head. Perhaps a shower would clear his thoughts. He turned on the water but realized he'd forgotten clean clothes. He jogged across his room to his closet and grabbed jeans and a fresh T-shirt. His bedroom doorknob clicked and rattled, like someone was trying to pick it. Did the door just scrape against the carpet?

His heart leapt into a sprint, but he was probably paranoid. Could be Rose coming to get his laundry. But she would knock and definitely wouldn't pick her way into a locked room. His dad or Jerry would have said something by now.

His heart tried to leap up his throat. That left Leon, Grisham, or some super-stealthy robber, and the last one was the least likely. Cameron eased his walk-in closet door shut and locked it. His hands shook. Maybe he was being stupid, but too much crazy stuff had happened.

He leaned against the door, listening. The soft swish of shoes against carpet sounded in his room. Fabric rustled—someone looking under his bed perhaps. The person grunted, and the shoes swished nearer to his hiding spot. Cameron scrambled backward several feet until he bumped into some shoes. The closet knob rattled. This time, Cameron's heart tried to jump through the top of his head. If he didn't have ticker issues before, he might now. He groped for a weapon and found a remote.

He hit the *on* button, and the robotic vacuum under his bed buzzed to life. Someone—was it Leon?—muttered a curse word. He couldn't hear footsteps over the buzz of the vacuum, but his bedroom door snicked shut. Cameron sank onto the carpet and tried to breathe.

He counted to twenty then opened his closet and shoved the desk chair under his bedroom door. With his retractable bo staff in hand, he jogged into the bathroom, locking that door too. As he undressed for his shower, his jeans clattered on the tile. It wasn't until he was drying off that he realized why his jeans made that sound—he'd shoved Tasha's bracelet with the flash drive charm into his pocket when Gabe had announced Bethany was missing.

That's what she wanted him to remember. In all the craziness, he'd forgotten. He checked his room for intruders, but the chair was still in place under the doorknob. Locked in—a prisoner in his own room. He needed to talk to his dad soon, whether Jerry agreed or not.

He locked himself—and his bo staff—back in the closet and plugged in Tasha's drive, using smart glasses to view the contents. It contained one video and numerous images of newspaper articles. He glanced through the titles:

Suspicious Death for Foster Med Corp Security Guard.

Police Investigate Odd Death. Only Find Dead Ends.

Investigation into Suspicious Death Killed.

The words thudded in the pit of his stomach. He could barely swallow. The video was titled with only a date—three years ago—so perhaps he should start there. He slipped in ear buds and hit play.

"You ready, Dad?" Tasha's voice sounded younger, lighter.

A deep voice answered. "I gotta stick this little camera on my forehead?" So that was Solomon. A grainy picture appeared.

"That's it," she said. "Move around so I can see how it looks on my screen."

The picture shifted up and down and around, as though Solomon was nodding. The image focused on a steering wheel, then a windshield and a big hood. A gearshift, rearview mirror, and two rows of seats behind him. Looked like Solomon sat inside an SUV.

The camera focused on a cup of coffee, and Solomon's brown hand grabbed it. A thick black notebook and a Bible sat on the seat next to him. He chugged some of his drink and put the car into gear. The SUV meandered through the empty parking lots, and he chatted with Tasha about her class project. "You see everything I see and hear it too?" he asked.

"Yep. I did it!" she said, her voice bubbly and happy. "I'll be sure to beat Bethany's grade on this project. I might be better at robotics than she is."

Solomon laughed. "I never doubted you."

Lights illuminated the mostly empty parking spaces. A white BMW and a few other high-end sedans sat near a building entrance. The timestamp read 10:30 pm, three years prior. Solomon's truck slowed and the camera focused on a sign: Building One, Foster Medical Corporation. "What do you see, princess?"

"A Mercedes coupe and a Toyota SUV in the parking lot on your right."

"That's my girl!"

Cameron gripped the phone tighter. FMC South. The place where Solomon had worked, the place where Tasha said he'd died. Cameron seriously needed his oxygen, but he stayed rooted in place.

"Did you get your homework done?" Solomon asked.

"Don't be a nagopotamus, Dad. I even restrained from correcting the teacher's spelling after Grammargate last week."

Solomon chuckled. "Take it from your old man, princess. Never let on you're smarter than your superior officers." He rounded the corner of Building Two. "Looks like I'm a couple minutes early—what's this?"

The security lights illuminated four men in business suits wheeling a long cart into Building Six. Shadows hid their faces. Dozens of white Styrofoam coolers were stacked on the cart.

Cameron paused the feed, staring at the rows of coolers. What would they be shipping in those? He twirled the retracted bo staff in his hands while his mind whirled. Could be medicines or vaccines. Those would require consistent temperatures. But there were other things that required refrigeration, like organs. He tapped the bo staff against his thigh. Guess it would make sense to receive a shipment of organs—the ghost organ protocol division used animal parts to build new DNA-compatible organs for humans. He started the video back up.

"Hang on a sec, princess," Solomon said. The sound of static must be from activating his security radio. "This is Unit 504. I've got a possible B and E in Building Six."

Solomon rolled down his window and leaned out. "Good evening, gentlemen. I need to see some security badges. We keep it tight in these parts."

Two of the suits stepped from the shadows. The looks on their faces lit a fire in Cameron's gut. They watched Solomon like starving junkyard dogs. Another guy whose face was still hidden raised a phone to his ear. Cameron fumbled his phone. The man wore a ring with a gamma sign on his right hand. A ring just like Grisham's. Cameron paused the video and enlarged the image. If he could clean up the picture, the skinny guy might turn out to be Grisham.

He started the video again. For a moment, the only sound was Solomon's ragged breathing. The camera swung around and focused on the passenger seat that held a Bible and a thin journal. Solomon groped for the journal. He pulled out a tiny scrap of paper. On it was written *Failstate. Organ protocol.* Solomon added the letters *FMC.* He rolled the paper up, unscrewed his pen, and tucked the paper inside.

"Dad, you okay?" Tasha asked.

Solomon yelped. "Great balls of fire, princess, you startled me."

"What's the matter? Who're those guys?"

"Hey, Tash, you ready to turn off your project? I'd better go."

The car jolted forward with a screech of tires. "Whoa! What in the name of—"

"Dad?" Tasha's voice took on a sharp, hysterical edge.

Solomon grabbed the wheel. The camera panned up, like he was checking his rearview mirror. The men in suits stood in a group, watching Solomon's vehicle.

The SUV lurched forward again, turning. "Hey, now! Whoa. The car's driving itself. Stop!"

The perimeter fence loomed ahead. The truck kept accelerating. The airbag deployed, but there was no collision. The truck whined. Air hissed out of the airbag, so the camera had a clear view when the truck smashed through the electrified fence. Blood spattered onto the dashboard. The steering wheel jerked, and the SUV flipped. Crackles of electricity danced around the truck's smoking interior.

"Dad? Dad?"

Solomon didn't answer.

Someone reached through the busted window. Long, tapered fingers, one encircled by the gamma ring, grabbed the notebook. A deep, gravelly voice came through the audio. "Sometimes it doesn't pay to be early, Solomon. But don't worry, we'll keep a close watch on your family, including your lovely daughter. If she or anyone else gets in our way, we'll make sure you're all reunited." The video turned to static.

Cameron jolted and whacked his head on the wall. He couldn't catch his breath. The ring guy's voice was deeper, harsher, but so much like Grisham's. He might've been trying to disguise it, but Cameron would bet it was him. How many people had that ring?

He stumbled from his closet and grabbed the cannula attached to the O2 machine, turning it on and breathing in deep, greedy gulps. He sank to his knees and glared at the tubing in his hands. What was he doing? He threw it across the room and pounded out a text to Jerry.

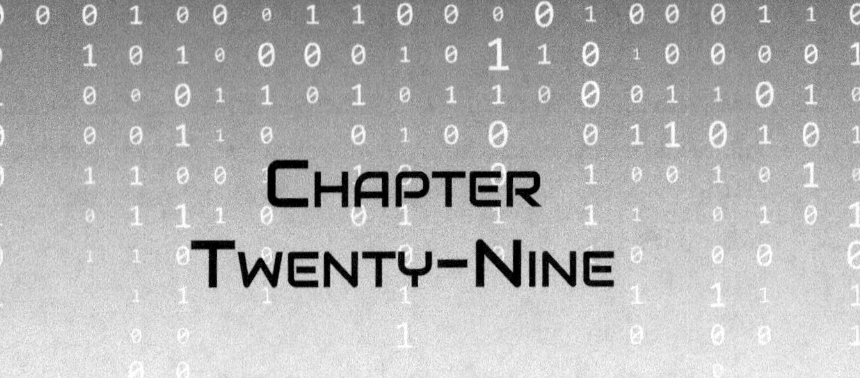

Chapter Twenty-Nine

Cameron

CAMERON PACED. THE GUY in the video had to be Dr. Grisham. He'd always been a weasel, but a dirty murderer? Why hadn't he seen it earlier? And what was he going to do about it?

"Hey, kid?" Jerry pounded on the door.

Cameron kicked the chair out from under the doorknob.

Jerry burst in, Taser ready to fire. "What happened?" Jerry's face contorted. "You need the doctor?"

"No." He glanced around. Time to get a grip. He wasn't a sick kid any longer. He was Nigel Cameron Foster IV, and if there was anything he'd learned from his dad, it was to master the world, not let it master him.

But he wasn't his father. He was a sheltered kid who played with computers and dreamed of being a hero.

"Cameron?"

He swiped his hands across his forehead. Grisham might be after him, but if he was the guy in the video, he'd threatened Tasha, so this was not the time to fall apart, not when she needed him. Her grandmother and Elvis only had so many bullets.

First, he and Jerry needed to leave the house—too much potential to be overheard. Cameron shoved two laptops into a bag, along with a few stacks of cash and prepaid credit cards from one of his bank boxes. His dad often told him to expect everything to go right but plan for everything to go wrong.

Jerry gawked but kept quiet.

Cameron stared at the money as it swished into his bag. When he was little, he'd loved to play with cash in all different currencies, sorting it, counting it. It had all seemed like a game.

Not anymore. No more games. He motioned for Jerry to follow him.

In the back hall, they ran into Leon outside the main floor laundry room. He did a double take at Jerry and tried to cover it by leaning one elbow on the doorframe and downing an energy drink. His gun peeked out of his suit jacket. A thin red streak ran from his temple to his cheek. A scratch? Leon raised his drink in a mock salute. "Hey, Junior. Whatcha doing?"

It took all of Cameron's self-control to stand his ground so close to that gun. "Field trip."

Beside him, Jerry shifted closer, his posture making it clear he was ready to throw down.

Leon kept those beady eyes on Cameron. "What kind of field trip? I thought you'd graduated."

Cameron's pulse thrummed. Leon shouldn't have been in this laundry room. His basement apartment had a washer and dryer. Could he have been looking for the data drive in Cameron's pants pocket? But how would he know it'd been there unless he'd been following Cameron? He flashed back to that guy he'd passed in the hospital IT hallway who'd reminded him of Leon. The black truck that followed him then hit Tasha. The pen that looked just like Jerry's. The shots fired last night. Could those all have been Leon? Cameron's skin went cold. "Where's Dad?"

"Meeting. He sent me to check on you. Guess he's worried you'll sneak out again."

Cameron did his best to laugh, but it sounded hollow. "You caught me."

Leon leaned against the wall, shifting to accommodate his shoulder holster.

Cameron gulped but straightened. "I didn't want to tell Dad, but I've been chatting with this college girl online. She's hot. Legs two miles long. She asked me for some help with a photography project. We're meeting at Turtle Creek."

Leon snorted. "Don't be a dupe, Junior. She's probably a forty-year-old man who made his profile picture some cute girl to see who he can rope in."

Yeah, someone as gross as Leon probably knew all about those guys. "No. Remember that scholarship dinner?"

Leon leaned in, his eyes curious and dangerous. "You met her there?"

Jerry went statue still.

Leon's interest had his hairs standing on end. As soon as Cameron spoke to his dad, he'd also ask him to fire this creep. For the moment, though, he held his ground and spun yet another lie. "No, but this friend of a friend of a person I met there knows her. She's the real deal."

Leon glanced at Jerry. "It's your day off. Shouldn't you be enjoying it?"

Jerry shrugged. "Came in for a change of clothes, and the kid, well, you see him. I figured I'd give him a few pointers and keep an eye out."

Leon swiped the side of his nose. "If it's pointers you want, then you've come to the right man." He lifted his chin to Jerry. "Why don't you head out, and I'll watch Junior."

"No!" Cameron's yell came out too sharp, and Leon's eyes narrowed to slits. Cameron tried to shrug it off. "Seriously. Jerry swore he'd hang back, blend in." He nudged Leon. "Besides, she might like you better." That was pushing it, with Leon being north of forty and…Leon, but he was conceited enough to buy it.

Leon lifted his chin toward Cameron's shoulder. "What's in the backpacks?"

"O2 and camera equipment." Cameron headed toward the garage. "Wish me luck."

"Okay. And Foster?" Leon said. Cameron glanced back as Leon eyeballed him. "Be careful. You never know who's watching."

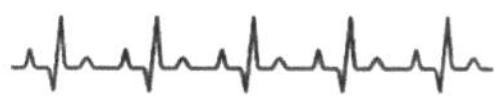

Cameron piloted his Porsche through the mansion-lined streets of Highland Park toward the Dallas North Tollway. It took ten minutes of driving before Cameron's hands quit shaking. Jerry said nothing, just ran a new bug sensor over the interior. He'd found two so far. Cameron zipped into a drive-through and ordered them breakfast. As he pulled out, he spotted the Porsche dealership and careened into the parking lot.

Jerry raised his eyebrows.

Over the perfectly quiet hum of the engine, Cameron said, "Is that a knocking sound?"

Thirty minutes later, they sped south toward Tasha's house in a loaner car, a Porsche Cayenne SUV. It didn't drive like his Nine-Eleven, but that was probably a good thing. The important part was that this one wasn't bugged. The Nine-Eleven keychain Jerry had given him for his birthday glinted in a beam of sunlight from the loaner's cup holder.

Jerry held out his fist for a quick tap. "Convincing the service manager not to call your dad because you didn't want them losing his business was brilliant. You got the Foster gift."

Cameron switched lanes and took a long swig of tea to drown the sick swirling in his gut. He handed Jerry his phone with Tasha's video still cued up. "Now that we're alone, you need to see this."

Though he couldn't see the video, each of Solomon's screams knifed into Cameron's chest. Jerry swore. "What happened with his SUV?"

"My theory?" Cameron asked. "Some cars have an external network that can be used to unlock the car remotely in case you lock your keys in it. Unfortunately, the external network can also access the steering, acceleration, airbag, and braking systems."

"You saying someone hacked the car and drove it into the fence?" Jerry asked.

"Yes. And I'm almost certain the guy on the phone was Grisham. At least he ordered it to be done."

Jerry glanced his way. "Why?"

"The ring. And did you notice the coolers?"

"Yeah—they looked like the ones they use to transport organs."

Cameron nodded. "FMC has an organ cloning research division. We make organs. There's a ton of money for those in the black market—maybe Grisham's been selling them on the side and wanted to hide his secret."

"Then I should send this to my superior at UNITED. She could—"

"Not yet. If this gets into the wrong hands, we risk getting Tasha killed." Cameron pulled off the interstate into a parking lot.

Jerry glanced around. "What's up?"

"You drive." Cameron's mind turned over info as they switched places. It was all making sense. "Okay, so say Grisham and Leon are working together to sell organs. There's a ton of money in it—like I mentioned, even the Mafia's got their hands in the organ trade worldwide. In fact…" Cameron's insides turned icy, and his mouth went dry. "Grisham could be faking my heart issue to get Dad to pour more money into funding FMC organ research. That would give him opportunity to produce and sell more organs."

Jerry shook his head and ran a hand over his chin. "But that's…I can't imagine."

Cameron started a search on Grisham's files he could access at FMC, but it would take a bit to get results. He rubbed his eyes. So many things to think about, including Grisham's past. Cameron pulled up the Dallas Morning News archives. He searched for his dad's name along with Dr. G's, excluding everything from the last twenty years.

His dad's name appeared all over the place. Society pages, news reports of the Fosters' generosity. Cameron stopped at the article *Local Oil Mogul Orphaned in Boating Accident.*

Dallas elite and others around the world experienced a collective gasp this morning as news broke of the terrible boating tragedy on Lake Ray

Hubbard, just east of Dallas, TX. Nigel Cameron Foster II (45) along with his wife Jacquelyn Foster (38), née Morris of the Newport Morris family, were killed at 12:47 pm yesterday in an explosion when their sailboat Jacquelyn's Pride *collided with a Jet Ski. Sole survivor and heir is their son, Nigel Cameron Foster III (16).*

Foster III, a senior at Phillips Exeter Academy in New Hampshire, was home on vacation and present with his parents. Rescue crews found young Foster about fifty feet from the boat.

According to Foster III, his parents had several drinks before and after boarding the boat. Both fell asleep and did not wake when the Jet Ski collided with their boat and exploded. The Jet Ski driver's body has yet to be found. No witnesses have come forward.

Rescue crews took Foster III to Dallas General, where he was treated for hypothermia and shock. He is reported to be in stable condition.

Exeter alumni and friend of Foster III, Charles Grisham, a sophomore at Harvard from New Haven, CT, gave this statement: "Nigel has suffered a great tragedy. We ask that people be patient and respectful of his privacy as he works through this emotional upheaval."

Grisham was a guest of the Fosters but had declined the boat ride that morning at the marina.

Cameron pushed his phone away and stared at the freeway floating by, but the display glowed in his lap, pulling his gaze. It should hold some deeper meaning. The doctor followed his dad around like a broken horse, and he had given up a promising career to become his dad's lapdog. What was that about? He ran a search about his dad, Grisham, and their school. Scrolling through several articles, he found information further linking them.

Grisham and Foster III first became friends on the Exeter debate team, but events drew them closer when tragedy struck Grisham's family. After a dramatic shift in the Grisham family holdings, Grisham's father, Conwell Grisham (52), killed himself, and Conwell's second wife, Glorianna "Glory" Grisham (23), moved back to Alabama with her family.

Grisham (22), still a student at Harvard medical school, was left alone and penniless, but Foster III stepped in and helped, even paying Grisham's tuition.

Grisham had lost everything as a young man and Nigel had come to his rescue. Was he thankful? Or did he resent Nigel's help and money?

Cameron dug deeper. Since Grisham came from Connecticut, he started with the New York Times. A slew of articles about Grisham's father came up, and they weren't nice—embezzlement, an IRS investigation, freezing of assets, fleeing business associates, along with some other scandals involving women.

Cameron searched the society pages. He came across a brief article about Grisham's mother. One anonymous source had said, *Mrs. Grisham was given to long bouts of depression and suffered from severe headaches.* Another said they weren't surprised at her untimely death. The family had refused an autopsy. The article concluded with:

Regrettably, the only witness to her death was her ten-year-old son, Charles. The two were enjoying afternoon tea when her heart gave out. Young Grisham thought his mother was sleeping, so her passing was not discovered until hours later when a maid attempted to wake her. New Canaan, CT, Police Department spokesperson stated no investigation is ordered at this time. An anonymous source close to the family said, "The boy is melancholy like his mother, and understandably, he hasn't been the same since."

Cameron rolled the stiffness out of his neck. He'd never spent time with a dead person, but it seemed odd to be having tea with someone and think they were napping when they were actually dead. But the guy had been a kid. During the time Cameron had been reading, he and Jerry had left the busyness of Dallas behind. Trees lined the two-lane country road. Jerry turned right, gunning the car around a slow-moving sedan. Cameron clicked on another article from the Dallas Morning News.

Dallas General Patient and Medical Resident Both Victims in Fire

Dr. Charles Grisham, MD (28), was found unconscious with minor burns in a patient room after an explosion caused a fire. Sprinklers put out the fire, but the patient died as a result of the explosion. Investigators believed the patient attempted to light a cigarette, and the oxygen tubing exploded. Grisham has no memory of the incident but was treated for minor burns. Grisham returned to work the next day, saying it was his duty to care for patients and prevent tragedies like the one that had occurred.

Family members of the victim expressed concern, saying their loved one had quit smoking several months ago. Investigators ruled the incident a patient accident and closed the case.

Friend of Charles Grisham, Nigel Foster III, CEO of Foster Medical Corporation and native of Dallas, commended his friend's perseverance and duty to his chosen profession.

Cameron leaned back. His dad and Grisham again. Outside, they passed an intersection with a gas station connected to Joe's BBQ Joint and a chiropractor. Everything else was grassy fields.

He rubbed his forehead and kept scrolling through information, including a minor newspaper article from Grisham's Exeter days detailing his award-winning pharmaceutical research on anesthetizing agents like midazolam for patients.

One more article caught his eye, this dating back several years before Cameron was born.

Viscus Medical Group Sale Halts

Successful cardiology practice Viscus Medical Group hoped for a lucrative sale until a Medicare investigation halted the process. One of the partners, Cardiovascular Geneticist Specialist Dr. Charles Grisham, is under investigation for Medicare fraud, reported for unnecessary procedures. Out of six-thousand stint procedures, Medicare labeled twenty-seven questionable. One colleague of Grisham, who wished to remain anonymous, calls the investigation a "bogus witch hunt. One millimeter could make the difference between life and death. How can a committee of jack-wagons possibly make such a judgment call, not having seen the patient themselves?"

Though Grisham has been cleared of any wrongdoing, Grisham stated in the interest of his own health he would take a research position at Foster Medical Corporation. Grisham filed for bankruptcy only three months after the investigation ended.

Grisham had filed for bankruptcy? Perhaps he resented Cameron's dad for having so much money. Cameron rolled the stiffness from his neck while Jerry piloted the car down a road covered with arching tree branches.

"What're you looking at?" Jerry asked.

"Information about Grisham."

"Anything good?"

"Depends on what you mean by good," Cameron said, "but I need to look into Leon too." He dug around for more on the guard. It didn't take long to find some real dirt. "Did you know Leon's got a couple million-dollar bank accounts offshore?"

Jerry slowed and glanced his way. "Where'd you find that?"

"Information's everywhere if you're willing to dig ditches with toothpicks."

"Who are you, kid?"

"A guy in big trouble."

Trouble…that reminded him of the EyeNet message he'd received in the parking lot just after they'd discovered Bethany had been kidnapped. The hacker with the handle Black Mask had sent some info. Cameron logged into the EyeNet boards and skimmed through Mask's message. Queasiness assaulted him. "Umm, listen to this:

> *If you're reading this it means I'm in trouble. This information is beyond dangerous, especially for a kind-hearted friend of mine.*

Cameron reread that part. His stomach dropped like the descent of a plane. Bethany came across as kind. Did Mask mean Bethany? How would he know Cameron was connected to her?

He kept reading.

> *It took some digging, but the danger seems to lead back to one place: Foster Med Corp. Their organ manufacturing plant isn't what my friend thinks, and I'm afraid he could be killed for it. Please help.*

The road outside looked like black tar about to consume them. "I was right. This is about FMC, probably about Grisham selling black market organs." But Mask had said he could be killed. If Mask meant Bethany, he would have said *she*.

"Who's this Black Mask guy?" Jerry asked.

Cameron dug his fingers into the fabric of his jeans. "He leads this hacktivism group that recruited me last year."

"What, they called and asked for a résumé?"

"No, he contacted my username—we'd crossed paths on another board. It was an organ bust I—never mind. He's been legit so far."

Jerry gave him a long look with plenty of raised eyebrows and frowning. It was obvious this wasn't the end of the EyeNet subject. "But you don't *know him* know him."

"Does that matter right now? We have to warn Dad."

"And say what? That some masked hacker guy sent you a cryptic message?"

"You're doubting this?"

Jerry pursed his lips. "I'm saying you need to let UNITED handle this, or you'll endanger both of you."

Cameron tried to read between the lines. What connected these pieces together, and why was Jerry so hesitant to expose these guys? He sucked in a breath as it hit him. "Is this connected to UNITED's investigation into the people you think are using FMC as a front? Wait…" He thought back to the coolers he saw on Tasha's videos. "Maybe organ smuggling?"

"You know I can't say, and need I remind you that you're a *seventeen-year-old kid*?"

Cameron clenched his jaw. "And I thought we were trusting each other. How much of this reason for waiting has to do with your investigation rather than Dad's safety?"

Jerry exhaled. "Just trust me that your dad is in good hands."

"Not good enough." Instead of picking a fight with his best ally, Cameron let his mind wander. His thoughts returned to sitting with Bethany and Tasha at the latter's dining table. How many times had he stared at the raccoon sticker on Bethany's computer? That memory brought up another—sitting in Whataburger across from Bethany. Her phone case and key chain were also raccoon themed. Cameron hit his forehead. "Bethany's Black Mask."

"Come again?" Jerry asked.

"Bethany. She kept asking me to link computers with her, talked like she knew all about hacking. I think that message is from her."

"Those aren't exactly straight lines you're drawing, *kid*."

If Jerry dropped one more comment about his age, Cameron was going to lose it. "My gut tells me I'm right."

"You and your gut—"

"Have been right before, and Bethany just got kidnapped."

Jerry tilted his head. "Okay, say it's true, that she's this masked hacker. Could someone else have known that?"

"I figured it out. Who's to say others haven't?" He shook his head. "Either way, we have to tell my dad what's going on. He could be in danger too."

Jerry drove the twists and turns of the country roads to Tasha's with ease. "His phone could be bugged, and you can't risk Grisham or Leon overhearing. We'll need to wait until he's alone."

"Why can't UNITED arrest Grisham and Leon? I've given you plenty of info."

"Wish it were that simple, but it's gotta hold up in court."

Cameron stared out the window. Fine. He'd find enough evidence to implicate them all.

They rounded the corner near Tasha's house. Red-and-blue lights splashed off the sprawling tree in her front yard. His hands went numb and seemed to evaporate. Had someone gotten to Tasha's grandmother? Cameron jumped out of the car before Jerry rolled to a stop.

Chapter Thirty

Cameron

CAMERON RAN TO THE porch. A splintered hole pockmarked the front door, and glass littered the steps from a shattered windowpane. He kicked something metal that rolled toward the rocker. Glancing down, he said, "Is that a bullet?" *Please, God, let them be okay.*

Jerry swore and yanked out his Taser. He looked both ways, like a soldier headed into a gunfight. Cameron banged on the door, his heart galloping. Tasha's mom, Sarah, jerked it open, glaring at him. "You are not welcome here, Foster."

Jerry stepped shoulder-to-shoulder with Cameron. "What happened?"

"Some creep broke in and stole my daughter's computer."

Cameron peered inside, past Sarah. Someone had shot through the TV, and mail was scattered all over the floor. Cameron's skin crawled at the thought of someone hurting Tasha's grandmother. "Is Hazel all right?"

"She's fine," Sarah said, "not that it's any of your—"

"Now, Sarah, don't be rude. Let the young man in." Gran snap-tapped her walker to the front door. The crocheted bag dangling from the front bar swung and stretched like she had a brick inside it.

Cameron let out a relieved sigh. "You're okay. Did he try to shoot you?"

Gran shoved the door open wider. "Heck no. Didn't give him a chance. He came in through the back, so it took me and Elvis a few times to get him." The old woman wrung her puffy, arthritic hands. "Still stings."

Jerry gave her an appreciative nod. "Nice shooting."

"Dang buzzard got away," Gran said, "but I grazed him good. He was probably hopped up on Drano, but it'll be a snowy day in Death Valley before he messes with this old lady again."

Sarah huffed. "Mom, I told you to stay back."

"What? I'm packing Elvis." Gran waved them inside. "And I always have time for my secret admirer."

Sarah's glare went from irritation to inferno. "You're the one who sent her flowers?"

"Mom, please." Tasha stepped out of the shadows, sounding tired. Strands of her golden hair hung loose from her ponytail, and she wore athletic shorts and a Batman T-shirt.

He wanted to hug her, but he didn't want to be vaporized by Sarah, so he stayed on the porch. "Why didn't you tell me about the break-in?"

Her eyes widened like she was pleading with him. "I didn't want to worry you. Did you get my other message?"

Cameron met her stare, his brain replaying Solomon's fiery crash. "Yes, I saw several things that concerned me."

Sarah blocked the door, glaring at Cameron. "Did your snake of a father send you?"

Something hot snapped inside him "My dad isn't—"

Gran grumbled. "Shush, all of you. It's my house, and I say get inside."

Cameron gave Tasha an awkward one-armed hug. He didn't need her mother going nuclear. "They stole your computer? Anything else?"

Tasha shook her head. "Not that I could tell."

From her chair, Gran said, "Good riddance to that devil box. I never used it myself. All the passwords gave me a headache."

Tasha rolled her eyes, but her lips quirked up. "How would you know about the passwords if you'd never used it?"

Instead of answering, Gran popped a piece of chocolate in her mouth.

"When did they break in?" Cameron asked.

"Around two in the morning," Tasha said.

"About the same time they loaded you into the ambulance. And they wanted your computer?"

Tasha pursed her lips and gestured him outside. "Maybe we should sit in the car."

Gran called after them, "No hanky spanky, kids!"

Cameron glanced over his shoulder at Gran giving him a one-eyed squint. "I both admire and fear that woman."

"Yep." Tasha followed him but paused on the porch. "Do you collect Porsches?"

"It's a loaner. Mine was bugged again." He turned on the a/c full blast and motioned her to the backseat.

She put on sunglasses and climbed inside. "Trying to lure me into the back of your car?"

"Definitely, another time." He pulled out his two laptops, handing one to her. Tasha rubbed her head like it hurt to think. He put a hand on her arm. "You okay?"

"Just a headache. Talking face-to-face with a closed window will do that. What're we doing?"

"Research," Cameron said. "Your password is *1l0veHe11oKitty%#!.*"

"I hate you." But her fingers moved over the keys.

Maybe he should start with the stuff about Black Mask. "I have something to tell you."

"Weirder than sitting in my driveway after my best friend gets kidnapped and Gran shoots some guy who steals my computer, which might all be related to your fake heart condition?"

"Well, when you put it that way…listen, I'm in this online group…thing."

"Like a virtual barbershop quartet?"

"No." He pulled up Black Mask's message. "Read this."

Tasha's eyes popped wide. She looked at Cameron and back at the screen, then back at Cameron. "You're Cardiac?"

It was his turn to stare. He glanced at the screen, but he'd only copied the contents of the message to show her. "Who said anything about Cardiac?" Heat spread from his chest to his arms. Tasha knew about the Cardiac. That was impossible, unless…

Tasha rubbed her face and groaned. "What does this have to do with Bethany?"

"I think Black Mask is Bethany."

Tasha shook her head. "No, Black Mask is some guy covered in tats who wishes he wore an actual mask. He recruited me to his EyeNet group…" Her voice trailed off.

"He recruited me too." He glanced at her Batman T-shirt. Earlier, she'd carried a Wonder Woman keychain. "You're Bellona!" The Roman goddess of war who in the DC comic-verse was

Wonder Woman's enemy. An uneasy flutter stirred in his gut. "Did you know Black Mask was Bethany?"

"No."

"What are the odds of the three of us being in the same group?"

"Um, super small?"

"She recruited you. Why?"

"Because I'm good."

"No," Cameron said. "What spurred her to invite *you*? Did you tell her you were interested in the organ trade? In hacking?"

"No, not directly." She dragged her hands through her hair and stared down at the seat beside him. "It was a while back…after the first FBI visit."

"The FBI visited you? More than once?" That was a story he needed to hear, but not now. "After that, you told her you were a hacker with the handle Bellona?"

"No, but Black Mask sent me a message and asked me to join the group."

"It's too weird," Cameron said. "Out of all the hackers in the world to bring into EyeNet, she chose us, and we all have the common connection of FMC. What was her purpose?"

Tasha's jaw stiffened. "Are you suggesting she's into something bad?" Her voice intensified with each word. "Last time I checked she was the victim, and if—"

"I'm not blaming her, and I think I know who has her, but I don't know where. Go get your mom and Jerry. We've got to see Gabe."

While Tasha jogged inside, Cameron set up a few more searches about Bethany. Perhaps Tasha wasn't the only one who'd been contacted by the FBI.

Chapter Thirty-One

Tasha

Of course, Cameron had awesome computers to spare. Jerry drove Cameron's loaner to Gabe's while Tasha's mom glared at everyone from the front seat. Cameron was too busy messing with his computer to notice.

When the four of them arrived at Gabe's, his puffy-eyed mom Veronica beckoned them into their family room where Gabe sat on the couch staring blankly at a cooking show. Tasha snapped it off, but he remained fixated on the black screen.

Cameron, though, set up his computers like some task force sergeant in a movie. Tasha flopped down next to Gabe.

"What are you doing?" Veronica asked.

Cameron hooked up his 3D image display and infrared keyboard to his phone. "I'm searching for connections between my dad's doctor and his bodyguard. I think they might have something to do with Bethany's disappearance."

Veronica stared at him, hands on her hips, mouth pressed flat. She tapped her foot. Was she going to throw them all out of her house, telling them to let the police handle this? In a flurry of motion, she cleared the framed pictures off the wall to create a white space for Cameron's 3D display and headed to the kitchen. "You work. I'll fix something to eat."

Cameron started two displays. "Look, this will take some time." He nodded at Tasha. "In that video you showed m—"

The last of Tasha's frayed nerves snapped in one big go, and the angry wolverine inside her snarled. "Shut up!" He wasn't supposed to tell anyone.

"It's relevant, trust me. The guy with the gamma ring on the video? That's Grisham." He turned his computer screen toward her. The display featured an image from that night, the night she wished she'd never shared with him, but the lighting was better. "See?" he said. "I worked on the image. I'm ninety-nine percent sure it's him."

She squinted at the screen. "But...no, he can't—"

Gabe chose that moment to come alive. He let out a groan that ended in a roar. "You keep making noise, but none of you are helping!"

Tasha huffed. "It's more than you're doing, sitting there like a freaking statue."

Gabe jerked forward. "Well, if you hadn't wanted to use your boyfriend here to screw his dad over, none of this would've have happened!"

Buzzing sounded in Tasha's ears.

Cameron looked between her and Gabe. "What do you mean?"

Tasha pulled her new necklace so tight it dug into her skin—deep, painful, shameful. "No, it's not—"

Gabe stood and shook his head at Cameron. "It totally *is*. She blames Nigel for her dad's death, always has. And she's been planning to take him down for years. It's the only reason she wanted to be with you."

Tasha pulled her knees to her chest, wishing she could disappear into the couch.

Cameron's hands stilled, and his phone dropped to his lap. His face was a dark storm of betrayal, the kind that destroys everything in its path. "You're using me to hurt my dad?"

"No—no, not anymore." Her gut pinched, and her mouth went dry. She tossed a glare at Gabe. "Maybe at first, but—"

Cameron stood and typed something into his phone then shoved it into his pocket. "Jerry, we're leaving." He waved his hand over the coffee table. "Keep the computers. Keep it all." He straightened his back, and his eyes went cold and dead. His normally sunny manner had been eclipsed by cruelty, the cruelty of terrible people—people named Tasha. She was no better than that doctor of his, using him for some dark purpose.

She stood. "Wait—"

Cameron and Jerry walked out the door without looking back.

Chapter
Thirty-Two

Cameron

CAMERON SLUMPED INTO THE Cayenne's passenger seat while Jerry drove. Thankfully, the big guy knew when to stay silent. Cameron squinted against the high midday sun that warred with the car's a/c system.

Cameron clenched his phone. He should've known better than to trust her, but Tasha had acted so unimpressed by his money that he'd fooled himself into thinking she was genuine. Ugh, he was so done with manipulative people. At this point, the only people he could trust were his dad, Jerry, and maybe Rahul, although that guy was still MIA.

To distract himself, Cameron scrolled through some of Rahul's favorite social media spots. There were a few posts about unplugging and heading to a beach. Nothing since.

The guy worked hard. Guess it made sense he'd want to unplug. Cameron glanced at the last DM Rahul sent him—a *Star Wars* picture of Jango Fett pushing Boba Fett on a playground swing. He exhaled. It reminded him of Cameron and his dad—two people, alone in the world.

His thoughts returned to searching Leon's emails, which he'd started at Gabe's house. If they could just figure out—no. He dropped his phone into the cup holder. "I should forget the whole thing."

Jerry nodded. "Yep."

But he couldn't. He might not want to see Tasha again, but Bethany was still in danger. Cameron grunted, grabbing his phone and opening Leon's email again. One stood out, from Beneficence Corp. He'd seen that name in Grisham's emails the night of the banquet.

He pulled up his search of Beneficence Donor Corp and found a trail of several dummy corporations, all coming from different Caribbean islands. He went through Leon's emails and found several of those corporation names. Each message contained only an address, perhaps for a drop off. Some in New York, some in Tokyo, all of them in cities they'd visited during the last two years. Even one in East Dallas. Cameron looked up the address in Dallas—it looked like a little Tudor-style house on Ridgedale Avenue just east of Central Expressway.

After some digging, he found it was owned by a corporation—Donneur d'Argent Entreprise, headquartered in St. Lucia. *Money Donor Corporation.* His palms itched. It was like someone had dared him to find this. A house owned by a dummy corporation where Leon made drops or deliveries would be a great place to stash a kidnap victim. Maybe Cameron was grabbing at the wind, but at least he was doing something.

He glanced at Jerry. They needed to check out that house. The only obstacle was tricking Jerry into it. Thinking of food turned his stomach, but Cameron said, "Can we stop to get something quick to eat?"

"Sure. Soon as I see a good place, I'll pull over."

Three texts came through:

Tasha

I'm sorry.

It's not what you think. Well, it was, but it isn't now. Ugh.

PLEASE call. I'll explain everything.

Cameron stared out the window, squinting in the glaring afternoon sunlight. His phone rang, but he turned it off. He couldn't talk to Tasha, not when the pain of her betrayal burned like a knife in his throat.

Jerry's phone rang a moment later. He glanced Cameron's way, forehead wrinkled. He answered and proceeded to say things like, "Yeah, I see," and "Seriously?" He thanked the caller and hung up. "That was the Porsche dealership. They found mothballs in your gas tank."

Cameron's head started to pound. "Think someone tried to kill me?"

Jerry pulled into a drive-through lane at a sandwich shop. "Mothballs simply increase the octane levels in your engine. They'll cause mechanical problems, but there are better, ah, worse ways to harm a person. More likely, someone wanted you to stay home."

"Dad would simply ground me again. Grisham would've told Dad I needed to be on bed rest, so that leaves Leon."

Jerry nodded and ordered for them.

The brown bricks of the sandwich shop blurred into a blob. As angry as Cameron was at Tasha, he didn't want her, Hazel, or her mom in harm's way. He couldn't give up now. "Hey, mind if I drive? I need to clear my head."

Chapter Thirty-Three

Cameron

While Jerry ate his sandwich, Cameron piloted the Cayenne north on Central Expressway.

"Where're we headed? That new store you were wanting to check out?" Jerry asked around a bite of sandwich.

Cameron's sandwich sat untouched on the console. "Nah, I'd like to drive around, see the sights, clear my head." A few more minutes and they'd be on Ridgedale near that address he'd found in Leon's emails.

Jerry sipped his drink. "About Tasha. I told you I was concerned—"

"Lesson learned."

Jerry held up a hand. "Lemme finish. I knew her dad."

Cameron glanced at Jerry.

"We both served in the Corps. Solomon was a good guy, the best. Quit cussing and drinking in honor of his daughter." Jerry chuckled at some unseen memory. "He showed us a picture of her once. One of the guys said something about how Solomon obviously wasn't her daddy with how different they looked. Solomon snatched her picture back and said what made a father a father was love and responsibility, not paternity." Jerry stared out the window. "He didn't deserve the end he got."

Cameron spoke around the boulder in his throat. "And that has to do with me how?"

"Imagine seeing your daddy die like that at fourteen and being afraid to tell anyone. Imagine how it'd eat you alive."

Cameron gripped the wheel tighter. He couldn't think of a response. He turned onto Ridgedale. The house sat at the end of the block, on the right. A white Tudor with a red front door and turquoise awnings over the windows. Way too cheerful for the darkness that might lurk inside.

Jerry went on. "The accident happened at FMC, so she had one main person to associate with that tragedy—your dad."

"My dad didn't have anything to do with it. You saw—"

"But she didn't know that. And in the last few weeks, she's stuck her neck out for you—that wasn't about revenge."

Cameron passed the house. The blinds were drawn, and a tall wooden fence blocked the view of the backyard. Was there a basement? Cameron circled the block for a second pass.

Jerry wadded up his empty sandwich wrapper. "Don't let bitterness rule your life. The only person it hurts is you." He nailed Cameron with a stare. "And you want to tell me why we're circling this street?"

Cameron pulled over halfway down the block from the house. "That white Tudor down there was built in 1928."

"Quit stalling."

"It's been sold three times in the last ten years, all to corporations with no real business ties. Current owner is one Donneur d'Argent Entreprise."

"You just Google that?"

"It's more complicated than that. Anyway, Donneur d'Argent Entreprise is part of a chain of dummy corporations all funneling money through banks in the Cayman Islands. Two other homes are owned by corporations in the chain I've traced—one in New York, one in Buenos Aires. These homes have all been used in business drops initiated by Beneficence Donor Corp."

Jerry's eyes grew bigger as Cameron spoke.

Cameron went on. "Leon receives emails about transactions and makes deliveries all over the world. He made a delivery here a while back." Cameron cleared his throat. "It's conjectural, but if he is Bethany's abductor, and if has access to the house—"

Jerry grabbed his phone. "There's a chance Bethany could be there."

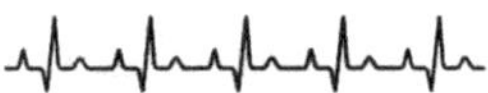

Within fifteen minutes of Jerry's call, a dark van passed their car and circled the block of houses. Cameron raised his eyebrows. "Surveillance?"

"Yep. They're checking the inside of the house for people." Jerry's words were clipped. "For the last time. I might not be your daddy, but I answer to him. We need to leave."

"Look, I'm sorry, but I can't let this go. I have to see with my own eyes if I'm right."

"And I need to keep you safe."

As they argued, a cable van rolled down the street. Within ten more minutes, a yard company and a maid service arrived.

A woman climbed out of the maid service car, tossing a tote bag over her shoulder. She wore khaki pants and a bulky blue uniform shirt that probably concealed a Kevlar vest. The sunlight glinted off something metallic in her bag.

Cameron was a tightly wound spring. *Get inside already.*

Two guys climbed out of a lawn service truck a few doors down. They wore dirty beige uniform shirts and green pants, but both had neat, expensive-looking haircuts and stiff postures that implied military training. One had a leaf blower.

Cameron turned up the Cayenne's a/c. "Guess UNITED doesn't lack funding."

"You have no idea, and you've seen enough. What if they start shooting?"

Cameron tapped the gearshift. "Then I'll hit reverse and floor it."

While Jerry grumbled, a broad-shouldered guy rounded the block with a German Shephard on a leash like they were out for a casual stroll, but the dog was wearing a Kevlar vest made to look like a harness.

Jerry groaned. "Your dad will kill me if—"

"So I should just sit at home waiting for Grisham and Leon to kill me and Dad? Dr. Zemke is dead. Solomon Jenkins is dead. Someone tried to kill Tasha and her mom. Grisham and Leon might be responsible, and they might also be stealing from FMC. You said you needed more evidence, so this is me working on getting enough to put them away for all they've done. I'm not leaving."

A tall man rapped on Cameron's window and claimed there was a gas leak on the block. He motioned for them to leave.

Nearby, a couple neighbors moved to their front lawns to check out the commotion. One even settled in a lawn chair.

Cameron pointed to them and raised his eyebrows at the UNITED guy.

At the other end of the street, the maid crept to one of the Tudor's windows. The German Shephard handler jogged to the front door and knocked. A moment later, he kicked in the door, and the dog darted inside, followed by the lawn crew who'd pulled out guns. Cameron held his breath, straining toward the windshield.

Two minutes later, a T-shirt-clad man jumped out of a window on the side of the house and darted across the front lawn, but the German Shephard came flying out of the house and took him down, jaws clamped onto the guy's arm.

Two large black SUVs zipped around the corner and screeched to a stop at the house. Guys with medical bags grabbed stretchers from the backs and ran inside.

A burning rush of adrenaline heated Cameron's neck. Was Bethany inside? He shoved out of the car, sprinting forward. He had to know.

Guys with guns held him back.

Moments later, UNITED paramedics pulled two people from the house—Bethany and a familiar-looking man, but Cameron couldn't place him. Both were strapped to stretchers.

He'd found her! For a second, he considered calling Tasha, but that brought a sour taste to his mouth. To the guard holding him back, he said, "Please, I know her."

After a conversation with Jerry, they let Cameron through. She looked up at him, eyes hazy, and moaned. "I knew you'd figure it out."

She put her hands over her face and made a choking sound. "They tied me to a chair, questioning me about EyeNet and what we knew about their organ operation."

One of the agents exited the house carrying a smashed laptop. The ragged remains of a Batman sticker held part of the case together. Cameron jerked his chin in that direction and called to Jerry, "I'll bet my Porsche that's Tasha's computer."

Paramedics rolled the other man past, and Cameron finally recognized his face. "Dr. Winn?" He was one of the doctors who worked in the ghost organ protocol division.

The doctor's eyes rolled until he could focus on Cameron, then they bulged wide. He flailed for Cameron's hand, muttering.

Cameron leaned closer. "What?"

Winn muttered again. "Find…twenty-eight." He gurgled and started convulsing.

Cameron shouted. EMTs pushed him back, rushing to help Winn. In the commotion, a glint of light reflected off a ring on Winn's other hand. It bore a gamma symbol, just like Grisham's.

Blood pounded in Cameron's ears. He dug his hands into his hair and backed up, glancing left and right. Had he been wrong? Was Winn the guy in the video?

EMTs rushed Winn and Bethany into ambulances. At some point, Jerry led Cameron to the passenger seat of the loaner car.

"You okay?"

Cameron couldn't seem to swallow. "That was Dr. Winn from FMC. He said to find twenty-eight. What does that mean?"

Jerry's forehead crinkled. "No idea."

Cameron stared ahead at nothing. "He was wearing a ring just like Grisham's."

Jerry pulled out his phone and began a conversation, relaying what Cameron had told him.

While Jerry talked, Cameron thought over his own conversation with Bethany. She'd mentioned EyeNet and said they'd asked "what *we* knew" about their organ operation, like she knew Cameron was a part of it. But Cameron hadn't mentioned his work with EyeNet to anyone but Jerry and Tasha. Unless Tasha had talked to her today, Bethany shouldn't have known Cameron was involved.

Jerry ended his call and slid the phone into the cup holder. He pinched the bridge of his nose. "Looks like we won't be able to ask Winn about the ring or what he meant. He's dead."

Chapter Thirty-Four

Cameron

More people dead. Where would this end? Cameron wanted to keep searching, but Jerry insisted they head home and regroup.

While Jerry drove home, Cameron studied the "drop off" messages in Leon's email. Someone smart had been sending those. They'd come from different machines, different servers, different IP addresses. Very difficult to trace.

His dad wasn't home when Cameron got back, so he checked over his search on Grisham, but the info wasn't what he needed. He spent a few hours trying to hack into FMC files through Grisham's logins, but he didn't find much, which meant the important files were stored on an internal server. Looking over some security blueprints of the facility, he noted a server room was located in Building Six along with a massive power grid.

Dallas General had used an internal backup system. FMC would use something similar for their sensitive files, especially with the secretive ghost organ protocol research. Difficult to access info—just another way for Grisham to cover his butt, but an unending source of viable organs would let them live like kings in a non-extraditing country. Had Dr. Winn been in on it too, or had he, like Solomon Jenkins, found out something he shouldn't have?

And how did Bethany fit into this? Her mom had worked with Dr. Winn.

At some point he must have nodded off, because he woke up to the sun streaming into his windows. Crud, he'd overslept. He checked his dad's location. Yep. Already gone. He wouldn't be available for hours.

Before he'd fallen asleep, Cameron had texted Jerry to see if UNITED was willing to investigate, but he still hadn't heard back.

He jumped into the shower. There had to be options that wouldn't put his dad in harm's way. That internal server at FMC could have the information he needed. If he could find some evidence that Grisham had been selling organs to the black market, at least UNITED could arrest him and the others, keeping his dad and Tasha's family safe. Bethany too. The problem was Cameron couldn't just walk into FMC and ask to see the servers. Unless…

He formed a plan. It was risky and stupid, but he had to know. Jerry's lack of response probably meant that UNITED wasn't willing to help, and he wasn't sure the police would believe him. Getting into the servers would mean search warrants and red tape that lawyers would block while Grisham destroyed data.

No, it had to be done as soon as possible, and who better than the CEO's son? At least it was semi-plausible that a Foster would be on site. And he did have a vested interest in the company, so this time he technically wasn't breaking the law.

Cameron rummaged through his closet and packed a bag full of the things he'd need. He grabbed the smart glasses that linked to his phone and some of his spy tech, including his new magnetic screen projector. He also packed the Autonomous Navigation Tire Sensors system, or ANTS System, that had come in the other night. It'd been a feel-sorry-for-himself purchase but might come in handy. He paused, stretching. His past self would never have believed he'd use this stuff for anything but entertainment.

He topped the bag off with his data card maker, a baseball cap, a wig, and more money. The rest he could get on the way.

Cameron sent Jerry a quick text, grabbed the loaner Porsche remote from under his pillow where he'd stashed it, and rushed down to the empty kitchen with his backpack over his shoulder. The bag pulled on him like a sack of weights. Was he insane to try to break into his dad's company? Maybe he should send his dad an encrypted message and be done.

Leon sauntered into the room and raised his chin to Cameron. "Why the sad face? And where's your oxygen?"

Cameron reached for the tubing on his upper lip—his bare upper lip. Guess running from death cured an oxygen habit. "In my bag."

"Seems like oxygen is necessary, with you being so sick." Leon yanked his gun and a spare magazine from his shoulder holster and set them on the table. He flicked open the clip and popped out the bullets, taking a moment to shine each on his sleeve before lining them up like little toy soldiers. Once Leon's army of death was all polished up, he snapped them back into place, eyes never leaving Cameron's face. With a final click, Leon shoved in the last bullet and flashed Cameron a gunpowder-laden smirk. "Health is a funny thing. Here one day, gone the next. Enjoy it while it lasts, eh?"

A dark, twisted feeling curled up from his chest and pushed into his hand until he formed a fist. He'd love to punch that stupid grin off Leon's face. Cameron shoved away from the table before he did something that got him maimed.

This would be a great moment for Jerry to arrive. Where was he anyway? He should look for him upstairs, but with the gun-toting Leon on his heels, Cameron rushed out the front door and jumped in the Cayenne.

"Nice wheels," Leon called.

He had to work through a few more details and make several stops along the way, but it was time to nail Grisham.

Chapter Thirty-Five

Cameron

It was amazing what people could buy on Craigslist.

Cameron had spent the better part of the morning shopping. He'd even stopped at a small specialty outfit that sold bug-detecting equipment. Yep, Leon had put more tracers on Cameron's loaner car. Cameron had flushed them down the toilet at a gas station. That ought to be fun for Leon to trace. Next, he'd dropped off his loaner Porsche at the dealership and walked six blocks down Lemmon Avenue where he met the Craigslist seller of a small white Ford work van. The thing was clunky, with balding tires and no rear seats, but it looked like something a repair technician would drive. Or a serial killer, but he tried not to think about that.

His plan was simple enough that it might work. FMC used hefty copiers and printers, and Cameron had been able to remotely sabotage the one closest to the internal server room—good thing FMC hadn't gone completely paperless yet.

He'd then used Grisham's logins to create a work order, which went to the dummy company Cameron had created. FMC probably employed in-house technicians who could deal with copy repairs, but Cameron hoped his work orders would grant him entrance. It was either genius in its simplicity or completely idiotic. Probably a bit of both.

He put on a pair of gloves to avoid leaving fingerprints and drove toward FMC South, stopping in a grocery store parking lot to make some modifications. The ANTS System had sensors, which attached to each tire to monitor speed and distance. There were also tiny cameras for the bumpers, hood, running boards, and top of the car. A simple plug-in for the van's computer system monitored and allowed for control of things like speed and braking. All of it connected to his phone where he could set the vehicle to drive itself using GPS and positioning software. Precautionary only. He hoped.

Digging through the morning's purchases, Cameron changed in the back of the van. After adjusting his wig, he pulled out his badge printer and printed a new ID badge for Ben Jameson, an employee of a copy service firm. Who knew he'd get so much use out of his sick-kid purchases?

He programmed his magnetic mini projector with the company logo and aimed it to the van's side door. Instant work vehicle. On his way out of the parking lot, he tossed all the bags and trash from the day's purchases.

He glanced in the rearview mirror. Not bad. The wig cast a different light on his complexion, and the cap hid his face. His khaki pants and black collared shirt looked plain enough to avoid notice. He'd stuck on a goatee to better hide his face.

For the last part of the disguise, he stuck a small plastic insert onto the roof of his mouth and a tiny rock under his left heel. The palate insert would alter his speech patterns and the rock in his shoe would change his gait. Same as when he accessed the hospital servers, he hoped anyone who saw him today would recall the absurdities of his costume and mannerisms rather than his actual facial features.

The security cameras would be more difficult to fool, but he planned to keep his head down and face in the shadows. He put his smart glasses in tinted mode and slid them on for more camouflage.

His feet went numb for the tenth time that day, but he started the engine, air on full blast. He was already sweating.

Around two in the afternoon, he stopped a mile short of FMC and pulled up a map of Building Six, memorizing the details. The front doors held several levels of security. A side entrance on the northwest corner boasted a covered car drive, but a repair guy wouldn't be given that sort of access. The basement of the structure stretched under the entire FMC campus, and a massive power grid fed the area. What did they do there?

He closed the maps. Cameron hadn't given God much thought, but in that moment he sent up a prayer for safety. He'd need it in case Grisham found out what he was up to.

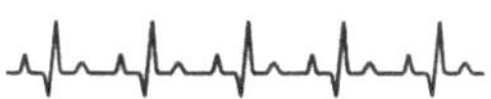

Security at FMC was tight, as expected. Two security guards stopped him at the gate. Cameras fixed on his face and several angles of his car. Thanks to the emails he'd sent via Dr. Grisham, Building Six should be expecting someone to fix their printers. Once inside, he'd have to find a way to plug into the server.

One of the guards inspected his badge, so Cameron checked his phone for something to keep him looking calm. No calls or texts from Jerry.

The other guard made a call and glanced at one of his security screens. Had Cameron missed a detail? There should be an email from Grisham granting Cameron temporary clearance and a security card. Maybe he should have sent it from his dad's email instead. The guard fingered his gun.

Cameron let out a long breath. *Stay cool.* Turning the tablet so the guard could see the mock work request from FMC, Cameron spoke with the Mumbaikar accent he'd worked on with Rahul. "Is there a problem? All I know is that I got this work request this morning, and I'm one of the few certified technicians in the Metroplex who can fix the R678I9 model."

Guard One sneered. "Is that so?"

Cameron was in huge trouble. He grabbed the gearshift but thought better of it. This was the best chance he'd get. He couldn't leave yet. He opted to bluff. "Fine. I'll leave." He bobbled his head and waved his hand around like Rahul did when upset. "My next opening is in two weeks. And you can explain to your boss why it's your fault no one here can do their jobs."

Guard Two rolled his eyes. "Don't be a jerk, okay? Building Six confirmed they have a copier issue." He handed Cameron a temporary pass. "Stay in the designated areas."

Cameron put the van in drive and hoped the guard couldn't see his shaking hands. "Yeah. Fort Knox. Got it."

Chapter Thirty-Six

Cameron

CAMERON STRAPPED THE BAG across his chest and waited for the front door of Building Six to buzz open. Four security guards met him at the entrance. The amount he'd been sweating earlier was laughable compared to the waterfall pouring between his shoulder blades now. The building better be arctic cold, or people might think he had a gland problem. Ahead, he spotted three sets of double glass doors, scanners, and ID checks. Security was way tighter here than in the other FMC buildings he'd visited.

The frigid air blasted him, and goosebumps rose on the back of his damp neck. A guard sent Cameron's bag through a scanner and pointed toward a rotating circular platform about two feet wide—a three-hundred-sixty-degree scanner. Two vertical posts resembling ski poles protruded from the base of the machine. The guard working the scanner didn't look up from his screen. "Hold the poles, please." He spoke in monotone.

The platform spun Cameron in a circle. Seriously? Security was probably necessary, but this was more intense than airport security. So how good of a picture did it take of his face?

No one said anything to him as he stepped off the platform feeling like he needed a shower. Considering there was no way his dad would subject himself to such a scan, the side entrance he'd seen on the map must belong to him.

Once through security, two guards joined him in the gray hallway. They led him through a series of double doors, all with security-card scanners.

Remembering the floor plans he'd studied, Cameron would have to go through several more doors to reach the server room in the heart of the building. Sweat pooled under his pits. What was he thinking? The hospital was a joke security wise, but this was *Men in Black* headquarters.

He'd never get into the server room, not with two guards hawking him. Any moment, he'd be shot—or worse, caught by his father. Although he was technically doing this for their family, Nigel Foster would not appreciate his son trying to break into such a heavily guarded area. Plus, Grisham and Leon would get wind of his plan, putting them all in more danger.

On both sides of the hall, robotic camera stands whirred and adjusted to follow him as he moved through another set of security doors. Screens on the wall monitored his heart rate and temperature and maybe checked his GPA. Cameron had swallowed an erupting volcano, and suddenly he had to pee. Awesome.

They passed through another set of doors into the central hallway. The guard pointed to a security checkpoint about halfway down the hall, guarded by a woman with a squint sharp enough to shape diamonds. She perched behind her island of a desk, gazing at Cameron like a dragon guarding her hoard, ready to flame him into crispy bits.

Behind Dragon Lady, a door swung open. A pale, middle-aged scientist slipped out of the doorway and swished past. At the end of the hall, he waved his ID badge over a sensor and pressed his palm to a reader. An elevator door opened, arrow pointing down, headed to the giant basement with its own power grid.

For a second, Cameron's feet failed him, trying to become one with the floor tiles. He stilled his racing thoughts. Grisham was dangerous and had to be stopped. He refused to wimp out.

In an alcove near the desk, he spotted a sink along with a coffee vending machine and snack machines. Beside those sat the copier.

Dragon Lady stood, nostrils flaring as she spoke. "Finally." The word came out razor edged. Man, this lady might even scare Tasha. She continued, each word like a bullet, "Your company promised this machine would be trouble-free, but they lied. It broke during a very important project."

Cameron set his bag down on the counter. He knelt in front of the copier and prayed for the second time in his life. He had no idea what to do next, so he dug around in his bag and opened a panel near the bottom of the machine.

Footsteps clicked down the hall. "We have the room prepped, Doctor."

"And the subjects?" The nasally voice turned Cameron's blood to hardened superglue. Dr. Grisham.

Cameron willed himself not to turn as a burning sensation spread through his gut. The machine parts swam in and out of focus and he seemed to float off the floor, losing his sense of direction. The doctor was in the lab today of all days? Maybe he'd discovered what Cameron was up to.

Thinking quickly, Cameron flicked the display in his smart glasses to connect to his phone's camera and angled the device to give him a clear shot of the hallway. Grisham and Leon spoke to some doctor. Those guys *were* working together. He had to get into that server room.

He held his breath until Grisham and his crew stepped into the elevator, then Cameron closed the panel. Careful to use the accent, he said, "Is there a server room nearby? I think the problem's with the network."

The clerk crossed her arms over her chest. "Can't you fix it from the machine?"

"I'm afraid not." Cameron looped his bag over his shoulder and sidled to the door, checking over the locks. He whistled like an artist appreciating a fine painting. "Is this the G2-8000 lock series? This is great tech." His work order had included instructions to unlock the server room. Here went nothing. He entered the code from the work order and held his breath. The door didn't open.

Umm. He swallowed. They hadn't bought it. He was not only going to fail but get caught.

Dragon Lady tip-tapped closer. "What are you doing?"

Cameron swallowed, his mind reeling. Time to run—wait. This looked similar to the lock his dad had installed on the Computer Graveyard. What if? He was in this deep, so he might as well go for it. He typed 8-6-7-5-3-0-9.

The door beeped open.

Cameron ducked inside and let the door swing shut before Dragon Lady could protest. The chilled air was a relief, jolting his brain back into gear. Soft blue lights glowed over the floor-to-ceiling cabinets filled with rows and rows of what looked like the backsides of computers—plugs and vents and input jacks.

He stared at the floor to keep his face out of camera range. About halfway down the first aisle, he located what looked like a laptop on a rollout tray. He pulled it out of the server rack and opened it to access the keyboard.

After typing for a couple seconds, he scratched his head and knocked his hat off. He crouched to grab it and pretended to fumble it against the machine. On his way back to standing, he made a show of checking the racks, like he was concerned he'd knocked something out of place. If security wasn't well-versed in computer maintenance, no one would see the thumbnail-sized transmitter he'd plugged in. Hopefully, no one would notice the downloads and the extra files he was putting into their system.

He typed on the keyboard one last time, looking for the file that served the copier so his movements would appear legit, but he only had to send a message from his phone to bring the copier back online.

The clerk banged on the door. It must have locked behind him. "Sir! Non-employees are not permitted in the server room unsupervised." Her voice was muffled but still managed to sound dagger edged.

"Coming!" He yanked the door open and pulled out his phone like he received a text. "It's my mom." Cameron winced. *His mom? Was he a complete idiot?* Too late to quit now. He typed *Be home for dinner*. In the hall, the copier sputtered to life. "All fixed."

The guards flanked the desk lady. She frowned but didn't argue.

He pulled up the dummy work order on his phone. "With your signature, I'll be out of your way."

The elevator binged while she signed. Cameron froze. He should have turned his back, but the lady was writing in perfect slow-as-an-overloaded-computer cursive. He was trapped.

The doors slid open. Grisham, flanked by Leon and a lab tech, looked up. His gaze met Cameron's. *Stupid, stupid, stupid!*

Grisham's eyes narrowed then widened with recognition. *He knows!*

Cameron was so dead. Grisham murmured something to Leon and stepped off the elevator. Cameron couldn't move—he was a deer caught in the path of a speeding car.

Any second, Leon would raise his gun and shoot Cameron. Or they'd kidnap him and take him to some remote location, making horrible grainy videos of him and extorting money out of his dad. Grisham would have Cameron killed and hide the evidence by selling Cameron piece by piece on the black market. Why had he thought this was a good idea?

The elevator doors slid shut behind Grisham, but before they closed completely, Leon glanced up. His eyes met Cameron's. Hot and cold flooded Cameron's body and his heart tried to crash to the floor.

"Excuse me, miss?" Dr. Grisham called.

Curse words banged around in Cameron's head. *So dead, so dead, so dead.*

Dragon Lady, still inspecting the work order, turned. Grisham motioned her over. She indicated Cameron and said, "But—"

Grisham waved Cameron toward the opposite doors, toward the exit. The look on his face was odd—furrowed brow and urging eyes, like he was scared for Cameron. Grisham said, "The guards will show the technician out, I'm sure. We need to discuss the…"

The doctor's voice faded behind the whomping in Cameron's ears. Why was Grisham letting him go? Was it a trick? It had to be a trick. Leon would be waiting in a quiet corridor. This was it. No escape. *Time's up, Cardiac.* But he couldn't die without someone knowing this information. Someone had to stop Grisham and the others.

Tasha. She would know what to do with this. His fingers flew over the phone screen as he worked to give her access to the folder he was downloading.

The guard beside him grunted and motioned him to the exit. Dragon Lady and Grisham still held a murmured conversation. Grisham said something about security. Cameron was going to puke, but he refused to look back.

As the guards swiped him through the first set of heavy doors, Cameron held his breath, waiting for Leon to ambush him. Each door he passed sent a metallic surge of adrenaline through his chest. Why wouldn't the guards move faster? It took all of Cameron's tai-chi-trained self not to sprint. They weren't anywhere close to the front door, after which he still had to make it through the parking security gates. Grisham might have let him go, but he couldn't take a chance with Leon.

They headed into the main hallway, where several scientists stood chatting. A door opened at the other end. A tall, dark-haired man stepped out, hand inside his coat jacket like he was reaching for a gun. Shudders stomped up and down Cameron's spine. Leon. He pushed past a clump of scientists and headed toward Cameron.

Cameron ducked around a corner, no longer caring about his guard escort. *Time to escape.* He pulled out his phone. If the batch program he'd uploaded to their server was doing its job, not only would he be getting files, but he'd have security access too. He typed in the code *On the way.*

One...two...three seconds later, a fire alarm sounded throughout the building. The guards paused. The fastest way out was to play up the moment. He gasped. "Is the place melting down? I don't wanna die."

The guard next to him shook his head. "Me neither." The three of them ran to the doors. One of them shouted into his shoulder radio. "Check the Eagle's office. Confirm. Is the Eagle in his nest?"

Stupid code words aside, Cameron dashed to the van and dove inside. He could only hope no one had tampered with the van while he'd been in the building. Fumbling the keys from his pocket, he cranked the starter. *Please start, please start, please start.* The engine sputtered and came to life. *Thank you, God.*

He roared toward the front gates, but one of the gate guards stepped in front of his van. "We've been asked to hold all traffic."

Maybe the fire alarm was a stupid idea, but he'd panicked and needed a diversion. He was not going to let them trap him. Cameron ignored the numb feeling on the tips of his fingers and pointed to his ears like he was listening to loud music. He shouted, "Sorry? Didn't hear you."

The guard moved toward the van's driver-side window to speak to him. "We're—"

Cameron stomped on the gas and swerved around the security checkpoint. He'd done it. Movement in the rearview mirror caught his attention. A black Foster Med Corp SUV followed him out of the exit. Cameron's hands were so slick he wasn't sure they'd stay on the wheel. Leon was coming.

Cameron

FIVE O'CLOCK TRAFFIC IN DFW sucked. Cameron dodged his way through thousands of cars up Highway 287 West toward Ft. Worth, with the Foster SUV close behind. At least they hadn't fired shots. Yet.

Once he got closer to Ft. Worth, the road ahead became a sea of red taillights. Side streets might be a better way to lose the FMC tail. He pulled off the freeway, taking sharp turns through business and residential streets, but every time he relaxed, thinking he'd lost them, the black SUV would appear again. He choked the steering wheel. How long before he ran out of gas and time? He called Jerry but got no answer. Cameron left a vague *call me* message in case someone had bugged the van while it sat in FMC's parking lot.

He careened around a corner, but the SUV in pursuit scooted through a slight break in traffic. It pulled close enough that Cameron could make out the SUV's front license plate in his rearview mirror—FMCS 15.

Cameron wound through a section of Ft. Worth filled with chain-link fences, empty buildings, and graffiti. Perfect place to shoot him and make it look like a mugging. Where could he go to escape? Already, his gas had dwindled to less than a quarter tank.

He jerked through a space between two cars and cut off another guy to take a sharp turn. Unlike his Porsche, the van was clunky and sluggish. Horns blared behind him. Something nagged at Cameron's mind—that weird look in Grisham's eyes as he urged Cameron to leave FMC. The more times he replayed it in his head, the more it seemed like the doctor wanted Cameron to escape. But that made no sense.

He caught movement in his rearview mirror. The Foster SUV jerked in and out of its lane.

Leon was getting closer.

Tasha

Tasha and Bethany sat together in the game room over Gabe's garage. Bethany hadn't said much since her kidnapping. Not that Tasha had wanted to converse. Her fight with Cameron yesterday had tanked any desire to interact with people. The only reason she'd come over today was Bethany's plea for company.

Gabe settled on the other side of the coffee table in one of his curved gaming chairs but didn't bother to turn on the TV. Tasha glared at him and his big, blabbing mouth. It was his fault she'd fought with Cameron. She blew out a stream of air. Well, mostly his fault. Actually, not entirely his fault. The back of her throat burned. It was her fault. But dang it, she still wanted to punch Gabe.

Against her will, Tasha sniffled and made the mistake of taking a deep breath. Gah! The room smelled like old socks and a boy's locker room. Several of Gabe's T-shirts decorated the low-lying coffee table and the end of the couch.

Their three laptops sat open on the table. Tasha plunked her computer back onto her lap. To avoid conversation, she tapped through some of her searches on Florencia, the drug cartel boss's missing niece. She hadn't spent much time on it lately, but she needed a distraction.

The young woman had visited the DFW area a few weeks before she disappeared, but her movements before that had been erratic—a road trip with a friend to California, a flight to New York, a return to El Paso. Then nothing. Not a dang thing she could find. Tasha wanted to throw the computer across the room. She sucked at everything lately.

Gabe's mom, Veronica, wandered into the game room, presumably to put something away but probably checking on them. She leaned over Tasha, inspecting the new heart necklace. "That's beautiful. Where'd you get it?"

Tasha's mouth twisted up like a fist, but she managed to choke out, "Cameron."

Veronica nodded. "I figured as much. I don't know anyone else who could shop at Tiffany's."

The metal around Tasha's neck suddenly felt hot and heavy. She fumbled with the clasp. "What kind of idiot buys me a necklace from Tiffany's?" She tossed the necklace onto the coffee table. "Cameron Foster is such a jerk!"

Veronica settled onto the couch. "Why do you say that?"

Tasha rubbed the feeling of it off her neck. "He just…why would he buy me something so extravagant?"

Gabe picked it up, turned it around in his hands, and glanced Bethany's way. "Maybe I'm the jerk because I can't buy stuff like this for you."

Bethany's eyes filled with tears. "You think that's important?"

Veronica snapped her fingers. "Stop it, all of you." She pointed to Tasha. "Do you remember in second grade when you bought that five-dollar watch for your dad?"

Tasha inspected the couch fabric. Of course, she remembered the dumb watch. Solomon had worn it like it was a flippin' Rolex until it turned his arm a funky color. Tasha's insides went tight thinking of him. Would it ever stop hurting? Would she ever stop missing him? She pinched her arm until all she could focus on was the physical pain.

Veronica went on. "For you, five dollars was a lot of money, but buying the gift for your dad made you happy." She paused. "One of the articles I read about your necklace-giving friend estimated his trust fund puts him in the top one percent of the top one percent."

"And what does that mean?"

Veronica headed toward the door. "It means that necklace is like your five-dollar watch. And someday you need to stop pushing everyone away, *mija*." She disappeared down the stairs.

"He's still a jerk."

"Because he cares about you?" Bethany wiped her eyes and sat up straighter. "While I sat tied to a chair, I had a lot of time to think. People and relationships matter. Family and friends matter. Maybe you should be glad you have another friend in this world."

Tasha motioned around the room. "What friend? I don't see him here. Do you?" No, Tasha's mistakes had seen to that. "Besides, associating with him could get us killed."

"Your dad was killed long before we met Cameron," Bethany shot back. "You can't blame that on him."

Tasha pulled her knees to her chest. Bethany was right. It wasn't Cameron's fault, but it was always easier having someone to blame. Grisham was bad news—they were all in danger for having crossed paths with him. "What good—"

Tasha's computer beeped with a notification from EyeNet. A personal message. She clicked on it, her heart climbing into her throat as she read.

"What is it?" Bethany asked.

"Cameron—he's crazy!" Tasha shoved all her stuff into her bag and waved. "I've gotta go."

Chapter Thirty-Eight

Cameron

Tasha's shrill voice blasted through his earbuds. "Cameron Foster, what did you do?"

Guess she'd seen the files he'd sent her. He gunned the van through a side street and tried to think of how to tip her off that someone might be listening without being specific. "Burgers for dinner?" He turned onto a main road and spotted signs pointing toward the TCU college campus ahead. Maybe he could ditch the van somewhere around there.

"You're being watched." She paused again. "I hear road noises—wait, are you being followed?" Her voice took on a hysterical edge, and she sucked in a breath. "Oh. My. Word. You freaking went to freaking FMC and freaking hacked their servers. Are you nuts? Do you want to die?"

"No." Yeesh, she needed to look at the files he'd sent her, not yell at him. "Just do your homework. I'll call you back."

"Oh, you will definitely call me back."

Traffic slowed for a light. The black SUV was five cars behind him. He pulled up the ANTS System on his phone screen, typing as fast as he could. This was the perfect setting for self-driving car technology designed to take over for commuters in heavy traffic. He entered coordinates that would take him to a grocery store near the TCU campus, then pulled up the Foster Med Corp servers. He hoped this would work.

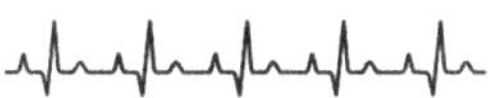

Tasha

Tasha pulled over and dug around with her phone until she could find a way to trace Cameron. Fortunately, he'd given her access to his location. Oh, that ridiculous boy! He was gonna get himself—maybe all of them—killed. And downloading files to her? He'd better be using proxy servers and bouncing that signal. The last thing she needed was to get in trouble with the FBI again.

The file names seemed to be numbers, probably some code they'd employed in case they were hacked. She could reference which files belonged to Doctors Phan, Winn, and Grisham, but there were thousands of them. If they had a team of FBI specialists reading stuff, maybe they'd come up with something, but did she want to spend the next five years looking through research files?

Maybe, if it helped her find out what happened to her dad.

She fingered the necklace Cameron had given her, tracing the heart-shaped pendant. It was the perfect gift. Though he seemed determined to be stupid lately, he had one of the biggest hearts of anyone she'd ever met, much like Solomon. She'd messed that all up, but here he was, sending a gazillion research files downloaded from FMC's internal server. Did that mean he'd forgiven her? Or did he just want her help the same way she'd wanted his?

She rubbed her temple, and light glinted off her heart pendant. None of that stuff was the real question nagging her. The real question was…once this was all over and Cameron had the world at his fingertips, would he still be interested in a neurotic, small-town girl whose goal in life had been to get revenge against his father?

She'd have to think about that once she found him. Knowing Cameron, he probably had some elaborate plan to break into FMC but hadn't thought through his exit. He was heading into Ft. Worth, so she drove in that direction too.

Chapter Thirty-Nine

Cameron

CAMERON'S VAN SQUEALED AROUND a corner. He slammed into the side door as the vehicle braked for a red light. Guess the ANTS system needed a bit of refinement. Up ahead, the abandoned graffiti-covered buildings gave way to storefronts and more signs for the TCU college campus. But the traffic was getting thicker and slower. He glanced in the rearview mirror. The SUV was about four cars back. With the snail-paced traffic and constant red lights, the dudes might get out and chase him on foot.

He scrolled through FMC data, searching for the security vehicles—that information was kept on the accessible server, he just had to find it. Of course, he'd only read about hacking cars, never actually tried it, but Solomon's work SUV had been hackable, so perhaps it would work again. If he didn't figure it out soon, he'd be in trouble.

Yes! He got into security's fleet-tracking system and found SUV fifteen. He only had to access the car's steering and braking.

He glanced up. The university's tan-brick and red-roofed buildings stretched ahead. That might be the perfect place to disappear. He unhooked his seatbelt and hopped into the rear of the van to change out of his technician disguise. He put on another hat and shoved everything else into his backpack before slipping the bag over his shoulders. Up ahead, the car would make a right turn and drive past a strip mall with several restaurants. If there were enough people on the street, he might have a chance to escape.

The van scooted around the corner. Cameron reprogrammed the ANTS System to drive east and squatted behind the passenger's seat, next to the door. He glanced ahead as the van inched forward in the heavy traffic.

People milled in front of a Thai restaurant to his right. Many more waited outside an Italian eatery two doors down. Behind him, the SUV hadn't turned the corner yet. Cameron jumped out of the van and ducked through the parked cars outside the restaurants, crouching behind a sedan while the van kept going.

The summer heat hit like a hammer, and the scent of tangy and sweet spices rolled over him. His stomach growled and reminded him that he hadn't eaten in hours, but he had to push the hunger away. The black SUV thundered past. Cameron waited until it followed his van through the next light then executed the command on his phone.

The sound of tires screeching stopped several conversations outside the Thai place. The Foster SUV jerked to a stop. The thing bounced and reversed, spinning toward the curb. He'd triggered the parallel parking feature. A second later, a loud metallic crunch reverberated across the area. One of the restaurant patrons said, "What kind of idiot tries to parallel park in the middle of the street?"

Head down, Cameron walked in the opposite direction. He felt bad for the poor driver who had rear-ended the SUV, but that should keep those guys occupied.

Cameron crossed the street and forced himself to walk at a normal pace toward the safety of the college campus.

He took his first deep breath in an hour, and his question returned. Why had Grisham let him go? Perhaps he hadn't recognized Cameron, but a tiny doubt wiggled around—what if Grisham wasn't trying to kill him? Yet a benevolent Dr. Grisham wouldn't explain Cameron's non-existent heart issues.

Or… His blood turned icy despite the hundred-degree weather. Grisham was trying to protect Cameron, his greatest investment.

All these questions were going to make his head explode.

When he reached campus, Cameron ducked into one of the large, older buildings. So far, he hadn't noticed any security cameras, but they could be hidden. If they recorded him, the FMC dudes could track his location. He slid into a nearby restroom and shed most of his costume. The smaller pieces went down the toilet, and he stuffed the wig into his bag.

Checking his appearance, he headed back into the hall. He tossed the hat under a desk in an empty classroom. Someone would assume a student had left it. He waited until the class next door let out and followed a group of students outside. After wandering around campus, he ditched his wig in a dumpster.

Settling near the campus's Frog Fountain, Cameron stared at the water pouring off the four lotus leaves in its center and tried to catch his breath in the shade. Two and a half hours had passed since he'd left FMC. He needed to talk to Tasha, needed to get back to his car, needed to figure out what was up with Grisham.

He called Jerry, but it went to voicemail again. Cameron's gut swirled. Why wasn't he answering?

Chapter Forty

Cameron

"Enjoying the view?"

Cameron jumped high enough to clear a two-story building. He whirled and blinked in disbelief as Tasha appeared in front of him with her hands on her hips. He glanced at his phone, closing search results on Bethany. "What're you doing here?" He put a hand on his chest and tried to rub away the pounding.

She sank beside him, dropping her backpack at his feet with a huff. "Saving your butt."

He wasn't sure whether to hug her or yell at her for putting herself in danger. Part of him wanted to kiss her, but the rest of him wanted to walk away. She'd used him and lied. Instead, he asked, "Why'd you come?"

She exhaled and leaned her elbows onto her knees. "Haven't you ever done the right thing for the wrong reason? Or started in one direction then realized you had it all wrong?" She met his eyes, and her hair slipped over her shoulder, cascading like a soft waterfall. "Haven't you ever regretted something and wished you could make it different?"

He refused to let her off easy. Growing up as a rich kid, he always expected people to use him to get ahead, but this was different. Worse. Tasha was the last person he expected to pull something like that. Out of everyone, he'd wanted to trust her. "How would you make it different?"

She unclasped her necklace, the one he'd given her. She held it up, letting the heart charm dangle and catch the light, and passed it to him. "For what it's worth, I'm sorry. I never should have used you like that. If I'd known I could trust you—"

"But I can't trust you." He refused to take the necklace back. Maybe he'd been a jerk to give it to her in the first place. If he were honest, it had, in part, been a test. Although he liked the meaning behind the heart, he'd also needed to check her reaction to an extravagant gift. She'd been reluctant to take it, but he'd mistaken that for a lack of greed when it was probably guilt about using him for information.

He took a long moment to breathe out his frustration. She watched his every move, biting her nails. Her eyes reminded him of a scolded puppy. Guess that made him the jerk in this conversation. He tried to swallow past the feeling that something spiky was lodged in his throat.

She let out a frustrated huff. "Maybe you'll never trust me again, and I truly regret that. For so long, I wanted to find someone to blame for Solomon's death, so I focused solely on your dad. Revenge became my obsession. I saw only what I wanted to see."

He could almost hear the "but" coming up next.

"But…"

Yep. Next, she was going to manipulate him into taking the blame for everything.

She met his eyes. "But I truly care about you, and I'm here if you want help."

Cameron stared at her. There hadn't been any layers of sarcasm or anger in her voice. This was a crossroads moment where his next move could determine the course of their future. What did he want? To see her walk away, or to suck up his pride? To protect himself, or take yet another chance?

Were he and Tasha that different? They'd both gone to great lengths, even crossed boundaries, to find the truth. Maybe he should take another chance.

He inched his hand forward, intertwining his fingers with hers. The tension left her body, and she sagged against his shoulder.

He let go of her hand and wrapped his arm around her, pulling her close and rubbing his cheek against her silky hair. She smelled like vanilla and flowers. His nerve endings stood on end, all straining toward her. Their thighs pressed against each other, each point of contact growing warm. He shifted to face her and pulled her close, kissing her until everything else faded—no more fountain, university, or danger. Only the two of them, together. She reached around his neck, digging her fingers into his shoulders.

A nearby snicker brought him back to the world. They pulled apart as a group of students moved past them, one of them smirking in Cameron's direction.

Tasha shifted away, fanning her face. "Just so we're clear, was that a 'we're all good' kiss?"

He unrolled her clenched fingers, unclasped the necklace, and placed it back around her neck. He traced the skin along the collar of her T-shirt. "Yeah, we're good."

She grabbed his hand. "Okay, so long as we're good, you want to tell me what you were thinking, pulling a brick-brained stunt like breaking into FMC?"

"You don't hold back, do you?"

"That was holding back."

Right. Guess things were back to normal. He rubbed his forehead and stared at the fountain behind them. It made a swooshing noise. Where to start? "I think Grisham and Leon are working together to sell FMC's manufactured organs on the black market."

After nibbling on her lip, she stood, grabbing her backpack. "Then let's go prove it."

Cameron rose to his feet, surprised at the stiffness in his legs. Must be the adrenaline wearing off.

A couple students walked past them carrying take-out boxes. The scent of roasted meat and sweet citrus wafted from their containers. Tasha took a deep breath and pointed. "How about we eat while we investigate?"

Chapter Forty-One

Tasha

Tasha scrolled through the stupid data files, cursing all scientists, lab experiments, Foster Med Corp in general, and Dr. Grisham in particular.

She took another bite of her orange chicken, *mm-mming* at how the spicy meat mixed with the salty soy sauce on her rice.

Cameron munched veggies while he searched for DNA donors to the ghost-organ protocol division to see if they could trace any buyers, but most of the files and subjects were numbers. The index helped some, but Tasha couldn't escape the feeling that they were just playing some murderous game.

He opened his fancy phone display onto the white tabletop in front of them but made a disgusted noise and dug his hands into the meaty part of his shoulder. Outside, the sun dipped below the horizon.

Tasha finished her last bite, wishing she had some chocolate. "What?"

"All these file numbers. It's impossible."

She tried to think of something awesome to say but ended up digging an emergency peanut butter cup out of her backpack and shoving it in her mouth. Maybe it would help her think. "Okay, this is a puzzle, right? There has to be a pattern."

Cameron leaned back, twirling a pen between his fingers. "There's no pattern here, only a bunch of stupid numbers." He threw the pen down. "Why did I think I could solve anything? I should just head home and talk to my dad."

"Why haven't you?" He'd been reluctant to talk to his dad from the beginning, but maybe it was a pride thing. Maybe Cameron wanted to know all the facts before he presented them to his dad, earning an atta-boy. Doubtful that Nigel gave those out often…or ever. Plus, it didn't seem like Nigel Foster was one for crazy conspiracy theories. For all she knew, Cameron was afraid his overprotective dad would have him committed for paranoia.

Cameron folded his arms. "I never see him, and when I do, Leon is always hanging around. Jerry told me saying something could endanger all of us, especially my dad. If Leon overheard my suspicions, who knows what he'd do? Jerry said he was taking care of it, but he's not answering his phone." He lowered his voice to a hoarse whisper. "When he's on duty, he always answers."

The peanut butter cup turned over in her stomach. "Do you think something happened to Jerry?"

Cameron met her eyes, his lips pressed flat.

Tasha tried and failed to swallow. The scream that always simmered under the surface since her dad's murder threatened to release, but she pushed it down. Like Solomon used to say, *the only way out is through*. They had to get to the bottom of this before more people were hurt. "Let's go through Grisham's files according to the dates."

Cameron pursed his lips again and tapped around. Files shifted across his big screen readout, but there were still a ton dating back twenty-five years. Tasha leaned over him and scrolled through the dates. So many files. She gave up and clicked on a random one. Inside the file was a lot of technical data, but a few words stood out: Cloning subject 027, pluripotent, stem cell.

Cameron stopped clicking his stupid pen and pointed to the display. "I think this might relate to what we saw on the video—the stuff in the coolers. They're talking about growing organs."

The orange chicken in Tasha's stomach caught on fire.

Cameron continued, "It makes sense, right? All kinds of tissues can be donated. Skin, corneas, kidneys, hearts, livers…" He scrolled through the article some more. "They mention pluripotent stem cells—those are sort of like raw dough that can be baked into different kinds of tissues."

"Yeah. Cloning stuff," Tasha said. "But that's so sci-fi, isn't it?"

Cameron shook his head. "No, but the technology is impressive—I've sat through numerous FMC presentations. It's expensive and experimental, but FMC has an astronomical research budget. They're doing a ton of this stuff." He scanned some more. "Maybe this is part of what we need to prove Grisham has been using stem cells to grow organs that he then sells on the black market. There's mention of cloning, but no legit sales that I've seen."

He kept talking, but Tasha couldn't hear him any longer over the ringing in her ears. She stared at a line toward the bottom of the report. *Subject 027, pluripotent, stem cell, no longer viable.* Terminated March fourteenth, three years ago. The day her dad died.

It was like someone had punched all the air out of her lungs. Her mouth went dry. "I don't…" She couldn't form the rest of her sentence. Why of all dates did it have to be that one?

Cameron was saying something about Grisham, but his face kept blurring. She cleared the rock out of her throat. "But you were having doubts about Grisham."

He hit his pen against the table. *Tap, tap…tap, tap, tap.* "It's a place to start." He glanced at her. "Hey, you okay?"

Tasha's eyes were hot, and she had the urge to run all the way home, but that was stupid. For the last three years, she'd wanted answers. Why, when information was possibly within reach, did she want to bolt?

She pointed at the screen. Her arm seemed to be made of an unmovable metal compound. "That was the day my dad died." She forced the words out, which opened a flood of memories. An image from the night Solomon died flashed through her head. Blood spattering on the already deployed airbag. A wave of nausea hit her, and she dashed to the bathroom.

She leaned against the metal stall but couldn't stop the slideshow of events ticking through her brain. Solomon hugging her after she'd won the science fair, that night at softball when she'd sprained her ankle and he'd carried her across five fields to the car, or the time in sixth grade when he'd taken her for ice cream to cheer her up after Zane Fredricks had called her Flatty Four Squared.

Tears poured down her cheeks. She slapped them away and scrolled through her phone to find a distraction. She stopped on her recent searches for Florencia but couldn't focus. Ugh. This was stupid, hiding in a gross public bathroom. Might as well face whatever Cameron was about to find. She inched her way back to the table.

The skin around his eyes wrinkled as he assessed her. "I'm so sorry."

Tasha let out her fakest laugh ever. "I'm fine."

He squeezed her hand but glanced down at her phone, his forehead scrunching up. He pointed to the picture of Florencia taken the last night she'd been seen. "Who's the girl with Grisham?"

Tasha blinked. Cameron's crooked doctor was with a woman who went missing soon after? Definitely not a coincidence. She swallowed. "Florencia's the niece of drug cartel boss Julio Cortez. This was taken the night she disappeared eighteen years ago. You sure that's Grisham?"

"It's grainy, but I've seen a lot of old photos of him and Dad." He started tapping on his phone. "Why're you looking into Florencia's disappearance?"

"Remember that EyeNet post about the FBI investigating Cortez for killing all those kids? It seemed more something the Wolf Brothers Cartel would do, so I started looking into it."

Cameron stopped whatever he was doing on his phone. "I thought the same about the Wolf Brothers." He had an intent look about him—pursed lips, dilated pupils. "Leon does these drop offs in the cities we visit—that's how I found Bethany. What if a member of the Wolf Brothers is meeting him and doing the distribution?"

She nodded. "If you could link Leon and Grisham to one of them, we'd be in a better position."

He tipped his phone in her direction. "See? A younger Grisham."

She swore.

Cameron stood. "It's time I talked to my dad."

Chapter Forty-Two

Cameron

Tasha dropped him off at the car dealership to pick up his Porsche, and after a kiss that led to several more, Cameron headed to his car. He pulled her in for one last kiss because he never wanted to forget the feel of her lips. "Talk to you later. Thank you, for everything."

Her eyebrows furrowed. "That sounded too much like goodbye."

Yeah, it did. With one last wave, he slid into the Porsche and took off. He glanced at the silent phone on the seat next to him. Where was Jerry? He never went this long without getting in touch. Had Cameron's stunt saving Bethany somehow caused UNITED to transfer him? An ache in his gut stirred. He hoped it was something as simple as a job transfer and not anything worse. No, he wouldn't think about that. He stared at the endless black sky. The dark evening seemed to open its jaws wide. Without Jerry, he was lost.

It was after midnight when Cameron got home. He tiptoed into the house, hoping his dad was busy—

"Nice of you to drop by."

Cameron jumped, clutching his chest. His father was sitting in the center of the main hall. Not good.

Nigel glanced at his watch and gave Cameron The Stare. No blinking. No emotion. It was like looking into the face of a dragon that hadn't decided whether to flame him or eat him.

Cameron gulped. "Uh…"

His dad nodded at the car remote still clenched in Cameron's fist. "You didn't hang it up. Leon, come here." Even though his dad didn't raise his voice, the oaf appeared as if he'd been lurking around the nearest corner. "Put Cameron's car remote where it belongs."

Cameron kept his hand fisted. "I'll keep it with me."

His dad stood and brushed off his suit. "A disorganized house makes for a disorganized mind."

Leon pried the remote from Cameron's hand. Had those same meaty digits tied Bethany to a chair? If it had been Leon, Cameron would find a way to sink him.

His dad waved Leon away and focused his tractor-beam gaze on Cameron. "Were you with Natasha Jenkins today?"

He should lie to protect her, but his dad wasn't the enemy. Still, Leon could be listening. What to do? He spoke in a low voice. "Can we talk?"

"Aren't we?"

Where could they speak without being overheard? The entire house could be bugged. He glanced toward the front door. "How about a walk?"

His dad blinked. "At this time of night?"

"Yes, please. I just… I have to—" How could he convince his dad to come outside? "Humor me."

"You've certainly piqued my interest." His dad led the way outside. The rose bushes threw prickly shadows on the stone walls of the porch. Ahead, the circular drive wound through the gates to the street. They'd only made it halfway down the drive when Leon lumbered out of the house, stuffing his gun into his chest holster.

Cameron lowered his voice. "Dad, please, I need to talk to just you. It's important. I'm worried about you."

His dad stopped walking. "Me?"

Before Cameron could say more, Leon caught up. "Where're we headed, Mr. Foster?"

His dad cleared his throat. "My son and I are going to enjoy the evening air. No need to accompany us."

Leon's fingers twitched, and Cameron held his breath. Would he try to shoot them? Finally, Leon nodded and turned back to the house, glancing over his shoulder a few times. As soon as they were out of sight, he'd probably follow them.

Cameron urged his dad forward. He'd have to be quick. They passed the neighbor's house, a sprawling beige monstrosity flanked by palm trees straight out of Beverly Hills. He glanced at the night sky. Instead of stars, planes with blinking lights circled overhead. It was a nice evening in the city. Quiet, not too warm. Why didn't he and his dad do these kinds of things anymore? Cameron pointed to the colonial mansion across the street. "Have you ever met them?"

"You wanted to talk about something serious."

"Right. I know. It's just…" He didn't know where to begin. While he tried to organize his thoughts, he waved his dad forward. They passed one more house, this one a turreted Disney castle. He'd never seen the people who lived there either. What did they do all day? Were they nice? Was he missing out for not having met them? Argh. He shouldn't be wasting these few seconds with his dad.

With Grisham being his dad's oldest friend, he had to tread softly. Maybe if Cameron made it seem like Grisham was a victim too, his dad would be more receptive to the bad news. "I think Leon is trying to hurt us by using Dr. Grisham and maybe others at FMC. They might be selling FMC ghost organs on the black market."

His dad slowed. "Why would you think that?"

"It all began when I saw this email a few weeks ago." He showed his dad the screenshot he'd taken of Dr. Grisham's email the day of his heart tests at FMC. "That corporation, Donor Beneficence Corp? It's a dummy front, maybe mafia controlled. It goes through several other false businesses. They might be selling your information, but most likely organs manufactured at FMC. And I think Leon's been following me. I've found bugs and tracking devices in my car. I think he even tried to run Tasha off the road. And you remember Dr. Zemke from the hospital?"

His dad wore an odd look on his face. "Yes."

"He died right after he tried to contact me regarding my test results. Did Dr. Grisham ever show them to you?"

"No."

"See? That proves it!"

"I'm not sure what it proves," his dad said, "but how did you get Charles's email?"

The use of Grisham's first name somehow humanized the guy. Cameron's tongue stuck to the roof of his mouth. What if he was wrong and got Grisham in trouble for nothing? He could ruin the guy's life.

Cameron swallowed. "Accessing email isn't what's important here." Cameron's heart climbed up his chest, but people were getting hurt, and he couldn't risk his dad being next. He cleared his throat, hoping and praying his dad didn't go ballistic when Cameron gave him the news. "I'm not sick. For whatever reason, Grisham faked my heart condition. All of it."

His dad stopped walking. Though it was difficult to see his face in the dark, his eyes popped wider and his lips parted, but no sound came out. Yep, he was shocked. "Why would you accuse Charles of such a thing?"

"Money. You've said in speeches that I was your inspiration to push into new areas of research like the ghost organ division. That alone could give Leon and others an unlimited supply of organs to sell on the black market."

"You think Leon has been controlling Grisham, making him falsify medical facts? Then they're selling organs on street corners like common drug peddlers?"

"There's a ton of money in the black-market organ indus-try—they could make far more selling organs than any doctor could make in his lifetime."

"But how would Leon control Grisham? I've seen his IQ. He's no criminal mastermind."

Geez, Cameron should've prepared a PowerPoint presentation. This was why he'd done so much research. His dad always wanted facts and more facts. "I've seen evidence Leon has Mafia ties. There has to be someone else behind this."

"For seventeen years?"

Warning lights flashed in Cameron's mind. His dad probably thought this was all some fantasy designed by a kid desperate to avoid heart surgery. He had to convince him. "I've been searching some files." Cameron's voice faded. And what? He still hadn't connected Leon to the Wolf Brothers cartel or any other organ smugglers, nor had he found specific information that anyone was selling FMC organs. His "evidence" was a couple weird emails, two sets of disparaging heart-test results, images of Leon with international mobsters, and Tasha's grainy video. Not enough to convince Nigel. Jerry was right—he should've waited to talk to his dad.

The sidewalk swam in and out of focus. How could he have been so stupid? He knew he needed specific proof but jumped before he had all the facts. His dad didn't believe him. He might even mention this to Grisham. Leon could be waiting at home to kill them both. Cameron's lungs were frozen.

His dad stared back at the house, the muscles in his cheeks flexing. He probably wondered if Cameron needed psychiatric help. The neighborhood seemed to shift, like it was still in the real world but Cameron was just a shadow, a figment of his own imagination. The too-familiar numbness crept up his arms.

Perhaps none of this was real. Maybe he'd already had his surgery and was in a coma and his subconscious had dreamed up Tasha and everything else. He clasped his shaking hands behind his back. His fingers were ice cubes.

After several pounding heartbeats, his dad spoke. "Fascinating." His voice held a dangerous, dark edge. He gripped Cameron's shoulder. "You were right to come to me."

It took Cameron a while to find his voice. Did this mean his dad believed him? It still didn't feel like this was happening. "What're we going to do?"

His dad headed back to the house with rapid strides. "We're going to return home, and I will take care of everything. I have plenty of security personnel besides Leon who can see to this issue."

"What about me? What can I do?"

"Send me all the information you've gathered. I think it will be quite useful." He paused, looking Cameron over. "You truly are my son, aren't you?"

The tension in Cameron's shoulders melted. Everything was going to be fine. Everything *was* fine…except that Jerry still hadn't called. "Hey, Dad? Have you talked to Jerry?"

His dad was already on a call and didn't seem to hear.

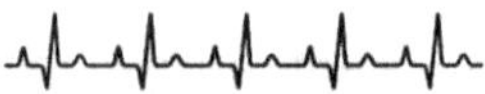

Cameron must have dozed off because he woke up to his phone buzzing. The display read four in the morning.

"You awake?" Tasha asked without saying hello.

"Sure."

"Um…" She paused and puffed out several breaths.

If Tasha was having difficulty with words, it couldn't be good. "What is it?" he asked.

"Is Jerry with you?"

"I can't get hold of him."

"You've got to get out of there."

Cameron rubbed his forehead, his entire body going numb. "It's four in the morning, and I talked to my dad. Everything's going to be fine."

"No, it isn't," she said. "Read the files I sent you. It's a lot worse than we thought."

Chapter Forty-Three

Cameron

THE FILES BELONGED TO Dr. Grisham and referred to Test Subject 030. Among the jumble of medical nonsense, he recognized words like "embryo," "nucleus transfer," and "maternal source." The main gist seemed to be about a cloning subject. The files referenced twenty-nine previous failures and a string of tests conducted on Test Subject 030. Cameron rubbed his eyes. So far, he hadn't seen mention of what organs they were cloning.

He glanced at the time. Still nothing from Jerry. In all the years Cameron had known him, the big guy had never gone this long without responding to messages. He stuck his chair under his bedroom doorknob and slipped inside his Computer Graveyard, locking that door too. He read more about test subjects and pluripotent cells, but the words ran together and blurred.

His phone buzzed. Cameron jerked up from where he'd slumped against the wall and fallen asleep. Gah, why couldn't he stay awake? His phone read five thirty-two AM. "Mmhm?"

Tasha's voice held a lightsaber's edge. "Did you read the stuff?"

"No, I—"

She groaned. "It's not just Drs. Grisham and Winn. It's dozens of scientists. The experiments in the basement of Building Six are about organ growth from stem cells, especially hearts. But there's more research going on down there. Some of it involves cloning."

He swiped a hand through his hair. "Yeah, their ghost organ division." What did she think they'd been talking about this whole time?

"You obviously didn't read far enough. Humans. Cloning humans. As in an entire person, not just parts. After hundreds of botched attempts over the years, there were thirty attempts with this one genetic donor. The first twenty-nine had issues, decreasing with each trial until Subject 030, born seventeen years ago. There's more—at least the digital files refer to more research—but that's stored on site. We can't get to it remotely."

"Uh…" His brain was stuffed with cotton. The conversation would go better after another eight hours of sleep.

Tasha kept talking. "You still don't get it." She exhaled, her breath creating static in his ear. "Tell me about your mother."

A wave of cold washed over him. His brain kicked into full processing mode, and he sat up straighter. "What does she have to do with anything?"

"What do you remember about her?"

"I told you. She abandoned me as a baby, took off as soon as she got a payment."

"Yeah, you also said she didn't take care of your health issues."

Cameron choked on his next words and pressed a hand to his chest. His perfectly normal heart beat a steady rhythm. *Thump, thump. Thump, thump.*

"Cameron, listen to me." Her voice softened. "There were surrogates involved in the cloning attempts. Surrogates no one has seen since." She paused, letting that sink in.

The thumping of his heart turned to a bass drum in his ears. He tried to laugh, but no sound came out. "This isn't funny."

She sniffled—was she crying? "No, it's not funny at all." She took a shuddered breath. "The person they cloned was your dad."

The floor seemed to be falling away underneath him. "You're wrong, and that has nothing to do with me." Lack of sleep had made her delusional. "My mother was a gold digger who neglected me, so Dad was forced to terminate parental rights."

"When?"

"I don't know. I don't care!"

She coughed and sniffled again. "You don't know because it never happened, but that's not important—"

"You're saying my mother was some nameless person paid to gestate me, but it's not important?"

"I thought you said I was wrong."

"You don't know anything." Cameron gripped the phone so hard his knuckles popped. His world spun away from him, out of control. Everything crashed around him, burning to the ground.

"*Please*, Cameron. I'm trying to—"

"Maybe I don't want to know—"

"Just let me—"

"No!" This wasn't true, couldn't be true.

"Subject 030 is you, Cameron. You're FMC's first perfect clone."

Chapter Forty-Four

Cameron

CAMERON DROPPED THE PHONE. The room blurred—maybe he'd fallen asleep, and this was a crazy dream. Yes, that had to be it. He pinched himself until the pain made his eyes water. His father never mentioned his mother. Cameron had never seen her picture because she'd hurt him, hurt them both. She'd neglected Cameron, only gotten pregnant for the money.

He paced, head pounding. His mother was not a surrogate. She couldn't be. He was not a clone. He couldn't be. That was some fiction Tasha's mind hallucinated, probably from all the poisonous fast food she ate.

His father wouldn't do that. A tingle shot from his toes up his calves. His chest hurt. He couldn't catch his breath.

A voice echoed from the phone on the carpet. "Cameron? Can you hear me? You've got to—"

He stared at his phone, a useless hunk of metal unless the wiring worked just right, and it was hooked into the vast cellular network. Sort of like a heart.

His heart. His heart that was supposedly busted but was actually healthy.

No, this wasn't happening. Online, he'd seen people joke about nightmares like they were back in high school and hadn't studied for finals. They would simply tell themselves it wasn't real and would wake up sweating and relieved. "Wake up, stupid!"

"What?" said a voice from his phone.

Cameron stared at the device. He wasn't waking up, and worse, his phone was talking to him. He kicked it away and stumbled to the bathroom. He turned on all the lights and faucets and stepped into the shower with his clothes on. That would wake him up.

All he got was wet. Water pooled into his shoes. He had nowhere to escape. He stared at his face in the shaving mirror that he'd bought more on principle than need. His face, so much like his dad's.

No, Tasha was wrong. The files were wrong. Cloning was sci-fi stuff. Normal people couldn't just clone another human being and make it work. Things went wrong.

Tasha's words came back. *"You're subject 030."*

He leaned against the wall of the shower, warm water from the multiple jets cascading over his head and down his sides.

What if?

No. Maybe.

Building Six with its separate servers. Building Six with its major security protocols. Building Six with its massive underground structure and power sources.

He cranked the water up as high as it would go and turned his face into the spray, but the thoughts wouldn't wash away.

Clone number thirty. That meant something had gone wrong. Twenty-nine times.

No, this was stupid. His dad could explain this. No way was Cameron some weird sci-fi experiment. Whatever was going on, Leon and Grisham were behind it. They were milking some scheme without his dad knowing it.

Cameron slapped the shower knob to turn it off. Yes, that had to be it. He would go downstairs and talk to his dad, and together they'd figure this out. His dad was just as much of a victim as he was.

He peeled off his wet clothes and left them in the shower. After he changed, he yanked open the bathroom door but stopped short of leaving his bedroom. Last time he'd checked, Leon and his guns were out there.

Phone in hand, he sank onto the bed. His dad wouldn't have any reason to get involved in something weird like cloning, but Grisham and the others would. He thought of the money they'd gain by perfecting the technology. Cameron punched his pillow.

That article Cameron had found earlier talked about Grisham filing for bankruptcy. Cameron took a long breath and plugged in his keyboard and 3D projector, hacking his way into Grisham's accounts once again.

It took a while to find financial information, but eventually, a picture formed. The guy made a decent salary at FMC, but his bank balance remained minimal. Part of it went to IRS payments for some past taxes and some went toward a modest retirement account. There were large amounts of cash withdrawals, but for what? The guy didn't have a social life. He wore the same black suits over and over, didn't take vacations, and only owned one small house. He had no other major expenses. No car payments, no mortgages, no credit card balances. Where was his money going? Cameron wasn't an accountant, but perhaps the doctor was funneling money into some offshore accounts. It was the only thing that made sense, but proving it would take more digging. Hacking was like the story of *Hansel and Gretel*…following breadcrumbs to find the witch's house.

He set up another search through Grisham's files and rubbed an aching spot on the back of his neck. His brain needed a break.

He paced and scrolled around some of his social media sites. One of the messages Rahul had sent caught his eye. Cameron stared at the picture of Superman and Superboy. Pain settled in his chest. He missed Rahul. As with Jerry, he'd taken for granted that Rahul would be around all the time. Where had he gone?

Because he wasn't ready to get back to researching the doctor, Cameron continued to scroll through Rahul's accounts. Aside from the "Unplugging at the Beach" posts, there were no other updates.

A dark storm swirled inside Cameron's gut. Using the guy's backward-birthdate password, Cameron looked up his last GPS location. He stared at his screen while his stomach dove to the basement.

The phone was at FMC South—at least the last time it had been powered up. Weird. What would he be doing there? Perhaps the phone belonged to FMC and Rahul had left it at the office, but something wasn't right.

Cameron hacked into more of the guy's accounts. No new phone, no recent money transfers. Nothing. Maybe he'd gone off the grid, but that made no sense. Rahul stayed in the spotlight like Texas did the sun. He had to figure this out.

Time to stop hiding and find some answers.

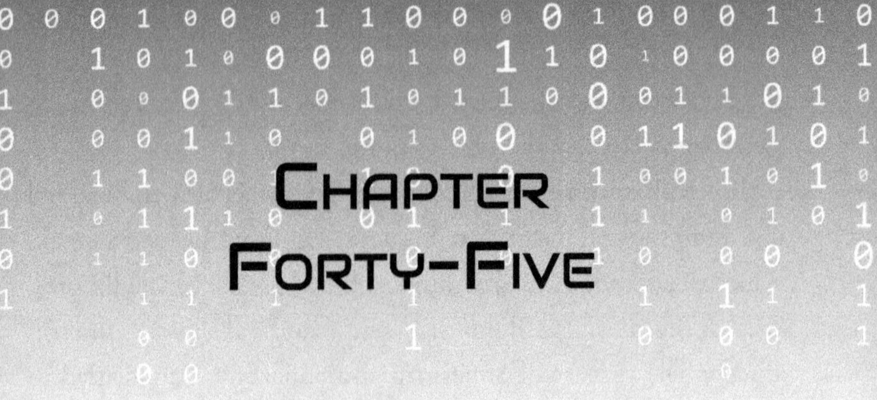

Chapter Forty-Five

Cameron

CAMERON SHOVED HIS PHONE pieces, wallet, and money clip into his jeans pocket. A quick check of the security system showed Leon in the basement. Cameron stuffed his lock-picking set and collapsible bo staff into a computer bag and jogged down the rear stairs, nearest to the main garage. How easy it had been to forget about his supposed heart condition now that he knew it was a lie.

Among his other problems loomed the need for a car. Leon had taken his Porsche remote, so that was probably under surveillance again, or worse. He stared at the car remotes hanging on the hook by the garage door. Leon had access to all those vehicles. Plus, the main garage bays were behind an extra set of security gates. Cameron could take care of the cameras, but Leon might hear the gate motors. He leaned against the wall and glanced back into the house's darkened caverns.

His dad kept the Tesla in the garage by his office. Leon probably didn't have access to that part of the house, but Cameron's dad could be a problem. He was a light sleeper, if he slept at all.

Cameron ducked into a bathroom and pulled up his access to the home security network. He paused the camera feeds on his dad's side of the house. He only needed a car remote. Sometimes, a neat-freak dad came in handy.

He jogged across the house. It took several heart-pounding moments to pick the lock on his dad's office, but it finally clicked open. The coach lanterns in the driveway glared through the office windows, their light scraping over the desk, shelves, and collection of sailing books. Odd how his dad kept all those reminders of sailing, considering his parents died in a boating accident.

He couldn't hear any movement, so maybe his dad hadn't heard him. He disabled the alarm chimes on the single-stall garage connected to his dad's office and glanced inside the Tesla. No remote. Darn it. It wasn't on the hook by the door, either. Where would his dad keep it?

He headed back into the office. If he didn't get the security system back online soon, it might trigger an alarm. He had to be quick.

Cameron swung around. His computer bag knocked over his dad's sailboat replica of *Jacquelyn's Pride*, but he grabbed it before it clunked onto the cabinet. Unfortunately, his bag flopped onto the floor and his bo staff rolled out. Fortunately, they all hit the rug, so they only issued a small *schnick*. He exhaled, waiting for his pulse to return to normal, but as he set the boat back on the shelf, the top slid off. Inside, the structure was hollow, and someone had crammed an old prescription bottle into the hull. What was that about? He jammed it into his bag so he could investigate later.

His hands were shaking so hard it took three tries to click the sailboat's top back into place. He scooped his stuff off the carpet and kept searching.

As he rifled through the desk for his dad's Tesla remote, each drawer revealed nothing and more of nothing. A few pens. A stapler. A bottle of pills prescribed to Nigel Cameron Foster by Dr. Charles Grisham. Cameron glanced at them. Digoxin—the same medicine Grisham prescribed to Cameron. Except none of his pills looked like these. Cameron stared at the bottle, his eyes unfocused. Why would this be here?

A soft click, like the closing of a door, sounded from somewhere in the house. A surge of adrenaline kicked through his veins. What was he doing wasting time?

Cameron shoved the bottle into his computer bag next to the one from the sailboat and checked a cabinet for the car key. The latch clicked and jangled. Cameron froze, the blood in his ears *whomp, whomp, whomping*. As quietly as he could, he glanced through the rest of the cabinets.

No keys. No keys anywhere. If he took any more time, he might as well run through the house with a set of cymbals and drums. His eyes swung around the room. *Quick.* He had to either find a way out or come up with a good story.

He glanced across the hall and down the corridor to his dad's closed bedroom door. His dad had strict rules concerning his room. Cameron had never been allowed to play in there as a kid, and he'd only been in the room a few times.

He peered down the hallway toward the kitchen and basement stairs. No lights were turning on. Was his dad home?

His dad's room didn't emit any noise either. Maybe due to the eerie silence or maybe due to the thought of Leon and his gun, chills ran in infinite loops up and down Cameron's back.

He swept his phone light around the master bedroom. Chairs and the other furniture cast long-clawed shadows. The bed was empty, but the covers were rumpled. He exhaled. Leave it to his father to get up before dawn. Nigel Foster was fond of saying that money didn't make itself.

He kicked some plastic tubing sticking out from under an odd cabinet. The structure was about three feet tall and two feet deep, and the sides were constructed with wooden slats like it needed to be ventilated. He bent to look closer, but the nightstand caught his eye—his dad's phone and Tesla remote sat side by side, abandoned. Business-first Nigel Foster did not make little mistakes like leaving his phone behind.

A light suddenly blinked on across the garden, in the kitchen. Cameron ducked and glanced out the curtains. Leon? He squeezed his eyes shut, but his head pounded. How did all this fit together? Grisham and Leon, FMC, cloning?

The next thought hit him so hard his muscles went rigid—his dad had promised to look into everything. Maybe he'd discovered the terrible truth and confronted Grisham and Leon. Had they killed his dad? He was going to throw up.

Cameron had to get out of the house and find Jerry. His connection to UNITED was the only way Cameron could think to get help. He snagged the remote and shot back into his dad's office just as a hall light came on. Heavy footsteps trudged closer—too clunky to be his dad's.

Cameron fumbled into the garage and popped the manual release on the bay door, easing it open. He darted to the car, but before he could climb inside, the interior garage door slammed open. Leon raised his gun and charged.

Chapter Forty-Six

Cameron

Dropping his computer bag, Cameron yanked out his bo staff. He spun it so that the sides popped out, giving him six feet of stick to work with.

Leon curled his lip, and the gun in his hand seemed to grow larger. He took a step closer. "End of the road, kid."

Yeah, no way, dude. Cameron whipped up the staff, whacking Leon's hand. Leon cursed, and his gun fired. The bang rang in Cameron's ears, and the light above the car shattered. Glass *plinked* over the concrete floor. Leon shoved further into the space and aimed his gun at Cameron's chest, but Cameron brought his bo staff down across Leon's hand so hard he heard an audible *crack*. Leon hollered as his gun clattered to the ground.

When Leon lunged for his gun, Cameron hit him with the staff once more, knocking him to his knees. Leon growled, and Cameron darted for the car, tripping over his computer bag and spilling some of its contents.

Cameron stuck out his hands to keep from face-planting onto the concrete, but the impact jarred his spine. Leon snagged Cameron's pant leg, yanking him backward. Cameron swiveled and kicked him in the face.

Leon swiped a hand across his mouth. "You and your dad are through, you hear me, freak? You're both dead!"

"No!"

Both of them scrambled up, and Leon barreled into Cameron, slamming him into the car. Pain exploded in Cameron's ribs and his sight went black for a second, but Jerry had once told him that pain could be procrastinated until one was out of danger. Cameron let out a yell and slammed his knee between Leon's legs. Leon grunted but swung his fist at Cameron's head.

Cameron ducked and used Leon's momentum to swing the guy's arm around, trying to push him to the ground. Leon bucked and slammed him back against the car. Cameron gulped, his lungs stuttering. Silver dots swam in his vision, and his back ached.

Leon shoved him into the wall. One more hit and Cameron would be down for good. Cameron swung wildly with his bo staff, missing Leon, who dove for the gun.

Someone shoved open the door, and a shaking flashlight shone into the garage. "Sir? Are you okay?" Rose's voice drifted into the silence.

Cameron's throat was dryer than sand. He tried to yell "run!" but all that came out was a strangled grunt. Leon grabbed his gun and scrambled toward Rose. He grabbed the poor woman's throat before she had time to scream. Her eyes bulged, and she gasped for air like a fish on dry land.

Leon spat. "Give it up, Junior. You can't win. Come with me, or I splatter her brains all over this floor."

Cameron had no choice. It was stupid, impulsive, and the thing Jerry said often worked. With a loud yell, he whirled the bo staff upward, driving it into the soft flesh under Leon's chin. The jerk's grip on Rose slipped, and she yanked free, whacking Leon with her flashlight.

Cameron slammed the staff down on Leon's gun arm. "Where's my dad?"

Leon chuckled. "You won't live long enough to find him." Blood and spittle foamed on his lips. Leon reached behind him.

That's when he remembered… Leon always carried more than one gun. Cameron rammed his bo staff into Leon's neck. While Leon staggered and gasped for air, Cameron whacked him on the temple. Leon sputtered and slumped to the ground. Cameron tossed Rose a wad of cash that had spilled out of his bag. "Run, and don't tell them where you are!"

He found some duct tape and secured Leon's hands and feet together. He slapped a strip over Leon's mouth, tossed his bag into the car, and backed out, shutting the garage door behind him.

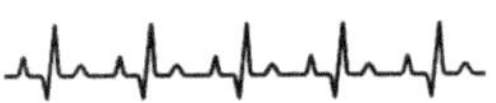

Tasha

Tasha's head was so full of information it was about to explode, but one thing flashed at the top like a giant strobe light. Cameron needed to get out of his house. Why didn't the idiot answer his phone? Jerry wasn't answering either.

She stared out the window, keys biting into her clenched fist. Should she or shouldn't she? Stubborn, stubborn boy, not wanting to believe her. Guess she had no choice but to convince him. She grabbed her purse.

Her hand was on the doorknob when Gran cleared her throat. "Going somewhere?"

Several lies ran through her head, but lying to Gran was like wrestling a crocodile—dangerous and foolish.

"Let me guess. This has something to do with Cameron." Gran stared at her with clear, cognizant eyes.

Busted. Tasha swallowed past the rock rising from her gut. "I…"

Gran leaned on the arm of her chair. "Listen, Natasha. I might be an old woman who doesn't know a GPS from a garden hose, but I know people, and your mom is right about something. Foster Med Corp is trouble."

Gah. Did the old woman have X-ray soul vision or something? "But Cameron—"

"Isn't like his father," Gran finished. "Yes, I know." She waited until Tasha looked her in the eye. "Do you care about him?"

Tasha's eyes watered as a burning pressure built in the back of her throat. Unable to speak, she nodded. Tasha ducked out the door and leaned on it, breathing hard like she'd been running. Her brain played a long and horrible stream of "what-ifs."

Gran and her mother would be devastated if something terrible happened to Tasha, but she had a bad feeling that Cameron was in danger, and since Jerry wasn't available, Tasha might be his only hope. If she wasn't too late.

Chapter Forty-Seven

Cameron

Cameron pulled into a church parking lot a few blocks from his house. He leaned against the steering wheel and breathed in giant, shaking gulps. What was he supposed to do? He stared at the large screen on the Tesla's console, but his mind screamed. His dad was missing, Jerry was missing, Rahul was possibly missing. What if they ended up like Tasha's dad?

On the opposite seat, he noticed the medication bottle he'd found in the sailboat had rolled out of his computer bag. Cameron scooped it up, glaring at the label.

It wasn't a prescription, but a manufacturer's bottle, the kind a hospital or pharmacy might stock. A drug called midazolam. He'd seen that before, but where? He used the Tesla's screen to look it up—an anesthetizing agent that put patients into a twilight state and wiped their memories. Warnings indicated that mixing with alcohol could cause the patient to pass out or worse.

Like a bizarre photo shoot, pictures popped into his head. The sailboat. The boating accident with his grandparents, Nigel II and Jacquelyn—they had been drinking and didn't wake when the Jet Ski collided into their boat. And hadn't he read some article about a young Grisham researching anesthetizing agents, including this one?

Grisham had been staying with the Foster family that fateful day but had a headache and declined a ride on the boat. Grisham, whose mother died from an untimely heart attack while drinking tea with him.

Then there was Dr. Zemke's strange expression at the hospital when he saw Cameron. Dr. Zemke, who'd been working in emergency at Dallas General for decades and had mentioned Nigel II, Jacquelyn, and midazolam on that flash drive he'd sent to Tasha's mom. There was also that photo of the old memo about missing drugs in the hospital supply closet.

Cameron's feet and hands went cold. His dad rarely mentioned his parents, and when he did, it was often in distaste, like the comment about Nigel being sent to boarding school because he interfered with his parents' yachting schedule. Did Grisham get rid of them in some sort of sick tribute to Nigel?

What was to stop Grisham from killing anyone he wanted? Maybe he'd already killed Cameron's dad too. Had he hired Leon to do it? Cameron swallowed a wave of nausea. He wanted to go home and…what? There was no escape.

No, he had to end this now. Cameron put the car into gear and pulled out of the parking lot. Tasha had mentioned more info about the cloning experiments was stored on site at FMC in Building Six. Maybe he could find something that would take down the bad doctor there.

He thought of Tasha, of all the broken bits of sorrow behind her beautiful face. He wasn't going to let Grisham hurt her or anyone else ever again. Grisham was going down. All Cameron had to do was find a way inside Building Six.

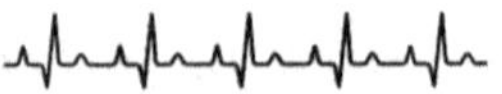

Cameron drove south and used voice command to dial Bethany. From everything he'd found in his searches, she didn't qualify as president of The Department of Trust-ability, but he needed her help to pull this off.

"Cameron, hey! How are ya?" Her voice sounded chipper, not at all what he'd expect of the mastermind behind a watchdog hacktivism group or a recent kidnapping victim, which were two of many reasons more was going on with her than it seemed.

He didn't waste time with pleasantries. She might hate him by the end of this conversation, but she'd cooperate. "Why'd you recruit me to EyeNet?"

"I—what?" She tried to laugh, but it was more of a sputter.

"You recruited me and Tasha, but why? Who told you to do it?"

The only sound coming through his car's speakers was her sucking in a breath.

"Be honest, if you can manage. We're all in trouble. Big trouble. There's no way the three of us working together was a coincidence, and there's no way you could have traced Cardiac's identity to me, so I'm guessing someone very powerful is behind EyeNet."

"But—"

She was going to lie again, and he didn't have time. "Just stop, Bethany. I'll fill you in on what I know so far so you can report it to whoever has you in their back pocket, then you can either tell me the rest, or I'll figure it out. The FBI caught you hacking like they did Tasha, except whatever you got into was worse. And you've been working for them since. How am I doing?"

She sniffled. "What do you want?"

Pretty much the reaction he'd expected. No acknowledgement of the truth, but no denials. Yet none of that mattered, because he was stuck, and Bethany was the one with the resources to pull him out. Besides, she genuinely cared about Tasha. He knew that as much as he knew there was more behind her choice to work for EyeNet.

"I want the truth, but for now we've got to work together. I figure for some reason you were asked to recruit me so perhaps whoever you work for could get a closer look at FMC. Since you have such a powerful contact, I know you can do it. Tasha's life depends on you cooperating. Though you might not care about me, I know you care about her."

Bethany remained silent for five, six, seven seconds, then exhaled. The sound rattled in the speaker. "Okay."

Cameron lowered his shoulders a few inches. By now, Leon could have gotten loose. He shook off the thought and said, "I'll tell you what we need. But first, call Tasha and convince her to steer clear."

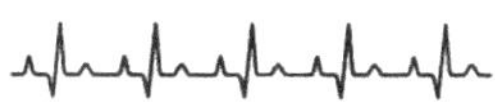

Cameron parked at one of the large, crowded strip malls about ten minutes from FMC. After his repair-guy stunt, he couldn't just drive into FMC. They might be watching for him. But Bethany's mom, Liana Phan, worked there. Using a trick he'd learned a few years ago, he sent Dr. Phan a message from his dad's number, asking her to meet with a safety committee at a local coffee shop. Then he settled in to wait.

Cameron wandered into a large retail store and made a few purchases. He stepped into a bathroom, changed clothes, and stuffed what he needed into his new backpack. After that, he stopped for a snack and a couple waters, then settled onto a bench that gave him a good view of the coffee shop.

Ten minutes later, Dr. Phan drove up and entered the shop. One minute after that, Cameron used his phone to hack into her car's external network and navigated his way into the internal network until he got the trunk to pop open. Glancing around to make sure no one was looking, he climbed inside the trunk and pulled it closed. He then sent her a message that the meeting had been cancelled.

In the moments that followed, the trunk morphed into a sauna. He chugged water, but even at this time in the morning, Texas was hotter than an overheated computer. After five minutes, Cameron was about to open the trunk and abandon the plan before he dried into a prune. Thankfully, she chose that moment to climb into her car. The machine roared to life. Though a little cold air reached him, he still felt like a polar bear trapped in the Sahara. Texas summers sucked. Why couldn't he have done this in January?

Despite her diminutive size and demeanor, Liana Phan drove like a demon. Apparently, she didn't believe in braking for turns or slowing down before stopping. Cameron silently thanked Jerry for all his strength training as he braced himself.

The car jerked to a sudden stop, and the engine shut off. Cameron's GPS read that they'd reached FMC. He accessed the security-camera feed and watched Phan stomp inside the building. He spent a minute gathering blank parking lot images, then looped those into the security feed. Once he'd fixed the cameras, he popped the trunk and jumped out.

He gulped the stifling summer air as his sweat dripped onto the pavement, but anything was better than that sauna of a trunk. Panting, he darted toward Building Six. Up ahead, a porte-cochere covered what had to be his dad's separate entrance, but a guard booth sat outside.

Dang it! He hadn't anticipated that, but… He squinted in the sun. The booth was empty. A trick? Too late to worry. Cameron ducked under the carport, restarted the parking lot security cameras, and took a moment to catch his breath. Above, a spider web glinted in the sun. Such finesse, such strength. Strands strung in every direction. Multiple cords wove together to catch invaders. The perfect trap.

What would he find here? A trap like that web? Information on Grisham? Something worse? For certain, the next few minutes would change everything.

Cameron leaned on the pillar and stared at the door lock. He might find answers inside. But did he want them? His earlier thought hit—why not disappear? He could walk away and live a happy life on some beach with the money he'd earned from his own security firm.

Or he could get inside and find proof his entire life had been a lie.

Nothing to lose, except everything.

He squeezed his fist several times then punched in the code his dad had used to lock Cameron out of his Computer Graveyard. 8-6-7-5-3-0-9. The door clicked open. The chilled air should have cooled him off, but his insides were already frigid.

What if Tasha was right, and he was a freaking clone? *Clone, clone, nothing but a clone.* The words choked all his air, but it was crazy, the kind of stuff that only happened in fiction. No way was it real.

Inside, a hall, an elevator, and more locks led to his dad's darkened office. The door closed behind him with a final-sounding whoosh.

The place suited Nigel. Opulent, but understated. Large antique mahogany desk, very few papers in sight. Polished furniture, rugs, oil paintings, even a wall clock, each of them worth more than most people's salaries and designed to last. Designed to intimidate. A wall of cabinets stretched along the right side of the room. A conference table, shining and stately, took up the other end. In the corner, Cameron spotted another plain, wood-slatted cabinet like the one in his dad's bedroom. It seemed out of place among all the antiques.

Cameron sat behind the desk, trying to decide where his dad would keep hidden information. He picked the lock on the nearest drawer, but it was mostly empty except for a black phone and a blue-faced Daytona Rolex with diamonds on the black bezel. A buzzing started at the base of Cameron's skull.

That looked like Rahul's watch. Could that be his phone? Cameron tried the phone, but it was dead. He plugged it in and waited while it booted up. No use, though. The phone had reverted to its factory settings.

With clammy hands and a sick feeling, Cameron picked up the watch, turning it over. No engraving, but not surprising. It proved nothing. How many Rolex watches like this existed? Thousands? He doubted a court would take a watch and a blank phone as evidence.

Still, Cameron's stomach tilted like he was falling off a building.

Why were these in his dad's desk? Did Nigel suspect Grisham of hurting Rahul and these were part of his investigation? Or had Grisham planted them here to frame his dad?

Cameron slipped the watch onto his arm. He would find out.

Under the desk, Cameron found a button. He pressed it and waited for sirens and guards with guns, but a wall opposite him opened, revealing another computer.

Cameron moved closer and turned on the machine, pulling up the batch program he'd loaded into FMC that would track passwords entered. He waited, but nothing matched. *Shoot.* Maybe this computer hadn't logged onto the network since then. Cameron ran his hands through his hair. He'd hacked his dad's computer at home, but this would be more complicated. He typed in his dad's old-school home password: IamTheDonor.

Didn't work. Argh. He should have brought a password decryption device. His heart thunked in his chest. He had so little time. He tried the door code. 8-6-7-5-3-0-9.

Nope. Cameron ground his teeth. He mentally scrolled through conversations with his dad, through the office at home, anything that would be meaningful to him but not to anyone else. The sailboat in his office obviously held meaning. Cameron typed in its name, *Jacquelyn'sPride.*

The computer opened. Cameron plugged his phone into it and started downloading files.

Chapter Forty-Eight

Cameron

CAMERON AND BETHANY MESSAGED back and forth, compiling information. The scent of expensive leather wafted into Cameron's nose every time he shifted in Nigel's office chair.

He kept glancing at the time. Would Grisham and Leon burst in before he was ready? He'd downloaded everything on his dad's computer but still had to put it all together in one cohesive "You're Screwed" presentation for Leon and Grisham.

So far, they'd discovered three of Leon's previous employers had ties to the mob. Two were serving time for money laundering. One, Sergio Valero, had been president of a bank and commerce institution that had financed and laundered billions for cartels, smugglers, and dictators. Another, Nikolai Kozlav, had been part of a Russian scheme with offshore banking.

And…yes! Leon had worked for Emilio Sanchez, who had ties to the Wolf Brothers cartel. If he dug deeper, Cameron bet he would find a tie between Sergio's bank and the Wolf Brothers. He filled Bethany in on what he'd found and asked her to look into Sergio, Leon, and the cartel.

A few minutes later, Bethany called. "I can't get a hold of Tasha." Her voice was breathless and raspy. "According to Gabe, she went up to your house to find you."

"No." Something inside him clanged. Of all the horrible, stupid, and utterly Tasha things to do. What if Leon had gotten her?

"She wanted to make sure you were okay. Gabe told her not to go." She gulped. "What about your guard Jerry? Can he check to see if Tasha got there?"

"He's not answering calls either." With shaking fingers, Cameron pulled up a new window and opened the security footage for his house. He scrolled backward in time until Tasha's Honda drove up. Leon met her in the driveway, gun in hand. He shoved her back into her car and took off. Cameron spat a string of curses.

"What, what, what?" Bethany shrieked.

"Leon got her."

Bethany gasped. "What do we do? I can't—"

"Report it to the people you spy for and keep working. It's the only way we can bargain with them." He pulled up a file with the blueprints for the FMC basement and looked at the clock. Almost out of time.

Chapter Forty-Nine

Cameron

CAMERON COMBED THROUGH files on his dad's laptop until he opened one called resumes. Three folders deep, he found a list of encrypted files.

A few minutes later, he was in, perusing a list of women's names. He stopped on Florencia Cortez, the girl Tasha had been researching.

He opened her file. Medical history, family history, specified diet, and other information that would make sense for a surrogate. There was also detailed financial history, some of it linking to an Edwardo Cortez who had received a large sum of money on the day Florencia disappeared. Had someone sold the poor young woman to FMC?

He paused when he reached a list of pictures, forty of them, one for each week of gestation. As her belly grew larger, she put a hand on her expanding middle like a protective and loving mother who cared for the baby inside her. The information stated she'd lived in a surrogate-care facility and had been kept in seclusion for the baby's health. All testing had been conducted in the basement of Building Six.

Cameron couldn't help himself. He touched the screen. Did this person count as his mother? Did she love him? Where was she now? Damp spots on his cheeks brought him back to the real world where he sat in an office in FMC trying to stop some very bad killers. He swiped at his tears and cross-referenced the list of resumes he'd decrypted with a missing-persons list.

As he worked, his stomach sank. All the women on his dad's computer had been presumed dead or found dead. Cameron couldn't be sure, but in his heart he knew the ones classified as missing, including Florencia, were dead too.

So many questions. So little time.

Cameron unplugged his phone from his dad's computer and slid it into his backpack, but the backpack didn't matter because all the information they needed was saved on an external server and had already been sent to numerous email accounts and backup files. It had taken a while to set it up, like that spider web outside—designed to trap and ensnare. The information was out there and unstoppable.

He wanted to puke, but instead found the elevator. If Nigel's files were correct, Cameron would find the rest of what he needed downstairs. While Cameron waited, he recalled Jerry's words: *"A good man puts others first, will lay down his life for those he cares about…only love can change the world."* This was Cameron's chance to be a good man.

The doors opened into a cold, dim hallway. Metal doors led to rooms on either side of him, all of them with security locks. He'd expected a mad scientist lab complete with bubbling glass tubes, a concrete slab, and Frankenstein's monster all prepped for a lightning bolt resurrection. This looked more like a military installation. He opened the first door. Test tubes and white boxes, like incubators.

The next room featured monitored glass cases full of pinkish blobs. He'd seen pig hearts compared to human hearts on a video at an FMC fundraiser a while back. Human hearts were shaped like a lopsided trapezoid, while porcine hearts appeared somewhat closer to the traditional heart shape a child would cut out of construction paper. The heart in front of him was porcine but so pale it was translucent, which was where the process got its "ghost" moniker.

Yet… He squinted. The thing was beating. Crazy. This was the ghost organ research in action, where animal organs were stripped down to protein shells then injected with the potential host's own DNA. Cameron took a few pictures and backed out of the room.

Grisham had talked about implanting Cameron with one of these hearts. But why? Surely there were better ways to trial the new organs, such as with patients in need of a transplant who had no other options.

Out in the deserted hall again, Cameron stopped. Where were all the scientists? Each footstep seemed to take more effort. This place could be the movie set for a horror film, and this would be the part where the audience would be screaming at him to run away. He opened the next door. Here was the Frankenstein-type lab he'd expected—tables, burbling test tubes, and glass cases full of body parts. Part of him wanted to run away, but the other half was drawn closer to the gruesome display.

Against the wall, several large glass cases held translucent masses, similar in color to the ghostly pig heart he'd seen. He peered into the nearest case. The organ inside was long and flat—maybe a liver. Clear liquid dripped through the pale tissue.

The next case held a kidney, but it had a pink hue, which meant it was close to being ready for a transplant. Further into the room, cases held recognizable human organs—hearts, kidneys, livers, even an eye, all of them the ghost-like color. He counted about twenty hearts. They were human, only child sized. The closest heart could fit into the palm of his hand, whereas an adult heart would be the size of a fist. A chill prickled his skin. These came from a human source. The question was—who had they been stolen from? His knees buckled. Could FMC be part of something so terrible, so horrific, so evil?

A computer sat on a lab table next to the heart, so Cameron opened it with his password-capture program. The most recent files on the computer referred to a heart. He plugged his phone into it to transfer all the files to his server, but as he skimmed through the information, his throat went dry.

These were indeed human organs…organs from twenty children. They'd been brought here and drained of all their proteins and were being repurposed. The organs arrived in a mass shipment three weeks earlier. Something clanged inside Cameron's head. The reports on EyeNet about the twenty kids being left for dead in the wilderness, all their organs removed. His vision wavered and he stumbled to the side.

No, it wasn't possible. FMC couldn't be a part of something so dirty. Cameron braced himself on the table. The cases around him seemed to be moving nearer, closing in on him. Ghost organs…haunting…children murdered for money. Cameron let out a yell and shoved the table in front of him. The table, the computer, and his phone crashed to the ground.

Cameron fisted his hands at his sides and squeezed his eyes shut, but he couldn't shut out the silent screams emanating from every corner of this room.

He opened his eyes again, but they were all still there, like ghosts of the murdered children. His family name was being used to sell organs stolen from murdered children.

This was what Tasha's dad had discovered. Grisham was using organs from murdered people. He'd read about a massacre three years ago. The Wolf Brothers cartel had been accused of killing dozens of children, but they'd bribed enough officials that the charges were dropped. Maybe FMC had financed those bribes.

He grabbed his phone, checking to make sure all the files had downloaded from the computer to his server. Finally, the link between Grisham and the Wolf Brothers cartel. He shoved out of the room. There wasn't a punishment dark enough for Grisham.

Bleating sounded up ahead at the end of the hall. Cameron's insides clenched. Did he want to know what lay behind those doors? This was like some freakish game show where each level held something more gruesome.

He crept to the end of the hall and slipped through the door onto a catwalk two stories off the ground. Cameron crouched and peered over the railing. Below stretched a room bigger than a football field with doors leading off it.

In the corner, a few people wandered between animal pens. They wore either white lab coats or protective bio-suits that covered their entire bodies, including their heads. Sunlamps shone on pads of grass and hay where goats munched, butted heads, and bawled. Some goats were hooked up to milking machines. Metal tanks stored and processed the liquid next to a lab station.

Enclosed in a glass case were four metal arms that rotated around and around, stretching strands of silky fabric like a taffy pulling machine. The goat's bleating sounds echoed throughout the chamber and clawed up Cameron's spine.

He edged along the catwalk. A suite of glassed-in rooms took up one wall below. In one room, two doctors in full surgical gear operated on what appeared to be a goat. Even from his perch, Cameron could see the blood spatters on their plastic aprons and gloves. The lady doctor held up an organ while the guy across from her charted on a computer.

Cameron had to hold his breath to keep from losing it. He scooted toward the other end of the catwalk, but movement below caught his eye. The doctors had finished their macabre surgery and were rolling the carcass out of the operating suite. Cameron froze, afraid to move and unable to look away. They toted their bloody corpse toward two square, black-stoned structures on the far end of the operating suites. What the heck? With their metal latch doors, they looked like giant ovens, the kind witches in stories like *Hansel and Gretel* might use.

The surgeons rolled their gurney to the opening and punched in a code. A long tray slid out. Together, the scientists dumped the carcass onto the tray. The small door lifted, and the inside was glowing hot. Cameron fell on his butt. That was an oven.

They slid the carcass inside and a loud whooshing sound rumbled to life. The cold floor of the catwalk seeped into his bones, but he was sweating. This was a freaking crematorium. Right here in the basement.

Cameron's heart pounded while he choked on thoughts of the ghost protocol room he'd just seen. All those kid organs. He stared down at the two doctors walking casually away from the crematorium like they did that sort of thing every day. The scientists here could burn whatever and throw it out with the trash.

The next thought hit him like shrapnel. Rahul. Cameron's best guess was he'd been killed, but obviously his body hadn't been found. He hadn't been around, no one had seen him, and he hadn't posted on any of his social media sites. The guy was gone. The last time Cameron saw him was at the hospital when Rahul noticed something odd in Dr. Zemke's notes. Who else had noticed, and what had he seen? It must have been bad.

Rahul's watch grew heavy and cold on Cameron's arm. Had Rahul been killed and disposed of here at FMC like that goat? *Not Rahul. Please, God, no.*

Cameron darted off the catwalk and into a nearby room. He pressed his back to the wall. No goats, no ghostly organs, no scientists, but a liquid-filled, coffin-like tube, about seven feet in length, sat on the other end of the room. It was hooked to at least ten machines, beeping and pinging in rhythmic bursts like a life-support system. He sank to a squat. What new horror would he find? He should look inside, but his body was too heavy to lift off the floor.

Instead, he used his projector to open the files he'd downloaded from his dad's computer, looking for key words. Nigel Foster was organized, so it wasn't difficult. Cameron started with the word "clone." The word was like a drumbeat that wouldn't leave him alone.

This was sci-fi stuff. Ridiculous sci-fi stuff, like the tank in front of him, bubbling and beeping. Like the ghost organs. He rubbed his temples and opened files from Nigel's computer into windows all over the room. In addition to info on the surrogate mothers,

Nigel had also kept information on all his employees, and not basic stuff like college degrees and work history. The FBI should be so thorough.

Cameron perused Jerry's history. It detailed his military service, including his AWOL status, his family, and where to find them. But nothing about his current employment with UNITED. Interesting. At least Nigel Foster couldn't reach everywhere.

In Grisham's file, Cameron discovered a malpractice suit against Grisham that had been dropped due to lack of evidence—evidence that had been lost. There were also documents detailing Grisham's income, actual and what he reported, his hidden bank accounts—plenty to get the guy imprisoned for tax evasion or buy him a private island—letters of warning for missing drugs in hospital pharmacies, and patient complaints that had gone missing. He also found a detailed police report about Grisham's mother's death, along with photos of an empty bottle of aspirin found near the body. Most likely, that was the bottle he'd seen on his dad's shelves in his home office.

Cameron opened the message Bethany had sent him regarding Grisham. Though Nigel's files were more detailed, it appeared to be much of the same information. Grisham had built quite the life outside the United States. He had several passports, including ones from the United Arab Emirates and Cape Verde, both non-extraditing countries. He even owned property in Cape Verde.

He opened Leon's files and found more pictures of Leon with known Mafia members. Also, offshore bank accounts and passports with fake identities.

Leaning back, Cameron stared at the files projected around the room. The information floated in front of him like vengeful spirits. All information Nigel could use to control and blackmail.

Cameron paced, moving past the person-sized tank. Inside, a flash of something dark caught his eye. He paused. Was that hair? No, couldn't be. But…what was it?

He took another look and lost the muffin he'd eaten earlier.

A small readout on the side of the machine read 028. This had to be a nightmare. It couldn't be real.

He forced his eyes open and stared at the thing in the tank. It was like looking at himself trapped underwater in a pool of death. Himself, only not himself—a ghostly and distorted apparition with eyes closed, eternally asleep. The body jerked from some sort of electronic stimulus, perhaps to keep the muscles toned. Alive, but not alive.

Cameron gripped his own chest like his heart would try to jump out. The thing inside the tank could not be what he thought it was, but Cameron's mind returned to when he'd helped rescue Bethany and the FMC scientist, Dr. Winn. The doctor's dying words replayed. *"Find twenty-eight."* Was this what he'd meant?

Clone.

He swished files around until he found the one titled 029, but he didn't open it, *couldn't* open it. Not yet. Instead, he went back to Nigel's file on Rahul. It was mostly empty, except for some bank account information. What exactly had Rahul found out at the hospital that night?

Cameron twirled Rahul's watch around his wrist and thought back. Rahul had called a few days after the movie-police-hospital-Dr. Zemke fiasco but hadn't left any specific messages. Instead, he'd sent Cameron messages on socials. Cameron scrolled through the last three. The *Star Wars* picture of Jango Fett pushing Boba Fett on a playground swing, the *Tron: Betrayal* comic book cover, and the GIF of Superboy.

What did they have in common? *Tron: Betrayal* was where Flynn replicated himself, causing all sorts of trouble. Superboy was a hybrid clone of Superman and Lex Luthor. Jango Fett had cloned himself to create his son Boba.

All of them were about clones.

This was Rahul's message.

The thing in the tank…

Cameron swallowed and started reading. A few facts stood out. They'd stored 029 at the FMC facility in Abu Dhabi. Heart tissue imperfect on 029. Improved over 028, but the transposition of the greater vessels remained. Damage repaired at birth as a backup heart. Pages of research and stuff Cameron didn't understand, ending with the next trial of 030.

Clone 030. Successful. No remaining heart issues. Birth date was Cameron's.

He was a clone, really and truly a clone. A thing from a sci-fi story. He stared at his hands, so much like his dad—Nigel's hands. *Clone.*

He almost laughed, thinking back to his fears of having a lab-created heart implanted into his chest. *He* was the lab-created thing.

All this time, he'd thought it was Grisham. Everything pointed to him, but behind Grisham stood Nigel. And Nigel Cameron Foster III was up to his eyeballs in this. He was a big, fat spider, spinning webs, tapping minions, destroying lives.

Cameron whacked his fists against the sides of his head and squeezed. His dad—no, not *dad*. Genetic donor.

Clone…

Did Cameron count as a real person? Or was he an experiment for FMC to see if they could make donors for sick rich people? He was a prototype—an organ donor created by The Donor.

So sick and twisted. If he did an MRI, would he see a "Property of FMC" tag inside him? Gah, he didn't have time for this. Tasha was still missing.

He rummaged in his backpack for the prescription bottles he'd taken from his dad's office, adding pictures of them to his files. Heat flushed into his arms as he stared at the label. His insides bottomed out. The heart medication Digoxin was prescribed to Nigel Cameron Foster *III*. Not IV. How had he missed so many details like this?

Nigel was the one with the heart condition in need of a new heart. His company had poured billions into organ and cloning development. The room spun, and he pressed a hand over his chest.

Cameron searched until he found Nigel's medical files. There it was. Transposition of the greater arteries. Surgeries had failed to repair the damage.

Head in his hands, Cameron's thoughts whirled like a hurricane. The last day Grisham ran those heart tests. Nigel, gasping for breath—not out of fear for Cameron's surgery, but perhaps because his heart was failing him. Nigel at the benefit, gripping his shoulder. Not indigestion, but probably oxygen deprivation.

Other realizations hit him, such as the fact that Nigel never went shirtless, even when swimming. Was that to cover chest scars from previous procedures? Who knew? And at this point, Cameron didn't care. But recently, when he went into his dad's bedroom searching for the Tesla keys, he kicked that plastic tubing connected to that odd cabinet with slatted sides. The same kind Nigel also kept in his office. Cabinets that looked like something inside needed good ventilation.

Now he knew what his subconscious had been trying to tell him—the tubing was the type Cameron had used for oxygen. Those cabinets probably housed oxygen concentrators.

Nigel needed a new heart—a perfect heart, the perfect transplant donor. How many of his late-night and all-day meetings had been him getting medical treatments?

What about all those years of Cameron's rigid eating, intense exercise, and supplements that Dr. Grisham claimed were medications? And that slipup in the hospital when his dad yelled about Cameron risking himself so close to "*our* surgery." Nigel had been obsessed with Cameron's health, not because he was an overprotective dad, but because he was planning to take Cameron's heart.

Curses exploded in Cameron's mind. There were no words strong enough. What kind of person did something like this? How did the man sleep at night or look in the mirror? Worse, how could Cameron have been so blind? Jerry had once said people will believe what's easiest and most convenient. And who in their right mind would suspect their "dad" of wanting to steal their heart?

But did Cameron's life matter since he was a clone? *A freaking clone.* Nigel didn't believe in anything other than himself, but Jerry believed in all that religious stuff. Would Jerry's God see Cameron as a real person? Would the law? Maybe it wasn't illegal for Nigel to take Cameron's heart because he was a thing, an experiment like those goats. A nothing-entity destined to become ashes once his usefulness expired.

Cameron leaned against the wall, head in his hands, and a thought struck him. He opened the file on clone 027. The final entry read *Terminated on March fourteenth.* Three years ago, the day Solomon had died after seeing Grisham loading up all those organ-transport coolers. Gah, he couldn't process this.

Cameron stared at the door, legs splayed on the floor. Once again, the instinct hit him: run. Run to the Caribbean, to Thailand, to one of the densely populated places around the globe where he could blend in and hide. He had the money and could live on an island, alone, away from this horror of a life. Sit on a beach, soak up the sun, and let the waves wash this nightmare away.

But he wasn't in this alone. Tasha, Jerry, Bethany, and Gabe. Even more: Tasha's Gran, her mom, Gabe's parents, Bethany's mom, Jerry's sister. None of them were safe, not with a psychopath on the loose willing to steal his own son's heart. Cameron couldn't protect them if he ran; they knew too much. He picked some lint off his shirt and tried to gather his wits. Jerry wouldn't run. Cameron drew a deep breath. Jerry would say only love and sacrifice can change the world.

Cameron

CAMERON WASN'T SURE HOW much time passed, but he felt like he'd been swimming laps for days when his phone binged with a text.

Nigel

It's time we talked. Come to my office.

Nigel had offices all over the world, but of course he knew Cameron was here. Such simple sentences, but so final. His "dad" didn't want a chat. Nigel had leverage and would demand surrender. He was going to get a war.

Cameron made copies of the files. He sent an email to Tasha and a last message to Bethany, giving both her and Tasha access to the files he'd downloaded. Shoulders back, he slid the phone and his backpack under the tank's monitoring system. If Bethany managed to send someone here, maybe they'd be found.

He headed to his dad's office. Several hours had passed, so most of the staff had gone home for the day. The majority of the basement lab stations were dim and deserted, except for the bleating goats. On the way to the elevator, he found a janitorial closet and grabbed a broom, loosening the pole out of the brush end. The elevator opened into his dad's office.

Nigel sat behind his desk, a king staring at his subject. Leon hovered behind him while Grisham stood to the side, staring at the ground—the weasel.

Ah, the empty guard booth made sense—Nigel had wanted Cameron to get into FMC. Cameron probably could've walked through the front door.

Leon gripped his gun while Grisham looked at anything but Cameron. Nigel gestured to the chair opposite the desk from him, as if conducting a friendly meeting. "Please, sit." He glanced at the broom but didn't comment.

Cameron eased the handle from the brush end and let the pole fall on top of his feet. No way would he go down without a fight. He sank into the chair, repeating Jerry's words over and over. *A man puts others first.* He nodded at the monster across the desk. "Dad. Or is that even what I should call you?"

Nigel let out a chesty laugh that would have impressed Jabba the Hutt. "Finally demonstrating the Foster brains." He leaned back and assessed Cameron over his folded hands. "I created you from my own genetic material. Therefore, I am your father."

Cameron's thoughts boiled. "How'd you fake a heart condition? I know Grisham did his part, but stuff like the oxygen? Wouldn't too much of that harm my heart?"

"Ah." Nigel steepled his index fingers and tapped them against his lips. Cameron flashed back to how cold his dad's hands always felt. Was that a symptom of his condition as well? "Yes, I could see how you would wonder. Your tanks were designed to give you the same oxygen a normal person needs but with the side benefit of less pollution."

"And my so-called low oxygen episodes? How did you manage that?"

Nigel chuckled like a fat, satisfied worm. "Basic psychology. I conditioned you to have frequent panic attacks. As you must have discovered, the symptoms can be similar."

"And the pills?"

"Supplements. For your health—our health. I thought you had this figured out."

"But Leon…earlier in the house, he said you and I were both going to die."

Nigel chuckled. "We are all going to die at some point. You sooner than me, of course. Leon played his assigned role to perfection."

"Why not one of your ghost organs?"

"The technology is still new, and I need the best. It will be a shame, though." He waved to Cameron like he was an object in a store. "You were just getting better at chess."

"Monster."

"And yet we are the same, you and I."

"We're nothing alike." Cameron hoped.

Nigel smirked. "True, I'm older and smarter, and I'm always going to win." He shook his head. "You spent all that energy looking for bugs in your car, never thinking to check that keychain you love so much."

Cameron was going to be sick—how could he have been so stupid? Gabe had even noticed the difference in color on the tiny Porsche keychain. All those precautions Cameron had taken were for nothing. Like an idiot at a Poker game, he'd played with a mirror behind his back.

Nigel took a ragged breath. "Your little friend would like to see you."

Cameron's body went tight. He strained to catch Tasha whimpering or moaning somewhere nearby. Nothing. "Where are they?" The force of his own voice surprised even Cameron.

Nigel's eyebrows rose. "They?"

"Jerry and Tasha. I know you have them both."

Nigel eyed the watch on Cameron's wrist.

Cameron's gut twisted. "You killed Rahul."

Nigel spread his hands. "A tragedy. Rahul will be difficult to replace." He was talking like Rahul was an espresso machine. Nigel didn't care about anyone, didn't care who he hurt.

"Where's Tasha?"

Nigel wiped at a smudge on his pristine desk. "She knows too much." Beside him, Leon looked ready to pounce and Grisham looked ready to barf.

The ice in Cameron's veins spread into his chest. "It was you who had someone sent to Tasha's house. You knew about the data drive from Dr. Zemke. You had her run off the road."

"Did you think there was anywhere you'd go I couldn't or wouldn't follow?"

"But she doesn't know," Cameron said. "She has no idea about your heart condition or how you, Grisham, and Leon have made a killing off the organ trade. Just let her go." Cameron leaned to the side of his chair. Leon's gun followed him, but Cameron waved it off. "You can't use that, so you might as well put it away." He pointed to his heart. "You don't want to risk damaging the goods." Cameron met Nigel's eyes. "Where is she?"

Nigel typed on a tablet in front of him. A video of a dark area appeared. Cameron couldn't see much, but he could hear muffled whimpering. Nigel gestured to the screen. "Any last thoughts before she dies?"

Where would Nigel think he was safe to kill her with no evidence? Cameron's stomach bucked, but he forced the feeling down. The crematorium downstairs. It made sense. At least it would make sense if he were a narcissistic psychopath like Nigel.

He couldn't catch his breath. They'd put her in there, probably while Cameron was in 029's room. Was it still hot? It took a couple hours for those ovens to cool down, but she was alive if the screen was to be believed. *Quick.* He glanced around the room. He had to do something, strike up some kind of deal.

Leon moved to block the elevator entrance. Cameron's heart jerked into seventh gear, but if he cracked now, Tasha might not make it out alive. He swallowed. "And Jerry?"

"There are two spots down there," Nigel said.

"How'd you get him?"

"Five milligrams of midazolam. It really is a marvelous drug."

Cameron forced himself to breathe. In. Out. He had to get them out of there. "I want to see them both."

Nigel laughed. "You are not in a position to make demands."

"You sure about that?"

Nigel's eyes darkened, but he didn't move.

Cameron gripped the sides of his chair. "You can't kill them. You'll go to jail, and there's no room service there. You'd hate it."

Nigel curled his lip. "You think the police can save you? They are unimaginative and limited by laws."

"I didn't bring a deck of cards to a chess game," Cameron said. "Check your messages."

Nigel tilted his head, his forehead wrinkling.

Cameron continued. "I can't do anything about Rahul, but if Tasha and Jerry, along with Gabe, Bethany, and the others, don't log into the accounts I set up for them and aren't seen at regular intervals, it all comes down on top of you."

"What does?" Nigel asked.

Cameron leaned over the desk. "Everything. Your murder of your own parents. Grisham drugging their drinks with midazolam so they'd sleep while you crashed the remote Jet Ski into their boat."

He pushed on. The rest were assumptions from his research on Grisham, but it all fit. "Grisham's drug habit—there was a memo about medications missing from a hospital pharmacy. I'd guess Grisham got caught stealing the meds, maybe even by the patient who conveniently died in that hospital-room fire."

The next part was more speculation, but like Nigel had always taught him, never let on you aren't certain about anything. "Grisham murdered his mother by putting aspirin in her tea, which gave her a heart attack. That old, empty aspirin bottle in your office at home will turn out to be the one missing from police evidence from the case. Your weakness is a thing for keepsakes, including the midazolam bottle I found inside the model of *Jacquelyn's Pride*."

He held up his arm, pointing to Rahul's watch. "I'm assuming you keep a little something special from all your murders." That also explained the detailed files.

Beside Nigel, Grisham shrank and ate half a roll of his ever-present antacids.

Cameron went on. "Then there's Solomon Jenkins's murder, the illegal organ sales I've tracked to Grisham and Leon, and not to mention tax fraud. Kinda hard to claim income on illegally sold organs. And don't forget all the secret offshore accounts, passports, and Grisham's new identity in Cape Verde. You all have plans to relocate, but you need the spotlight, people to adore you. I'm guessing you'll go to Abu Dubai. They don't extradite, after all."

He paused, his throat oddly tight with emotion as he thought of Florencia. "And let us not forget the missing surrogate mothers who gestated all your clones."

Nigel gave him that snake-stare, void of any emotion. Leon tensed.

Cameron flexed his foot under the broom handle that was partially hidden by the desk. Maybe he didn't have proof about all of it, but he had enough evidence to cause trouble. "Your passports, finances, everything will be locked down and dispersed to thousands of charities if you don't let them go. The Mafia, FBI, NSA, CIA, and a host of other acronyms will come looking for you. And even if you survive, you'll have nothing."

Grisham sank to a chair and leaned over his knees, hands plunged into his hair.

"You're all screwed."

Nigel nodded to Leon. "Burn the girl. Make him watch."

"No!" Cameron kicked the broom into his hands and rushed Leon. He whacked Leon's wrist, sending the gun spinning, then smacked his nose. Blood spurted from Leon's nostrils, and the big guy fell to his knees, cursing.

Cameron pointed the handle toward Grisham. The doctor whimpered and held his hands up. "I'm sorry. I'm so sorry."

Cameron glared at the doctor's bare fingers. "Your ring is missing." He sucked in a breath. "You planted that ring on Dr.

Winn. You suspected Solomon had made a recording and that your face might not be in it, but your hand might've."

Grisham dropped his eyes to the ground like a young kid caught stealing cookies.

Nigel dove for Leon's gun. Cameron whacked Grisham over the head and used Leon's back as a springboard. He grabbed the gun first. It felt like an anvil in his hand—heavy and cold.

Nigel edged closer. "You aren't a killer."

Cameron did the only thing that made sense. He pointed the gun at his own heart.

Nigel's eyes widened, and his hands curled into fists. "You don't want to do that."

Chapter Fifty-One

Cameron

Cameron and Nigel locked stares, and Cameron heaved a prayer of thanks when Nigel's phone buzzed at the same time as Dr. Grisham's and Leon's. All three exchanged a glance and pulled their phones out of their pockets.

"That will be a message from my friend, Black Mask. If Tasha and Jerry aren't released, all my information goes viral."

Grisham swayed and Leon cursed.

Nigel tossed his phone onto his desk. "Leon, kill Jerry and Tasha and inform your men to shoot Dr. Liana Phan and bring me her daughter Bethany. And blow up Hazel Watt's house while you're at it." He glanced at Cameron. "Shall I go on? I'll continue to dispose of people until you undo everything you've set in motion."

"Stop!" Cameron sneered at his farce of a father. Nigel was worse than a monster. He was a demon in a custom suit. "I'll make a deal with you."

Nigel folded his hands together. "A deal? This should be entertaining."

"You created me for my heart. Take it. Only let them all live."

"With that kind of leverage? Never."

"We're all trapped, Nigel." Using the monster's first name felt better, like Cameron stood on equal ground. "It's checkmate on all sides. They tell, you retaliate and have them killed. You hurt them, your life is over. No one wins. Only I lose."

"You think they'll let me take your heart?"

"My heart is mine to give in exchange for them, but if they disappear or come to harm, your life is over. The information is there. If they don't check in periodically to the program I created, it goes off like a bomb." Cameron made an exploding noise and pantomimed a mushroom cloud expanding. "This is your best chance, and you know it."

"What's to keep them from exposing this information?"

Cameron shrugged. "There are no guarantees in life, *Dad*, but who cares as long as you get what you want, right?"

Nigel took a shallow, wheezing breath. How had Cameron missed the shortness of breath? The gray undertone in Nigel's skin? So much evidence right before his eyes. So much he'd ignored in his refusal to believe the terrible truth. So easy to swallow lies. People see what they expect to see.

Nigel nodded to Leon. "Have the others brought up." He gestured to Dr. Grisham. "Let's go."

Cameron swallowed, his knees suddenly made of jelly. "Where are we going?"

Nigel paced around the desk and put a hand on Cameron's shoulder. "Don't worry. It's not far. Not for you. But you can rest well knowing you will live on...in my heart."

A few tears squeezed out of Cameron's eyes. He bit the inside of his cheek until he tasted blood. No way would he cry in front of this guy. Yet he couldn't help but wonder. "You had your chance to live, and you could have any heart you wanted out of your factory. Why this?"

Grisham pulled out a medical case and gave Cameron a pinched look, like he was apologizing for being a murderous devil. Did he expect Cameron to be consoled by the fact that the doctor felt slightly bad? *Yeah, no.*

Nigel shrugged, as if this meant nothing to him. "I have a lot yet to accomplish in this life, and I can only accept the best. This was the best way I could ensure my body wouldn't reject it."

"Then I hope the best keeps you warm—of course, where you'll eventually end up, you won't lack for warmth."

"Clever." Nigel glanced at the door as though impatient to get on with his murderous scheme. Leon was busy stuffing papers into a computer bag. Nigel continued, "Life is full of death. The sooner the masses accept that, the easier their miserable lives will be."

"*Their* lives, huh?" This guy believed himself so far above everyone else. How had he missed it? "What about your parents? Did they deserve their fiery end?"

Nigel glanced up and to the right. "They lived bored lives, always seeking the next thrill. I simply gave them what they wanted."

Cameron shook his head, fighting the thickness in his throat. "Why not at least give me a ghost-protocol heart? Give me a chance?"

His donor's mouth turned down. "I hate loose ends." With a wave, Nigel motioned Leon toward Cameron, and the big idiot zip-tied Cameron's hands together behind his back. Leon jerked the plastic tight.

This was it. The end. Funny how he'd always expected to die young, but this was the first time he'd had someone to live for. After all he and Tasha had been through, would she be comforted by the knowledge that Cameron truly cared about her? He glared at Nigel. "Are you even human?"

The corners of Nigel's mouth edged up. "I am…better. And now it's my turn to ask questions. Did you want for anything?"

"Seriously? You kept me completely isolated from the world. I didn't have any friends."

"Friends complicate everything." Nigel tilted his head like a robot dog trying to figure something out. "All the same, I believe your death will be a tragedy."

"You're causing it!"

Nigel took a shallow, wheezing breath and staggered. He leaned on his desk. "I have given you a good life. It's your turn to offer the same to me."

"I hate you."

"Another frivolous emotion. Only clouds your mind." Nigel moved back to his desk as though dismissing a servant.

"You know if you do this, it'll change you forever."

"That is the point." Nigel glanced at the clock.

Grisham inspected a hypodermic needle, checking the dosage. Cameron's hands were slick with sweat. Why had he agreed to this? It was an attempt to be noble, but at this moment, nobility sucked. He nodded toward the doctor, anything to divert him until he could come up with another plan. "That email from Donor Beneficence Corp about the cryo units. What was that about?"

Sweat formed a ring around the doctor's forehead. He stared past Cameron—what a coward. "Cryo storage for…" His voice evaporated.

It took Cameron a moment to comprehend the disgusting picture. He glared at Nigel. "You're going to store my spare parts after you take my heart? Waste not, want not, *Dad*?"

His hands shook, and he wanted to wrap them around Nigel's throat and squeeze, but he needed to focus on what was important. He had to try one more thing to ensure Jerry's and Tasha's safety. "Just in case you are planning to double-cross me, which we both know you are, UNITED is looking for Jerry and Tasha. I don't know how big of an agency they are, but they seem to be extremely well-funded."

Nigel's head snapped up. His eyes widened and his face froze, corpse-like, before he seemed to catch himself and rearrange his face into its usual bored, haughty expression. But Cameron didn't miss the shock and something else he'd never seen on Nigel's face—fear. "Interesting." Cameron let out a mocking laugh. "You didn't know Jerry worked for them, but you know who they are."

Nigel didn't respond, but his lips tightened.

Cameron leaned forward. "They're coming for you."

Nigel snapped at Grisham. "Shut him up."

Grisham popped another antacid and jammed a hypodermic needle into Cameron's arm. Cold liquid burned through his veins. "What's that?"

"Versed, also known as Midazolam," Grisham said. "It'll relax you, and you won't remember another thing, just like your grandparents."

"I don't want to…" Cameron's head seemed to be floating away. His limbs were heavy, like they were made of tingly rubber. The room blurred in and out of focus.

Nigel spoke softly from across his desk. "Goodbye, Cameron."

CHAPTER FIFTY-TWO

Tasha

THAT MISERABLE PILE OF puke. That horrible felonious ogre. Tasha had always known Nigel Foster was lower than diseased rat droppings, but never had she imagined he would have his minion Leon strap her to a giant oven tray like the witch from *Hansel and Gretel*.

Her breaths came in shallow gasps. Her head spun and throbbed at the base of her skull where Leon had knocked her out. She kept her eyes squeezed tight, couldn't open them or she'd start screaming again. The smell of ash burned her nose. Duct tape seemed to cover her entire face, and every second she could feel the walls of this giant oven shrink.

Would they turn on the fire? Burn her to a crisp? Would she die quickly? She thought of Solomon, the only dad she'd known. Would he meet her as soon as it was over? Would God be mad at her for all the years she'd spent furious at him? *I'm sorry, so sorry for everything.*

She shifted her arms around, but the duct tape held firm. Her hands were numb, past the horrible pinprick-and-needle stage. Tears burned the cuts on her face. She'd fought the orc Leon as best as she could when he grabbed her in Cameron's driveway, but that needle jab and hit on the head had ended it all.

Why had she gone to Cameron's house alone? What did she think she was going to do? She was five feet tall in her Converse. Prickly as a cactus, true, but what good is a cactus against a bulldozer? *Way to go, Super Genius.* Tasha hadn't intended to take them on, not really. She'd only wanted to help Cameron. Where was that super-pumped bodyguard? Or was he just as evil as the others? She sent up a prayer. *Please, God, I don't want to die.*

Her poor mom—she'd lost so much already. Now Nigel would murder Tasha, and her mom would never know what happened. Who would give Gran chocolate? Bring her healthy meals and keep her feet warm? Check her O2 level?

And Cameron…so much regret. It sucked that her last big accomplishment in life was being a manipulative snot. And falling for him…that hadn't been in her scope and sequence. But head, heels, and heart—all of her had fallen for Cameron Foster IV.

What would happen to him? It didn't sound like his dad had good plans. More tears dripped down her face. She remembered the lopsided grin, his spectacular shoulders. His wonder at every-thing, like it was all new. The gifts he'd given Gran. No one made her feel special like him, not since Solomon. Cameron had been too good to hope for, too good for her. And it was too late for both of them.

She'd never insult him or call him Golden Boy again. Never get to hold his warm hands again. Never kiss those adorable, awesome lips.

Tasha's chest burned. Her throat constricted. *I'm so sorry, Cameron. So sorry I used you, so sorry I wasted so much of the little time we had being angry and stubborn and…me.* She prayed, *God,*

I'm so sorry for everything. Behind the duct tape, she choked back a sob. Her heart fisted in her chest. If only she'd had more time with Cameron, she truly would have loved him.

The door thumped. Her entire body went stiff. This was it. They were turning on the oven. Time to die. *Please, God, don't let it hurt. Let me die really, really fast, like instantly. And don't be mad at me for…everything. And take care of Cameron.*

The door yanked open. A rush of cool air tainted by the smell of barnyard hit her. Where were they? Nearby, a few goats bawled, unconcerned about her predicament.

Was it the cops, rescuing her? Gabe's dad? Someone slid her out of the oven like a batch of cookies. She exhaled, relieved, until she stared into the face of Leon. She squirmed against the tape and yelled insults, but all that came out was, "Mumph mmph mmm."

Tasha heard more shuffling beside her and a deep groan. Cameron? She moved her still throbbing head with care. Black skin. Black T-shirt. Major muscles. Jerry was tied to the oven shelf next to her. Tasha sobbed behind her gag. If they had Jerry, did they have Cameron too?

Leon leered over her. "That stupid Foster brat says he's got us trapped, that he can protect you and this jerk and the rest of your people, but he's wrong if he thinks I'm going to let you live." He yanked out a gun that made Gran's Elvis look like a dollar-store water pistol.

Jerry thrashed and groaned. Leon glared at him. "Shut up or she suffers."

What had Cameron done? Had he tried to save her? She squirmed. Maybe she could roll off and get loose somehow. Leon raised the gun like a club. Tasha squeezed her eyes shut again.

A *bang* echoed through the cavernous basement.

Tasha squealed behind her gag. Waited for pain. Maybe she was dead already, but why wasn't she flying to Heaven and having a cappuccino with Jesus at the Pearly Gates?

Something thudded against the ground. She checked Jerry, but he still sprawled on the oven tray next to her. He focused on something across the room and up. Tasha followed his gaze.

Above them, Nigel stood on a catwalk, gun in his hand. Had he shot Leon? Tasha craned her head but couldn't see the floor. Chills covered Tasha's skin and her thoughts spun. Who would be next?

Nigel finally spoke. "I'm so sorry Leon did this. I had no idea he was such a criminal."

Jerry groaned beside her.

Nigel leaned on the railing, waving his gun as though it were a casual cup of coffee. "It seems we have a predicament."

A *predicament*? Heck yeah, it was. Was this guy insane? They weren't seated at a table in Starbucks. She and Jerry were strapped to an oven rack in his basement, and Nigel just stood there like a fat cat.

"Leon intended to harm you, intended to harm us all," Nigel said. "Sad, but true."

Did he hear himself? In a psychiatric textbook, this conversation could cover the lesson on gaslighting.

Instead of calling the police, Nigel turned off the lights. The entire room went coffin-in-the-ground dark. "Proceed with caution." Nigel's voice had a deep, dark edge to it. "I would hate for Cameron to be affected by your choices." His footsteps clicked away and disappeared.

Tasha screamed after him, but her throat was already raw, and the duct tape held her lips together. What had he done with Cameron? Did he mean he would harm Cameron if they called the police? They might be stuck here until they died from dehydration.

Beside her, Jerry grunted and rolled off his tray. He made all kinds of commotion when he hit the floor and wormed his way around. Should Tasha do the same? Worm-crawl to an exit? And then what? She had no idea how much time passed. Five minutes? An hour? The darkness grew inky, heavy. Like glue. It leaked into her eyes and ears and nose, weighed her down, drained her of everything.

Jerry swore and groaned. Wait, he swore. Was his gag off? "Hang on. I'm coming." His voice sounded hoarse. "Let me get some light."

A small beam from a tiny flashlight yawned into the darkness, but all around, horrible shapes swallowed the light. No haunted house, no ride at Six Flags, nothing could be creepier than this house of horrors and its giant oven.

Jerry shone the light on her and cut her arms and ankles loose. At first, she couldn't move, like it had been too long and her limbs would never work again.

"This is going to hurt." Jerry put pressure on her face. No, wait, was he going to pull off—

A sharp pain lit her lips on fire. Tasha screamed. "You just ripped my gag off, no warning?" Did her lips rip off with it? Words tumbled out. "What are we going to do? Where are we? What happened to Cameron? Was Nigel the one—"

"Shh. If I'm right, we're in the basement of Building Six at FMC. And we've got to move if we want to save Cameron."

An insane drummer with steel hammers had used her as a xylophone. She sat up but lost her balance and tipped off the tray.

Jerry caught the back of her shirt, but not before her hands hit the hard, dead chest of Leon. She screamed, scrambled backward, and let Jerry pull her up. Reality ran her over like a bus, and tears erupted. "How can we save him?"

Jerry limp-dragged her across the room with only the small source of light to guide them.

She tried to gather her wits. "What is this place? Smells like a barn."

"FMC has been cloning goats. They found a way to get the goats to excrete spider webbing in their milk. They're experimenting with medical uses for the mesh."

"Bethany mentioned that once." Tasha's mind rebooted. "What about the human cloning division? Cameron is Nigel's clone. I saw the records. He's the thirtieth attempt."

Jerry hit the lights. She blinked to adjust to the searing brightness. Lab stations lined the basement. White tables, strings of what looked like spider webs. And in the corner, the ovens. Leon. Blood.

Tasha's knees gave out. Every night from now on, she would dream of this place. Never would she forget the oven, the charcoal smell of it, the residual heat drying her into a raisin. Her guts twisted and turned inside out.

Jerry waited, then offered her a hand and pulled her up the stairs. Tasha leaned against a doorframe and gasped for breath. "Maybe you should go without me."

"We've got to find Cameron, but I don't have my phone. You have yours?"

"No, Leon took it, probably smashed it and left the pieces somewhere." She grabbed the doorknob for support, but someone had left it ajar. It tipped open and Tasha stumbled inside.

The lights came on. A long tank bubbled in front of her, like a life pod from a sci-fi movie. Jerry stepped past her and swore when he looked inside.

Tasha stumbled over to join him. She repeated his apt choice of words. "Wait." She glanced around. A sign said simply 028. *Oh, dang it.* "That's clone 028. They kept them. What are they doing with them?" Tasha inspected the monitoring equipment while she rambled. "Does that mean there are more? Cameron is subject 030, so where is 029? And where is Cameron?" She scooted close to a monitor on the tank, but there was no computer.

Something rumbled nearby, perhaps a giant truck driving by the building.

Jerry peered back into the hallway. "We need to get out of here."

Tasha followed Jerry, but her foot kicked something hard, and it skidded across the room. She gasped and knelt. "That's Cameron's phone." She checked under the equipment and spotted a black bag. "And maybe his backpack."

She grabbed both and turned on the phone. Hope against hope, she tried the same login he'd set for the computer he'd gotten her. The phone opened. She turned on the keyboard and monitor projectors, but before she could comment, another rumble shook the complex. Long trails of dust fell from the ceiling.

"They're blowing up the place!" Jerry grabbed her arm and jerked her to the hallway.

They bolted down a corridor that seemed a mile long. All around them, the ground shook. The lights flickered several times then went out. Red emergency lights came on, leading toward a door all the way at the end of the hall.

Jerry motioned her onward. "Faster!" He yanked open the door labeled Building Three.

A boom sounded, the force of it knocking her off balance. Dust rained over them. A terrible groaning noise and vibration shook the stairwell, and a crack opened in the wall in front of her.

Jerry sped up. "Move, move! We're almost out."

They climbed two flights of stairs and slammed through an exterior exit. They surfaced between Building Three and Building Two, smack in the middle of the FMC complex. The different buildings on the property formed a two-by-six matrix grid, with parking lots running in between the buildings and ringing the perimeter. It reminded her of a downtown area with tall, identical buildings laid out in two neat rows surrounded by concrete. She glanced up. The sun had dipped behind the horizon. It would be pitch dark soon. Tasha took a long breath of hot, non-laboratory air, but Jerry grabbed her shoulder. "Keep going."

Another explosion hit. Tasha's ears rang, and the world shook so hard she fell over. All around them, the ground had turned into liquid waves pushing up and down, everything threatening to fall in. Gravel dug into her knees. She scrambled back to her feet, dusting away rocks and skin as blood dripped down her calves.

A booming noise swept across the parking lot, and the side of Building Two crumbled. It collapsed in slow motion, like the structure was folding in on itself. Rocks pelted her face, biting and scratching. Her already sore head pounded. They skidded to a stop and sprinted in the opposite direction between Buildings Three and Four.

More explosions hit like drumbeats, and the parking lot beside them caved in. She and Jerry sprinted around the backside of Building Three, scrambling toward the outer edges of the parking lot, but they were at least an acre from the exit, and the entire parking lot was protected by fencing too high for Tasha to climb. Jerry yelled over the rumbling. "The whole place rests over that basement. It's all going to collapse."

Tasha looked around, her heart thudding like a drummer on speed. What to do, what to do? Next to Building Three, she spotted a row of black SUVs, part of the FMC security fleet. That gave her an idea. She pointed and took off running for the nearest one.

While they dodged fallen debris, she scrolled through Cameron's phone. He'd told her about hacking those SUVs earlier. Please, please let him still have the links he'd used. Jerry pulled her forward as another section of the parking lot disappeared. Behind them, Building One toppled over. The thudding concrete was so loud she couldn't hear whatever Jerry yelled at her.

She typed on Cameron's phone. Come on, come on, come on. Hurry up. She hit the ignition on one of the SUVs, but none of the cars in front of them turned on. Another explosion collapsed the parking lot between them and the cars. No! She couldn't do this.

A memory bubbled to the top of her mind—Solomon smiling at her. "Sometimes, baby, you gotta remember—the only way out is through."

She took a huge breath and tried another car. The one on the end lit up. They were still so far from it. While they dodged a pile of crumbled concrete, Tasha put the car in reverse and engaged the acceleration system to get the car to come closer to them. This was so much harder on a phone, but she could do this. She had to.

The car skidded close to a collapsed brick wall. Tasha scrolled through two screens before she accessed the braking system—this wasn't like some well-designed video game. Jerry yanked her around a crater. Pain ripped through her leg, but she didn't have time to look. She steered the SUV closer, but before it reached them, another explosion buckled a line of concrete between them and the SUV. This was impossible! Every time she had an idea, something of Nigel Foster's tried to kill her.

Jerry grabbed her arm. "Run for it!" He yanked her forward, and they scaled the buckled portion of the parking lot. They'd almost made it when another boom dislodged a chunk of concrete under her. Her ankle twisted, and she fell forward, hands and knees scraping on the rough ground. Force propelled her into a roll, and pain screamed through her entire body. Cameron's phone crunched, and the screen cracked. She grabbed the device, cradling it to her chest.

Jerry hefted her off the ground, carrying her like a football. He yanked open the car and tossed her inside, climbing in after her.

He hit the gas. "Nothing's happening!"

She still had control of the car, and it was stuck in reverse. No time to figure it out. Tasha squinted at the cracked screen and hit what she hoped was the accelerator. Behind them, a section of the fence had collapsed. Tasha aimed in that direction and the SUV propelled backward into the open field next to FMC's property.

Her mind flashed between the present and the video of Solomon hitting the fence. Someone screamed in the background—probably her, but she could hardly tell over the explosions in her memory. In the field, brush and rocks pelted the vehicle, but it bounced over a curb and landed with a jerk and a squeal on the road. Tasha slammed against the passenger door but pushed the SUV backward, further down the road. In front of the vehicle, flames erupted from the destroyed FMC complex.

The engine whined, and Tasha let the SUV coast while she backed out of the car's computer system. Her hands shook so hard she could hardly see the screen. She let out a sob. Where was Cameron?

Jerry took over the wheel and held out his hand. "Will that phone still make calls?"

Tasha set the phone on call mode and handed it to him, thinking over what Leon had said about Cameron trying to save them. What had he been up to in that clone room?

When Jerry handed back the phone, Tasha checked Cameron's sent messages. One was to her.

> *Tasha,*
>
> *I'll be dead when you read this. I only regret…lots of things. Dying, for starters. More than that, I didn't feel like I'd lived until I met you.*
>
> *Not fair.*
>
> *Here's where I should say something awesome like don't let your heart stay broken forever. But what I need to say is don't let them get you too.*

I've done all I can to ensure your safety and the safety of the others. I'm planning to make a deal with the devil. It's the only way. Follow my instructions and watch your back. I'm not sure who you can trust. There's something Bethany's not telling you. Beyond that, know that Nigel will try to find a way around this bargain. You have to stay ahead of him, and since you're far cleverer than me, you'll be able to put him away.

I wish you weren't involved, that I hadn't pulled you into this, but the one thing I'll never regret is meeting you. You made even this sucky death worth it.

All my heart,

Golden Boy

Tasha stared at the words, eyes blurry. She swiped at her tears. What kind of a bargain had he made? He'd attached a bunch of files. Tasha opened them one after another.

Newspaper articles on Charles Grisham. Articles on Nigel. Nigel's files on Leon. Cloning papers she hadn't been able to access. Reports on the heart condition of each clone. A medical file for a Nigel Cameron Foster III treated by Dr. Zemke thirty years ago. Transposition of the greater vessels. Scar tissue on the heart.

Tasha's own heart drummed in her chest. Cameron didn't have a heart condition. Nigel did. Cameron said he'd made a bargain. And he'd signed the letter, *all my heart.* "Jerry!"

Chapter Fifty-Three

Tasha

Tasha paced in a gray office suite at UNITED headquarters while Jerry made phone calls and the room filled with people wearing suits, badges, and guns. A few of the suits plugged into the laptop in Cameron's backpack with some tech that would've impressed even Golden Boy—no, she wouldn't refer to him in past tense. Tasha wrung her hands. Where was he?

Jerry argued with a gun-suit lady in the corner. They bantered in Russian, probably assuming Tasha couldn't understand.

Wrong, *dourak.*

The agent lady kept saying no, this wasn't part of the mission, not part of their jurisdiction. Jerry argued that a kid's life was in danger. The lady said kids died every day. Well, that lady could go die every day herself and see how she liked it. Tasha opened her mouth, but Jerry, with his weird-ninja-sixth sense for bad behavior, glared her into silence.

Tasha kept skimming through Cameron's files on his phone and thought back to what Cameron had said at dinner that first night when they'd discussed his upcoming surgery. He'd mentioned Abu Dhabi. She searched through the files he'd put together and...yep, there it was. She spoke over the Russian argument. "There's an FMC facility in Abu Dhabi, which is in a non-extraditing country. I bet that's where they're going."

She caught the attention of one of the suits.

The guy watching her had sandy blond hair and a beard, looked to be in his late thirties, and wore dark-tinted glasses. Name badge around his neck read Roger O'Brien.

Jerry's argument with the suit lady ratcheted. They switched to a language Tasha didn't know, but Jerry must have won because he moved closer to Tasha and motioned to Roger. "I'm heading to Abu Dhabi. O'Brien will set up a protective detail for your family."

"I thought protecting kids was out of your mission parameters," Tasha said.

The Russian-speaking lady's eyebrows climbed to her forehead, but O'Brien gestured to Tasha. "She's one of DAST-M's brightest students."

Tasha glared at him. "How would you know?"

"I'm on the board. We see big things for you going forward."

This guy was no educator, but Tasha wasn't about to quibble. "Right now, you better see me going to Abu Dhabi."

O'Brien tilted his head and stared at her like she was an unassembled puzzle and he was looking for a corner piece. "You want to go to the Persian Gulf. Just like that?"

"Yes." She motioned around her. "Your organization is big enough to hire this many suits and to own schools and who-knows-what else. You're big enough to make this happen and then some. I can tell from the tech your minions are using that funding's not an issue. Do you want enough info on Nigel and Grisham to lock them away? Then put me on a plane."

Tasha typed a message to her mom and prepared herself for the major grounding that would take place if or when she returned. She also pulled up Cameron's email and typed a message to Dr. Grisham. She would blast him with texts and emails and missiles if she had to. If he didn't help her, there would be nowhere he could hide.

Chapter Fifty-Four

Tasha

NOTHING DULLED THE MIND like watching a patient sleep, and Foster was a champion sleeper. Nurses traipsed in and out of his room, checking to make sure she wore the protective garb required for germ-free-ness. Outside the room, UNITED's suits prowled in different shifts, pretending to be bodyguards provided by her concerned "father" Roger O'Brien. UNITED had been fast to issue some interesting fake identities. Tasha leaned back in her chair. She didn't plan to move until Foster woke.

Three days she'd waited for this. He'd stirred in and out of sedation but was never conscious enough to recognize her. The nurses said he would wake soon. She leaned over the side of his bed, waiting and waiting for his brown eyes to open.

A nurse peeked into the room. Tasha gave her doe eyes, blinking and sniffling. She spoke English in her best Texas accent. "Will he wake soon? Is he going to be okay?"

The nurse nodded but left the room without any comment.

An hour later, Foster blinked a few times, eyes wobbling like the last two brown M&Ms in a glass jar. Tasha leaned as close as she could and pulled off her mask. "Hey. I've been waiting for you."

Nigel Foster focused on her, and his gaze narrowed. His heart monitor beeped faster, which was a big show of emotion for a psychopathic creep like Nigel.

Tasha yanked her mask back on. "Don't get excited. You'll ruin everything."

A nurse peeked in the door. Tasha faked some tears and grabbed Nigel's hand. "He's awake. My dear, sweet uncle is finally awake. You've saved him."

The nurse turned her lips up but gave Tasha a stern look. "Not long. He must sleep."

Tasha waited until the nurse left and kept her voice low. "Listen, you sorry son of Sauron, you may have gotten your way, might think you'll always get your way, but the game has changed."

Nigel groped around on the bed beside him.

Tasha held up the nurse-call button. "Looking for this? I'm almost done." She tossed it on the floor. "You aren't holding all the pieces anymore. Grisham is so terrified of you that he wouldn't play by my rules, so I upped the ante. I'll let you discover the fine print as you recover, but suffice it to say, I have a few nasty friends who owe me big, and they don't care about little things like politics and non-extraditing countries."

Nigel blinked, then kept his eyes closed for a few seconds. She waited until they reopened before continuing. "Remember Cameron's surrogate mother? She was the beloved niece of a cartel boss who owes me a favor since I got him out of some trouble with the law and found his missing niece. At least what happened to her."

She stood. There were things in her past that she wasn't proud of, but fighting to save Cameron was something she'd never regret. "You're slippery enough to escape the legal mess you're in, but never forget: we are everywhere, and we're watching." She offered him a cold smile. "Oh, and I'd make sure your heart is good and healed before you look at all your bank statements. Goodbye for now, Nigel. I'll never stop working to bring you down."

Chapter Fifty-Five

Cameron

STABBING CHEST PAIN JOLTED Cameron from sleep. The room shook, which only made the pain worse, like he might crack in half. He blinked. Hazy, too-bright images swam in his vision. He lay in a hospital bed under a white, curved ceiling. Square airplane windows with the shades down. Loud engine whine. An IV pole wavered in and out of focus above his head. He sucked in a breath but couldn't get enough air. A machine beeped nearby.

Tasha leaned over him. "Hello, sunshine."

"Are we on a plane?" He sounded like someone had stuffed a fist-sized wad of cotton into his throat. Felt like it too.

Tasha held a spoon to his lips. "Thirsty?"

When he opened his mouth, one tiny ice chip melted on his tongue. He groaned. "More?"

She gave him another tiny spoonful. "How're you feeling?"

"Like I've been gutted by a tiger and then mauled by bears."

"Sounds like a textbook description of a heart transplant victim."

A jolt passed through his gut. "Transplant? I had the surgery?" He scrunched up his eyes like he'd be able to see the memory.

Some important piece of information was missing. Everything was so fuzzy.

Cameron shifted around to sit up. Hot currents of pain seared his chest as if a crazed poltergeist stabbed him with an icepick. He fell back, teeth clenched. "Did they give me a heart made out of lava?"

Tasha and Jerry exchanged one of those glances that meant they had information and weren't sure whether to share.

"What're you hiding from me? Where's Dad?"

A nurse leaned over his bed. Tasha's mom? Cameron gulped, which ended with more stabbing in his chest. Tasha's mom put a cold towel on his forehead and pulled out a small vial to inject into his IV stream. "I think we need some more pain medicine."

"No, wait. Where am I? What happened? And why are you here with us on a plane?" Maybe he'd had surgery and the medication was causing delusions? Maybe he was dead and this was some weird form of torture?

Sarah pursed her lips. "You're a bit confused. That's normal after major surgery. First, some of the pain is the…device we implanted in your chest."

"What?"

Tasha rubbed the back of her neck. "You know I'm into robotics—"

"Are you saying I'm a freaking cyborg?"

Tasha chirped a laugh. "No, and shut up. Lemme explain. This man I met, Roger O'Brien, connected me to the robotics research division of Jerry's super-secret organization—"

"Sounds like they're not so secret," Cameron said. But…something she said was out of place. "Wait. Roger O'Brien? He's no agent. He's a guy Dad knew at Harvard."

"I guess we all have weird secrets, but that doesn't matter right now." Tasha shoved another piece of ice into his mouth. "What matters is that Roger had the doctors implant this little device in your chest that will stimulate the regeneration of damaged tissue. Plus, the transposition of the greater vessels issue was fixed on *this* heart soon after the birth of the..." An army of shadows marched across her face. "The...donor." She gulped a breath. "The point is, you might get back to your sexy, bo-staff-wielding self once you recover from surgery."

Images crashed through his head. His dad, Grisham, Leon. His dad's office at FMC headquarters. The clones. Tasha and Jerry in the crematoriums. Cameron's body went stiff. "My dad—Nigel. He did this. But he wanted—I don't—"

Tasha put a hand on his shoulder. "The short version: Nigel tried to kill us. You made a deal to save us. Leon tried to kill us anyway, so Nigel killed Leon, then took you to Abu Dhabi and gave you some drugs to slow your heart to make you look dead, and—"

"And how am I not dead?"

"Keep all arms and questions inside the car until the ride stops. I contacted that squealing piglet of a doctor and offered some incentive to change their plans."

"Incentive?"

"I thought you were going to stay quiet," Tasha said.

"I thought you were going to explain."

"I sort of know this drug cartel guy named Cortez. He owes me a big favor for saving his butt from the Feds."

"Wow, you're really getting to the point."

She shoved the spoon back into his mouth. "His beloved niece Florencia was...um, your mother. And Cortez knows what Nigel did to her. Suffice it to say, your genetic donor is rather vulnerable at the moment." Her face pinched, and tears bubbled in her eyes. She inhaled a shuddering breath. "I think I did something terrible. Maybe not. I don't know. Maybe someday we can dissect the ethics, but I couldn't lose you. Not after—I just couldn't—"

Though it took as much effort as lifting a giant barbell, he groped for her hand. "Did you have Nigel killed?"

She let out a snorted breath. "No. Worse, I think."

"How so?"

"I just—I thought Grisham would cancel the surgery, but instead he…he found an alternative heart source."

"For my dad—donor?"

She shook her head. "I wish I'd had enough leverage, been able to see him in person…"

"Just tell me."

"You saw clone 028 in Dallas," she said.

Cameron's mind spiraled with images of that body in the tank, lying there, lifeless yet alive. He didn't respond to Tasha, and his body shuddered like a car with engine problems.

Sarah jumped up and checked his stats. She pulled out a vial. "I'm going to give him lorazepam to keep him calm."

Tasha nodded. Her mom squeezed her shoulder, and Tasha continued. "Clone 029 was stored the same way they kept 028, but in Abu Dhabi. His heart wasn't as perfect as yours, but like I said, it was mostly fixed at birth." Tasha let out a sob. "I couldn't stop Grisham from taking your heart. I did my best, but I just…I didn't know he'd do something like this."

The lorazepam made his head feel like it floated off his body. Her words seemed to be about someone else. "What are you not saying? That I have my…brother's heart?"

"Yes, and Nigel stole yours."

Cameron couldn't digest that. His thoughts were tiny bubbles floating above him and popping, but a profound sadness settled over him.

Tasha's mom took over. "We moved you out of there as soon as you were stable. You have some tough days ahead of you, but with the implant, you should make a decent recovery. Jerry and this UNITED group have seen to that."

Even with his fuzzy vision, Cameron didn't miss the strained look on Tasha's mom's face. Sarah leaned in and whispered, "I don't trust them, but now's not the time to argue." She raised her voice back to normal. "When Tasha texted to say she was traveling across the world and another Federal Agent showed up on my doorstep, it wasn't hard to figure out you were involved. I volunteered my nursing services."

Cameron moaned and wished he didn't feel like there was a chainsaw in his chest. "What about Nigel? Can't they use the evidence at FMC to get him?"

Tasha shook her head. "FMC South Building Six blew up two days ago. They're searching through the rubble, but I doubt any of the important equipment is still there. UNITED has all your evidence, so we can only wait and see what they do."

Cameron's eyelids weighed ten thousand pounds, but he shoved them open. "I don't want anything to do with him, ever again."

Tasha snuffled. "Well, there's where you're going to be even more upset with me. I'm also sort of blackmailing your dad. Or I did."

Sarah muttered something and rubbed her forehead.

Tasha went on. "It was legal…mostly. You're now the poster child for FMC's organ research department. And you sort of own the place."

Cameron wheezed. "What?"

Tasha wrung her hands but hardened her eyes. "After your surgery, I released a statement to the press all over the world detailing FMC's desperate attempt to save you, to change your heart condition. After all the stress, your dad retired, leaving the company to you."

Cameron's chest burned. "Why would you do that?"

"I wasn't going to let Nigel ice you. He got you into this, so he's going to pay for it."

Tasha blurred in and out of focus. "You're pretty," Cameron said. "Wanna go onna date? I hear Whataburger's good."

Jerry leaned over him on the other side. "You've got this."

Behind Jerry, a vaguely familiar brunette sat next to a guy with glasses. "You look—seen you before," Cameron said.

The woman moved to his bedside. "Yes, I'm Janet Dover, a colleague of Roger O'Brien's."

A hazy memory of Janet bobbed to the surface of his brain. "The benefit." He blinked, forcing his eyes to focus. Expensive suit. Military posture. She had an unreadable face—two faces… No, that was the meds. He blinked again. "You're not who you say you are."

Janet nodded. "You are a Foster."

"Who do you work for?" he asked. "Jerry's group? Roger too? Were you two spying on Dad? Does everyone work for you?"

Cameron wasn't sure if Janet nodded or if she wobbled with the motion of the plane. "We're called UNITED. United Nations International Threat Elimination Division. Think of us as a global security task force." She patted Cameron's hand. "We'll get acquainted as soon as you're recovered."

Something about Janet and the entire situation bothered him, but he couldn't... She blurred and morphed into three people. A haze covered her face and then a purple monkey appeared to be tap dancing on her shoulder.

Tomorrow...he'd figure out Janet tomorrow. He closed his eyes but forced them open again, meeting Tasha's gaze—the color of a Texas sky in the summer. "You should walk away while you have the chance."

Tasha snorted. "You are not breaking up with me after I committed some major international crimes to keep you alive."

Cameron groped for her hand. "You have so much ahead of you. I don't have anything to offer you except Nigel's money, and—"

"I don't want his money."

"I know." He gestured with his hand, but moving hurt. "Look at me. I'm completely busted. The only thing I can offer you is a broken heart."

"Don't be ridiculous. By the time we finish with you, this heart might be better than your last one."

"But..."

Her eyes turned liquid, like a clear lake. She leaned closer, her voice low and husky. "See, Cameron, that's the strange thing about matters of the heart. They don't make sense."

"But I'm worthless."

She turned his face to meet hers. "No matter what shape you're in, you're worth more than Tiffany necklaces, Porsches, Whataburger, or anything else to me."

He squeezed his eyes against the heat in her gaze. It was too bright. He might burn up.

"Besides"—Tasha laughed, soft and sultry—"I think I like you better this way."

"Broken?"

"Chipped, cracked, humble." Tasha leaned in closer, her breath on his ear. "I sorta think this would be a great time for you to kiss me, but my mom would freak out that I might give you germs." She kissed his forehead instead. "Think of that as a deposit on a very long future."

His body sank into the bed, and his eyes refused to stay open. "Is this the way it's going to be? You telling me what to do?"

"You have to ask?" She leaned her forehead against his palm. "You know what they say about piranhas. You just have to tame them, and they're yours forever."

"I've never heard that." But he did remember some joke…thingy…she'd said about her personality and piranhas. Wait, what was he thinking? He needed sleep. Stupid surgery. "You're awesome." A thought stirred. "Hey, I have Comic Con tickets. Want to come?"

She kissed his forehead. "Sure. It's a date."

He relaxed into the pillow. The future opened wide, but it had some sharp teeth. Yet unlike the beginning of the summer, he didn't feel alone, and for the first time he saw the possibility of many tomorrows. He planned to grab life with both hands and fly. "I don't know much about piranhas or anything else, but I know this: I love you."

Tasha held his gaze for several heartbeats. "I know."

Chapter Fifty-Six

Tasha

FOR THREE YEARS SHE'D been lost, chasing justice with a side heaping of revenge. And now it was over. Tasha wasn't sure what to do next. She sat in her idling car—one leg in, one leg out—and stared over the sea of gravestones. The car's air conditioning spewed out cold air, but the stifling August heat wouldn't surrender. Sweat trickled down her back. Sunlight reflected off the plastic-wrapped bouquet in her lap.

Four rows over and five up marked Solomon's grave. She hadn't visited since his funeral, but that day was forever etched in her memory. Her mother sitting in front of the coffin, face ashen and staring at nothing, saying nothing. Gran kissing the flag draped over the coffin, tears streaming down her face. And the rows of quiet men in uniform, whispering among themselves. He'd survived so much overseas. Why this? Why now?

A gaping hole had ripped open inside of her that day, and she'd tried to fill it with vengeance. The hole still burned. Yes, knowing Grisham and Nigel were to blame for his murder helped, but would the world ever know the truth? She glanced into the sky, bright and blue and clear. Maybe it didn't matter what the world knew. What mattered was what Solomon would think of how she'd spent the last three years.

Tasha chewed her cheek. Maybe he wouldn't be proud. Did he know? Had he been looking down on her this whole time, shaking his head and wishing she'd followed his example and chosen to love instead of hate? The man had grown up in a world that sometimes judged him for things like the color of his skin, yet he'd told her the only way to change the world was through love. Would he be disappointed in her?

Maybe, but it was time to stop running. She gripped the flowers and shoved out of the car. Her feet were made of lead and the sun blazed against her skin. She was panting by the time she made it to the grave marker. She sank to the ground in front of the stone, tracing the letters with a finger. *Lt. Solomon Nathan Jenkins. Beloved husband, father, and son. Faithful warrior. Forever cherished.*

"Well, Dad. Here I am. I'm not sure what to do next. Bethany and Gabe are excited about school next year. We're getting transferred to the advanced campus—college. They promise I'll get to take MIT classes. Mom is busy working, and Gran…you wouldn't believe all she's up to. I'm sure you remember Jerry—he said you two met in the service. He's good, visiting his mom and sister."

She paused and stared at the flowers in her hand. Sitting there, as close as she could be to her dad, the hole inside shrank. Cameron was still recovering but already making changes at FMC, including appointing Gran and Jerry to the board. The move had caused some uproar, but he said he needed people who would speak their minds and safeguard ethics moving forward. The job came with several perks, including a self-driving car for Gran. That guy knew how to make an old woman's year.

Tasha laughed, and the hole diminished a bit more. How she loved that boy. And sticking it to his dad…that wasn't her most noble action, true, but Tasha grinned each time she remembered the look on that snake's face. They still hadn't unraveled the whole mess, and there were secrets they'd yet to uncover, including what Bethany was hiding. Once Cameron recovered, they'd keep digging.

She paused. A year ago, she'd never have imagined herself planning a future with some guy. She'd been so lost she couldn't think straight. But with Cameron, her heart felt light again. The world was better, worth fighting for.

Tasha set the flowers against the gravestone and turned her face to the sky. "You were right, Dad. Love does change the world." She stood. "I'll tell Mimi you said hi."

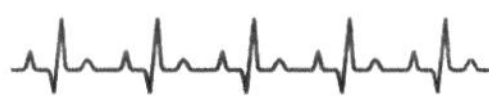

Cameron

One month later.

> Cameron,
>
> Ready to get your life back and more? I have a job for you…
>
> -Janet

Author's Note

While I did my best to research and ask questions of people far more talented than myself, any mistakes are mine. I took a few liberties with medical facts and technology, but my friend Amy who lived with transposition of the great arteries assured me it was fiction after all. Amy, I wish you could have read the finished version of this story.

Regarding panic attacks and anxiety… I have struggled with anxiety my entire life, and I distinctly remember my first severe panic attack. I was in graduate school, stressed with deadlines, a relationship breakup, and an eating disorder. While driving on the freeway in Dallas (which is dangerous on a good day), my arms, then legs went numb, my chest got tight, and I couldn't catch my breath. I was convinced I was having a heart attack, which made the panic worse.

In the years since, I've gone through stages where panic attacks come and go, but to anyone suffering from this: I see you. You're not alone. It's hard, but there is help. I regularly see a counselor. There's no shame in experiencing anxiety and panic attacks, but I urge you not to suffer alone.

Discussion Questions

1. Do you think hacking can be ethical? Can you think of a situation where Cameron and Tasha used their skills ethically? How about instances you felt were unethical? What would you have done in their place?

2. What do you think about the statement: People only see what they want to see? What important details was Cameron overlooking? How would you have done it differently in his place? And how would that have changed his choices?

3. How would you feel if you were in Cameron's position in chapter fifty-five? In regards to his situation, do you think forgiveness will be necessary for him going forward?

4. How does Tasha's determination to seek justice for others shape her choices?

5. Jerry tells Cameron: "A good man puts others first, will lay down his life for those he cares about." And, "Only love and sacrifice will change the world." Do Cameron's actions in chapter fifty reflect this?

6. Jerry has a noble yet troubled past. How do you think his past shaped his choices?

7. Jerry sometimes acts protective of Cameron but also sometimes stands back and lets Cameron lead. What do you think of their dynamic? How do you think Jerry's desire to see justice affects his choices?

8. In the middle of chapter fifty-five, Tasha says, "I think I did something terrible… Maybe someday we can dissect the ethics…" What conversations do you think will take place in the future?

Acknowledgements

Thank you from the bottom of my heart for spending time with this story. With all the great choices out there, I'm honored you spent time with Cameron and Tasha's story. No one writes a book in a vacuum, and a village of amazing people helped bring this story to life. Thank you!

As always, I'd first like to thank my Lord and Savior, Jesus, for the gift of creativity. Amid many things hard in this life, my imagination has been a source of joy and a way to process emotions.

To Madame Publisher, thank you for taking the chance on me and for the friendship we've forged. For those fun texts when you first read Cameron and Tasha's story, and for asking that last question, "What happens next?" You have encouraged and spurred me forward in so many ways. I am truly grateful I stopped to chat with you about your dragon stickers at Realm Makers!

To Denica, thank you for all your editing advice and the multiple reads. A writer is only as good as their editors, and I appreciate you! To Brittany, Amanda, and all you lovelies at Q&F, thank you for your fun messages about pickles, your prayers (especially as I cared for my mom this past year), and your encouragement. Y'all are the best.

A thousand thank yous to Mom and Dad. From those early days of reading to me and my sister, to sharing your Agatha Christie and Sherlock Holmes books with us, and all the ways you helped me attend writing conferences and classes. I could not have done this without you. Mom, it breaks my heart that you didn't make it to the publication date of this book, but you cheered me on until your last day. Love you forever, and I can't wait to see you on the other side. To Bonnie, thanks for always encouraging me. You're the best big sis ever.

To my husband for the endless emotional and tech support, brainstorming, and plot-hole help. And thank you for your endless patience with *all* those, "I just have a quick question" moments that were rarely quick and usually required detailed explanations. And thank you for continuously encouraging me to keep writing just because I loved it. Thank you and love you.

To Lauren, for helping me overcome my anxiety, for encouraging me to continue, and for your help with brainstorming and graphic design. You are one of my biggest blessings in this life, and I am ever and always so proud of you. To Joel for your encouragement and for listening to me yammer on about things like love stories. I am ever so grateful Lauren brought you into our lives. To Rachel, though you face so many challenges, you almost never stop smiling. You remind me what perseverance looks like and you've made me a better person a thousand times over.

To my amazing CPs: Kristen Joy Wilks, Lana Pattinson, and Tosha Sumner, I'm so grateful for your quick and repeated reads, your insightful comments, and your friendship along our writing journeys.

To Meghan O'Flynn, thank you for your wickedly sharp editing pen and for the countless hours of talks, advice, and all the times you've encouraged me to keep moving forward. You are supremely generous, and I remain so glad you said yes to coffee group all those years ago.

To my Author Media and Red Herring Society fellow authors and classmates: thank you for asking great questions that I didn't know I had, for encouraging comments, and for the community you have formed. To Mary and CJ at The Writer's Sanctuary: thank you for the countless hours of advice, mentoring, and love you have given me and so many in your bookish family. You two ladies are the best!

To Amy. You have already been in Heaven for two years as I'm writing this. Thank you for all the years of friendship and mentoring you gave to me and so many others. You taught me so many things, but I hope to never forget that index card where you wrote your life's goals: To know God. To serve God. To lead others to him. You never let an opportunity to laugh pass you by, and although you had a lifelong challenge with transposition of the great arteries, you never let that stop you from living each day to its fullest, including dragging your oxygen tanks with you to jazzercise. Thank you also for answering my questions about TGA and for assuring me it was okay to take some creative license in this book.

To my amazing and generous early readers: Nova McBee, AJ Skelly, Karyne Norton, Candace Kade, Katherine Briggs, CJ Milacci, Amber Kirkpatrick, and Sara Anderson. Thank you for giving of your limited time and for your words of encouragement along the way. Your support means the world to me. Also, thank you for taking time to answer my questions regarding so many things authorly.

To Dani, Jeremy, and Dena, thank you for being amazing beta readers. Jeremy, thank you for your hacking advice and for the numerous texts, phone calls, and reads. You helped me in so many ways–I claim all mistakes as my own, but a thousand thanks for the inaccuracies you helped me correct. I so appreciate you all and the encouragement you give me. Dena, you have been a constant cheerleader for over two decades, always reading, always pushing me to keep going. Thank you.

To creators like The Shawn Ryan Show, the Darknet Diaries, the Julian Dorey Podcast, and Andrew Bustamante "The CIA Spy," thank you for the hours of informational content. (Note to readers: the content in those shows is not always PG–13, and the opinions expressed are not necessarily mine).

To the amazing bookish community on IG, my readers, my launch team, and all you bookish people who encourage writers daily, thank you for spending time with my words. You are the reason this is such a rewarding endeavor. As a person who reads and writes in multiple genres, thank you for stepping into this thriller. I can't wait to share more stories with you soon. Be sure to stop by JenniferDyerBooks.com and IG @JennDyerBooks for a visit.

Much love,

Jenn

ABOUT THE AUTHOR

Jennifer Dyer is an award-winning author of speculative fiction, including thrillers, romantasy, space opera, and cozy fantasy. With a background in martial arts, Jennifer loves weaving action into intricate plots filled with fierce heroines, found family, and swoony kisses. Her short stories have been featured in various publications, including the bestselling *Meet Me at Midnight* anthology. When not writing, Jenn bakes gluten-free cookies and eats far more of them than she should. Connect with her at JenniferDyerBooks.com and on Instagram @JennDyerBooks.